Jacob's Way

Other Books by Gilbert Morris

Charade

Jacob's Way

Edge of Honor

Jordan's Star

God's Handmaiden

The Spider Catcher

The Singing River Series

1 | *The Homeplace*

2 | *The Dream*

3 | *The Miracle*

4 | *The Courtship*

GILBERT MORRIS

Jacob's Way

ZONDERVAN.com/
AUTHORTRACKER
follow your favorite authors

Jacob's Way

Value Edition 978-0-310-28797-1

Requests for information should be addressed to:
Zondervan, *Grand Rapids, Michigan 49530*

Library of Congress Cataloging-in-Publication Data

Morris, Gilbert.
Jacob's way / Gilbert Morris
p. cm.
ISBN: 0-310-22696-1
1. Peddlers and peddling—Fiction. 2. Women immigrants—Fiction.
3. Southern States—Fiction. 4. Jews—Russia—Fiction 5. Jewish women—Fiction.
6. Grandfathers—Fiction. I. Title.
PS3563.O8742 J33 2001
813'.54—dc21 00-068051

Published in association with the literary agency of Alive Communications, Inc. 7680 Goddard St., Suite 200, Colorado Springs, CO 80920

Interior design by Todd Sprague

Printed in the United States of America

08 09 10 11 12 13 14 • 10 9 8 7 6 5 4 3 2 1

To the elders of Christian Life Church and their wives—
true servants of Jesus Christ and a joy to my heart.

Aaron and Sherry Wren
Michael and Renea Broussard
Mike and Evelyn Young
Billy and Leslie Berrey
Kevin and Angie Noe

Far below lay the frozen earth, but the graylag goose had lost all sense of time and place. Overhead, the witless stare of the opaque sun flickered into nothingness, rimming the abyss of the printless earth beneath. Somewhere deep in the ancestral memory of the faltering graylag, all that remained was a dim instinct that kept the mighty wings beating the frozen air. The piercing cold and the biting wind that drove sharp fragments of frozen mist into the bird's remaining eye had drained him of all but a blind obedience. Once there had been warmth and food and communion with his kind. All of that was but a flicker of a memory now, but it was enough to drive the goose forward in an erratic flight toward the south.

A thin sheen of ice covering his feathers pulled the graylag earthward. The feeble rays of early dawn revealed the broad silvery zone on his upper wing, and the feather strips formed a series of thin white transverse stripes. The black tail made a startling contrast with the white rump and the gray-brown upper body. The beak was pink with a whitish hook, and as the lungs strained, the beak gaped open, taking in frozen air and fine particles of ice.

A primal and feeble memory came to the bird, of the time before he had been shot. Flight then had been a joy, a matter of strength and skill—finding a place in the V-formation, beating the air with powerful pinions through milk-white clouds that drifted across azure skies. And then coming down on a warm pond or a quiet river, the flock quacking and splashing, diving tail-up for the food that made rich, red blood.

But all that had changed with a single explosion and a terrible pain. The pellets had torn the muscles of his breast and gouged out one eye. He had floundered into the swamp where the sounds of the pursuing hunters came to him, but he had survived. His world destroyed, the graylag had fed on whatever food he could find as he mended—but he could not fly.

All during the late summer he had been able to stay alive, but in the fall when every instinct told him *Go! Go! Fly away!* he could not get himself into the air. Time and again he would flounder, half-running over the water, only to fall back, his right breast and wing weakened and almost made useless by the torn muscles.

Endless time had passed, and then one morning, the leader had given the special call. The graylag had watched as the flock had risen into the gray sky, making a V-formation. Frantically he had tried again to join them, struggling to slip the iron bonds of earth—but had fallen back into the water. With his one remaining eye he had watched them disappear, then later other flocks had passed overhead, dim patterns in the cold sky.

Slowly the graylag found himself able to struggle into the air for short flights, but it took many weeks before he was able to gain the upper reaches of the sky. He could not fly for long, nor could he attain the heights he loved—but he was free from earth.

The winter had come, grasping the Russian steppes in a mailed fist of ice, when he finally began his journey. He flew less than ten miles his first day, but managed to find a stream not yet frozen. There he landed and found some food and rested. The next day he covered almost twenty miles before exhaustion brought him to the land.

So it had gone, but the cold had grown worse, so that the streams and ponds and lakes were frozen. Food was so scarce that he grew feeble, unable to cover more than a few miles.

Now as dawn broke in the east, the graylag struggled to keep altitude. He had eaten almost nothing for three days, and the pain in his breast beat like a steady pulse. His flight was a jagged, lop-sided movement, his body unable to keep the position that allowed him to slice through the air.

Finally a blast of air stopped him in flight, and though his wings beat with what strength he had left, he began his descent. Down, down, down he went, striving to keep his neck straight and his legs folded. The land seemed to rush up to meet him, much faster than he had ever known, and the ice coating his one good eye half-blinded him.

As he rushed toward the earth, the faint memory from the dim past came to him. He had made the journey to the southern lands three times, and now he seemed to feel the warmth of the sun and to hear the cries and splashings of the flock, the taste of rich, abundant food...

But even as that feeble memory rose from the dim past, the wounded graylag sensed an object in front of him. He made one effort to throw out his wings and break his flight, but it was too late. As he crashed into the solid rock, he knew one blinding flash of pain—and then all was silence.

Part One

One

Reisa Dimitri always slept soundly through the latter part of the night and on into the morning, but a sudden loud thumping noise very close to her head brought her awake instantly. Confused and frightened, she sat up in her narrow bed and stared wildly around the room, trying to pull her thoughts together. She knew that it was morning, for a pale milky light filtered through the single window of the room. As the biting cold struck her, she shivered, pulling the covers up to her neck, afraid to lie down again.

It could be robbers!

The thought brought her completely awake, and she swung her feet over the bed, slipping them into the bulky leather boots that she kept beside her cot. Standing up she listened hard, but only silence came echoing back to her. Drawing a deep sigh of relief, she murmured, "It's not robbers—and I don't think it's soldiers."

The thought of soldiers was even more disturbing to Reisa. After all, robbers would only come in and take your possessions—but soldiers of the czar would seize people and carry them away to some frightful place where they would never be seen again. Such a thought always lurked deep down in Reisa's subconscious. She had heard terrible stories from her grandfather about the pogrom that he had survived in his youth. The Russian government had sent cruel cossacks through villages, killing Jews, slaughtering them like cattle, then taking the survivors away to prison camps where they died lingering deaths.

Waiting silently in the room, Reisa became calmer. *Not robbers and not soldiers. Soldiers would have broken the door down, and robbers would have tried to be silent. But I know I heard something.*

Standing up with a swift motion, she pulled a heavy overcoat over her thick woolen gown, buttoning the two buttons with numbed fingers. She plucked a white scarf from a peg, then moved quickly across the small room as silently as possible. She was alone, her grandfather spending a rare night away from home sitting up with an old friend whose wife was dying. Somehow the isolation had not troubled Reisa while it was light, but now the mysterious thumping sound worried her.

Unbolting the latch, she stepped outside. The cold pierced her to the bone, for though there had been no fire in the house, it had retained some heat. Outside, however, the frigid atmosphere touched her face with ghostly fingers cold as death. Blinking her eyes against the fine particles of frozen mist, Reisa scanned the area outside the house, but saw nothing. Then remembering that the sound had been close to her head, she walked around the corner. There on the ground lay a bundle of some sort. As Reisa approached, she realized that it was the body of a large goose. Drawing her breath in, she ran at once and knelt beside it.

The bird had been injured somehow. Strong compassion swept through Reisa. She loved animals almost fiercely, and indeed her grandfather, Jacob, had scolded her for bringing home crippled animals and birds half-mangled to death by cats. Yet she knew that this side of her character pleased her grandfather.

She leaned closer and rolled the goose over. Seeing an empty eye socket and the breast terribly scarred and denuded of all except the finest feathers, she cried out, "Poor bird! You were left behind, weren't you? Some hunter shot you, and you couldn't leave with the rest of the flock. How terrible to be left alone to face winter when your fellows were all flying away!"

Her fingers touched the bird's injured wing, and she leaned forward to look more closely. The goose gave a convulsive lunge and uttered a hoarse sound. Reisa jerked her hand back, afraid of the large bird's beak. The goose gave a shudder and seemed to grow still. She knelt there undecided. What should she do with such a large bird? Often she had tended sparrows and other small birds, keeping them until they were able to fly. But what could she do with this battered creature?

As she knelt there weighing the alternatives, the goose opened his beak and uttered a small sound. Somehow this brought a firmness to Reisa. Carefully she lifted the bird in her arms, then made her way to the small barn occupied by her flock of chickens, two goats, and the milk cow. Lifting the latch was difficult for her, but she managed, and as she stepped inside the usual greetings from the chickens rose as they gathered around her feet. Ignoring their cluckings as well as the nudgings from the goats, she placed the half-dead goose in a manger filled with hay. The long neck flopped over, but the good eye was fixed on her.

"I'll be right back," Reisa whispered, then turned and left the barn. Going into the house, she quickly built up a fire, then drew on two petticoats and a brown woolen dress. As soon as the fire was hot enough she put on a kettle, then waited as the flames licked the vessel. Finally a breath of steam appeared, and she at once poured boiling water into a small saucepan. Moving quickly, she grabbed a worn towel, plucked up the lantern, and left the house.

As soon as she stepped inside the barn, she hung the lantern on a peg, then opened a wooden box fastened to the wall. With her hand she scooped up some of the oats and dropped them into the hot water. The cold was so severe that the boiling water was already only warm. Moving to the goose, she began stroking him with the towel, intent on her task. She had seen flocks of this sort high in the sky, and twice a neighbor who hunted had brought her grandfather birds he'd killed as payment for a debt. Reisa had dressed and baked the birds, and even as she removed the icy scales from the goose, she thought, *Grandfather would expect to eat this goose.*

The thought troubled her, for survival was not easy in such hard times. If the goose died, she would certainly give thanks for God's provision, and it would become food for them. Yet somehow Reisa hoped that he would not. Broken and dying, the great goose had come into her life, and now as she dried him she hoped that he would live. She was aware that most of her neighbors would laugh at such a foolish wish. "Geese are made by the Eternal One for people to eat," they would say. Reisa knew they were right, and it certainly gave her no problem to behead one of the chickens from her small flock. Yet somehow this goose was different.

"Ruler of the Universe," she whispered, "this poor fellow is crippled and half-blind. He is lost from all his kind and has no help but me. You brought him into my life, and now I would see him well and able to continue his journey to join his flock. I am a foolish girl, but I ask you to give him strength to complete his journey south..."

As Reisa prayed (feeling rather foolish praying for a dying goose), suddenly the great bird began to move his wings. He lifted his head, and his one eye fixed itself on the face of the girl.

Reisa uttered a glad cry and leaped at once to pick up the pan of warm oats. As she approached, the bird lunged to his feet and spread his wings. She saw that the right pinion was damaged, but she held out the pan, saying, "Now, eat some of this." The goose shook his head and tried to fly, but Reisa reached out and caught him. She forced his beak into the oats, wondering if she could make him eat such foreign food, remembering how difficult it had been to get other wounded birds to eat. Warm hot mush had worked for sparrows, but she was not certain that a goose would eat it.

For several minutes, she restrained the bird without success, but finally managed to force some of the oats into his beak. He was no doubt frightened and confused, but he was also starving. He swallowed the food, then when Reisa forced his beak into the pan, he began to take the oats, swallowing convulsively. He ate ravenously, his bill tapping against the bottom of the pan, so that Reisa laughed. "Don't be such a glutton!" She rose and studied the bird as he faced her. She could see the naked breast with the jagged scar, and wondered what sort of determination had brought him this far.

She turned to feed the chickens, then milked the nanny and the cow, pausing frequently to glance at the goose. He had settled down on the straw with his good eye closed. Reisa felt a thrill of accomplishment, and nodded with satisfaction. *You rest, goose, and after I fatten you up, you can go find your mate.*

Carrying the two pails of milk, she returned to the house. The small fire and the feeble sun overhead had brought some warmth into the room, and she felt happy. As she moved around the room doing her housecleaning chores, she wondered what she would do if her grandfather chose to kill the goose for food. The thought bothered her, but she was a cheerful young woman, so put the thought out of her mind. She had never been denied anything that was in her grandfather's power to give her. If someone had said, "Reisa's learned to manipulate her grandfather," it would have bothered her. But nevertheless, she began to plan a way that would make him less ready to sacrifice the goose.

This problem occupied her as she boiled water for tea. Then as she drank the scalding beverage, she suddenly said aloud, "I know! I'll cook one of my chickens! If Grandfather is full of nice stewed chicken, he'll be happy enough to let me nurse my goose!"

Satisfied, she planned the meal, not pausing to give the doomed chicken one thought of pity. If she had been asked about that, she would have replied, "Chickens are made to lay eggs and to be eaten, but the great goose is made to fly high in the heavens."

Happy with her decision, she returned to the barn, killed the fattest of the chickens, plucked its feathers, then returned to the house satisfied that her grandfather would be happy.

Looking down at her bloody hands, a thought came to her: *I'll take a bath!* The thought stirred her, for she loved bathing, and in the summer nearly drove her grandfather to distraction by bathing every night. In the winter, however, with fuel scarce, it was more difficult. She laughed aloud suddenly, saying, "A bath I will have!" and quickly began the preparations.

She moved to the stove, the family's pride and joy. It was made of heavy iron, built by her father, Ivan, who had been Grandfather Jacob's only son. She had heard the story many times of how Ivan had become a blacksmith and had built the stove for his parents' twentieth anniversary. Now as Reisa quickly built up the fire which had been banked the night before, she ran her hand over the hard cold surface and thought of her parents. She remembered them with sorrow and grief, for they had been a cheerful, loving pair. They had both died of an epidemic before she was ten, but Reisa kept their memories alive by thinking of them often. And now, as always, a warmth came inside her that matched the fire that began to crackle inside the stove, and she whispered, *"Got tsu danken."*

She spoke the words in Yiddish, for that had been her mother's native language. Gretchen Moltman had been of German descent, and had spoken Yiddish so much that the rest of the family had learned it along with their native Russian. Her grandfather Jacob had taught Reisa Hebrew. While not fluent in this language as he was, Reisa could read it and even speak it rather haltingly. Over all of this was a layer of English. One of the villagers, Yuri Pavlov, had emigrated to the United States and stayed for several years. He had come back to take care of his aged parents and had brought several books with him. Living next door to Reisa and her grandfather, he had been amused at her interest in America and had taught her the rudiments of English. He had also let her read in English two books that he had brought back—*Great English Poetry* and *Uncle Tom's Cabin.*

When the fire was built up, Reisa put the large kettle and the large iron pot on the stove, then filled them with water. Going back outside, she fetched an iron pot used to wash clothes. It was heavy, and she puffed as she brought it inside and set it down on the floor with a thump.

While the water heated, she busied herself with the chores around the room which served as living room, dining room, and kitchen. The only other room was a bedroom and study where her grandfather kept his books and slept. She herself slept on a cot that folded up against the side of the wall in the larger room.

Finally her work was interrupted by the bubbling of the water and the whistling of the kettle. Moving over, she poured the boiling hot water into the large pot and added some cold water. She loved baths as hot as she could bear.

She bolted the door and drew the curtain over the window. The yellow light of the lamp illuminated the room as she stripped off all of her clothes and stuck her toe into the water. "Ooh, that's good!" she whispered, then slowly immersed herself. The water came up to the edge of the pot so that only her head and knees were out. She lay there soaking up the delicious heat for a time, then finally straightened up and pulled the pins from her hair so that it cascaded down her back. She had beautiful black hair that came down to her waist, but no one ever saw it. She kept it done up and covered by a scarf, as all respectable Jewish women did.

The soap was rough and almost gritty, but she managed to work up a lather as she washed her hair, then soaped herself all over. Filling the smaller pot with warm water, she rinsed herself and her hair. Finally she stepped out.

Being completely undressed embarrassed her, even though she was all alone. As the daughter of an Orthodox Jew, she had arrived at the notion that the body was something to be covered and not exploited. She toweled herself dry and for one moment stared down at her body, thinking, *I must have grown. I'm taller.* Indeed, she was a tall young woman, with the prominent curves of young womanhood. She had long legs and a rather short upper body, and her muscles were firm, although lean rations had kept her very slender.

She put on the underwear, the *gatkes*, then quickly donned a long gray woolen dress. Finally she sat with her back to the fire combing her hair and letting it dry. This was a time of peace for her, and she hummed under her breath. Finally, her hair dry, she moved over to the small mirror and began plaiting it so that she could put it under her scarf. Without meaning to do so, she studied her face. She was not a vain young woman, and would have been astonished if anyone had called her beautiful. Her hair was black as the blackest thing in nature, and her eyes were enormous—a strange gray-green color, with a beautiful, faintly oriental shape. She had an oval face with high cheekbones and a wide mouth. But one feature she always noticed was the widow's peak, the tiny "V" of the hairline that dipped down on her forehead. She touched it and said playfully, "I ought to cut you off!"

Finally she emptied the large pot a basin at a time, throwing the water out the door, then carried the pot outside. She felt strange about taking baths, for none of her neighbors seemed to enjoy the ritual—but she was determined to have this one pleasure.

Hunger gnawed at her, and she moved quickly to prepare herself a small meal. She made tea in the samovar, heated a little of the beet soup that they had had for supper, and after she had eaten that she found a bit of *taiglech*, a small cake dipped in honey.

She ate one of them, then Boris, her cat, came purring roughly and shoving his blunt head against her leg.

"Oh, Boris! Are you hungry? Here, I saved you some fish." Quickly she took the fish out of the cupboard, laid it out, and watched as he ate, stroking his coal-black fur. He looked up from time to time licking his chops, his enormous green eyes studying her. When he finished, she broke off a piece of the *taiglech* and offered it to him. "Do you like sweet cakes, Boris?" She laughed when he ate it. "Of course you do. You like everything."

Reisa rose and moved to the cage that her grandfather had made out of small branches, opened the door, and fed the small bird that was regaining his health. He had been mangled by a cat, and Boris was under suspicion. Reisa was always torn between her love for birds and her love for Boris. She often said to him, "Boris, you're a *mamzer!*" This was the Yiddish word for trickster that she had heard her mother use many times.

Reisa put on her coat, then picked up a package wrapped in brown paper. As she started for the door, Boris came at once with his nose stuck in the crack. "No! You can't go," Reisa said.

Boris looked up at her—and grinned.

Reisa laughed aloud at this ludicrous sight—as she always did. "You're the only cat I ever saw that could grin." Indeed it was true. Boris, for whatever reason, had learned to bare his teeth when he wanted something—or when he was in trouble. It was not a snarl, for the corners of his lips were turned up. It was a feat that never ceased to amaze and amuse Reisa, but now she picked him up firmly and moved him away from the door. Putting him down, she said, "Smile all you want to, but you're not charming me. I'll be back soon."

She left the house, pulling the door closed behind her. The biting cold struck her like a fist as she made her way against it. The small village was only a hundred yards from the little house she shared with her grandfather. As she came to the first house, it never occurred to her to think what a pitiful sort of village it was, for it was all she had ever known of the world. Basically the main street of the *shtetel* was composed of two rows of ramshackle houses. All of them were weathered and made of makeshift material, and now thin tendrils of smoke curled upward from the chimneys into the cloudy sky. She passed by two starved-looking dogs that slumped away when she spoke to them, and once a hammer-headed yellow cat emerged from a small space between two of the houses. She knelt down and stroked his fur for a moment, toying with the idea of taking him home. But this would not do, so she quickly moved on.

The streets were frozen mud, and she stumbled a bit over the ruts as she passed through the village and headed toward the mayor's house. She paused two hundred yards from the main part of the *shtetel,* and glanced fearfully at a stiff body hanging from a roughly built gibbet. A rusty chain encircled the middle of the body, and the face of the man was blue. The eyes of the corpse, staring and wide open, looked like frozen marbles. The body turned slowly, the chain creaking as the wind caught it. The criminal's body had frozen over during the night, and now a few drops of congealed moisture fell on the ground beneath.

Reisa shivered and turned her eyes away, a feeling of disgust welling up within her. *What good do they think that does? Putting a corpse on a gibbet won't keep men from stealing and killing. Other thieves laugh at it, thinking it won't be them.*

Disturbed by this gruesome symbol of rough justice left by the military who roamed the countryside in large bands, Reisa hurried along. She heard her name called and turned to see Yelena Petrov emerging from her house, which was set a hundred feet back off the road. Yelena was a short, heavyset girl with a ruddy face and a pair of shiny dark brown eyes. She had a bad reputation in the neighborhood for going out with wild young men, and was what Orthodox Jews called a *vildeh moid*—a wild

Jewish girl. She even went out with the czarist soldiers, but her parents let her do as she pleased, apparently not caring.

"Reisa! Come in and get warm."

"I can't, Yelena. I've got to go take this blouse to the mayor's wife."

"Always working! Always working!" Yelena grinned. She was missing one tooth, and there was a vitality in her that seemed to leap out. "You know who came to see me last night?"

"Who?"

"One of the sergeants. His name is Retzov. We went over to the next village and danced until nearly two o'clock. I think I drank a little bit too much."

"You shouldn't do that, Yelena. You're going to get in trouble."

"Life's too short to worry about that." Yelena turned her head to one side and reached over and tugged at Reisa's sleeve. "Come and go with me. The soldiers would go crazy over those green eyes of yours."

"I can't do that."

"I know what you're thinking, Reisa. I saw your grandfather talking to the *shadchen* last Monday."

"The matchmaker? Oh, that's nothing. They're good friends."

"Good friend, my eye! Your grandfather's looking for a good deal. I think he wants to marry you off to Ivan Tankoff."

Reisa laughed shortly and shook her head firmly. "I'd just as soon marry a *goy*, a Gentile, as him."

"Well, he's got lots of money."

"He's got three children, and he needs a new wife. He's worn out two women already, now he's ready to start on a third. No matchmaker for me! I've got to go."

Yelena called out after Reisa. "You'd better come tonight. We're going out sleigh riding. I can have my fellow bring you a friend."

Reisa shook her head and moved steadily down the road. She came to the mayor's house and knocked on the door. The mayor himself, Vassily Trecovitch, opened the door. He was a large man of fifty with a round, pale face and muttonchop whiskers. "Ah, it's you, Reisa. Come in out of the cold."

"I brought the blouse for your wife, Mayor."

"Fine. She only has twenty more, but she won't be satisfied until she has a hundred." He took the package and stood looking at her for a moment. He was not a Jew, but had been a good friend to her grandfather and to many of the other Jews. His wife had given Reisa a great deal of work, and the mayor himself had always been pleasant enough to her. His wife was a thin, dark woman who was sharp and rather harsh. Reisa much preferred dealing with the mayor himself.

"Reisa, do you still study English with Yuri?"

Surprised by the question, Reisa blinked, then nodded. "Yes, sir. I do."

"Why do you do it?"

"Oh, I don't know, Mayor. I just like it. It's fun, and it's such a *strange* language. The sounds they make are so funny."

Trecovitch nodded and pulled at his muttonchops. They were fine and long, and he was rather vain about them. "I'm glad to hear you're trying to better yourself. It may be a good thing."

"A good thing to study English?" Reisa asked, puzzled. "Why is that?"

But Trecovitch merely shook his head. "Here," he said, fumbling in his pocket and coming out with some change. "I put a little bonus in there."

"But your wife hasn't even looked at it. She may not like it."

"You always do good work." He smiled.

"Thank you, Mayor."

As Reisa turned to go, the mayor said, "Reisa, where's your grandfather?"

"He's teaching Hebrew at the synagogue."

"Have him come by and see me before he goes home."

"Yes, sir. Shall I tell him what you want to see him for?"

"No," Vassily said, and his eyes refused to meet hers. "Just have him come by."

"Of course, Mayor. Thank you very much."

Reisa left the house somewhat puzzled by the behavior of Mayor Trecovitch. He was a jolly sort of man—yet there had been something almost furtive in his behavior. She could not understand it, and as she made her way down the street and headed toward the synagogue, she was puzzled. More than once she looked up at the gray skies and thought of the goose that she had found. The thought of how he had eaten and was now sleeping pleased her. "My fine fellow—soon you'll be well—then I'll set you free and you can fly to the warm south. You'll be honking and pulling at the green grass with your fellows."

The thought of the goose's long journey south intrigued Reisa. She loved geography, but knew little of the great world. The mayor had a book filled with beautiful maps, and several times he had gone over them with her. As she moved along, she tried to think what it would be like to travel. She had never been so much as ten miles from her village, but since childhood she had dreamed of strange lands far away. Perhaps she was so determined to see the great goose make his way to a distant place because she herself would never do so. Once it had pained her to think that she would live and die in her small village, never seeing anything of the great world the mayor's book had revealed to her; now she had moved past that thought, putting it away with other girlhood fancies.

If I can't see the great world, my goose can! The thought cheered her, and she smiled as she made her way through the village.

Two

Reisa sat in the outer room which had been added to the synagogue, waiting for her grandfather Jacob to finish his Hebrew lessons with five bored and unruly boys. Across from her sat Reb Chaim Gurion, the spiritual leader of the small congregation. He was a thin, worn man with kindly brown eyes and sunken cheeks. His voice was soft, and there was a gentleness in his spirit that Reisa had always liked.

"And how goes your Hebrew lessons, Reisa?"

"Oh, I'm keeping up as well as I can, Reb Gurion. I'm afraid I'm not as good a student as I should be."

"Nonsense." Gurion waved his thin hand in a gesture disclaiming her answer. "You were always smarter than any of your grandfather's students."

"I'm pleased you should think so, but I'm afraid I didn't get my grandfather's brain."

The rabbi smiled suddenly, which made him look younger than his forty-five years. Time and troubles had lined his face and bent his thin frame, but his eyes were clear and sharp. "Tell me, Reisa, I know your grandfather's giving you different subjects in the Torah and the Talmud. What are you studying now?"

"For the last month he's had me looking up passages on the Messiah."

"Indeed! Fascinating subject. Let me test you then. You're familiar with Moses Mamonides?"

"Yes, indeed. He was the famous Jewish scholar of long ago."

"And how many articles are in the creed of this famous scholar?"

"Thirteen, Rabbi."

"I would have you recite them for me."

Reisa began reciting:

"I believe that God alone is the Creator.
That he is absolutely one.
That he has no body or bodily shape.
That he is the first and the last.
That only to him may we pray and to no other.
That the words of the prophets are true.
That the prophecy of Moses is true, and that he is the father of all prophets.
That the Torah now found in our hands, was given to Moses.
That this Torah is not subject to change, and that there never will be another Torah from the Creator.
That the Creator knows all the thoughts and deeds of man.
That he rewards and punishes according to the deed.
That the Messiah will come; though he tarry I will expect him daily.
That the dead will be resurrected."

"Very good indeed, daughter! You have a fine memory. And so the twelfth item is that the Messiah will come. Your grandfather has you studying that."

"Yes. It has been very fascinating."

"Yes. One day he will come. He who will deliver Israel and the nations from all the troubles of the world."

"Yes. I believe that, Rabbi."

"It has been a part of Jewish faith since biblical time. Has your grandfather told you of the origin of the word *Messiah?*"

"No, sir."

"The word *Messiah* is derived from the Hebrew *Mashiah.*"

"And what is the meaning of *Mashiah*, sir?"

"It means 'the anointed one.' Originally it meant a designation for a ruler king."

Reisa leaned forward, very interested in all of this. "And what will the Messiah bring, Rabbi? In what form will he come?"

"Ah, that is a matter of some disagreement—that and other questions such as what phenomena will accompany the Messiah's coming. How does the Messianic age relate to the end of history? I'm sure your grandfather will take you through all these questions step-by-step."

Reisa showered Rabbi Gurion with questions, and he, with a smile, answered them as best he could.

Finally she said, "I think my grandfather's view of the Messiah is different from those I have heard from others."

Rabbi Gurion was interested. Leaning forward, he folded his hands. "How so, Reisa?"

Reisa could not answer this exactly. She thought for a moment, then said, "So many that I have heard about believe that the Messiah will be a victorious political leader who will lead Israel into battle and win."

"Many do believe that. Your grandfather does not?"

"He is puzzled by the passages in the Torah and in the prophets that refer to suffering—that the Messiah will be a suffering one."

"Those are troublesome passages for all of us. And what are his conclusions?"

"I do not think he has reached one, Rabbi." Reisa smiled shyly. "Perhaps you could tell me."

"I do not think one tells another about things like this. Each individual must study and wait on God, believing that one day God will speak."

For some time Reisa continued this conversation. She could hear the vague sound of the boys reciting Hebrew in the main room of the synagogue, but as she continued her conversation, she seemed to find something troubling in the expression of the rabbi. He was ordinarily a calm man with a ready smile, but there were few smiles today, and she saw that he was worried. She wanted to ask him what was wrong, but it seemed ill-mannered for one of her age and sex to interrogate the rabbi. So she simply determined to say extra prayers for him.

Finally there was the sound of running feet. Reisa said, "I think the lesson is over."

She looked to the door. As her grandfather came in, she stood and asked, "How was the lesson?"

"They seem to be determined to remain unchanged."

Jacob Dimitri smiled as he spoke. He was a spare silver-haired man, but he did not look his age, which was sixty-five. Long ago he had wanted to be a university professor, but he had been forced to abandon his studies to support his brothers and sisters after the death of his parents. Instead of a professor, he had become a tutor of Hebrew to other men's children. "Has this worrisome young woman been troubling you, Rabbi?"

"Not at all! She is a fine scholar."

"And a good cook. I think I would starve to death if Reisa were not there to care for me."

"She has been telling me of your views about the Messiah."

"I think it is a subject that every Jew should be concerned about."

"I agree. Perhaps we can get together one evening this week and compare notes."

Reisa spoke up suddenly, "Christians believe that Jesus is the Messiah." She spoke before she thought (as she sometimes did) and saw that both men's faces changed.

"That is what they believe," Jacob said soberly. And then, as if to terminate a conversation of something unpleasant, he said, "We must go, Reisa."

"Good-bye, Rabbi."

"Good-bye, Reisa. Good-bye, Jacob."

The two stepped outside of the synagogue. As they walked back toward the village, Reisa said, "I have a surprise for you. I can't wait to give it to you."

"A surprise? What sort of surprise?" Her grandfather's warm brown eyes gazed down at hers, his mobile lips curving in a smile.

"It's a present," Reisa said. She returned his smile, linking her arm through his.

"Well, I always think I deserve surprises, but I usually don't."

"You deserve the very best, *Zaideh.*" This was the Yiddish word for grandfather, which Reisa often used as a term of endearment.

"Well, do you have it in your pocket?"

"No. It's much too big for that." Reisa's eyes sparkled, and she squeezed his arm. "What would you think of a feast tonight?"

"A feast! I'm always in favor of that, but where is it to come from?"

"It came from God." Reisa smiled. "All blessings come from him, *Zaideh.*" Suddenly she could not wait for the evening. "I killed the fattest chicken, and tonight we will have a feast!"

"That sounds wonderful!"

"I thought we would ask Yuri and his parents over to share it with us."

"That would be a blessing for them indeed. They would be most grateful, I'm sure."

Chatting happily, the pair passed through the food market that had been set up on one end of the main street. During the winter there was no problem of food spoiling. In the open square a food market to serve all the area contained the hanging carcasses of animals, including cows, sheep, and fowls. There were fish, too, all frozen like silver stones. As they passed through the market, they greeted the bearded merchants and peasants, most of whom wore the Muscovite costume, long heavy cossack pants and fur caps. Jacob spoke to many, and more than one young man came to give a word to Reisa. As she responded briefly to each of them, Reisa remembered what Yelena had said.

"A little bird tells me you've been talking to the matchmaker, *Zaideh,*" she said, a smile in her eyes and on her lips.

A look of surprise swept across Jacob's features, then he laughed. "Oh, yes. He's thinking of having his boy join the school." He turned to look at her, a question in his eyes. "Were you thinking I was looking for a husband for you?"

"The thought did pass my mind."

"What would I do without you? You'll have to have a husband some day, but not now."

"Good! Who needs one of those troublesome things anyway?"

Just then Yelena darted across their path, laughing as a young soldier chased her.

"I worry about Yelena," Jacob said. "She's headed for trouble."

"Yes. She's a wild young girl. There are many such."

Jacob put his arm around her. "But you are a good girl, Reisa. I thank the Creator of the Universe for you every day."

Reisa felt the warmth and returned his hug. Suddenly she remembered the mayor's message. "Oh, the mayor wants you to stop by."

"Indeed?"

"Yes. I dropped a blouse off for his wife. I got a bonus for it, too. Now we can buy you a new pair of gloves."

"Better a new dress for you."

The two argued amiably until they reached the mayor's house.

It was a short visit, and Reisa sat quietly waiting until her grandfather came out. He said nothing, and his silence worried her. *First the rabbi,* she thought, *and now Grandfather. What is troubling them?* She knew, however, that it was no good to ask, for he was a man who knew how to keep his problems to himself. She concentrated on the feast that would come that evening, thinking of what a fine time it would be.

The smell of stewed chicken filled the room, and Reisa poked at the bird with a knife. She had made a rich gravy which simmered on the stove, while another pot held the chicken liver soup, which was a favorite of her grandfather.

Across the room Yuri Pavlov sat speaking with her grandfather in an animated fashion. Yuri was a sturdy peasant in his late forties with a shock of dark brown hair and a square face carved, it seemed, almost out of granite. He spoke rapidly and waved his arms around a great deal, often laughing at something that Jacob was saying.

Yuri's parents sat quietly at the table. They were very elderly now, and Reisa sadly thought that it was unlikely that they would be alive much longer. She knew of Yuri's devotion to them, for he had left a profitable business in the United States after emigrating there. He had come home to take care of them when his other two brothers had both died and there was no one else.

Jacob, as always inquisitive, was pumping Yuri for details about America. It was a subject that fascinated him. "Why do you say such evil things about America, Yuri? You made money there."

"Yes, I made money there—and I lost my religion there."

"I cannot believe that!"

"Then you do not know America. It is not like here, Jacob. It is a godless place."

"But there are many Jews who have gone to America. They have not *all* lost their religion."

Yuri clapped his meaty hands together and leaned back in his chair, which creaked under him. He sniffed the air and said, "Reisa, how much longer do I have to wait? My stomach thinks my throat's been cut."

"It's all ready," Reisa said. "Everyone come to the table."

Since Yuri's parents were already at the table, the two men took the other two places. They had made a place for another, and Reisa said, "There's not room to set this beautiful bird down. Just give me your plates. Tell me what part you like best."

"Don't give me the part that goes over the fence last." Yuri grinned.

"You shouldn't talk like that, Yuri," Mrs. Pavlov said. Her voice was feeble, and her mind sometimes wandered. "It isn't nice in the presence of a young lady."

"Oh, I'm sorry! Did I hurt your feelings, Reisa?"

"You do that every time you open your mouth, Yuri," Reisa teased. "Now, what do you want?"

"I'll have dark meat. How about the leg?"

Reisa skillfully sliced the leg from the chicken and put it on Yuri's plate. "I made fresh bread last night," she said, and went to get it out of the oven. "Yuri, you slice it while I serve the others."

The feast was soon on the table, and there was a moment's silence. They all waited for Jacob, as always, and he prayed, "Oh, Father of the Universe, we thank thee for this food which came to us from thy hand. As the servant looks to the hand of his master, do our eyes look unto thee, O mighty and everlasting and almighty God. We love you for what you have given us, and we give you praise and thanks for every blessing. Amen."

Yuri picked up a huge leg at once, took a bite, then yelped, "Ow, that's hot!"

"Things are usually hot when they come right out of the fire, Yuri," Reisa laughed. "Now, why don't you let it cool a little bit."

"I can't. I'm too hungry."

Reisa saw that the others were served, then sat down. "What were you saying about America?" she asked. "I can't believe all Jews lose their faith."

"Not all, perhaps," Yuri said grudgingly. He took a bite of the dark meat, chewed it with evident relish, and swallowed, then waved the leg around as if it were a baton. "They forget that they are Jews. They cut off their earlocks. They don't eat kosher food. They don't go to the synagogue."

As the meal progressed, Yuri did most of the talking, with Reisa and her grandfather listening carefully. America was almost another planet to them, and Yuri was the only real contact they had—that and the two books he had brought back. The book of poems had delighted her. But the other book, *Uncle Tom's Cabin*, grieved her greatly. She asked, "The black slaves in America. Are they still beaten like Uncle Tom?"

"No. Of course not. The war settled all that."

"What war was that? Did America fight against an enemy?"

Yuri took another bite and chewed lustily. "They fought themselves," he said. "Half the country believed in slaves, the other half didn't. So they had a war, and those that believed in slaves got whipped."

"Good!" Jacob said firmly. "No man should be a slave."

"Nor no woman either," Reisa added with a smile.

"Right you are, my daughter."

The meal went on until they were all stuffed and warm and full. Reisa carefully divided some of the meat for the elderly Pavlovs to take back with them. Yuri stayed for a while to help Reisa with her English. He listened as she read from the book and corrected her pronunciation as best he could.

"Now, let me test your vocabulary. What is the English for *pipek?*"

Reisa's hand flew to her mouth, and she said in a shocked tone, "You shouldn't say things like that!"

Yuri's eyes danced with humor. "Well, you've got to know what to call things. What's *pipek* in English?"

"I don't know. I have no idea, and I don't want to discuss it."

"Must you speak of such things, Yuri?" Jacob protested. "It isn't nice."

"The English for *pipek* is belly button. Don't you suppose Americans have belly buttons? Of course they do! If you went to America, you couldn't call them a *pipek*. They wouldn't know what you were talking about. You've got to know belly button."

Despite himself, Jacob laughed. "You are an *awful* man, Yuri Pavlov! I think I do not want you to teach my granddaughter anything more intimate than belly button."

"As you will, Jacob."

"What are the women like in America?"

"The Jewish women?"

"Just any women."

"They're like women here. Some of them are very bad, but I'm sure you wouldn't want to hear about bad women. They're like Gentiles here, I suppose. *Goys* are the same everywhere."

"But do the Jewish women keep their hair covered?" Jacob demanded. "Do they wear scarves?"

"The more Orthodox do, but even when I was there a new movement was going on."

"What kind of a movement?"

"It was called the Reform Movement."

"I've heard of it." Jacob leaned forward with interest. "What do you know about it?"

"Not much—except I was against it. Why should we change the ways of our fathers? Would you believe they have services in English and not in Hebrew?"

"I can't believe that!" Reisa exclaimed.

"It's true enough. And they say there's no need to eat kosher food. Why, would you believe I've seen Jews eating meat and then washing it down with milk?"

"It's an abomination!" Jacob exclaimed. "They could not be good Jews."

"They think they are. Anyway, I was glad to get back here where men still hold with the old ways of God."

For some time the three sat there in companionable silence. Finally Yuri rose and said, "I must go sleep this off. Thank you so much for the fine feast. It was good of you."

"It was Reisa's chicken." Jacob smiled.

"No. It was God's chicken," Reisa said quickly.

Yuri came over and shook Jacob's hand and then turned to Reisa with a smile. "I give honor to your chicken who has brought comfort to me and my aged parents. I will see you tomorrow."

After Yuri was gone, Jacob said, "That was a fine meal. You can cook as well as your mother—or your grandmother, for that matter. A claim I would not make of anyone else."

"Why don't you sit down and have some more tea?"

"I believe I will. I haven't been so stuffed in years."

He sat down and began to read while Reisa poured tea out of the samovar. "Here. Taste some of this."

As Jacob sipped the tea, Reisa said, "A funny thing happened this morning, *Zaideh*. A huge goose fell into our yard, half frozen."

Jacob listened, then suddenly smiled broadly. "Now I know why you sacrificed one of your precious chickens. You were too tenderhearted to kill that goose."

Reisa laughed aloud, her eyes sparkling. "You're too clever for me! I can never fool you."

"You try it all the time—but I like it. Do you think the goose will ever be able to fly again?"

"Yes! I will feed him and care for him until he is strong. Then he can go south to join his flock."

The two talked for some time, but finally Jacob fell silent. Reisa knew that something was on his mind and just simply waited.

Finally Jacob sighed heavily and turned to face Reisa. "Daughter, I have some news that is not pleasant."

"Is it something the mayor told you?"

"Yes."

"I knew he gave you bad news. What is it?"

"It may never come, but I must have you prepared, my Reisa." Jacob had trouble framing the words, but finally he took one of her hands in his. "There may be trouble coming from the government."

Instantly Reisa understood. "A pogrom, *Zaideh?*"

"Yes."

Neither of them spoke, and the only sound in the room was the sputtering of the fire. Every Jew lived under the shadow of the pogroms—government attacks on the Jewish community. They were frightful persecutions, including the massacre of entire communities of Jews.

Boris got up, arched his back, and came over to nuzzle Reisa's calf. She picked him up and stroked his fur. "It will be all right. The Master of the Universe will take care of us."

"You believe that, Reisa?"

"Yes. Does it not say in the book of Deuteronomy, 'If a bird's nest chance to be before thee in the way in any tree, or on the ground, whether they be young ones, or eggs, and the dam sitting upon the young, or upon the eggs, though shalt not take the dam with the young.' So if the Eternal One cares for a little bird, he will care for us."

Keeping one hand on Boris's thick fur, she stretched out the other, putting it on her grandfather's thin shoulders, and stated again firmly, "He who cares for a tiny bird—or a big goose—will care for us!"

On the Wednesday after the feast, Yelena Petrov appeared early at Reisa's door, her broad face flushed with excitement. "You must come with me, Reisa," she said urgently. "My cousin Sonya is getting married today in Kitzel."

Reisa smiled at Yelena, but shook her head. "I've got too much to do, Yelena."

"Don't be such an old woman! You need to get out and have some fun."

"My grandfather would never let me go."

Yelena grasped Reisa's arm and shook it urgently. "My father would never let me go alone, but he said if you'd go with me, he'd consent. There'll be lots of good food and dancing and music. There'll be some good-looking men there, too." Her eyes sparkled and she urged, "Let me talk to your grandfather. I can talk him into letting you go with me. Where is he?"

"He's studying, but—"

Reisa's protests were cut short, for Yelena simply hustled her inside and began at once to bombard Jacob with pleas. Jacob listened with amusement for a time, then said, "How will you get to Kitzel and when will you be back?"

"My uncle is going to the wedding, and we can ride in his wagon. We can stay at my cousin's house. We'll be back tomorrow before dark, I promise. Oh, please, Reb, let Reisa go! She needs to have a good time."

Jacob was well aware that his granddaughter had few pleasures, and after inquiring into the arrangements carefully, he said, "Very well, but have your uncle stop by before you leave."

Reisa went to her grandfather and gave him a hug. "Now promise you won't worry about me," she said.

"I won't promise that, but you have a good time."

"I'll bring you some of the wedding feast," Yelena said. "Now, get your things ready, Reisa. My uncle wants to leave soon."

The two girls made their preparations, and shortly before three, Yelena's uncle, a tall thin man named Fedor Varvarinski, pulled his wagon up in front of Jacob's door. Reisa was ready, dressed in her best dress, and she turned to kiss Jacob's cheek. "Be sure and eat enough," she prompted. She climbed into the wagon and seated herself beside Yelena. As they set off she waved at Jacob until the wagon took the curve that hid their house.

"We're going to have a good time," Yelena said with satisfaction. "My cousin Boris Babin will be there—he's Sonya's brother. So good-looking! He'll fall in love with you, I'm sure! Then we can have another wedding..."

The village of Kitzel was only five miles away, but the horses were old and slow, so that the sun was low in the west before Fedor nodded his head. "There's Kitzel, right over that rise."

The party reached the village just as dark was falling, and Yelena saw to it that she and Reisa were settled in the house belonging to the bride's father. They arrived in time for the evening's festivities, and Reisa thoroughly enjoyed the music, the food, and the dancing. The celebration went on until nearly eleven, and Reisa found that Boris Babin was indeed fine looking and a good dancer.

Shortly before midnight, the two girls were in bed, weary, but too excited to sleep. Yelena whispered about the men she'd danced with until Reisa finally could not stay awake. She fell into a deep sleep in the middle of Yelena's talk and slept dreamlessly.

Reisa awakened as the first gray light of dawn slanted through the small window, touching her face. She sat up, stretched, and then reached out and shook Yelena, who was sleeping soundly. "Wake up!" she commanded. When her companion grunted and tried to burrow deeper under the blankets, she yanked the covers back. "It's time to get up," she said firmly.

Yelena groaned, but emerged with her hair swirled wildly and her eyes half-open. "It's too early," she complained, but at Reisa's urging, she sat up. "I'm hungry."

"You're always hungry—even after you've had a big meal," Reisa laughed. "Now, let's get dressed. I think I can smell breakfast cooking."

Yelena sniffed, then exclaimed, "It smells good!" She leaped out of bed and began to dress, shivering in the cold.

Reisa pulled her clothes on hurriedly, including her coat, for the room was cold. Turning to watch Yelena, who was lacing her boots, she said, "I slept like a log! It's going to be—"

Reisa never finished her remark, for the sound of many horses traveling hard came to her. She straightened up and went to the window at once. The room was on the second floor, and she could see in the pale light of dawn a dark mass driving down the street. "Soldiers on horses!" she gasped. A sudden fear ran along her nerves.

Yelena darted across the room and took one look at the street. "Cossacks!" she whispered hoarsely. "It's a pogrom!"

"We've got to get out of here," Reisa exclaimed. The stories she'd heard of the horrible things that had befallen Jews caught in a pogrom flashed in her mind. "Come on, Yelena!"

The two girls fled their bedroom and dashed down the stairs. By the time they reached the door, screams of terror filled their ears. "We can't go out there!" Yelena gasped. "They'll kill us!"

"We can't stay here!" Reisa's mind raced, and she grasped the handle of the door and pulled it open. "We can run to the woods and hide."

The two young women stepped outside, and Reisa saw a mounted cossack ride his horse into a young man. As the force of the blow knocked the man down, Reisa saw that it was Boris Babin, the brother of the bride. She halted and watched helplessly as the young man rolled over in the dust. He came to his feet, his eyes wide with terror. He cried out, "Please—don't kill me!" But the cossack, a huge man with white cross straps over his chest and a black fur shako, lifted his saber, laughed wildly, and brought it down with all his might. Reisa grew sick as the blood spurted from the falling victim. Babin kicked his legs and tried to stem the flow of crimson, but only for a moment, then grew very still.

The cossack spotted the two young women and cried out loudly, "Here we are, comrades! Two young pigeons. I'll take the tall one!"

Reisa was paralyzed with fear as the broad-bodied cossack dismounted in one smooth motion and started toward her. She could not seem to move, but she was aware that other cossacks were coming.

At that moment, Yelena gave her a shove. "Run, Reisa—run!" she cried. She threw herself at the huge cossack, and he grabbed her and began ripping at her clothing.

"Ho, a fighter! So much the better! I like spirit in a woman!"

Reisa knew that Yelena had sacrificed herself to give her a chance. She tore her gaze away from the pair, whirled, and darted down the street. Heavy footsteps were behind her, but she was fleet of foot. As she ran, she was aware of the slaughter that went on all around her. The cossacks spared neither young nor old. She saw a child no more than two years old impaled on the saber of a wildly laughing soldier, and two elderly men wearing prayer shawls were cut down.

Reisa had always been a fast runner, and now she ran with all her strength. The sounds of the heavy boots fell behind her, and she risked turning to see two large cossacks lumbering after her. Seeing her turn, one of them yelled, "You won't get away—you Christ-killing Jew!"

The taunt spurred Reisa, and she took a turn between two rows of houses. The woods lay close by, and she knew if she reached them, she would be safe. Her greatest fear was that men on horseback would chase her. The screams of terror and agony followed her, but as she reached the woods, she saw that she was not being pursued. The cossacks, she knew with a sickening certainty, had plenty of victims without her. She turned east and ran until the sounds of the dying faded, but she knew that everything had changed.

They will come to our village—we must get away!

She walked as fast as she could, and when she reached her house, she fell inside, almost unconscious. Jacob started up, his face filled with fear, and as she fell against him, she cried brokenly, "Grandfather—the soldiers. They have come!"

Jacob grabbed her by the shoulders. "Is it a pogrom?" He listened as she poured out the story, her voice choked with fear.

"We must leave at once, Reisa," Jacob said evenly. "I must go at once to the mayor."

Reisa wiped at tears and looked up at her grandfather. "Do you think he can protect us from the soldiers?"

"No, not even he can do that. He is a good man and has love for our people. We have talked of this terrible thing, and he has told me that if we are forced to flee he will buy all that we have—our land and all our possessions."

Reisa took a deep breath. "But what will we do, *Zaideh?* Where will we go where the soldiers cannot find us?"

"We will go to America. I have thought much about this, and I know we will be safe there. Now, listen to me carefully, Reisa. We must leave right away. The soldiers could come at any time. I will go at once to the mayor for the money, and I will return with Adrik Meshone. He will take us to the coast in his cart. While I am gone, you must pack for our journey. We will take only a few things, what we can put into the two trunks. All else I will sell to the mayor."

Reisa pulled herself up and stood straight. "I will have everything ready when you return, *Zaideh.*"

"That's my brave girl!" Jacob took her hands and said, "Let us put ourselves into the hands of the merciful God." He bowed his head and Reisa clung to his hands as he said, "O Master of the Universe, you are our hope in this dark hour. David once fled for his life, and when all earthly hope was gone, he said, 'But thou, O LORD, art a shield for me; my glory, and the lifter up of mine head. I cried unto the LORD with my voice, and he heard me out of his holy hill. I laid me down and slept; I awaked; for the LORD sustained me. I will not be afraid of ten thousands of people, that have set themselves against me round about.' O great and almighty God, keep thy servants safe as you kept David safe!"

Reisa looked up and saw the faith in her grandfather's fine eyes. Reaching up, she touched his cheek and whispered, "Salvation belongeth unto the LORD: thy blessing is upon thy people." She dashed the tears from her eyes, then gave him a gentle push, saying, "Go now, and when you return, all will be ready!"

Three

A sullen sun sent its dim beams through the single window of the room, and suddenly everything seemed unbearably sad to Reisa. She was alone, for her grandfather was already outside supervising the loading of the trunks onto the small wagon that they had hired to take their luggage to the coast. Reisa had sorted through their possessions hastily, but deciding what to take and what to leave was hard for her. There was a terrible sense of finality about everything, for she was saying farewell to the only life she'd ever known.

Now standing in the room she had lived in all her life, her throat grew thick, and she had to blink to keep the tears away. She ran her gaze around the room. Poor as it was, it was home to her. *I'll never sleep in that bed again—I'll never cook another meal on my stove—I'll never watch my grandfather sit beside the window and read...*

"Reisa, we're ready."

The sound of her grandfather's voice brought Reisa to herself, and she tightened her lips, then turned to leave the tiny house for the last time. Picking up the carrier that held Boris, she stepped outside and found her grandfather standing beside the wagon.

Adrik Meshone, the driver whom they had hired to convey them to the coast, was already in the seat. "You're taking that cat to America?" he demanded.

"Yes." Reisa could not say another word, and for a moment stood there as if paralyzed.

"It's time to go, my dear," Jacob said gently.

"I know." Reisa climbed up into the wagon and sat down holding tightly to the carrier. Jacob followed more slowly, and when he was seated, nodded to the driver. "All right, Adrik."

The driver spoke to the horses, who leaned forward with a protesting groan. He wheeled the team around, and the hard frozen earth crunched under the rims of the wheels.

When they had gone a short distance, Reisa turned around, holding Boris tightly to her breast. She took one last look at the plain, rather dilapidated house, and her spirit seemed to grow weak. "Good-bye, house," she whispered, pressing her face against Boris's fur. She could say no more, for the enormity of the undertaking overwhelmed her.

Jacob did not turn back. He set his jaw and said nothing. The two of them sat holding on as the wagon lurched over the uneven, frozen ruts.

Reisa glanced at the two small trunks containing all their earthly possessions, and Jacob caught her eye. "It's sad when you compress all of your life into two small trunks," he murmured.

Reaching over, Reisa took his hand in both of hers. They were both wearing gloves, for the weather was still freezing, but she squeezed his hand, saying as cheerfully as she could manage, "*Zaideh,* God will be with us." She looked down at her hands and asked quietly, "What will happen to the others?"

"The word is out, and many are fleeing, as we are," Jacob said. "Some do not believe the soldiers will come, or they have no place to go, so they stay. We must pray much for our people."

The wagon rumbled on, through the small village, and then to the outskirts, where the cemetery lay. Jacob called out, "Adrik, stop the horses!"

Startled, Adrik pulled the horses to a halt and turned around. "What?" he demanded, as if he had been insulted.

"Wait here," Jacob commanded. He stepped down from the wagon seat and reached up, saying, "Come, Reisa."

Reisa looked surprised, but handed the cat up to Adrik. "Hold him for me, please."

Rather affronted, Adrik took the cat, and for some reason Boris decided he liked the driver. He looked up and bared his fangs. Adrik laughed hoarsely. "A cat that laughs! I've never seen such a thing!"

Reisa took her grandfather's arm, and the two of them walked to the Jewish graveyard. It was set off from the main part of the cemetery. There were no flowers this time of the year, of course, but in the spring and summer Reisa would bring wildflowers of all kinds to place on the graves of her grandmother and of her parents. The three were buried in a small plot at the outer edge of the graveyard.

Jacob and Reisa halted at the stones. The stone over the grave of Reisa's grandmother was well carved, for her own father had done that before his death. Jacob knelt down. Taking off his gloves, he ran his fingers over the stone. He said nothing, but Reisa knelt beside him. Her eyes went to the two stones that marked the graves of her parents.

"*Zaideh,* will we see them again?" Reisa whispered.

Jacob reached out and put his arm around Reisa's shoulders, drawing her close. "Yes. For does not the patriarch Job say, 'For I know that my redeemer liveth, and that he shall stand at the latter day upon the earth: And though after my skin worms destroy this body, yet in my flesh shall I see God: Whom I shall see for myself, and mine eyes shall behold, and not another.'"

Jacob's voice suddenly thickened, and Reisa felt his arm tighten around her. She waited for a moment, then when he rose, she reached deep into her pocket. Pulling out a small glass jar and the knife that she always carried, she loosened a little of the dirt on her grandmother's grave and then from each of the graves of her parents. Putting it in the jar, she tightened the lid. Then she looked up. Her eyes were suddenly confident, and she put her arm again around her grandfather. "When we find our place, *Zaideh,*" she said, her voice strong, "we will put this in it. Now, come, we must go."

The two made their way back to the wagon. After they had climbed in, Jacob said firmly, "All right, Adrik. Take us to the coast."

"It is a long journey to Odessa—over a hundred miles on rough roads," Adrik remarked. He shook his head doubtfully. "Isn't there a closer place?"

"No, Adrik," Jacob said firmly. "Odessa is where the big ships come that go to America. We must go there."

Adrik shrugged and handed Boris back to Reisa. He lay down at once in her lap, going to sleep instantly. Adrik clucked to the horses, and they set off once again.

Turning toward her, Jacob studied Reisa's face, seeming to see the sorrow there. He suddenly asked, "Where do you suppose your goose is right now?"

Reisa brightened momentarily. She had tended the injured goose until he was strong, and just before the wedding had taken him out of the barn. She had watched as he took to the air, then wheeled and headed south. Now she said, "He's on his way to his new home, *Zaideh.*" She leaned against him, murmuring, "Just as we are."

The wagon lurched on for some time. As they left a stand of trees and entered an open road, Reisa asked, "Do you have the paper?"

"Oh, yes. Right here." Jacob removed one glove, put his hand into his pocket, and pulled out a leather wallet. Opening it, he extracted a sheet of paper. "Right here. The name is Laban Gold."

"Can we find him, do you think?"

"Yes. We will find him."

Reb Gurion had given them the name of a relative of his who lived somewhere in New York. He did not have the address, but when he had given Jacob the paper he had said, "You can find Gold. He's a good man, and he will help you get started."

Folding the paper carefully, Jacob inserted it into his wallet, then put the wallet back inside his coat. He sighed, and as he settled himself down, lines appeared in his forehead. He had said nothing to Reisa, but he had been gravely disappointed in the price that he had been able to get for all their things. He was not a businessman—nor ever had been—but now that they were stepping out across a sea to settle in a strange place, he knew that God would have to help him, for he had begun to feel his age. He had never been a strong man physically, but this had never concerned him a great deal. Now, however, he alone was responsible for this young woman who sat beside him and he prayed silently, *God, give me strength to see her settled. Oh, Maker of the Universe, give me strength to see her settled.*

Odessa was a busy place, bustling with people rushing from place to place. The journey from their small village had taken a week, and both Jacob and Reisa were exhausted. Now that they had arrived, Jacob tried to feel satisfaction, but he was drained of strength.

"How do you feel, *Zaideh?*" Reisa asked anxiously.

"Fine, daughter. Fine."

Adrik looked around and said, "We're here at the dock. What will I do with your trunks?"

Jacob said, "We will go find a place, and then you can go back." With these words he climbed down out of the wagon, and Reisa accompanied him. It was noon, and the two of them had been worn thin by their journey. Jacob had slept poorly, for the nights had been bitter cold. They had huddled up under all the blankets that they could bring, but it was not like being in their house.

Now as the two looked around noting the confusion, so different from their simple village, Jacob finally said, "We must buy tickets."

"Yes. Let me ask that officer," Reisa said.

Reisa approached an imposing-looking man in a uniform of some sort. "Please, sir. Where does one buy tickets to go across the ocean?"

The officer looked down at Reisa. He was a handsome man with a sweeping mustache and twinkling black eyes. "Going to America, are you?"

"Yes, sir."

"Well, the ticket office is right over there. You see that sign?"

"Yes. Thank you very much."

"Good voyage."

Reisa and Jacob made their way to the ticket office, where they waited in a rather long line. There was a babble of voices all around them, and Reisa was aware that most of the potential travelers were as poor as they were. *All leaving for America*, she thought. *We're not alone*.

Finally they reached the official who sold tickets and made their purchase. Jacob paled when he heard the price, but there was no alternative. After he paid for the two tickets, the wallet that he put back inside his pocket felt very thin.

"We must buy food," Reisa said.

"But food is included," Jacob protested.

"I do not trust them. Come. We will buy things that will not spoil." She led him to the stores that lined the waterfront and bought cheese, dried beef, and hard bread that would survive the voyage.

Finally, going back to the wagon, they found Adrik holding Boris, who seemed content enough.

"You'll never get on with this cat," he said. "Animals are forbidden."

Reisa whispered, "I've got to take Boris!"

"I will take him back to the village with me if you like. I like a cat."

"No. I can't do that. He must go with us."

"But, child," Jacob protested. "It's against the rules."

"I'm not leaving Boris here." A stubborn light shone in Reisa's eyes, and her lips grew tight. "Come. I will find a way."

Indeed, Reisa did find a way. It was not terribly difficult, for the sailor who looked at their tickets paid little attention to the baggage. Adrik carried on first one of their trunks and then the other, but it was Reisa who carried Boris aboard in his carrier. She walked by with her heart beating, and finally they were on board the *Jennings* along with their trunks.

"Here, Adrik. I thank you, my dear brother," Jacob said as he handed the sturdy peasant three coins.

Adrik took the coins and shoved them into his pocket. "You're going to get in trouble with that cat—but have a good time in America." He nodded at them and left.

Reisa turned to Jacob. "Grandfather, let me go find where we will stay. You stay with the luggage and with Boris."

Jacob was tired, and his strength was almost gone. "All right, Reisa. I will wait."

Finding their place was not difficult, for upon asking one of the sailors where to go, he winked at her and pinched her arm. "Well, a pretty girl like you could stay with me." He laughed at her angry reaction, then said, "Go down that ladder right over there."

Reisa left him at once and went below. She found a dark place lit only by several lanterns, and it was already crowded. The smell was terrible, and her heart sank, for there seemed to be no place for a young woman with an old man. But she knew that she had to be strong not only for herself, but for her grandfather as well. He was too weak and too old for this trip, but there was no other way.

Wheeling, she climbed back upstairs. She spotted a fresh-faced young man, a passenger, for he was wearing no uniform. He leaned on the rail, gazing down at the activity on the dock below.

"Excuse me," Reisa said. "Could you help me?"

The young man turned, and his eyes brightened at the young woman. He said at once, "Yes. What is it?"

Reisa introduced herself, and in exchange the young man said, "My name is Petya."

"I've just come on board, Petya, my grandfather and I. We have two trunks. Could you help us get them down below?"

"Yes. Of course," Petya said eagerly. He followed her, and when they reached Jacob, Reisa introduced him. The young man pulled his cap off at once and nodded. "Good day, sir. Let me help you with this luggage."

Jacob smiled with relief and said, "May the good God bless you, my boy."

Petya picked up one of the trunks and left, then came back for the second. "Plenty of room," he said cheerfully. "Come along now."

Jacob followed the young man with Reisa holding onto his arm. He was taken aback by the smell and the noise in the steerage compartment, for everyone seemed to be talking at the top of their lungs. Petya, however, had found them a place where their trunks could be stored against the side. There were bunks going from the floor to the ceiling. Petya said, "You'd better stake these out at once. They'll all be full before the ship leaves."

This proved to be true, for passengers kept coming on. Men and women and children, whole families all bound for the New World, filled the compartment.

Jacob lay down and went to sleep at once. He slept all afternoon, but Reisa stayed awake getting acquainted with her neighbors.

Finally Jacob awakened, and Reisa said, "The ship is leaving soon. Would you like to go up on deck?"

"Yes. I think so."

The two moved up the ladder holding on carefully. On deck, the sailors were busy with the sails. Neither Reisa nor Jacob understood a thing about seamanship, but they watched with interest as the sails began to drop, and they heard one of the officers crying out something about the anchor.

"We're moving," Reisa said. And sure enough, they felt the stirring of the ship as the winds caught the sails. Overhead the sky was gray, and marked only by the flight of noisy gulls circling the vessel.

As the ship picked up speed, both Reisa and Jacob watched the shore as it receded. Others were there, and the rail was lined with passengers, their eyes fixed upon the land. There was something magnetic about the sight, and every head was turned toward the disappearing line of flat land which represented their old home.

As the land grew fainter and fainter, and as the night began to come on, Jacob said, "Reisa, I know you're sad. But remember Abraham must have felt like we do at this moment." He smiled despite the discomfort of the sharp wind and his weakness. "He had to leave everything—family, friends—all that had been dear to him, but he knew that God was commanding him. And so he went out from his home into a strange country."

Reisa held onto the rail, ignoring the piercing cold. "Do you think God is sending us, Grandfather—as he sent Abraham?"

"Yes. I know he is, Granddaughter!"

Jacob Dimitri found out on the first day of the voyage that he was no sailor. Almost at once, as soon as they reached the deep rolling bellows and the ship began to dip, to fall, and to rise, Jacob felt his stomach lurch.

Reisa saw his face grow pale. "You'd better go lie down, Grandfather."

Jacob obeyed without comment, but even lying down the motion of the ship was terrible for him. He began to vomit, but he was not alone. Reisa was there to help, to bathe his face, to be sure he was as comfortable as possible. But there was actually little that she could do. The passengers were all huddled together almost like cattle, and the narrow bunks were not enough to take care of the overload. Many had to sleep on the hard deck wrapped in blankets.

For those first few days, it was all Reisa could do to care for her grandfather. She had to force him to eat, but the food that was prepared and served out twice a day was not fit in her mind for a sick man.

The dark filthy compartments in the steerage were filled with people with vomiting fits, and a confusion of cries became almost unbearable.

"I wish we had never left home," Jacob moaned one day.

"It's all right, Grandfather," Reisa said, moistening his lips with a damp cloth. She herself hated the ship. Now glancing around, she saw people jammed like rabbits in a warren into the ill-smelling bunks. The odors of scattered orange peelings, tobacco, garlic, and even worse blended together to form a horrible stench.

The next day she decided to try to wash some of their clothes, but it was a miserable failure. There was no fresh water available for washing. The best she could do was to rinse out a few of their clothes in salt water.

The young man, Petya, helped her a great deal. He was a cheerful young man convinced that he would become a millionaire in America. As they were on the deck washing as best they could, his face glowed as he said, "You just wait, Reisa. I'll get rich in America."

"Is that very important to you, Petya?"

"Important! Of course it's important!" Astonishment swept across the young man's face. "Everybody wants to be rich."

"I don't."

"Well, you're a woman. But you'll want to marry a rich man."

Reisa smiled and looked over at Boris, for she had brought him on deck with her. No one had made any complaints about him, and he seemed to be quite a seagoing cat. "You don't want to be rich, do you, Boris?"

Hearing his name, Boris grinned broadly and said, "Yow!"

"See? He wants to be rich," Petya laughed.

"I don't think it's going to be as easy as you think."

"Oh, there's lots of money to be made in America."

Reisa was not at all sure about this. She finished the washing and went downstairs.

After she had made her grandfather as comfortable as possible, Reisa turned to one of her new acquaintances, Ivana Chapaev. "Are you feeling better, Ivana?"

Ivana was not feeling better. She was a middle-aged woman not in the best of health. She and her husband, Ilya, were traveling with their three children. Both of the adults were very ill and seasick to an incredible degree, and it had been Reisa who had taken over the care of their three children.

She took care of them now, seeing that they were fed and washed as much as was possible. The food was dished out of large kettles into dinner pails provided by the ship. They all ate like starved wolves, and Reisa herself had never had a better appetite.

As the days passed, Jacob grew better, and the weather seemed to improve. The ship still plunged on, and sometimes waves came crashing over the top of the deck, filtering down to steerage below. Ship life was hard, but it was endurable.

Reisa was busy and had found ways to make herself useful to many of the passengers. One thing troubled her, however, but she never mentioned it to her grandfather.

She had gone to stand in the bow of the ship often during the voyage, especially late in the afternoon or early in the morning. It gave her, somehow, a feeling of exultation to stand there watching the boundless ocean before her, knowing somewhere ahead was America. But she had become aware that a man was often there watching her. She had seen him first early one morning, and had been somewhat frightened. There were few sailors on deck, and it was quiet except for the hissing of the water along the side, and the ropes trilling with the pressure of the wind. She had turned and seen this huge figure of a man, and a start of fear had taken her. He had not spoken and neither had she, but his eyes, almost hidden by the wild tangle of his beard, were steadfast as they watched her.

Reisa had slipped away, but it had happened more than once. And even worse, she noticed him when she went to get food and at other times. He never spoke, but she feared him and determined never to be caught alone.

Jacob got better each day, but the rough food was not doing him much good. Reisa finally went to the galley where she spoke to the cook, a German named Schultz.

"Herr Schultz," she said. "Could I heat some soup and make some tea for my grandfather?"

Schultz, a thin man who always dressed as if it were summer due to the heat of the galley, agreed at once. "Yah," he nodded. "I like some tea myself once in a while."

As the cook prepared the tea, Reisa spoke with him freely. He seemed to be an approachable man, and she finally asked him, "Who is that big man with the bushy black beard?"

"Oh, you've seen him? His name is Dov. That means 'bear.'"

"What do you know about him?"

"Nothing. He never says anything." Schultz turned to her suddenly, his eyes narrowing. "Why? Has he bothered you?"

"No," Reisa admitted. "Not really. But he watches me sometimes."

"Stay away from him. He looks like a bad one. And he's not the only one on this ship."

Reisa took the soup and the tea down, and it took some expertise to manage the ladder. But when she got there she found her grandfather talking with Ilya Chapaev. "I brought some tea and some soup, *Zaideh.*"

"Oh, that smells good! But there's not enough to go around."

"Oh, that's all right. We've had plenty," Ilya said. He was a large man, though somewhat shrunken by work. His face was worn and his hands were hard, the typical peasant. "What would you think, Rabbi? Will you do it?"

Reisa looked up quickly and saw her grandfather shake his head. "I am not a rabbi. You must not call me that."

"Well," Ilya said rather stubbornly, "you are the closest thing there is to a rabbi on this boat. Will you do it?"

"What do you want him to do?" Reisa asked as she dished out some soup for her grandfather.

"He thinks we should have a service—all of the Jews on the boat," Jacob said.

"I know you're not a rabbi, but you're a teacher—a learned man. We don't need a rabbi to have a service, do we?" Ilya asked.

Jacob blinked, and as he took the bowl of soup, Reisa saw that he was thinking hard. "It might not be a bad thing," he said. "I will do what I can."

"Good. I will tell the others. When would we have it?"

"Whenever you say, but it will not be like being in a synagogue."

"Abraham was not in a synagogue," Ilya said. "A synagogue is wherever the chosen people meet."

Jacob suddenly smiled. It was the first time Reisa had seen him smile since they had gotten on board the ship.

"I think it would be good," she said, pouring tea into a tin cup. "Here. Drink this."

"I think it may be," Jacob mused. "I will have to ask permission though."

"They don't care what we do down here," Reisa said.

"You're right enough about that. So, right here will be the synagogue."

The crowd that gathered for the worship was surprisingly large, at least fifteen men—and since ten men were necessary for any sort of service, that was sufficient. All of them were wearing something that resembled a yarmulke—although some were obviously rigged for the moment. The small caps on the head of every man seemed to bring some sort of pleasure to Jacob, and he noted that many of them were wearing the tallis or prayer robe. His own tallis was made of fine silk, and for the service he had bound a small black leather box to his forehead and another to his arm. They contained small pieces of parchment with quotations from Scripture.

As Reisa watched, she remembered what he had told her so often. *The tefillin on the forehead reminds Jews that they must love God with all their might. The other is worn on the arm facing the heart, which reminds us that we must love God with all of our heart.*

The service itself was rather simple. Jacob began by saying a prayer and was joined by others. "And I, due to your great kindness, will come into your house, and in awe of you I will worship, facing toward your holy temple. How good are your tents, Jacob, your dwellings, Israel!"

Reisa was sitting back with the other women. In a synagogue they would have been in a balcony, but there was no place for that here. So now she listened and repeated the prayer that she had heard so many times: "And I, due to your great kindness, will come into your house, and in awe of you I will worship, facing toward your holy temple. Lord, I love the dwelling of your house and the place where your glory rests, and I will worship and bow and bend my knee before the Lord, my maker. And as for me, may my prayer come to you in an acceptable time; God, in your great countenance, answer me with the truth of your salvation."

It was unlike any *Shabbat* that any of the Jews gathered below deck in the dim light of the lanterns had ever known. The oldest of the Jewish holy days, the Sabbath was important to all of them. If she had been at home, Reisa would have cleaned the house and draped the table with a clean white cloth before the sun set on Friday. She would have lit two candles, and the meal would have begun when her grandfather recited a blessing called the *kiddush*. They would have taken wine and sung hymns and had special food, always including two loaves of bread called *challah*.

All of these elements were there, for someone had produced a bottle of wine, and each of the worshippers had taken a sip. Some of the hard bread that Reisa had brought served as the food.

There in the dim light Reisa's eyes rested on her grandfather constantly. She had always known he was a man who sought after God with his whole heart, and she felt unworthy, for she did not have that drive.

Sometime during the service Reisa turned to her left, and there in the gloominess lightened by the lantern she saw the huge man named Dov. He was in the shadows, and he was watching her so steadily that her heart missed a beat. She turned quickly away and threw herself into the service, but she could not forget him.

~

The day after the *Shabbat* service Reisa left her place below deck to get some fresh water. This was doled out in small portions, and it had to be accounted for.

Out on deck, she noted that sundown had come, the sun sinking into the horizon in a blaze of red. She moved along toward the cook shack where the water was kept and doled out by Schultz. Suddenly a pair of arms went around her. She had the impression of a terrible smell and hands were going over her, touching her in a way that no man ever had. A guttural voice coaxed, "Come now, sweet, 'ere's a man for you!"

Reisa opened her mouth to scream, but a hard palm clapped over it, and she felt herself being dragged along the deck. Kicking and trying to scream, she tried to break the hold. The tin pitcher she had brought fell to the floor with a clanging noise, but there was no one to hear.

She saw ahead of her another passageway and knew that it led down to where the sailors slept. They passed a sailor who was coming down the rat lines, and he laughed, saying quietly, "Take her below for some fun, Max—I'll be right there."

"Now don't be fightin', sweetheart. You're going to love it! You ain't never 'ad a man the likes o' me."

Reisa's mind was blank with terror. She began to pray frantically, but the only thing she could pray was, *Oh, God! Oh, God!*

Suddenly she felt herself released. The abruptness of it caught her unaware, and she fell to the deck. Turning swiftly and coming to her feet, she saw two figures. One was the huge figure of Dov. He had grabbed the sailor by the back of the neck and with a tremendous, brute strength had lifted him up. The sailor kicked and was crying out hoarsely, but Dov simply held him there as easily as Reisa held Boris.

Dov did not speak for a long time, and the sailor began to beg. "Lemme down! You're—breakin' my neck!"

Evidently Dov's hand began to tighten, and he put his other hand on the front of the man's throat. For the first time Reisa heard him speak. "You leave this woman alone or I will tear your head off."

He spoke in Russian, so the sailor had no idea what he was saying. In any case, he could not answer, for his windpipe was clamped shut. The sailor tugged futilely at Dov's massive hand, but he might as well have been pawing at steel.

Another sailor came up and said urgently, "Come on! Let him go, Dov—you're killing him!"

Suddenly Dov released his grip, and the sailor fell to the deck. He scrambled to his feet, holding his throat. He reached under his coat for a knife, but the other sailor said urgently, "Leave him alone, Max. Come on."

Reisa watched as the second sailor hauled her attacker off, and then she took a deep breath as relief washed through her. Turning to the big man, she said, "I—thank you."

Dov did not speak but simply stood watching her. He nodded but said nothing.

"He would have hurt me if you hadn't come."

"Yes. Very bad man."

An impulse came to Reisa. She said, "Would you come with me? I want to tell my grandfather what you've done for me."

Dov's eyes opened, but he did not object.

She put her hand on his arm and said, "Come. He will want to thank you."

She led the huge man downstairs, leading him directly to where her grandfather was sitting on a wooden case reading a book by the pale yellow light of a lantern.

"Grandfather, this is Dov."

Jacob rose and studied the huge figure of the man. He listened carefully as Reisa told him what had happened, and then he put out his hand and said, "I am forever grateful to you, my son."

And then Dov did something that Reisa never forgot. He took the hand of her grandfather, and she saw that it was almost hidden in the huge hands of the giant. He fell to his knees, leaned forward, and kissed the hand of her grandfather. Jacob leaned forward and put his hand on the mat of dark curly hair and prayed a quick prayer for his safety. Finally he asked, "Are you Jewish, my son?"

"No, just Christian man. Russian Orthodox."

Dov rose, and without another word he left.

"God uses strange people to help us, doesn't he, Reisa?"

Reisa was still not over the shock. She well knew what her fate would have been down in that dark hold, and she put a trembling hand in her grandfather's. "Yes. He doesn't look much like an angel, but he was to me."

From that moment, Dov became Reisa's protector. There was no more trouble, for his huge, massive form was not far from the young woman wherever she went. The sailor named Max kept far away, and word spread throughout the ship of what had happened. And it was the cook, Schultz, who said, "Well, Reisa, you found yourself a protector, and a mighty good one, I'd say!"

Four

The galley was one of the few warm, cozy places aboard the *Jennings*. Reisa loved to visit with Carl Schultz, and he seemed to welcome her. Schultz was ordinarily gruff, running the sailors out of his galley with curses, but something about Reisa's appealing manner seemed to melt his crustiness. He had helped her with Jacob by warming soup on the stove, and several times had allowed her to make tea, which her grandfather had sorely missed.

Now as the ship rose and fell, the warmth of the stove soaked into Reisa, and the air was sweet with the odor of freshly baked bread. She wished that she could share this with Jacob, but he felt too weak to join her in the galley. Beside her sat Petya, also pleased to be included in the company.

"So, you have learned the words I gave you yesterday, yah?"

"Oh, yes, Herr Schultz!" Reisa responded quickly. "Petya and I worked hard on them last night. Go on, Petya, say the words for Herr Schultz."

Petya was highly pleased to be included in the English lessons, for he knew this would be a skill he must acquire—and the sooner the better. He had very little English, but he was a quick learner, and now he ran over the members of his body reciting precisely: "Ear—eye—throat—mouth—head, haar—"

"It's *hair,* not *haar.*" Schultz was peeling potatoes, and he grunted after Petya's recitation. Dropping a potato in the bucket, he picked up another one saying, "That is *gut.* You are a bright young fellow. Well, Reisa, what would you like to learn today?"

"Oh, whatever Petya would like."

Petya asked, "Ask him how to say *ben* and *bas,* Reisa."

Reisa said, "Oh, I know that! *Ben* is *son.* You know, Petya, like *Rabbi Ben Ezra* means 'the son of Ezra.' *Bas* is *daughter.*"

"What about an unmarried man?" Petya demanded. Reisa asked this of Schultz, who grinned.

"In English is *bachelor.*" Then he said, "You need to know the word *slob.*"

"Slob? What means *slob?*" Reisa asked.

"Someone who ain't got no manners and is rather nasty."

"Oh." Reisa smiled, her eyes laughing. "We have that word. It is *zhlob.*"

The lesson continued, with the two students pumping Schultz as he peeled potatoes. Finally Petya asked, "Ask him how to say *krassavitseh* in English." His eyes were fixed on Reisa, and he smiled at her.

Reisa flushed. "How do you say in English a woman who looks good?"

"Ah ha!" Schultz laughed, tossing the last of the potatoes in the bucket. "A beautiful woman."

"Beautiful woman," Petya repeated. "Now, I can say 'beautiful woman' and 'slob.'"

"Be sure you don't get them two mixed up," Schultz laughed. "Now, that's all the English for today." He paused and said, "How's your grandfather, Reisa?"

Reisa's face clouded. "Not well, Herr Schultz. I be glad when we get to America."

"Not I *be* glad. *I will* be glad," Schultz corrected.

"Yes. *I will* be glad." Reisa smiled her thanks.

"Well, let's make him up some soup and some hot tea. Maybe he'll feel better."

"Oh, thank you, Herr Schultz!"

Petya went over the list of English words that he wrote carefully down in a notebook while the two prepared the light meal for Jacob. He looked up occasionally. Finally he said in Russian, "I think the weather's getting worse."

"What'd he say?" Schultz said.

"He say wind getting strong. Very bad weather."

"Well, he's right about that. I don't like the looks of it. I've been at sea twenty years, and I can smell a blow. We've got a bad one comin' on."

Reisa and Petya went down below, where they found Jacob sitting with his back against the bulkhead. He smiled when he saw them, but his face was drawn. He was very pale and his eyes were dark hollows. "Ah, you have been getting favors from Herr Schultz again."

"Yes, he's a very nice man. Now, eat this soup while it's hot."

Jacob took the bowl and began eating. He had little appetite, Reisa could see, but she insisted that he eat it all. He did enjoy his tea, however, and as he sat there drinking it he asked if she had heard how long it would be before they arrived.

"I think maybe another week." Reisa poured herself a small cup of tea and sipped it while stroking Boris. She had brought him some scraps of meat, and he ate hungrily. She looked over to where the Chapaevs were huddled together. Both Ilya and Ivana had felt the rough usage of the voyage and had little strength. Reisa went over to share some of the tea with the two.

"Oh, you are good," Ivana said as she drank the tea greedily.

Ilya's face was an unhealthy pallor. "I wish we had never left home," he moaned.

"Don't be foolish, Ilya. We'll be all right. It's just going to take a little while," Reisa said.

She had brought enough soup to share with the young children, and each of them got several spoonfuls of it out of the pot. They clung to her, for they had grown very dependent during the long voyage, since their parents were unable to care for them. Now Reisa sat down and told them a story, a fairy tale her grandfather had often told her in her youth. They huddled close to her, and she hugged them tightly as she whispered the story. It did not matter what story she told them, and she often made them up as she went along.

Finally she became uneasy. The ship was falling more deeply into the waves, and along with the rise and the fall, the ship seemed to be rolling.

"I think I'll just go up on deck, *Zaideh,*" she said, "and see what I can find out."

"Be careful." Jacob smiled wanly.

"Oh, I will. Don't worry, and try to sleep if you can."

She made her way down the crowded hold, feeling as always a strong compassion for the passengers. She had known hardship most of her life, but this voyage had been far more difficult than she had dreamed. Her skin felt scratchy, and she wanted to claw at her scalp. Bathing, of course, was impossible on the ship. Fresh water was doled out in meager amounts only for drinking. As Reisa made her way up to the deck, she thought, *If I could just have a bath, I think I would be happier than I've ever been in my whole life!* But she shook off that thought, knowing that there was no point in dreaming of such things.

When she reached the deck, she was somewhat shocked. The waves were smooth, but she could tell that they were *much* larger—huge like rolling hills, and almost as solid. She could feel the roll and the pitch of the *Jennings* as it forged its way through the sea. Looking overhead, she saw that the sails were all full, and the ship was making good headway.

Making her way with difficulty to the bow, Reisa noted that almost all of the passengers were below. She saw, however, at the very tip of the bow a small group she had often seen before. They were listening as one of the men spoke to them. She knew they were a group of Christians, for she had found out this much. She was curious about them, for she understood they were not the Russian Orthodox that she had known in the village where she had grown up.

Reisa did not join them, of course, but listened until finally they started singing a song. She did not know the melody, but they were singing in Russian, so she understood the words. She listened as they sang in a strong cadence:

Jesus lead thou on
ill our rest is done;
And although the way be cheerless,
We will follow calm and fearless;
Guide us by thy hand
To our father land.

There were many more verses, and they all sang lustily, with happiness on their faces. Reisa saw a calm and a peace that she admired. They were poor people, about twenty in all, half women and some children. For some reason these people fascinated her, and she listened as they sang several more songs.

"They sing pretty well, don't they?"

Startled, Reisa turned to find a tall young man with piercing blue eyes standing beside her. He was one of the officers that she had often seen, but she had never spoken to him. "Yes. They sing very good," she said, struggling with her English.

"Oh, you speak English! Well, that's unusual."

"I study very hard for long time. Make many mistakes."

"You speak very well. My name's Ellis Carpenter. I'm the second officer."

"I am happy to know you. My name is Reisa Dimitri."

"First time on a ship like this, Miss Dimitri?"

"Oh, yes. I never away from my village."

"Well, it's a long way to America." Carpenter smiled. He began asking her questions and complimented her on her English more than once.

"You'll have an easier time than most," he said, nodding at the small group. "I've made this trip twice, and we've put people off who couldn't speak a word of English. I don't see how in the world they make it."

"Are you from America?"

"Oh, yes. From Boston. Do you know it?"

"Boston? No. I do not know him."

Carpenter smiled. He was an engaging young man. "You mean I do not know *it. Him* is for people. *It* is for things—like countries."

"I do not know *it.* Thank you." Reisa nodded to the group who was singing. "Those peoples—I mean *people*—singing, who are they?"

"I don't know much about them. They're very religious. They're Christians, but I don't know what kind. They're going to start some kind of religious settlement in America."

Reisa considered this, then suddenly a strong gust of wind caught her. She grabbed the rail to hang on, then looked up at the skies. They were gray now with dirty clouds scudding along. She turned to face the young man. He had very blue eyes, the bluest she had ever seen, and she wondered if all Americans had eyes like his. "It is very bad—the weather," she said.

"Yes. The glass is falling."

Reisa grew confused. "The glass? It has fallen?"

Carpenter smiled. "We have an instrument that we call the glass. It tells us when there's going to be bad weather. So when we say 'the glass is falling,' we simply mean there's a blow coming on."

Reisa hung on to the rail as the ship rose, heeled over, and then rolled to the other direction. "We will not zink?" she asked.

"We never have," Carpenter replied, "and it's called *sink*, not *zink.*" He looked out at the sea and the sky, and a worried expression swept across his lean young face. "I hope we don't. I'd hate to die. My parents were religious, but I'm not." He turned to face her fully, and his eyes were troubled. "I'm in no shape to meet God."

Reisa did not know what to say to this, and finally she said, "I pray that we will not sink—and that you will find God."

"Thank you, Miss Dimitri. That's a kind thought. You'd better go below. It's going to get worse, and you'll get soaked. I think we'll probably take on some water."

"Take on some water? What means that?"

"That means when the waves get high enough they'll break across the deck, and they'll go down through those openings. In very bad weather, water will come down below."

Reisa was alarmed. "Water will come down where we are?"

"Yes. It'll be very uncomfortable." Carpenter nodded. "But don't worry. It'll drain down below the deck where you are, and the sailors will pump it out."

"What is 'pump it out' mean?"

"It means we have a—" He struggled for the word. "We have a thing that will take the water out of the ship and put it back in the ocean. That way we will not sink as long as the pumps work."

Reisa nodded, understanding little of this. "I will go see to my grandfather."

She left Carpenter, who turned and went back toward the stern.

When she reached her grandfather, she sat down beside him. "It is going to be a storm," she said in English.

Jacob was not as good at the new language as she was and had not picked up much English. "Very bad storm?" he said.

"One of the mens who drive the ship tells me that it will be. He was very nice." She repeated her conversation, and then said, "He told me he was not ready to meet God."

"Most people are not," Jacob said heavily.

"There are Christians on this ship going to America. They are going to make a new village or something like that."

"So, it is not Jews only who flee for their lives but Christians also," Jacob mused. "That is strange." He looked at her, and in the darkness illuminated only by a few lanterns, her face seemed to glow. "Did you talk to any of them?"

"No. But they sang a song." She repeated as many of the words as she could. "They sang very well," she said. "They did not seem to be afraid."

Jacob leaned his head back against the wooden bulkhead and closed his eyes. "No man is so old that he thinks he may live another year," he said. "People always get religious when danger threatens. Someone said if the devil got sick, he would become religious himself." He continued to speak softly, and, as always, Reisa listened. His voice was quiet, and he showed no alarm as the ship pitched even more strongly, wallowing so wildly at times that the possessions of the passengers shifted and had to be replaced. "There is no way of knowing the time of one's death, my Reisa. So the secret," he murmured, "is to be ready at all times."

Reisa never forgot the storm that overtook the *Jennings*. It was a phenomena beyond her experience. She could not believe the fury that struck the ship, driving it, at times, sideways, and at other times thrusting its bow so far into the icy waters it seemed that it would never rise again.

As the fury of the storm struck, their first plunge sent her entire bow deep under the green water. The whole ship pitched at such an angle and with such force that Reisa was thrown forward, as was Jacob and the other passengers.

The wind howled outside like a wild thing, and a cascade of water flooded the compartment. Screams and cries of terror broke the air, and many were praying aloud at the top of their lungs. Children were weeping, and parents were trying to calm them.

How long this went on Reisa never knew. As the water flooded the deck, everything was soaked. No one was dry, and the cold had everyone shivering. On and on the torment went until it seemed there would be no end. The wind did not lessen, but howled in a fierce incantation of doom. Finally Reisa put her arms around her grandfather, and the two held on as the ship rolled and pitched.

Jacob said nothing, except once when the storm was at its height. "I am not afraid to die for myself, Reisa, but I pray that the Ruler of the Universe will save us so that you and the other young people on board and the sailors will have a chance at life."

As the storm continued with no letup, Reisa looked up to see the young officer Ellis Carpenter enter. He called out, "We need some strong hands to run the pump! My men are exhausted."

Reisa at once got up. "You need men?"

"Yes." He peered at her by the feeble light of the single lantern. "If the water isn't pumped out, the ship will sink. Can you speak to these people and see if you can get us some volunteers? Some strong men."

Reisa immediately followed him, interpreting his words. Suddenly, as they moved, the enormous form of Dov Puskin was at her side. "I am strong," he said simply.

Carpenter looked at the huge man and nodded. "Good. Come with me." He left with Dov and the three other volunteers among the men. Reisa said, "I'm going with them, Grandfather. Will you be all right?"

"Yes. Go see what you can find out."

Reisa followed the officer and the men until they reached the pumps. It was a simple enough piece of machinery, two poles with men sitting on opposite benches facing one another. While one pushed down, the other pulled up. This drove another slender pole down into the bowels of the ship. The water was pumped out, but the men had to pump for all they were worth.

"Here, you men take a break. We've got some volunteers." Carpenter had to shout over the screaming of the wind. Dov said, "You three sit there."

The three men took positions, and Dov sat down alone across from them. He put his heavy hands on the handle and pushed down with apparently no effort. The three volunteers were all young men and relatively strong, but the huge form of Dov dominated the scene.

Up and down, up and down they pushed the handle. Dov was tireless and seemed to be doing all the work himself.

"I never saw such a man," Carpenter murmured. "He's strong as a bear!"

"That is what his name means. It is good to have a man like him at a time like this." She hesitated, then said, "Will the ship go down?"

"I don't know. It's in the hands of God."

Reisa saw the trouble on the officer's youthful face. He was soaked to the skin, and the driving rain pelted all of them as they stood on the deck. She heard a sound, looked around to see where it was coming from, and was startled to see the small group of Christians that had been there before.

Carpenter said tersely, "Tell that bunch to get down below! They could be washed overboard. I can't speak their language."

"I'll tell them."

Reisa held onto the railing until she got to the small group. There were only about eight of them, all men except for two women. They sang lustily, and she listened to the words as she moved toward them:

The people down in darkness sat
A glorious light have seen;
The light has shined on them who long

In shades of death have been.
For unto us a child is born,
To us a son is given,
And on his shoulders ever rest,
All power on earth and heaven.
His name shall be the Prince of Peace
For evermore adored,
The Wonderful, the Counselor,
The great and mighty Lord.
His righteous government and power
Shall over all extend;
On judgment and on justice base,
His reign shall have no end.

The words of the hymn caught at Reisa, for they were familiar to her. Her grandfather had read them often, and she knew them almost by heart. They came from the book of Isaiah, which was one of her grandfather's favorite sections of Scripture. Now, for some reason, she stood there with the wind whistling through the yards, and above, the sails all taken in but one. And even as the ship rolled, and she hung on, something troubled her heart. *How is it that Christians sing of the Jewish Messiah?*

She moved closer to the man who was apparently the leader, and shouted in Russian, "The officer says that you should go below. He is afraid that you may be blown overboard."

The leader smiled, and there was not a trace of fear in his expression. He raised his voice over the screaming wind. "Our people are not afraid to die."

Confused by this, Reisa said, "The song—it comes from the Old Scripture from the prophet Isaiah."

"That is true. You know your Bible."

"You are Christians, yes?"

"Indeed we are. We are followers of the Lamb."

"But why do you sing the Jewish prophets?"

"Have you read Isaiah, daughter?"

"Yes. And my grandfather has read it to me."

"Then I say unto you that the one of whom Isaiah spoke, the Prince of Peace, the Wonderful, the Counselor, he has come to this earth and his name was Jesus Christ. It is to him we sing." The speaker examined her face and seemed to find something there that interested him. "Isaiah speaks of the Messiah, and it is the Messiah of God that is in our hearts. It is he who tells us not to be afraid."

"How does he speak to you?" Reisa asked in wonder.

"He speaks in his words, the Scripture, and in our hearts through the Holy Spirit."

Reisa had no answer for this. It was something far beyond her, and she looked away, somehow troubled by the encounter. Something about the simplicity of the man and his utter confidence amid the raging storm both troubled and interested Reisa. She wanted to ask more questions but did not have the courage. "The officer asked me to tell you," she said quietly, and then turned and left.

~

Finally the winds fell, and the terrible swells of the ocean smoothed out. The sun, which had been hidden for days, broke through the clouds, and many of the passengers that could, came up on the deck. Reisa, standing beside Petya, glanced over to the group of Christians who also were on deck. She was holding tightly to Boris, who clung to her with his claws digging into her arm. She repeated the details of her experience to Petya and ended by saying, "They think that Jesus is the Messiah of whom Isaiah spoke."

"They cannot be good people," Petya said firmly.

"Why not?"

"Because it is the *goy*, the Gentiles, who have slaughtered our people. How could they be good?"

Reisa kept these things in her heart. She did not have the courage to go to the leader of the small group, but she did listen to their singing, which never failed to stir her. They awakened some sort of longing in her, and she realized, being an honest young woman, that she had been terribly afraid during the storm. She had been afraid of death. Time and time again the words of the leader of the Christians came to her. *Our people are not afraid to die...*

Six days after the storm had passed, Reisa was awakened by Petya, who was shaking her shoulder.

"Come! We are here! We are in America!"

Reisa at once sat up and awakened Jacob, who was dozing fitfully.

"We are here, Grandfather," she said. "We are here! We are in America."

"I must see," Jacob said. He got to his feet shakily, and Reisa and Petya helped him up the ladder.

They found a place on the deck, and Petya, having the keenest eyes, said, "There, you see? It's land."

The ship was under full sail, and everyone was crying out, "It is America! We are here!"

Jacob's eyes were not good, but finally even he could see the dim, gray line that broke the horizon. He said quietly, "The Eternal One has brought us here, Reisa." He thought for a moment, then turned to her and smiled. "He guided your goose to its place, and now he has brought us to this land safely."

Reisa Dimitri stared at the long gray line of land that was approaching very rapidly. Overhead the sun was shining brightly, and the warmth came to her. She studied the horizon, and as she did the thought came to her, *I wonder what God will do with us here in this place?*

Five

By the time the *Jennings* had dropped anchor at Castle Garden and furled all the sails, the deck was crowded with passengers all anxious to set forth on a new world for the first time.

Jacob, however, was too weak to fight his way through the crowd, so Reisa said, "We'll wait until it's easier, *Zaideh.*"

"You want to say good-bye to people. I'll wait here for you. Go on, Granddaughter."

Reisa made her way up to the deck where the passengers were filing off. She knew many of the passengers and shook hands with as many as possible. As the Chapaevs got off, the three children clung to her. The smallest, being only two, started crying. Reisa knelt and said, "Don't worry, Poppy. We'll be seeing each other. You're in America now." She hugged the small girl and then stepped back, saying good-bye to Ilya and Ivana. "We must keep in touch," she said, but wondered if that were likely.

"I don't know," Ivana said tearfully. "It's such a big place."

"We'll be in the same city, and I imagine most of our people will find their way. We'll be a small community. If you have a chance, find the family of Laban Gold. That's the family we'll be looking for."

"Is he a relative?" Ilya asked quickly.

"Not to us, but he's the relative of a friend we had at home. I'm sure you can always find him in the Jewish part of New York."

She waved good-bye as the family departed and watched as the Christian group began to leave. The men wore shabby coats and vests, and one of them boasted a ratty bow tie. The women all wore skirts that reached to the floor and handkerchiefs tied over their heads, as did Reisa herself. One little girl no more than three had eyes like saucers and curly black hair. She smiled and waved at Reisa.

Suddenly the leader of the group, whose name she did not know, came over to her and nodded. "This is good-bye."

"Yes, but perhaps we'll see each other in New York."

"No. We're leaving for the west." He hesitated for only a moment and then nodded as if coming to some sort of agreement with himself. "God spoke to my heart last night and told me to do something."

A little disconcerted by this, Reisa blinked. She was not accustomed to meeting people who heard directly from God. A little nervously, she said, "What is it?"

"He told me to give you this." Ramming his hand into the oversized pockets of his bulky coat, the man pulled out a small package wrapped in oilskin.

"This has been a treasure to me," he said softly. "And now God wants it to be a treasure to you."

"Oh, I couldn't take it!"

"You must, my sister. It's God's will." He forced the small packet into her hand, then said, "God be with you. May the Messiah speak to your heart!"

Bewildered, Reisa watched the group leave. The leader reached the shore, then turned to look back at her. Reisa never forgot that look. There was a yearning look in the man's eyes as if he sought something from her, but she could not imagine what it was. As they made their way into the crowd streaming away, she opened the waterproof covering and looked inside. It was a small, thin book, and when she opened the first page, she read the title

The Gospel of John. It meant nothing to her, but she turned a few pages rapidly and saw the name of God mentioned many times. Quickly she rewrapped it and stuck it into her pocket.

The incident, for some reason, troubled Reisa. In fact, her encounters with the Christians had been disturbing to her. She had tried to push her feelings aside, but she kept thinking of the Christians, especially at night when she tried to sleep. Now, however, there was much to do, for the crowd was almost all ashore.

Going below, she found Dov standing beside her grandfather.

"Dov, I've been looking for you. I wanted to tell you good-bye."

"I help." Dov motioned toward the two bulky trunks that contained all the worldly goods of Reisa and Jacob.

"Oh, Dov, that's so nice of you!" Reisa had been troubled about how to get the trunks ashore. She patted the man's huge arm, and he looked down at her, his small black eyes opaque. But behind them Reisa thought she saw a faint warmth. It was hard to read the man! His face was covered with black, bushy whiskers, and he wore a fur cap pulled down over his forehead. His small eyes were the only sign of concern that she could discover.

Suddenly Petya appeared. "I've been looking for you, Reisa," he said. "I thought I'd help you two get settled. I knew you'd need some help with your trunks. I don't have much myself, you see." True enough, he had only a small bag stuck like a sausage under his arm. He smiled faintly at her and said, "I'm starting out light in the new world."

With the baggage taken care of by Dov and Petya, all Reisa had to do was carry Boris and help her grandfather. The cat had become well adjusted to the ship, and now as she stooped to put him in his carrier, he suddenly grinned at her and said, "Yow!"

"You and your grins!" she exclaimed, then snatched him up and draped him over her left shoulder. With her other hand she reached down and helped her grandfather to his feet. "Put your coat on now. It's still cold outside."

"Anything will be better than this, won't it?" Jacob murmured. He moved very slowly, but Reisa did not hurry him. Slowly they mounted the ladder, Jacob taking them one at a time. Finally when he stood on deck he took a deep breath. "Beautiful! The Architect of the Universe has created a beautiful world."

Indeed, it was beautiful. It was the second day of March 1871, a day Reisa knew she would never forget. The sky was a cerulean canopy overhead. Odors from the land came wafting across to them, and after the fetid stench of the quarters below deck, they smelled like rich perfume to Jacob Dimitri. He inhaled again and again as they moved toward the gangplank, drinking in the sea, the air, and the land where he had come to end his days.

"Miss Reisa, Mr. Dimitri, it's good to see you both." Ellis Carpenter had come to stand beside the gangplank. He smiled at Reisa and her grandfather broadly and said, "Welcome to America."

"Thank you, sir," Jacob said. "You've been very kind to my granddaughter and to me. May the God of heaven richly bless you."

Carpenter's face changed somehow, and he shot a glance at Reisa. "Your granddaughter is a persuasive young woman. I'm afraid if I stayed around her too long, I would become a man of God myself."

"Indeed, that would be something to make you proud." Jacob smiled. "It is a good thing for a young man to find God and walk with him all of his days."

Reisa put out her hand, and it was swallowed by the sailor's large one. "Thank you so much, Mr. Carpenter. And I do trust that God will bless you and keep you safe."

Carpenter nodded without speech.

As they headed on down the gangplank, Petya whispered, "That fellow is stuck on you, Reisa."

"No. I don't think so," Reisa whispered. "I think he's stuck on God—that he's afraid God will find him."

As they stepped off on the firm earth, Jacob abruptly laughed aloud. "It's odd. I've been moving for so long that to stand still on firm earth almost makes me dizzy."

All of them experienced some of the same effects. The novelty of walking on a surface that did not tilt or rise or heave was delightful to them, although it did give them a strange sensation.

"How do we go about finding Mr. Gold?" Jacob said. "Look at this crowd."

Indeed, the docks were swarming with people of all nationalities. Other boats were unloading their passengers, mostly from Europe. There were Greeks, Albanians, Germans, Englishmen, some wearing costumes such as none of the small party had ever seen before.

"Perhaps we can find a policeman," Reisa said timidly.

"I don't much trust soldiers," Petya said. "They haven't been kind to us at home."

"This is America," Reisa said quickly. "The police and the soldiers here will be good."

They quickly found that they were not permitted to leave. The docks were surrounded by a high fence, and everyone was being channeled into different lines.

"What are these lines for?" Petya wondered.

He had not long to wonder, for a guard wearing a dark blue uniform was urging the swarming masses into lines.

Gathering her courage, Reisa went up to him. "Please, sir, what we do now?"

"You'll have to take an examination."

"What is this examination?"

"A doctor will look you over and be sure that you're healthy."

This was a puzzle to Reisa as it was to the others, but she submitted to it. It proved to be a very simple examination. Two doctors were waiting, and they seemed to be looking mostly at the eyes of people. When Reisa, the first in line of her party, reached the doctor, he glanced over her carelessly and said, "You speak English?"

"Yes—not too good."

"Open your mouth." He looked inside her mouth, held up some fingers, then said, "How many fingers?"

"Four," Reisa answered quickly.

He looked carefully into her eyes and then nodded and waved her on. Reisa stood waiting while the other three were processed. When they regathered outside the immigration offices, they found that the streets of New York were unlike anything they had ever imagined. Coming from a tiny village, they were overwhelmed with the confusion. Carriages, wagons, and men on horseback crowded the streets. The sidewalks themselves were filled with people, walking rapidly and apparently with great purpose. They all wore very fine clothes—or so it seemed to Reisa. She stood there helplessly.

Dov said in his deep bass, "Policeman."

Reisa looked, and sure enough, there was a man who was either a soldier or a policeman. He had on a domed cap, his buttons were brass, and he carried a stick attached by a thong to his wrist.

"Go ask him," Petya whispered quickly. "You speak good English."

Reisa swallowed hard and then moved over to stand before the policeman. He turned to look at her and smiled. He had a red face, bright blue eyes, and a sandy-colored mustache that dropped down over his lip. "What might I do for you, miss?" he said.

"Please. We are looking for Mr. Laban Gold. Do you know him?" In Reisa's village everyone had known everyone else, but when the policeman laughed she suddenly realized her mistake.

"No, lass, I don't know him. Where does he live?"

"In the Jewish section."

"Ah, that I can help you with." His eyes ran over her companions, resting on Dov longest, but then he turned to Reisa and said, "See that street?"

"Yes, sir." Reisa listened hard as he gave what seemed to be complicated instructions.

Seeing her confusion, the policeman said, "Don't worry. You head in that direction. If you get lost, ask anyone how to get to the Jewish section. They'll point you to it."

"Thank you, sir."

"You're welcome. And you're welcome to America."

Reisa relayed the instructions of the policeman to her companions. "We go this way, I think," she said uncertainly.

The journey from the docks to their destination was fascinating. All of them looked until it seemed their eyes would hurt. They had never seen so many people in one place in their entire lives.

"How can they live with this many people so close?" Jacob whispered.

"I don't know, but I think we will have to learn."

They traveled slowly, making adjustments for Jacob's weakness. Finally, after asking several people, they found themselves thoroughly lost.

"What will we do?" Petya said in dismay. "We'll never find it."

"Look!" Reisa said. "There, *Zaideh*. He will help us."

Jacob glanced in the direction of Reisa's gesture and saw a small man wearing black. What caught his eye was the long curling earlocks. "A Hasidic Jew!" he exclaimed. He moved forward and said in Hebrew, "Greetings, sir."

The small man stopped and smiled, taking in the group. "You've just arrived?" he said.

"Yes. We are looking for a Mr. Laban Gold in the Jewish section."

"That will not be difficult. Where have you come from?"

"We come from Russia."

"You will find many of your companions here. Come, I will take you there myself."

Delighted with their find, Jacob led the way chatting with his newfound friend, who led them to their destination. Finally he said, "This is Hester Street, the section where most of your people live. I do not know Mr. Gold personally, but there's a large population here. If I were you, I would simply walk down the street and ask. Somebody will be sure to know him."

"Thank you so much, my friend," Jacob said warmly. "Where is your synagogue?"

"Ah, that is good. You ask that first," the man said. He gave directions, which Reisa wrote down on a slip of paper.

"That was good. Surely God above sent him to us."

Petya was anxious. "Why don't you wait here, Mr. Dimitri. I'll go find the Golds and then take you to them. There's no point in all of us going."

"Do you think you can do that?" Reisa said.

"I can't carry a ton like Dov here, but I'll bet I can find a family for you. Look." He pointed, and they saw what appeared to be a small cafe. "Why don't you go get something good to eat, and I'll be back soon enough."

"Good," Dov said. "I'm hungry."

Indeed, they were all hungry. The three made their way to the cafe. When they looked up at the sign which was in Yiddish, Reisa said with delight, "Good. They speak Yiddish."

"Indeed. I think most people do in this place. Haven't you heard the people as they pass?" Jacob said.

When they entered, a fat man with a smiling face came and greeted them in Yiddish. "Welcome. Sit down, and I will serve you myself."

"Thank you," Jacob said, answering in Yiddish.

"My name is Micah Pankoff," he said. "Today we have *borscht*, and we have *k'naidelch.*"

"You have *k'naidelch!* My favorite!" Jacob said with pleasure. This was a round dumpling made of matzoh meal and cooked in soup.

"Yes. And we have *k'nishes.*"

Dov asked, "What is *k'nishes?*"

"It's baker dumplings filled with potato, meat, and liver."

This was food such as they were familiar with, and they sat down eagerly while the proprietor brought them the steaming bowls. They ate heartily, Dov wading through several helpings and eating a complete loaf of round black bread.

As they ate, Micah came back from time to time. Reisa asked him, "You do not know where Mr. Laban Gold lives, I suppose?"

"Do I not!" Micah's eyes opened wide. "He lives two streets down from me. You know Mr. Gold?"

"We have never met him, but his uncle said we should see him, and that he would help us get established."

"He's a fine man, Laban Gold, a businessman, and his wife a wonderful woman. They are good people. We go to the same synagogue."

A feeling of relief swept over Reisa. She had been afraid of what would happen to them in America, but now at least there was one family that they could turn to. She felt much better.

When they had finished eating, they paid their bill, and Reisa insisted they wait until Petya came back.

Finally Petya did return, his eyes excited. "I have found them!" he exclaimed.

"Good," Reisa said. "Now, sit down and eat."

"Good. Anything is better than that ship food."

They waited while Petya ate, and then the two men shouldered their baggage, and they left.

"I will see you on the Sabbath day," Micah said.

"Yes. God be thanked. We will be there," Jacob replied.

Following Petya, they soon came to a very busy street. The buildings rose on each side five or six stories high, all with iron balconies. On every balcony clothes were hanging out—shirts, long underwear, trousers, petticoats. The streets were thronged with peddlers, so that it was difficult to make their way through. More than once the small party was besieged by peddlers wearing boxes suspended in front of them by a string around the neck. They sold such things as cherries, laces, glasses, ties, and almost any other item that could be carried in such a small compartment.

Finally they came to a street that was less congested. Petya led the way to the house of Laban Gold. Jacob knocked on the door.

Almost at once it was opened by a very attractive, heavyset woman. She had a wealth of brown hair, but most of it was hidden under her kerchief. "Yes?" she said.

"I am looking for the home of Mr. Laban Gold."

"I am Mrs. Gold. You want my husband?"

"Yes. If you please."

"Come inside."

The four stepped inside and found themselves in a very small parlor with doors on three sides. On the right was a passageway with a set of stairs leading up. They passed through another door in what was the home proper of the Golds. It was to them a very attractive room, with carpet on the floor, framed lithographs on the wall, and a chandelier of brass that lighted the room. It was evidently a sitting room, for there was a couch, three chairs, several tables, and two floor lamps. "I will get my husband," Mrs. Gold said as she left.

"I feel embarrassed throwing myself into this home," Jacob said.

"Don't worry, *Zaideh,*" Reisa replied. "Reb Gurion said his nephew is a very generous man and that he would welcome us."

Almost at once the door opened, and a small man with dark eyes and rather thick glasses entered. He came to stand before them and smiled, bowing slightly. "I am Laban Gold. You wish to see me?"

"My name is Jacob Dimitri. This is my granddaughter, Reisa. This is Dov Puskin, and this is Petya Ivanov." Jacob hesitated slightly, and then said with some embarrassment, "We have a mutual acquaintance—Rabbi Chaim Gurion."

"My uncle!" Mr. Gold exclaimed. He nodded energetically, which seemed to be a habit with him, his head going up and down rapidly. He turned to his wife. "Rachel, these are friends of my uncle Chaim."

"I heard, Laban." Mrs. Gold had been studying the oddly matched quartet. "You have just gotten off the ship, I take it?"

"Yes," Jacob said. "We know no one else in America." He said this simply and without any attempt to ask for favors.

At once Laban seemed to grasp the situation. "Oh, yes. We have been able to help many of our countrymen. Have you found a place to stay?"

"No. We've come directly from the ship."

"Well, we can arrange that, can't we, Rachel?"

"Certainly." Mrs. Gold smiled. She came forward and said firmly, "You may stay with us. We have room in our home for you, Mr. Dimitri, and your granddaughter. And three houses down my neighbor, Mrs. Epstein, can take two more boarders."

"We unfortunately have very little money."

Gold threw up his hands in a gesture of disdain. "We will work it out. We must stick together, we Russians."

From that point on it became relatively simple. Mrs. Gold was an active woman accustomed to managing things. Mr. Gold took Jacob off to an inner room that he used for a study, where the two were soon deep in conversation. Rachel Gold showed Reisa the small room that would be hers and another for her grandfather.

"They are very small, but at least you will have a window in your room."

"We're so thankful to you, Mrs. Gold."

"Supper will be ready soon. You get yourself settled and go invite your two friends. You must have your first meal together in the new world."

ಸ

The meal was delicious. Mrs. Gold served *gefilte* fish, fish stuffed with onions and seasoning and cooked in salt water.

There was much more, and the wanderers were made to feel very much at home. Reisa was interested in the Golds' children. Zillah, age fifteen, was well shaped and a fine-looking young woman, and Joseph, age eighteen, was a head taller than his father but very thin. They were both lively young people, plying the visitors with questions.

Joseph was sitting next to Reisa and paid her many compliments. "You speak English very well."

"Well, thank you. I had a good teacher."

"You will like it here in America. Perhaps you will permit me to show you around the neighborhood."

Reisa was not sure if this would be proper, but she felt it would be impolite to say no. "That would be very nice," she said.

Finally the meal was over, and Jacob, Reisa could see, was exhausted. "Time for you to go to bed."

Jacob said, "I am a little tired. It was a wonderful meal. Absolutely kosher and delicious, Mrs. Gold."

Reisa said good night to Dov and Petya, agreeing to meet them the next morning and explore their new world. She made sure that her grandfather was comfortable in his small room, and before she left, she knelt beside him, and they said a prayer of thanksgiving for their safe journey. Rising, she went to her own room, undressed, and washed as thoroughly as she could from the basin, using the entire pitcher full of water. It was not like a bath, which she determined to have somehow or other, but it felt wonderful. She pulled on her woolen nightgown and slipped into bed.

As she leaned over to extinguish the lamp, a thought came to her. She threw back her covers, went to the table where she had piled her things, and found the oil-soaked package that the man had given her. Back in bed, she unwrapped it carefully. She was exhausted and her eyes were gritty, but she was curious about the book. Opening it, she saw that it was in English, which pleased her. She saw that one passage had been underlined, which drew her eyes to it.

"Behold the Lamb of God that taketh away the sin of the world."

Reisa read this, and it seemed to echo in her mind and somewhere deeper down in her spirit. She was thoroughly familiar with the Old Testament Scriptures which dealt with the sacrificial ritual of the Jews. The Paschal Lamb had to be perfect, without blemish, and was slain during the Passover. The custom, of course, was no longer possible, but her grandfather had drilled into her the teachings of the Talmud as well as the Old Testament and the Law.

She closed the book slowly, wondering what the passage meant. Putting the book under her pillow, she pulled the covers up, leaned over, and extinguished the lamp. The darkness closed in on her. While she was tired almost to exhaustion, she could not sleep for a time. The passage she had read kept running through her mind like a song.

Behold the Lamb of God that taketh away the sin of the world. She knew that the priest in the Old Testament was connected with the sacrifice. The family that brought the sacrifice would confess their sins, the priest would lay his hand on the lamb, and then it would be slain. *But that would only be for the sin of the family*, Reisa thought. *How could one lamb take away the sin of the whole world?*

She was still thinking of this when sleep seized her. It came over her like a blanket, and she fell into a deep darkness, warm and soothing.

Six

A hoarse humming sound in her ear and a tentative touch on her cheek brought Reisa out of a sound sleep. Smiling, she opened her eyes and saw Boris lying beside her as closely as he could. As soon as she opened her eyes, he reached out his paw and put it on her eye carefully. It was a tradition between them, a ceremony to be observed each morning on Reisa's waking. Reaching out, she stroked the ebony fur, the blackest thing in nature, and for a time lay there thinking as she woke up fully.

"Enough already, Boris!" She shoved him away, pulled the covers back, and got out of bed. She dressed quickly and made the bed, then went downstairs. There she found Mrs. Gold in the kitchen already busy with breakfast. "Good morning, Mrs. Gold."

"Ah, good morning, Reisa. You're up early."

"Yes. I expect Grandfather will sleep late. He's very tired." She looked around at the kitchen and said, "Let me help you. I love to cook."

"That's good. You can make the *taiglech*. Do you know how?"

"Oh, yes! We often have *taiglech*, my grandfather and I." Reisa set about mixing the dough for the cakes that would be dipped in honey, and as they baked she set the table. By the time the food was ready, she heard stirrings outside.

Mrs. Gold said, "We're a little late this morning. We must hurry."

Rachel Gold finished frying the *feinkochen*—scrambled eggs. There were also *tsimmes*, or sweet carrot compote, left over from the meal the night before, and *blintzes*, small rolls filled with cheese.

Mr. Gold came down dressed in a shiny, rather worn black suit. He greeted Reisa warmly. "Ah, you slept well, I trust."

"Yes, Mr. Gold. Very well indeed. It was good to be on a bed that wasn't rocking back and forth."

Zillah came in wearing a light blue dress. She wore a kerchief, as did her mother. She greeted Reisa, then sat down. Joseph seemed to be very sleepy. He wore a yarmulke, the small cap on his head, as did his father. After Mr. Gold had prayed over the food, they all plunged in. She discovered that Zillah was off to school, and that Joseph was working at a tailor shop. She asked him about his work, and he said, "One day I'll own my own shop. I'll be rich, won't I, Papa?"

"If God wills."

"Oh, God wills it all right," Joseph said.

The meal was quickly over, and Mr. Gold went off to his work, the others to meet their responsibilities. Reisa helped Mrs. Gold wash the dishes, and as they did she said, "My grandfather and I have very little money. I will need to go to work soon."

Mrs. Gold nodded firmly. "I expect you will."

"What would I do?"

"Oh, there's plenty of work." Mrs. Gold frowned suddenly. "The trouble is, it's all long hours and pays little. When you're ready, my husband will help you find a place."

Reisa knew that her grandfather might sleep very late, so she asked tentatively, "It was so dirty on the ship. I need to take a bath if there's any way."

"Oh, yes. We have a tub you can take to your room. Heat water on the stove here."

Reisa busied herself with this activity, and soon had the tub filled with hot water in her room. Stripping off her dirty clothes, she took the soap and sat down with a sigh of relief. She washed thoroughly, soaping herself and washing her hair. She had brought extra water to rinse with, and standing up, she poured it over her hair and let it run down her body. Finally she stepped out, dried off, and put on only one petticoat. The weather was growing warmer already, and she thought it would be all she needed.

Finally she emptied the bath water, and by the time that was done Jacob was up and eating breakfast in the kitchen. She greeted him with a smile. "Did you sleep well, *Zaideh?*"

"Yes. Very well."

He finished his plate of eggs and started to rise, but she pushed him gently back into his chair.

"Sit down. You must eat more. You've lost weight."

She saw to it that her grandfather had a good breakfast, and then he said, "I think I will go down to the synagogue and see if I can find some work teaching Hebrew."

"I think that would be good," Reisa said. "You need to meet the rabbi and the other leaders of the synagogue."

After she got Jacob off, she gathered their few spare items of clothing and set about boiling water and washing. Then she helped Mrs. Gold clean the house. The work was easy for her, and it was good to be moving around.

Later that afternoon Petya came by. He was excited. "I think I found me a fine job. I start tomorrow working with a tailor. He's going to teach me everything. There's a fortune to be made in it, Reisa!"

"I'm glad you found something. I know you'll do well."

"Dov has a job, too. He's unloading the ship down at the docks." He laughed. "I was with him, and they took one look and hired him. He can do the work of two men. I heard one of the foremen say so."

"I'm going to get a job, too, as soon as I can," Reisa said.

"Not today. Let's just take a walk around and see this new world we're in."

They took a tour of their part of the city, and once again Reisa was almost stunned with the city itself. It was not a clean place, she saw at once. There were dark hallways and filthy cellars, all crowded with dirty children. They clustered on stoops and fire escapes and in wash-hung courts, and in the trash-laden alleys they played their little games with balls and sticks.

As they made their way along, the sidewalks whirled with the tides of the city life. Men and women everywhere were shouting and bartering in a dozen tongues. The city was actually an open-air marketplace where storekeepers competed with push carts, wagons, and temporary stands.

"They sell everything out here on the street, don't they, Petya?"

"Almost, it seems. I don't see how they all make a living. Some of the stuff is so cheap." He pointed out that bandannas and tin cups sold for two cents and peaches a cent a quart and damaged eggs for practically nothing.

They made their way along, with children slipping through the turmoil like eels, and the sounds of what seemed like a dozen languages always on the air.

Finally, back at the Golds' house, Petya said good-bye.

"Come by tonight, and we'll work on your English," Reisa said.

"I'll do that, Reisa."

Reisa found that her grandfather had returned, but he did not have good news. There was an unhappy look on his face as he said, "There are many who teach Hebrew. I do not think it will be possible for me to find employment."

"Don't worry, *Zaideh*. We will find a way. I will find a job—and God will not leave us!"

The sun was going down now, and the city growing cooler. It was like living in a canyon, Reisa thought as she sat on the steps. The buildings on both sides rose up to cut out the pale sunlight. For a time she sat there watching the children play and then thought: *I don't like this place. It's dirty and crowded and people are so rude!* She knew, however, she could not say anything like this to Jacob, for he was already discouraged.

That night she sat with Jacob, Dov, and Petya giving them English lessons. They were joined by Joseph, who was helpful, and he began teaching Reisa how to write in English. Reisa was a quick learner.

After Dov and Petya had left she said, "Thank you, Joseph, for teaching me."

"You're very quick, Reisa." Joseph nodded. "You must learn how to speak well and to write well. This is not Russia. We must put all that behind us."

"Must I?" Reisa said wistfully. "I have good memories of my home there. It was hard, but I miss it already."

Joseph smiled and waved his hand in the air. "You will forget it soon. There's so much to do here, and you will marry a rich man and have a big house."

"I don't think so," Reisa said.

"Oh, yes! You are a very attractive young woman. You will have many suitors."

"Well, I don't think of that." Reisa smiled a little.

"Of course you do. Doesn't every woman think of a husband?"

Joseph was teasing her, she knew, and she wondered for a time if he would be one of those suitors. But it was as if he had read her mind, and he held both hands out palms up. "Not me," he said. "I'm going to marry a rich woman."

Reisa laughed. "I believe you will. She'll probably be fat and ugly."

"Doesn't matter," Joseph laughed, his eyes sparkling, "as long as she's rich."

"Will you help me find work, Joseph?"

"Yes. It won't be a good job. You have to have training for that, but I know that you and your grandfather need money immediately. I will look around tomorrow."

"Thank you, Joseph."

The day had been tiring, and Reisa said good night to her grandfather. "Joseph has promised to find me a job," she said as she stood at her door.

"I regret that you have to work, Reisa," Jacob said sadly.

"I'm strong, and I expect to work. Good night."

"Good night, Reisa."

Quickly Reisa prepared for bed, but she found herself unable to sleep. She had brought a newspaper home and practiced her reading. The main story was about a terrible fire that had destroyed much of a city called Chicago. As she read about the death and devastation, her heart went out to the people that she had never seen. She could almost see the children who had lost parents, and parents weeping over their dead babies.

Quickly she moved her eyes to another part of the paper, which concerned something called a circus by a man called P. T. Barnum. It was opening in New York for the first time, and for a fleeting moment she wished she could go. She had never been to a circus, but traveling acrobats and trainers with bears trained to do tricks had come through the village once. Now as she read about the circus with the strange animals and many different acts, she thought about asking her grandfather if they might go. But she knew it would cost money, and there was none to spare.

She put the paper away after a time, and her eyes fell on the small gospel of John. She picked it up and opened it and began reading. The section she read told the story of the prophet Jesus who met a woman at a well. This fascinated Reisa, for she well knew that women in biblical times had almost no honor or position. No man would speak to a woman in the open, so as she read that Jesus spoke to one, she became engrossed. She followed the story, amazed that Jesus knew about the woman's life without ever having met her! She knew that the woman was not a good woman, for she was living with a man not her own husband. Finally she reached the parts that said, "Ye worship ye know not what: we know what we worship: for salvation is of the Jews." This thrilled her and surprised her, for she had not known that Christians thought this way. Of course, she knew that Jesus himself was a Jew.

Finally her eyes fell on the verse that said, "God is a spirit: and they that worship him must worship him in spirit and in truth."

She thought about this verse for a time. *God was a spirit. Anything other than this was idolatry.* She was pleased with this thought.

Then she read the next verse. "The woman saith unto him, I know that Messias cometh, which is called Christ: when he comes, he will tell us all things."

Reisa's eyes fell on the next verse, which hit her with more force than she had dreamed. "Jesus saith unto her, I that speak unto thee am he."

No! It can't be true! Jesus cannot be the Messiah. He died!

The story itself had interested Reisa, but the thought of Jesus being the Messiah that would free all Israel deeply disturbed her. She tossed the book down determined to read it no more, but as she tried to sleep the verse kept echoing in her. *I that speak unto thee am he...*

Seven

"Almost quitting time. I'll be glad to get out of this place."

Reisa, who was sitting on a stool tying strings around the necks of small bottles, looked up at the girl who spoke. Her name was Hannah Marsh. She was a plain girl of seventeen years old, and fatigue had bent her shoulders and drawn lines in her face. "We can go home and rest up," Hannah said.

Reisa straightened her own back, aware of the pain there. She had been working at the medicine plant, which was simply one floor of a large brick building, gloomy and airless and dark. She had been eager to come to work to make money, but Joseph had warned her that it would not be pleasant.

Indeed, it had been most unpleasant. The hours were long, from six in the morning until six at night. The work was boring and monotonous, tying strings around an endless series of small bottles containing a dark liquid. Reisa had learned on her first day that the medicine was worthless—colored water with a few things added to make it taste extremely bad. Sitting in one cramped position for twelve hours with only brief breaks three times a day was almost more than Reisa could bear.

But the worst thing was the owner, Mr. Oscar Trunion. He was a greasy-looking man of fifty who apparently never bathed and who took liberties with the young women who worked for him. Reisa had recoiled the first time he had laid his hand on her shoulder, but he had laughed at her, exposing stained teeth. "You little rabbit," he said. "You and I will get better acquainted."

Each day grew worse, and Reisa woke up dreading the job—not so much the hard work and the long hours, but the unwelcome attentions of the owner.

But there was nothing else to do, and she had to work. Besides, she had been assured by Hannah that other jobs were just as bad. She longed for the times back on her small farm when all she had to do was milk the cows, tend the garden, and do the housework. She wished often that they had never come. However, she never complained of this to Jacob, who asked her often how her day was. She would always say, "It was fine, *Zaideh.*"

When Friday came, Mrs. Gold was busy all day cleaning the house and cooking, for the next day was the Sabbath, a day of rest, when no work nor cooking could be done. When Reisa arrived home tired and discouraged, she smelled the odor of good food cooking. She went at once to her room, washed, and lay down on her bed until the evening meal. She actually fell asleep, so that a knock on her door caused her to start.

Her grandfather called, "Reisa, come. We're ready."

Reisa pushed aside Boris, who did not smile at her but grunted and growled deep in his throat. Coming off the bed, she quickly pulled off her old dress and put on her one good dress, a garment that had once been dark green but was now faded. Well aware that the Sabbath began at sunset on Friday evening, she hurried downstairs.

The *shibak* dinner was the most important dinner of the week, and she entered the room to find that the table was already set, covered with a clean white cloth. Everyone was there, and her grandfather smiled at her. "We're waiting on you, Reisa."

"I'm sorry, Grandfather," Reisa said.

"It's all right," Mr. Gold said quickly. "Plenty of time."

"Would you recite the *kiddush,* friend?"

Jacob took the cup of wine and said a long blessing. "God blessed the seventh day and pronounced it holy, for on it he rested from all the work which he had created to set the universe in motion.

"You are blessed, Lord our God, King of the Universe, who creates the fruit of the vine. You are blessed, Lord our God, King of the Universe, who has made us holy with his commandments and desired us and who, with love and good will, has made us inherit his holy Sabbath—a remembrance of the work of creation. Today is the day which is the beginning of all holy celebrations, a remembrance of the departure from Egypt. For you have chosen us and sanctified us from among the nations, and you have made us inherit your holy Sabbath in love and good will. You are blessed, Lord, who makes the Sabbath holy."

"Amen," Mr. Gold said, and then they ate their food. The meal was the same that they had always had on the Sabbath: chopped liver, chicken soup with dumplings, roast chicken, and two loaves of bread called *challah* especially baked for the Sabbath.

Reisa was so tired she could scarcely keep her eyes open. Although there was much talk among the family, she finally excused herself and went to bed. As she went to sleep, she wondered how she would stand the factory. She looked forward to the *Shabbat* the next day, but beyond that came the factory, which was always a nightmare to her.

The din of the factory had given Reisa a terrible headache that would not go away. All morning she had suffered in silence, and at the half-hour lunch break she ate her meager lunch sitting all alone. Closing her eyes, she tried to ignore the throbbing pain, and memories of her old home in Russia came to her. She was able to see the cozy little house and summoned up pictures of her tiny stove and the narrow bed which had been hers. Suddenly she thought of the goose she had nursed back to health, and wondered what had become of him. *I hope you're happier than I am, goose!*

Her thoughts were rudely interrupted when she felt a hand run over her shoulder and down her arm. Her eyes flew open and she saw Oscar Trunion's greasy smile as he bent over and leered at her. Without conscious thought, Reisa struck out, and her open palm caught the owner on the cheek with a meaty sound.

"Why—you little cat!" Trunion glanced around, and noted that other workers were watching him. His face flushed, and he said loudly, "You're fired! Get out of here!"

Reisa came to her feet, anger racing through her, and she spoke in Russian without being aware of it. "You are a mangy dog of a man!" She shoved Trunion aside and almost ran out of the room. She stopped long enough to pick up her coat, aware of Trunion's angry voice shouting curses at her. Leaving the factory, she took a deep breath, then forced herself to calm down. As she made her way home, she found herself praying silently. *Father of the Universe, forgive me for my anger. You have said that your people are to be humble, and I broke that law. Forgive me, and please, O great Maker of all things, make a way for me and my grandfather!*

Jacob had been surprised to see Reisa come home early. He listened while she told him that she had left her job, then said, "It's all right. We will find a way. God will help us."

Reisa took a quick breath and wondered if she should speak. For the past two weeks she had suffered at the factory, and every day had spent an enormous amount of time trying to think of some way out. She had listened to the girls at work and to the conversation at the table. She had talked with Dov, with Petya, and with others that she had met, and out of all of this had come what amounted to a dream. She had nurtured it and worked it out in her mind, waiting for the right moment to come to speak to her grandfather, and now she felt that the moment had come.

"Grandfather, I think I know how we can make our bread."

"What way is that?"

"I think we should become pushcart peddlers." She saw his look change to one of immense surprise, and hurriedly spoke as if to head off his objections. "I've been talking to some of them and to Mr. Gold, and I know we can do it."

"But we know nothing about it. We have nothing to sell."

"We have a little money. A pushcart can be rented for ten cents a day, *Zaideh*. I've already seen to that. All we have to do is buy enough merchandise for one day. We will sell it, and then we'll have enough money to buy some for the next day. If others can do it, we can do it as well."

Jacob was shocked into silence. He had never thought of such a thing. He was well aware, however, that they could not go on as they were. He thought for a long time, his face intent, and finally he lifted his eyes. "It is a gamble, Reisa."

"Not so much as you think. We will sell things. I have met a street peddler named Jake Cantor—"

"Yes," Jacob interrupted. "I know him. He has been to the synagogue often."

"Well, he has offered to teach us. It will take all the money we have, I know, but God will be with us."

Jacob nodded, his face worried but resolved. "Well, my Reisa, we will do it. Tomorrow, as soon as possible, we will take to the streets!"

Reisa was a busy young woman for the next twenty-four hours. She asked Jake Cantor to help them, and early in the afternoon, Cantor arrived at their rooms. He was a short, fat, balding man with rather merry brown eyes and a cheerful air. "Ah, Miss Reisa. You are ready to launch into your new profession?"

"Yes, Mr. Cantor. We are so grateful for your help."

"There is not much skill to it. Come, I will take you, and we will buy your stock."

The entire day was spent in buying stock. They had to buy carefully and in small amounts, but they got a sampling of everything, including razors, carpet slippers, snuff boxes, tobacco, spectacles, sassafras, peppermint, needles and thread, ribbons, and suspenders.

"You can't sell out of an empty wagon," Mr. Cantor said firmly as they collected the merchandise. "It's a funny thing, you may have the greatest bargain in the world, but if it's the last thing in your cart, nobody will buy it. But if you have a full cart, people will always buy. I've never understood it, but I always try to keep my cart full."

~

The next morning Reisa and Jacob took their purchases and rented the cart. Reisa arranged it neatly, and by seven o'clock they were ready to go out on the street. Reisa felt some fear, but she never showed it to Jacob. "Come, *Zaideh,*" she said. "We will go now and sell on the streets."

"May the God of heaven be with us," Jacob said. He was even more reluctant to go than his granddaughter, but they had no choice. They had burned their bridges.

The next two hours were a trial, for despite many people stopping to look, no one bought anything. Reisa's heart fell, but she kept a smile on her face. She chatted constantly to Jacob to keep his spirits up, and finally when a woman stopped and bought three ribbons for twenty cents, she turned to Jacob and said, "See, we're already successful!"

The morning passed quickly. It was noisy, and Reisa's legs and feet grew tired. She sent Jacob home at twelve o'clock, for she could see he was weary. "You go home and rest and get something to eat."

"All right, Reisa. I'll come back this afternoon, then you can take a rest."

Reisa moved the pushcart several times, and more than once men stopped to flirt with her. Nearly all of them were Jewish. When the first one, a thin man wearing a fancy suit, made an improper suggestion, Reisa moved closer to him and stared him straight in his eyes. "Would you, a good Jew, show such disrespect for a daughter of Zion?"

The man flinched as if Reisa had struck him. He mumbled, "No offense," and bought a pair of house shoes.

Reisa found this to be almost inevitably a good way to turn away those men who stopped at her cart. She was the only woman on the street with a pushcart, and some men seemed to feel that she would be easy.

Reisa had been prepared for this, and finally it ceased to be a problem. All she had to do was raise her voice so that those around would hear. "Would a good Jew show disrespect to a daughter of Zion?" she'd exclaim. And the man instantly would flinch and start to turn away. She discovered quickly that these men would buy out of embarrassment, if for no other reason.

Jacob came back and kept the cart and was pleased at her success. She left, got something to eat, then lay down for half an hour. But she worried about Jacob and soon was back. She sent him home very soon, for he obviously felt ill at ease.

Late that afternoon, when it was almost time to close, a burly policeman stopped by her. He had a red Irish face, red hair, and bright blue eyes. He twirled his stick and said, "Well, girlie. How's business?"

"Very good, sir."

"I'll tell you what. After you get off I'll take you to a nice place, and we can have a talk."

Reisa had spotted the wedding ring on the man's left hand. "You don't need me," she said. "You should buy something nice and take it to your wife." She smiled at him and saw his confusion. "I'll bet she's a good wife to you. You ought to appreciate her."

The policeman laughed. "Well, faith and she is. I'll take that brooch."

It was the most expensive thing that Reisa and Jacob had invested in, and she insisted on wrapping it up neatly in a piece of paper.

"You give her this and a big kiss, and you tell her how pretty she is, and what a good wife she is."

The policeman stared at her and shrugged his shoulders. "You're all right, miss. I'll keep my eye out for you."

Finally the day ended. When Reisa turned in the pushcart, she was able to carry the remainder of the goods back in one sack. When she got home, she went to Jacob's room and found that he was worried about her.

"Not to worry," she said. "Look." She pulled out the purse where she kept the money and poured it out on the small table by his bed. It was almost all in silver. Jacob stared with astonishment.

"Reisa! All this money?"

"Enough to buy more things. You can't sell out of an empty wagon, *Zaideh.*"

He laughed. "No," he agreed, "I guess you can't!"

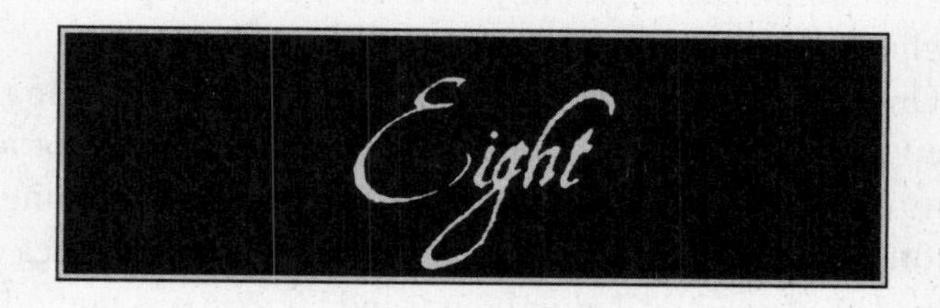

Eight

Rare indeed were the moments of pleasure that came to Reisa during her first weeks in New York. One of these, however, came on a Friday afternoon. Friday was a half holiday with many of the Jewish workers, and Reisa took a half day off to attend a wedding of a young woman who lived just down the street from them. Donning her only good dress and her best pair of shoes, she joined the wedding celebration. Dov was there, strangely enough, and she went to him at once.

"You like weddings, Dov?"

The black beard parted for her to see strong white teeth as the huge man grinned at her. "Like food and music," he rumbled.

"So do I," Reisa said. "Stay with me, and we'll eat them out of house and home."

They were soon joined by Petya, and the three of them moved among the guests and the wedding party. The celebration took place in a vacant courtyard. The space was small, and the participants were many, but Reisa didn't care. A trio composed of an accordion, a flute, and a zither were playing vigorously, and the cheerful music seemed to brighten the air. It was the second day of May, and a festive atmosphere was everywhere.

Reisa moved about greeting those she knew and making new friends. She had become quite outgoing since taking to the street with a pushcart, and now she smiled as Joseph and Zillah brought some of their friends to her.

One of these friends introduced by Joseph was a young man named Zuriel Benjamin. He was a husky young man of about twenty-five, Reisa judged. His hair was black and glistening, and he wore a beard, which he kept trimmed short. His eyes were dark and shadowed by darker brows, and his skin was tanned dark by the sun.

"You are lately arrived from the old country, I suppose," Zuriel said.

"Yes. We've just been here a few weeks."

"How do you like it?"

"To be truthful, we came because we had to. There was a pogrom, and my grandfather and I had to leave."

A shadow crossed the young man's face. "I left for the same reason." He brightened then, saying, "You may be lonely now, but you'll make many new friends here." He bowed suddenly, and his eyes sparkled. "I hope that I may be one of them."

He was a very bold young man, and Reisa guessed that he had had much success with young women. She asked him if he worked in one of the factories in the district.

"Work in a factory! No! God deliver me from such a thing." Genuine horror was in young Zuriel's eyes. "I worked in a factory when I first came here, for six months. It nearly put me in my grave working seventeen hours a day, six days a week! No factory for me! What about you?"

"My grandfather and I sell out of a pushcart in the streets."

"Oh, yes. I did that myself for a while. But it was too hard, so I quit."

Reisa had learned something about that. The pushcart furnished a bare living, but the peddlers were often victimized by brutal police methods. Every day several peddlers were accused of crimes such as obstructing street corners or peddling without a license. To avoid these arrests, the peddlers paid extortion. One of Reisa's acquaintances, a man named Seth Meyers, had refused to buy five one-dollar tickets to a police clam bake. He had been arrested the next day and stayed in jail until his fine was paid. While he was in jail, his pushcart had been thoroughly ransacked.

"It is hard," she said feelingly.

"Too hard for me. What I did was leave the city. I'm still a peddler, but now it's with a pack on my back."

Reisa had heard of men who filled packs with goods, strapped them on their backs, and made their way into the rural areas, dispensing all sorts of goods to the farmers and dwellers of small towns.

"That must be very hard," Reisa commented.

"Hard? No, indeed! It's nothing like a pushcart or a factory."

"But don't you get tired?"

"Oh, if I do, I stop and rest a day. There's always someone willing to take you in for a bit of cloth or a silver spoon."

Reisa listened to him carefully, and finally Zuriel winked at her. "You ought to try it, Miss Reisa. But then you're a woman—I've never known a woman back peddler."

"I could do it," Reisa said abruptly. "I can walk as far as almost any man."

"That may be, but it wouldn't be kosher for a young woman to walk alone."

"I could take my grandfather with me. We could go together."

"That would make it all right, I suppose." Zuriel rubbed his chin and said, "I don't recommend it. Maybe I made it sound too easy. Sometimes it gets wet out there when it storms, and you have to take refuge in a barn. Other times it gets so hot you think you're going to melt. Sometimes there are bad dogs. It's not all fun. I wouldn't want to mislead you."

"Tell me more about it, Mr. Benjamin."

"Call me Zuriel. All right. Here's the way my days go..."

Reisa listened for the next half hour to the young man's tale. He made it sound almost romantic, and when he finished, she said, "Is it expensive to get started?"

"No. Not at all. You can't carry more than fifty dollars worth of merchandise in your pack. You pack it, you go out and walk to the villages, the farms, around the city, and then when you sell out, you come home and rest up."

"How much can a person make doing that?"

"You'll never get rich," Zuriel said regretfully. "But it beats the sweat shops, and it beats competing with all those fellows in the streets with pushcarts lined up for a mile."

At this time the music rose again, and the wedding procession emerged from one of the buildings. When it reached the center of the courtyard it halted. A canopy was stretched over the principal figures. Prayer and benedictions were chanted. Finally the groom put the ring on the bride's finger, dedicating her to himself according to the Law of Moses in Israel. More prayers were recited. The bridegroom and the bride received sips of wine. A plate was smashed, and everybody cried as loud as they could, "Good luck! Good luck!" The band struck up a lively tune, and everyone went to congratulate the couple.

Reisa said good-bye to Zuriel, who promised to call on her. She smiled but gave him no answer.

Dov found her and said, "Come. We eat." She held onto his huge arm as he led her to the tables. The wedding meal was quickly devoured, consisting of stuffed cabbages, stuffed potato cakes, chopped meat, and *schneken* or coffee cake. There was only a little wine, which Reisa did not take.

The party began to break up, and Reisa said good-bye to Dov and Petya. She made her way back to the Golds' house and sat out on the back balcony of the house thinking a great deal but giving only minimal answers to Zillah, who had joined her.

She went in later to help Mrs. Gold with supper, and afterwards she sat on the steps, still silent. Petya came by, and when he asked her to walk with him, she did. They walked down the streets, and she was astonished when he suddenly said, "Why don't we get married?"

Reisa's eyes flew open. She turned to face Petya, who was staring at her intently.

"Married! Why, Petya—"

"I know it's sudden, and you haven't thought of it. But I'm going to get ahead in this world, Reisa. I don't ask that we be married now, but we could be promised until I make enough to keep us."

Reisa did not expect a romantic courtship, but the suddenness of Petya's offer took her by surprise. She, however, did not have to think about it, for her answer was already there. "I will not marry. Not for a long time, Petya. I have to take care of my grandfather."

"I understand that, but when I make my way—"

"Besides," Reisa interrupted him, "I don't think we have the right feelings for each other."

Petya was confused. "What do you mean by that? You like me, don't you?"

"Well, yes, I like you, but that isn't enough. You must feel something very strong for the person you're going to spend your whole life with."

Petya was downcast. "I think you're romantic."

"Romantic? I don't believe so," Reisa said. She felt very sorry for Petya and said, "You will make a lot of money, and you will find a good woman who will make you happy."

They said no more. It was her first offer of marriage, and later that night she told her grandfather about it.

Jacob Dimitri listened as Reisa related the incident, and finally he said, "You do not care for Petya?"

"Oh, not like that."

"Well, then you gave the right answer. Somewhere there is a man for you, and the two of you will find great happiness."

Reisa was sitting across from him in the small parlor. He had been reading to her from the Hebrew Scripture, and she had interrupted him to tell her story. Now she said, "How will I know him?"

"You must ask God to reveal it to you. Many a man looks good when he's young, but he does not wear well. The same is true of women, I suppose. When I saw your grandmother for the first time, I had no idea she would be my wife. It was almost a year before I realized that I loved her and asked her to marry me."

Reisa took all this in, and finally she said, "Maybe I will never marry at all."

"That would be a waste for a true daughter of Zion! No, you will have a husband and children."

Reisa did not speak for a moment, then she said, "*Zaideh*, I have something to say."

"Well, what is it?"

"I met a young man today at the wedding. He's a backpack peddler." She went on to describe Zuriel Benjamin's occupation, and when she finished, she said, "I think we ought to try that. I believe it would be better than a pushcart."

Jacob threw up his hands and laughed aloud. "What in the world will you think of next? First it was a pushcart which no woman does—and now you're proposing to go out into the country when you know almost nothing about it. It would be too dangerous."

"I do not think so," Reisa said. "It would be hard, but you and I could catch one of the coaches out to the edge of town. Then we could get out and go through the farms, to the homes of those who live in small villages. Zuriel said that they are always glad to see peddlers. It makes a break in their day. We could carry things that they couldn't buy at their little stores in their communities."

Jacob refused to consider such a thing. Reisa did not press him, but she resolved that she would not let the matter drop.

Two weeks passed, and each day Reisa kept her plan before Jacob in small ways. She would just mention the advantages of it and ignore the disadvantages, of course! Little by little she saw a change begin to take place in Jacob's mind. Finally, at the end of the week when she approached the subject again late one night, he said with resignation, "I see that we're going to have to try your plan or you will drive me crazy."

Reisa apologized. "I'm sorry, but it's something that I think will be good for both of us. If we don't like it, we can always go back to the pushcart."

That then settled the matter. The weather was fine, and Reisa began to collect the items. The next day Reisa purchased two used backpacks, one from a store and another from an elderly man who had once been in the business. Both were well worn but serviceable.

Selecting the merchandise was a matter of great thought. She made list after list, and as she had been told you can't sell out of an empty wagon, she determined to choose items that were light, small, and rather unusual. Her first items were the practical things such as needles, thread, and pins. She added ribbons for children and small shiny jewelry that brightened the drab monotony of the isolated people she would be selling to. She bought a few pairs of suspenders, a considerable amount of inexpensive jewelry, snuff boxes, combs, a few pair of spectacles, hair brushes, samples of peppermint, wintergreen, and cloves, a few spoons—not many because they were heavy—caps for men and boys, neckerchiefs and handkerchiefs for women, and bunches of bright-colored beads. She shopped for four days before her inventory was complete.

When she had all of her merchandise, more than enough to fill the two bags, she practiced putting it into the bags. In order to do this she divided things into smaller bags plainly marked with different colors. She knew that each of the backpacks would have to be unpacked, and the merchandise set out for the customers to see it all, or as much as possible. For over a week she worked on this project after she and Jacob got home from their pushcart sales.

Finally she said one evening, "We're ready, *Zaideh*. Tomorrow we will become backpack peddlers."

"God help us," Jacob smiled. "What will you think of next?"

But Reisa could tell that he was not unhappy. She worried that night as she got ready for bed. "Maybe I made it too rosy. Perhaps it will be too much for him." She had packed the two bags carefully so that Jacob's contained the lightest material, hers the heaviest. Still, no matter what Zuriel Benjamin said, it was a new world for the two of them.

That night she knelt beside her bed and said her prayers, then read for a time. She looked at the gospel of John but decided not to read it. *I can't believe all of that.* She was doubtful about the miracles of Jesus, turning water into wine, healing the blind. It was more than her mind could take in. Despite the fact that she was drawn to Jesus Christ, still she knew that such a thing was dangerous for a good Jew. She had always been told so. She had seen young boys being chased by Gentiles who yelled, "Christ killer! Christ killer!" and beat them badly when they caught them.

She turned out the light and got into bed and waited until Boris came and plopped himself down beside her. She stroked his fur saying, "You'll have to be good until I come back. It will only be a few days, Boris."

She closed her eyes and wondered at the audacity that such an adventure seemed to take. As sleep came upon her, she thought again of Jesus, and how he healed people and seemed to love everybody. She found herself wishing that the story in the little book were really true. And then sleep overtook her.

Nine

Reisa and Jacob stood still, packs on their backs, as the sun began to rise. It was very silent. Nature seemed to be struck dumb with no sound at all. And then Jacob heard the sound of a dove making its peculiar, poignant cooing sound. He did not know what sort of bird it was, for he had never seen or heard one in Russia. It saddened him for a moment, for it was a sad cry.

Then the moment passed as the world began to be bathed in morning freshness, a bright cleansing light. As they stood there, the horizon made sharp lines in the distance.

"How quiet it is and peaceful," Jacob murmured. "You know, Reisa, I heard once of a man who was sent to a prison camp in Siberia. He was a musician, but there was no piano there. The way I heard the story, he carved the piano keyboard with a nail on a piece of wood and for long hours would sit there playing the piano—but the music was made entirely of silence."

Reisa took his arm. "Come," she said briskly. "We'll make our first sale in that house."

"You're sure of that?" Jacob smiled. He wore his pack on his back, and his eyes fastened on the house that lay ahead of them not more than two hundred yards.

"Oh, I think so. We'll think it about every house. We'll think, *This is the woman or the man who will buy something from us.*"

The two moved toward the house. It was set back twenty yards from the road and surrounded by a white picket fence. Inside the yard, bright tulips paraded up the pathway to the door. Hearing a faint sound, they glanced upward to see a flight of geese headed south.

"Look, *Zaideh*—geese!" Reisa studied the V-shaped flight and murmured, "I wonder where my goose is? I wonder if he's happy?"

"We'll have to think that he is. It's beyond us. You did all you could for him, and now he's in the hands of the Master of the Universe—just like all of us."

Reisa commented, "You know, I think people who live in the country are happier than those who live in the city." She did not elaborate, but Jacob understood that she was making some sort of a statement about their life in New York. He felt the same himself, and just being out in the rural area surrounded by green grass, towering trees, and running brooks seemed to lift his spirits. He missed his native land, but would never say as much to Reisa or anyone else.

As they approached the white fence, a cinnamon-colored dog with stiff fur and a large bullet-shaped head came from around the house. The pair halted immediately as the dog came to the gate and stood there, fixing them with his pale eyes.

Nonplused, they did not know what to do. The dog looked dangerous, and although they liked animals, Jacob and Reisa did not know whether they could trust this one. This was one of the dangers that Zuriel Benjamin had warned them about.

"Maybe we'd better go to the next house, Reisa."

"Wait—someone's coming."

Just then the door opened. A short, dumpy woman wearing a gray dress and a white apron stepped outside. She paused on the porch giving the pair a curious look, then came down and spoke sharply to the dog. "Get away, Mickey!" She did not give the dog a second glance, and he slumped away and plopped down in the grass. "What do you want?" she asked curtly.

"Good morning," Reisa smiled. Despite her words, the woman did look approachable. She had a round, red face, light blue eyes, and taupe-colored hair that was in rather a disarray. She was a working woman, Reisa saw, for her hands were red and chapped. There was nothing fine about her, and for some reason this encouraged Reisa. "Could we show you some nice ribbon this morning? Or perhaps you're running low on spices."

"You're a peddler?" the woman said with surprise washing across her face. "I've never seen a woman peddler before."

"My name is Reisa Dimitri, and this is my grandfather, Jacob. We have some lovely things."

The woman hesitated, then nodded. "My name is Mrs. Dortch. I don't think I'd like anything this morning."

"Oh, please! Couldn't you look?"

At that moment a group of children came tumbling around the house—two boys and two girls, healthy, and their faces flushed with exercise. "Mama," the oldest girl pleaded, "Please let us look."

Mrs. Dortch hesitated. "Well, I don't suppose it would hurt anything to look. You'd better come into the house though."

This was better than they had expected. Reisa gave Jacob an encouraging smile, and the pair followed the woman into the house. They were flanked by the children, and as Reisa set her pack on the floor and opened it, they crowded in to see what she had. Reisa and Jacob both opened their packs eagerly, and soon the floor was covered with their merchandise.

"You don't have to unpack everything. I can't afford much."

Reisa was encouraged by this "much" for it did not mean "nothing."

"Look at this." Reisa held up a brightly colored neckerchief to the oldest girl. "That would look nice to shade your head from the sun."

"Oh, Mama, can I have it?" the girl cried. She put it on her head and tied it. "How do I look? Can I have it, Mama?"

"How much is it?" Mrs. Dortch asked cautiously.

"It's usually twenty-five cents, but because this is our first sale, you can have it for fifteen."

"Very well. I'll take it," Mrs. Dortch said.

This, of course, was a trigger for the other children, for they would not be left out. Mrs. Dortch wound up buying three dollars worth of merchandise. After they had repacked their merchandise, Mrs. Dortch insisted they have coffee or tea, whichever they preferred.

Thirty minutes later they left the house, and Mrs. Dortch walked to the gate with them. "That next house down the road, the white one over there. My sister lives there. Her name is Gretchen Kleinman. Go tell her that I sent you." Mrs. Dortch grinned broadly. "She's got plenty of money, although she'll act poor. That husband of hers has made a miser out of her. Make a good sale there."

"Thank you so much, Mrs. Dortch. I hope that we'll see you again," Reisa said.

Mrs. Dortch nodded, and the two left the yard. When they were out of hearing distance, Reisa smiled, her eyes sparkling. "Didn't I tell you, *Zaideh?* What a wonderful way to start our day!"

"Yes, and I have the idea that if we sell something and the people are nice, we could ask them who lives down the road. It means something, I think, if you go call someone by name."

They found this to be true. Mrs. Kleinman bought over five dollars worth of merchandise and sent them to her neighbor, Mrs. Heller. She sniffed, "She's not a good neighbor, but can well afford to buy some things. I wish," she said, "she would buy something to fix herself up. She goes around looking like a wet dish rag! A shame for a woman to let herself go like that."

Jacob and Reisa exchanged glances and smiled. Not only was their new venture making money—but they were enjoying themselves too!

ꕤ

A little brook was stirred by the wind, its clear water chuckling in the clump of willows, as the two passed over it on a wooden bridge. Both Jacob and Reisa were exhausted, for it had been a long day. Their packs were considerably lighter, however, and the silver from their sales jingled in Jacob's pocket with a comforting sound and a reassuring weight.

Reisa glanced at her grandfather, distressed by the fatigue on his face. She realized that she should have called a halt two hours ago at least, but her grandfather had not complained, and she had been excited with the success of the day's peddling. "I think we'd better think about a place to stay, *Zaideh.*"

"I would not mind something to eat and a bed, but there's no bed here."

"Zuriel told me that he often traded some goods for a night's lodging. That's a big house up there. If they don't have too many children, perhaps they will trade us a room or at least a place in the barn with some blankets for something we have that they like. We'll try it. Come along."

They approached the house, which was a large, rambling, white two-storied structure. A barn stood out behind it with several cows grazing, but happily there was no dog to greet them. They stepped up on the porch. Reisa noticed how slowly Jacob moved, and her heart smote her. "I should have been more watchful," she said. "We'll not work this late again."

At her knock the door opened, almost as if someone had been watching them. A tall thin man well up in years stood there, and his eyes took them in carefully. "Good evening. You're out late," he said.

"Yes, sir," Reisa spoke up. "We've been traveling all day selling our goods to your neighbors. We just left Mrs. Williams' house. Would you have a few moments to look at what we have?"

The man turned and said, "Mama, would you like to look at what these people have?"

The woman who came was as small as the man was tall. No more than five feet two inches, she had snow-white hair and a pair of kindly brown eyes. "Well, come in. We're just fixing supper."

"We wouldn't want to intrude," Jacob said quickly.

"Oh, my land, it's no trouble at all. Come into the parlor and put your packs down."

"My name is Elmo Tarkington. This is my wife, Judith." The tall man listened as Reisa gave her name and Jacob's, then said tentatively, "Mama always cooks like all of our children was at home. Be proud to have you sit and join with us."

"That's very kind of you," Jacob said and hesitated. "But we are Jewish, you see, and there are some foods we can't eat."

"Is that a fact? Well, come and sit down. I don't know what you eat, but I'll bet Mama can find somethin' like it."

"Why don't you go wash up first," Judith interrupted. "The road's been dusty today."

It was a relief for the two to wash their face and hands. They dried off on clean white towels.

When they came to the table, Elmo Tarkington said, "Sit down over there, Mr.—I didn't catch your name."

"Jacob Dimitri, and this is my granddaughter, Reisa."

"Dimitri! You're not from around here, I take it?"

"No. My English is not good. We are from Russia."

"Well, I swan!" Mrs. Judith Tarkington said. "All the way across the water! Well, isn't that fine! Now you set down there, and we'll find you something to eat."

The table was spread with a red and white cloth, and in the center was a baked ham. But there were vegetables and there was bread.

As they sat down, Mr. Tarkington said, "Reckon do you say a blessing like we do?"

"Oh, yes," Jacob said quickly. "Always we give thanks."

"Well, why don't you say it, brother," Tarkington said, and the pair bowed their heads.

Jacob was taken aback but bowed his head and said at once, "We thank thee, oh great Maker of the Universe, for this food. I thank thee for this generous couple and for their hospitality, and I ask that your peace and your rest and your safety might fall upon them and upon their children. Amen."

"Well, what can you folks eat and what can you not eat?" Judith Tarkington asked.

"We're not allowed to eat pork," Reisa said. "But we can surely eat the vegetables."

"Well, we got plenty of them." And there on the table were corn on the cob, a huge bowl of peas, and fried squash.

Reisa and her grandfather ate hungrily, and throughout the meal Elmo, who was a curious sort, asked them question after question about Russia. Finally his wife said, "Will you hush, Elmo, and let them eat. Do you have to know everything in the world?"

Grinning, Tarkington said, "She gets on me because I want to know about things, but I think it's natural."

"It ain't natural to ask a thousand questions to guests. Now you hush up."

Reisa smiled. "We don't mind in the least. You have such a lovely home here."

"Well, it was plumb full at one time," Mrs. Tarkington said. "We raised all eight of our chillun here, but they're all married and gone now."

"Are they far away?" Reisa asked.

"No, not far. All except Bud and Janie. They're gone off—Bud in Pennsylvania and Janie to Massachusetts. But they come back, and we have reunions."

Elmo laughed. "House gets plumb full. I've got fourteen grandchildren. I don't mind bein' a grandpa, but I sure hate bein' married to a granny."

"You hush your mouth, Elmo Tarkington!" Judith said sharply. "You ought to be satisfied that I've stayed with you all these years."

"How long have you been married, if I may ask?" Jacob said.

"Fifty-three years," Elmo said, and winked at Jacob. "And I've enjoyed every second of it."

Judith sniffed at this. "I can remember a few times you didn't appear to be enjoyin' it too much."

"Well, I've got a good forgetter. Now, let's have some of that blackberry cobbler you made. Are you folks allowed to eat that?"

Indeed they were allowed, and both guests filled themselves up on the succulent cobbler that came steaming from the oven with light flaky crust. Then they washed it down with cups of coffee laced with sugar.

Finally Reisa said, "We would like to pay for the meal."

Elmo stared at her. "I don't reckon so, miss. It'll be a sad day when a guest has to pay in my house."

"Come into the parlor, and let us see what you have." Judith smiled. "I've been needing some new ribbon for a dress I'm makin' for my youngest daughter. You got anything like that?"

The evening passed quickly. The Tarkingtons evidently were starved for talk, and they paid for their merchandise, which was a considerable assortment. Afterwards they sat in the parlor and talked.

Finally Mrs. Tarkington said, "Well, it's too dark for you to go anywhere tonight."

"That's right. There ain't no hotel close either. We got six bedrooms in this house. I reckon one of them ought to suit you."

"Oh, that's so kind of you," Reisa said.

"Glad to have company," Elmo said. "Mama, why don't you show them their rooms and let them get to bed. You've about talked their ears off."

"I think Mr. Dimitri and this young lady knows who does the talking around here." She smiled, got up, and took them to their rooms. "I hope you will make yourself at home. Good night."

After Judith Tarkington had gone downstairs, Reisa turned to her grandfather, her eyes glowing. "What wonderful people they are!"

"They are indeed." Jacob was so tired he could hardly stand up. He said, "We can't expect this kind of treatment everywhere. God is good. Good night, Reisa."

The next two days passed quickly and pleasantly for Jacob and Reisa. The weather was fine, and they learned more each day about their new profession. They found lodging both nights with families much like the Tarkingtons, and marveled at the hospitality of Americans. But their stock dwindled, and just before they went to bed on Thursday night, Jacob said, "It's time to go back to New York and restock. And I could use a rest."

Reisa glanced at her grandfather, noting the lines of strain on his face. "Yes, that is what we must do," she said firmly.

They left the next morning and made a leisurely journey toward New York. They asked for lodging each night, and insisted on paying their way. Reisa adjusted her pace to suit Jacob, who was very tired indeed. She resolved in the future to be more careful of his well-being.

When they reached the outskirts of New York, Reisa turned to Jacob, her eyes shining. "The Master of the Universe has been good to us, *Zaideh!* Here we are, safe, with money in our pocket, and a home to go to."

Jacob took her hand and nodded. "Yes, God is always good."

~

"Well, look who's here!" Rachel Gold came sweeping in to greet Jacob and Reisa. She had the dust of flour on her hands and wiped them on a napkin before she reached out and hugged Reisa, then shook hands with Jacob. "We've wondered and wondered where you two got to."

Laban Gold came in holding a newspaper in his hand. He smiled at them and greeted them warmly. "Did you have a successful trip?"

"Oh, yes!" Reisa said at once. "We made more in three days than we would have made in two weeks with the pushcart."

"Fine! Fine!" Laban said. "Well, come in, and we'll stir up something to eat, and you can tell us all about it."

"I want to go see Dov while you eat, Grandfather."

Laban chuckled. "That big fellow's been worried about you. Came every day to ask for you."

Reisa left the house and went two houses down, where she found Dov sitting on the doorstep. He jumped up at once, and his eyes glowed with pleasure. Reisa put out her hands, and they were swallowed by his huge, massive paws. "Reisa!" Dov said, his voice rumbling deep in his throat. "You're back."

"Yes. I've missed you, Dov."

"I missed you, too. Sit down. Tell me all."

Reisa sat down on the steps and shared her experiences with Dov, and then finally he asked, "You go soon?"

"I'm afraid so." Seeing the sadness come into his dark eyes, Reisa reached over and took his hand in both of hers. "It'll only be for a few days. We're doing so well, Dov."

"Nobody bother you?"

"No. God took care of us."

"I like to go with you some time."

Reisa laughed. "Maybe you can."

She left Dov, promising she would see him the next day, that they would go out after he got off from work, and she would buy him a meal at a cafe. This pleased him, and he patted her shoulder clumsily with his hand.

Back at the Golds for dinner, she found that the whole family was anxious to hear about their experiences. Reisa did most of the talking, and finally she said, "God was with us. And we learned so much."

"Indeed," Jacob said. "It was much better than I expected."

"What did you learn mostly?" Zillah asked.

"Oh, just little things," Reisa answered. "For one thing, next time we'll take some small, inexpensive toys so that when the parents buy we can give them to the children."

"Yes, even if they don't buy," Jacob said. "We found this one woman in a very poor house. She had three children and no money at all. You could see the longing in her eyes." His glance went over to Reisa, and he smiled. "The woman obviously loved a locket, and guess who simply gave it to her?"

"But, *Zaideh,* she wanted it so much, and she had so *little.*"

Jacob laughed then, reached over, and patted Reisa's hand. "We'll never get rich. You'll give away all of our profits."

Being very tired, Reisa and Jacob went to bed early. When she lay down, Boris came at once. He climbed up on her chest as he always had and stood staring at her with his huge green eyes.

"You missed me, did you?"

"Yow!" Boris said and bared his teeth at her in his grotesque grin.

"Well, you'll have to miss me a little bit more. You can have me for two days, but then we'll be leaving again."

She stroked Boris's fur, and then began thinking of the profits that they would make. She was not a greedy young woman, but she knew that when cold weather came they would have to go back to the pushcart. Her grandfather, she knew, could not stand the bitter cold weather. He had always been sickly during the winters, and they would not be able to make their trips then.

For a long time she stroked Boris, then rolled him off, turned out the light, and went to sleep.

A dream came to her some time that night. She was not a young woman who typically remembered her dreams, but this dream was clearer than any she had ever had. It was a simple thing. There was a man there, and she could not see his face. But she could hear his voice. She was standing before him, and he was saying, *"You must go south."*

She woke up abruptly, shocked at the clarity of it. Her dreams were mostly formless and meaningless. "What does that mean?" she said. "We must go south?"

The next morning she told Jacob her dream, and asked if he thought it meant anything.

"Dreams sometimes mean something," he responded. "But usually they don't."

This satisfied Reisa, and she said no more.

ஃ

By the time June came, Reisa and Jacob had done very well. They had made five trips and sold a great deal of merchandise. They had also learned a great deal about what to buy and what not to buy. It was quite an art, and Reisa realized that the longer she was at it, the more successful she would be.

The thing that troubled her the most was the recurring dream that she had. She had it five times, and the last two times it had been different. She had been walking down a road with Jacob at her side through a field of blossoms so white that they almost hurt her eyes. And they had passed by people, but they were not like people she had ever seen, for their faces and hands were all black. Always as they walked down the road, she could see the man before them, and he was always saying, *"Go south."*

The dream troubled her, especially since she had it repeatedly. She said no more to Jacob, but one night she prayed, "God, if this dream is from you, please make it clear!"

Ten

"Reisa!—Reisa!"

Hearing her name called, Reisa turned quickly and saw Zuriel Benjamin making his way through the crowd. He was wearing a light tan suit, a white shirt, a blue tie, and a straw hat with a wide brim that covered his brow.

Coming forward, he took her hand and said, "Reisa, I'm so pleased to see you!"

"Zuriel, what are you doing here?"

A band was playing loudly not fifty feet away, so Reisa had to shout her words. They had come to the village of Benton on the Fourth of July and had spent the morning selling their goods in an open space. She had left Jacob there while she wandered around to see the sights.

Zuriel smiled broadly. His white teeth gleamed against his darkly tanned skin, and his black hair glistened as he removed his hat. He had curly hair which he had allowed to grow rather long, and now he held onto her hand tightly. "I'm so pleased to see you. Come. Let's get away from all this noise."

Reisa allowed herself to be led away, noting that he did not release her hand. This brought a smile to her lips, for she remembered that, from what she had heard of Zuriel, he was very successful with young ladies.

"Now," Zuriel said as he drew her down to a bench a hundred yards away from the center of activity. "Tell me how you've been. You look wonderful."

"Thank you, Zuriel. You're in good health, I see."

"Oh, yes. I never get sick." He reached over and took her hand again in both of his and leaned forward. "I had forgotten how pretty you were."

Reisa laughed aloud and pulled her hand back. "And I had forgotten what a romantic young man you are. How many young ladies have you been after since I saw you last?"

For a moment Zuriel looked confused, but he was a good-humored young man, and he laughed. "It's all a game, Reisa. They smile at me, and I smile back. And then they run, and I chase them. Isn't that what you do?"

"No. I don't do anything like that."

"Then how do you expect to get a husband?"

"I don't expect one. If the Master of the Universe wants me to have a husband, he knows where I live. And he knows where that young man lives. He will bring us together."

Her words amused Zuriel. His black eyes sparkled with humor, and he shook his head, saying in a pseudo-mournful tone, "You'll never get a husband. You're too romantic."

"Never mind how romantic I am. Tell me what you've been doing."

"No. You tell me first."

The two sat on the bench. Around them there were games and booths set up, and far off on the other side of the small park young boys were exploding squibs. The firecrackers went off like miniature cannons, and the squeals of pleasure from the boys came to them as they sat there.

"We took your advice and have gone backpacking, Zuriel. It's been very good. God has been very good to us."

"I told you, didn't I? It's the only way, being a back peddler. You've made a lot of money?"

"Not a lot. And when bad weather comes we won't be able to travel."

"Oh, I don't know, I do pretty well. People are lonesome in the wintertime. I sometimes sell more in the winter than in the summer. People are anxious to see someone and have someone to talk to." He thought for a moment and said, "There are many lonely people out there. I've learned to spot them. They're anxious to have you in their house and find out what's going on in the big world."

"I've noticed that. It's a little sad."

"Well, all of us get a little bit lonely at times." He reached out and touched her shoulder and winked. "Even you romantic people, eh?"

Reisa could not resist his good humor. "Yes. Even us romantic people," she said. "Now, tell me about yourself."

"Oh, I'll tell you later. Let's go join in the festivities. I've got a pocket full of money. Come along, I'll buy you a taffy apple."

"What is a taffy apple?"

"They put a stick in an apple then dip it in hot taffy. It sticks to the apple. Come along and I'll show you."

Taffy apples did not sound particularly good to Reisa, but she found that they were delicious. She got her face and hands covered with the sticky candy and had to go to the pump to wash it off.

The two spent an hour going around to the different stalls and booths. Zuriel was an amusing young man, quick and always easy with his smile. Finally Reisa took him back to Jacob, who was very glad to see the young man.

"You go look around for a while. It's rather fun, *Zaideh.*"

Jacob left her with their small stall that they had rented for twenty-five cents, and while he was gone she and Zuriel talked easily. She was glad to see Zuriel again, for he had been kind to her.

Later in the day there were patriotic speeches and a drill team by men dressed in the blue uniform. Reisa watched all this and listened, not understanding much about the war that had passed over America. Zuriel explained it to her. "It was over slavery. The South wanted to keep slaves, but the North felt it was wrong."

"Then the North was right."

"Yes, they were."

"People from the South must be very bad."

"No, they're really not. I've just come from there. I have a friend there, a cousin actually. He says they're very warm-hearted people. Generous and quick to help, for the most part. They were just wrong on the one issue. It cost them dearly, though."

Reisa stored this in her mind, for she was always anxious to learn about America.

The rest of the day was spent pleasantly enough, and that night they treated themselves by staying in a hotel. They had made a great deal of money, for people were free spenders during the celebration.

Zuriel insisted on buying their supper in the crowded dining room. There was the usual struggle of finding something that was kosher, so they settled for vegetables and dessert.

"It's inconvenient not having kosher food," Jacob said. His eyes fell on Zuriel, and he smiled suddenly. "I suppose you always stick with the kosher diet."

For once Zuriel Benjamin was somewhat taken aback. "Well, as much as possible," he said carefully. "Of course, sometimes a fellow has to have something to eat. You know how that is."

Jacob laughed. "You are a scoundrel, Zuriel, but a charming one. Do the best you can, my boy, and God will look after you."

Jacob went to his room soon after this, but it was early yet.

"Come. Let's take a walk," Zuriel said. "It's very nice out tonight."

The two walked out of the hotel and down the main street. The booths were still up, and many couples were walking up and down the sidewalk. A band was playing, this time not stirring martial music, but a softer tune. They walked to the end of the street, and over to their left a grove of trees rose up into the sky. The stars were sparkling overhead like tiny dots of fire.

"It's so quiet here," Reisa said. She stopped and listened, for a man had started to sing. He had a clear tenor voice that sounded very beautiful to her.

"What's that he's singing, Zuriel?"

Zuriel listened for a moment and said, "It's a song the southern soldiers sang during the war. It's called 'Lorena.' It's still very popular, even in the North."

The two stood there and listened as the words came floating on the summer air.

The years creep slowly by, Lorena,
The snow is on the grass again,
The sun's low down the sky, Lorena,
The frost gleams where the flowers have been.
But the heart throbs on as warmly now,
As when the summer days were nigh;
Oh! the sun can never dip so low,
Adown affections cloudless sky.

"How beautiful!" Reisa was vaguely aware that Zuriel had moved closer to her, his arm touching hers. She was caught up with the song as it continued:

We loved each other then, Lorena,
More than we ever dared to tell;
And what we might have been, Lorena,
Had but our lovings prospered well—
But then, tis past, the years are gone,
I'll not call up their shadowy forms;
I'll say to them, "Lost years, sleep on!

Sleep on! Nor heed life's pelting storms."
I'll say to them, "Lost years, sleep long!
Sleep long! Nor heed life's pelting storms."

For some reason the pathos and sadness of the words touched Reisa's spirit. She stood there as the words came to her. The singer continued in the same sad strain. She felt tears rise to her eyes, but did not understand why.

Sensing her mood, Zuriel turned her around and held her by her upper arms. Leaning forward, he saw her tears. "Why, Reisa, you're crying!"

"It's—it's so sad!"

Reisa's mood was so strange that she could not remember a time like this. She felt Zuriel's arms go about her and pull her close, and the softness of her body pressed against him in a way that she had never pressed herself against a man. All of the sweetness and the richness that was in her seemed to rise, and as he bent his head and put his lips on hers, she returned the pressure of them. She was aware of his needs as a man, and perhaps for the first time in her life she was aware of what it meant to be a woman. He held her closer, his lips demanding, and she found herself responding. Her own arms had gone around his neck—and then suddenly she realized what was happening, and it frightened her. He no longer had her, and she turned her head aside and placed both hands on his chest.

"Reisa, you're so sweet!"

"You—you mustn't say those things."

"Why not? They're true enough."

"Good night. I must go." And she turned and walked away.

The next morning Reisa blushed slightly when she met Zuriel at breakfast. To her relief, he said nothing about the previous night, but kept his talk on business.

"I've got a new plan," Zuriel announced. "I'm going to go down to the southern part of the country."

"You would leave the North?" Jacob said. "Why is that?"

"Well, for one thing, I like it there. For another, my cousin down there tells me that it's good right now for peddlers. No competition. The stores charge high prices, and people are quick to look for a bargain."

"How long will you be gone, Zuriel?" Reisa asked.

"I don't know. All depends on how I do." He smiled at her and winked. "You wait until I get back. Don't be marrying up some rich old man."

Reisa's flush deepened, but she managed a smile. "I don't think you'll have to worry about that."

They parted from Zuriel and for the next two days made their way back by another route toward the city. By the time they reached home, they had sold at least three-fourths of their goods.

"If we could just take a pushcart with us, we could sell out of that," Reisa said.

"It would never do. Where would we keep it at night?" Jacob replied.

That night back at the Golds' Reisa slept well. She was awakened by Boris pushing his nose against her cheek. It was cold and wet, and she put her arms around him and hugged him, shaking him back and forth. "You rascal," she whispered. "What a life you have! Just eat and sleep and get petted. *I* should have such a life!"

All day she was busy helping Mrs. Gold with the housework, but after supper that night she had a visitor. Dov found her walking along the street just for a change of scene. His huge form towered over her as she greeted him warmly, as always giving him her hands. It gave her a strange pleasure when his huge hands enveloped hers, and she always remembered how he had protected her on board the ship.

"How are you, Dov?"

Dov did not answer, and Reisa could see that he was troubled. "What's wrong?" she said. "Are you sick?"

"No sick." He struggled with words, and she knew he was trying to find the proper English word. He was not quick with language, but he did the best he could.

"Take me with you," he finally said slowly.

Reisa was confused. His hands tightened and hurt her own, until finally she said, "You're hurting me, Dov." He released her hands at once, and she reached up and put her hand on his massive arm. It was like putting her hand on an oak tree. "What do you mean?"

Dov tried to speak but gave up on English. Finally he began speaking in Russian. "Two nights ago I had dream."

Instantly Reisa tensed. "What kind of a dream, Dov?"

"I dream of you and the reb. You are walking along the road." He closed his eyes for a moment as if to refresh his mind. When he opened them they were troubled. "You are on a road with white flowers all around, and—and there are black people everywhere. They are staring at you and the reb."

Reisa was shaken. It was the same dream, in essence, that she herself had had repeatedly. She saw the trouble in Dov's features and patted his arm. "I won't leave you, Dov. Tell me again about the dream. Don't leave anything out." She listened as he repeated it almost word for word, and then said, "It's just a dream. I won't leave you."

Dov's massive chest heaved with relief, and he patted her shoulder clumsily. He began to tell her about his day at the dock, but Reisa did not forget about his words. Indeed, she kept his dream in her mind for two days, and even as she and Jacob left to go on another tour, she thought of little else. Finally on their second night, when they had found a family willing to give them a room in exchange for goods, she mentioned Dov's dream to

Jacob. He sat quietly while she spoke, and finally he said, "What are you thinking, Reisa?"

"You remember Zuriel's plan to go to the South? I think God is telling us to do the same thing."

Jacob stared at her. "It's impossible! Our people are here. We don't even know that there are any Jews there or synagogues."

"Yes, there are. Zuriel's cousin told him so. Not many but a few."

Jacob was highly disturbed by this suggestion, and Reisa knew better than to argue. "It's something to think about," she said. "Maybe it's nothing."

But the seed was planted. Although Jacob said nothing about it, she knew he was thinking of it.

ॐ

Jacob was so quiet at dinner the following night that Laban Gold asked him, "Are you not feeling well, Reb? You say almost nothing."

"Oh, I'm very well. Just thinking."

"Do you feel bad, *Zaideh?*" Reisa joined in.

"No. I just feel the need for God." He nodded to them, excused himself from the table, and climbed the stairs to his room.

Every time Jacob Dimitri had problems he would flee for refuge to the Scriptures. He knew them almost by heart, having read them over and over again throughout his long years. Many times he could remember finding a Scripture that would seemingly give him an answer. This was difficult because, at times, he was not quite sure if he simply chose the Scripture, or if God had caused his mind to focus on it.

All day he stayed in his room, going over the Old Testament Scriptures. He read until his eyes grew weary and he had to lie down and rest.

When he awoke the following day, he had a strong impression that he needed to read the book of Joshua. All day long he read carefully.

He had gone almost all the way through the book of Joshua, and finally he reached the part that had to do with Caleb and his daughter. He had read this before. Joshua had divided the land among the Israelites, and Caleb, being one of the heroes with Joshua himself, had gotten the choice of land. He began reading the section which said:

> *And Caleb said, He that smiteth Kirjath-sepher, and taketh it, to him will I give Achsah my daughter to wife.*
>
> *And Othniel, the son of Kenaz, the brother of Caleb, took it: and he gave him Achsah, his daughter, to wife.*
>
> *And it came to pass as she came unto him, that she moved him to ask of her father a field: and she lighted off her ass; and Caleb said unto her, What wouldest thou?*
>
> *Who answered, Give me a blessing; for thou hast given me a south land; give me also springs of water. And he gave her the upper springs and the nether springs.*

Jacob suddenly felt a very strange emotion run through him, just like the other times when God had spoken to him through the written word. He read the passage again, and then for the third time. The verse that moved him most was the phrase, "Thou hast given me a south land; give me also springs of water."

With trembling hands, Jacob pressed his eyes. He began to pray silently and remained absolutely motionless. Finally he read the section again, and he knew that the phrase "Thou hast given me a south land; give me also springs of water" would be on his mind for days.

Finally weariness overtook him, and he went to sleep. It was late when he woke up without any warning. He turned on the light and blinked until his eyes grew accustomed to it, then looked at his watch that he always kept beside him. It was three-thirty, the middle of the night.

But Jacob was wide awake. He rose and dressed and then sat down in a chair. He had gone to sleep thinking of the phrase that had so burned into his mind, and now he thought, *It may be nothing. I will read more of the Scripture. It may be only my idea.*

He left the book of Joshua and began reading at the beginning of the next book, Judges. He read the first eleven verses and then suddenly the words jumped out at him. "And Caleb said, He that smiteth Kirjath-sepher, and taketh it..."

It was the identical passage! Jacob sat there quietly, his hands trembling as he completed the passage. It was the same, word for word. "Give me a blessing: for thou hast given me a south land; give me also springs of water."

Something seemed to click in Jacob's mind. He had always said, "It is impossible to know always the will of God—but sometimes he speaks to us so plainly we cannot mistake it."

Jacob Dimitri was not a mystic. Nor was he in the least an impulsive man. He believed in waiting and thinking things through, pondering and meditating on them. But now he suddenly knew that he must share this with Reisa.

Reisa started, for a sharp knock on her door had broken through her sleep. She sat up, pushing Boris away, thinking perhaps it was a sound from somewhere else in the house, but it was repeated—not loud, but with intensity.

"Just a minute," she said. Getting out of bed, she put on her robe and moved barefooted to the door. She unlocked it and opened it. Seeing Jacob there, her eyes grew large. "Are you sick, *Zaideh?*"

"No, but I must talk with you."

"Come in." Stepping back, she allowed her grandfather to pass. He held the Scripture in his hand, and she saw that his face was troubled. "What is it?" she demanded.

"I—do not know, Granddaughter," he said, and his voice was slightly above a whisper. "Something has come to me. I have thought much about what you have said about the South, and now it may be that God has given us a confirmation."

Reisa's heart began to pound, and she reached out and took her grandfather by the arms. "What is it? What has God said to you?"

He said, "Come. Let me sit down and read to you."

Reisa watched as he sat down on the single chair beside the bed. She sat down as close to him as she could get and listened as he said, "This is from the book of Joshua." He read the Scripture with an unsteady voice. "When I read this verse 'Thou hast given me a south land; give me also springs of water,' it seemed to burn into my spirit." He looked up and said, "I was troubled by this because I do not ever want to mistake God, and it is easy to do so."

"You think it is from the Lord?"

"I went to sleep at once, but an hour ago I came awake very suddenly—completely awake. You know how slowly I come out of sleep, Reisa. But I was wide awake, and I picked up the Scripture. I did not want to read Joshua anymore, so I started reading the next book, the book of Judges." He put his finger on the spot and turned the book toward her. She read it aloud, "Give me a blessing: for thou hast given me a south land; give me also springs of water."

The two sat there hushed, each waiting for the other to speak. Finally she said, "You must decide, *Zaideh*. I am only a woman."

"Do not say that, child," Jacob said quickly. He reached out with his free hand and took her hand. "I have been troubled about your dreams."

"And then there is Dov's dream..." Reisa said.

"I think," Jacob said slowly, "that we must go. If God is calling, we must answer. It will be hard, but then Abraham went out and did not know where he was going. He was simply told by God to leave his kindred, his family, and God would provide the place." Jacob smiled tremulously.

"We will be the children of Abraham. We will go out though we know not where we go."

The two sat there, and both knew that something tremendous had happened in their lives. Neither of them understood it, but somehow a tiny seed of faith had been planted. And it was Reisa who said, "We will go south. Abraham is our father, and God is our God. He will take care of us."

The two bowed their heads and prayed, and as they did Reisa Dimitri knew that her life would never be the same again.

Part Two

As Reisa leaned on the railing of the *Dixie Queen*, the cascade of sparkling drops showering from the huge paddle wheel delighted her. During the two-day trip that had brought them from New York to Virginia, she had spent hours fascinated by the rise and fall of the paddle wheel. She listened now as the wheels churned in the water, and far below she could hear the throbbing of mighty steam engines. The boat shivered and quaked beneath her feet, but it was a thrill to her.

Mr. Gold had decided that they should take a boat down the coast to Virginia instead of going by coach or railway. The fare had been much cheaper, and they had been able to bring their trunks with them. Since these contained all they had left of their home, neither Reisa nor Jacob could bear to leave them behind. Now they were stowed safely somewhere in the hold of the ship with their names firmly attached to them.

The trip had been a delight. They had slept well both nights, Jacob and Dov sharing a cabin, while Reisa shared one with a lady named Frances Milhouse, a middle-aged woman going to Georgia to meet her husband. She and Reisa had found each other good company, but both were wondering about how they would like the South.

"I've heard so much about the mistreatment of the slaves," Mrs. Milhouse said one day as they stood on deck, watching the river pass beneath them. "I just don't want to see such things."

"But the war ended all that, didn't it?"

"It was supposed to, but we will see."

Dov came to stand beside Reisa, his huge form dwarfing her. He turned and smiled through his thick beard, his white teeth flashing. "Boat is good in water," he said. "Better than wagon."

"Yes. Much better," Reisa said.

"Where we go now?"

"We'll get off at a city called Norfolk."

Norfolk had been the destination decided by Reisa and Jacob after studying a map carefully. It had become their plan to get off and make their way westward, maybe past Richmond. They had no real reason for doing this, but not having another plan they had made this one. And now as Reisa stood beside Dov watching the silvery drops fall back into the churning water, she hoped they had made the right decision. All any of them knew of Norfolk was that it was in the South.

Dov was silent. He was quiet as a rule, but there was something comforting about his presence. Reisa knew that she would never be afraid of any physical danger as long as he was there. Her grandfather, she knew, felt the same, for he had said once, "God has sent Dov to take care of us. He is one of God's innocents."

Now Reisa glanced up at the huge man and smiled. "Do you miss home much? I mean, back across the big ocean?"

"Sometimes," Dov said. "But this is good land, and I have two good friends."

Reisa patted his hand and smiled. "You'll have more than that. God will send us many friends."

Even as she spoke, the whistle gave a mighty blast, and Reisa straightened up. "I think we're coming to Norfolk," she said. "One of the sailors told me it wasn't far."

Indeed, the banks were lined more and more with houses, wharves, and other buildings. "We'd better go get Grandfather," she said. They moved away from the deck and found Jacob engaged in a conversation with one of the deckhands. He smiled and said, "This is Mr. Anderson. His sister married a good Jewish man, and we've been talking about how he should treat his new brother-in-law."

Anderson was a short, muscular man with a tanned face and a pair of bright blue eyes. "To tell the truth, I was worried. I didn't know nothin' about Jews, but meeting your grandfather here, well, it's given me a change of mind."

"God will bless your sister, and may God bless you, too, Mr. Anderson."

"We'd better start getting our things together," Reisa said. "We'll be docking soon."

"That's right," Anderson said quickly. "I'll go down and see to your luggage if you'd like."

"Thank you. Dov, would you go with him and help him carry the trunks?"

Dov nodded and the two men left. Reisa went to her own cabin where she stroked Boris. He had not liked the ship for some reason, and now he yowled piteously. "It's all right, Boris," she said. "We'll be on firm ground soon enough." She got out the canvas carrier with the thin wooden bottom. She had sewed net over one end of it, and when she put him in he settled down reluctantly. She tied up the drawstring on the end, picked it up by the handle, then picked up her light canvas carpetbag that she had bought in New York to carry some of her clothes.

Leaving the cabin, she went to the deck where the passengers that were to disembark were gathered. There were not many of them, no more than a dozen. Soon Anderson and Dov emerged from the hold, each carrying one of the trunks.

"I'll help you put these on shore, Mr. Dimitri," Anderson said.

"Very kind of you, I'm sure." Jacob turned to Reisa, whispering, "This is such a kind man. If all Southerners are like this, we will do well here."

The *Dixie Queen* nudged its way carefully into the dock. They watched as the deckhands lowered the gangplank that was situated in the bow. About twenty bales of cotton were located there, and Captain Creighton came by, giving orders. "All passengers ashore!" He had spoken to Dov before. He was from North Carolina and had taken an interest in the big man, marveling at his size. "Well, friend. You ought to do well here, a strong fellow like you."

"He's very strong," Reisa said proudly, looking up at Captain Creighton, who was a tall man. "I've never seen a load he couldn't pick up."

Anderson grinned. He had stopped and put the trunk down. "I bet he couldn't pick up one of them bales of cotton."

"No indeed!" Creighton exclaimed. "No man could do that."

"Yes, he could," Reisa said firmly. She had unbounded confidence in Dov's strength.

"I'm sorry, miss, but I don't know any *two* men who could pick up a bale of cotton. We have to wheel them off on two-wheeled dollies. They're very heavy."

Reisa felt a twinge of puckish humor. "I'll tell you what, Captain. My grandfather doesn't let me make wagers, but I'll make a bargain with you."

Creighton smiled at her. "What sort of bargain?"

"If Dov can carry one of those things of cotton ashore all by himself, you'll buy your family something from our kit."

The several sailors waiting to unload the bales laughed. Creighton said, "What do I get if he can't?"

Reisa thought for a minute. "Then I'll let you pick anything from our pack as a gift for your wife."

"Sounds like a bet to me," Captain Creighton said. He stared at the big figure of Dov, then put his eyes on one of the bales of cotton. "Might as well get out the most expensive thing you've got."

Reisa turned and said, "Dov, pick up one of those things and carry it ashore for the captain."

Dov nodded. He moved over to a bale of cotton, pushed it with his hand, and it gave. It was bulky, and he looked around and asked for something in Russian.

"He wants a rope," Reisa said.

"Plenty of those on board ship," Captain Creighton said.

A rope was soon produced, and Dov threw it around the bale. He tied it in a firm knot, then backed up to the bale which was standing on end, putting the loop over his shoulders. He tightened the knot so that it fit snugly, then he simply leaned forward. The bale tilted and rose off the deck.

"Well, I'll be—!" Creighton and the sailors stared as Dov moved slowly down the gangplank. There was no hesitation in his movement, and a cheer went up from the deck crew. At the end of the gangplank, Dov leaned back, and the bale settled down. He slipped out of the rope, loosened it, and brought it back up. Handing it back to the captain, he smiled but said nothing.

"Well," Creighton laughed. "Open your pack. Let's see what I'm going to buy."

Reisa quickly grabbed one of the packs. They had packed two small ones for herself and Jacob and one enormous one for Dov. They were carefully packed with all sorts of things. The passengers quickly gathered around, as well as the crew and the captain, and before they had left they had sold over thirty dollars worth of merchandise.

Reisa put her hand out to the captain and smiled up at him. "Thank you so much, Captain. It was a good trip for us."

"You're going to sell your goods in Virginia?"

"Yes."

"I'm afraid it won't be so easy as here. This country's been hard hit. People don't have much. But good luck and God bless you."

The three left the *Dixie Queen*, turning to wave at the captain and the first mate and the rest of the crew.

"That was very good, Reisa, but it sounded like a wager to me," Jacob said.

"No. We had nothing to lose. I knew Dov could do it." She smiled at the big man and then looked around. "Now, what will we do with our trunks? We can't carry them with us."

"That's true," Jacob said. "I don't know what we'll do with them. We'll have to store them somewhere."

Reisa had learned to be quite active in handling things like this. She found the office for the steamship line and got permission from the agent to leave the trunks until they found a place to store them. He agreed at once saying, "They'll be very safe here, miss."

A thought came to her, and she asked, "Is there a synagogue in this place?"

The agent, a thin man with gray eyes and gray hair to match, gave her an odd look. "A synagogue? I think there is. I've never been there myself, of course."

"Could you tell me how to get there?" She listened carefully and nodded. Giving her thanks, she went at once to Dov and Jacob. "They will keep our trunks until we come back for them. And, *Zaideh*, we have found a synagogue. The man told me how to get there."

Jacob beamed. "That is good, Granddaughter."

The three of them made their way away from the harbor to the inner city of Norfolk. They noticed at once how different the city was from New York. The trees were different, being a variety that they had never seen before, and there were few high buildings such as in New York.

Finding the synagogue was simple, and when they entered they were greeted by a middle-aged man with black hair and black eyes to match. His eyes took in the three at once, and he waited.

Jacob greeted him in Hebrew. *"Boruch hashen."*

The rabbi smiled at once and replied, *"Tzu eich bagaigenen."* Then he interpreted himself. "A great pleasure to meet you. My name is Isaac Tichler. Welcome to Norfolk."

Jacob quickly introduced Dov and Reisa, then said, "Excuse my English. It is not good."

"Better than mine when I first arrived." Tichler smiled. "How can I help you? I hope you've come to settle here. We need more good men and women in our synagogue."

"Unfortunately we will be moving on." Quickly Jacob explained their plan and then ended by saying, "We need a place to store two trunks until we find out where we will be."

"That will be no problem. I have the use of a wagon. Where are they?"

"At the dock," Reisa said quickly. "If you would, Dov and I will go get them."

The reb was pleased to do this for them, but he insisted that they stay for a talk and for a meal afterwards.

Dov and Reisa rode in the wagon to the docks and returned in half an hour with the trunks. Rabbi Tichler had Dov place them in a storage room and promised, "They will be safe here for as long as you care to leave them. But come, we will have a good meal."

"I hope it won't be eggs." Jacob smiled. "When we are on the road, we eat so many eggs that I'm starting to cackle. It's hard to find kosher food."

"Well, we will do better than that."

Indeed, the rabbi did better—much better. His wife greeted them warmly, and an hour later they were sitting down to a meal of *grieven*, fried chicken skins, which they had not had since they left their home in Russia. There was also lox, *tshav*, delicious sour leaf soup, and for dessert, streudel that melted in the mouth.

"I fear that you may find difficulty by and by," Tichler said. "This land was devastated by the war."

"But that was over almost six years ago," Jacob said. "Has it not recovered?"

"Not by any means. Virginia was the site of many battles, and many homes were destroyed. Those men who survived came home to find nothing but a pile of ashes with everything gone. They literally started from the ground up."

"That was not so in the North, was it?" Reisa asked.

"No. Almost all battles took place in the South. The land was truly devastated. It was as if a huge scythe went over it—especially in Virginia and down through Georgia. General Sherman destroyed everything he could. To this day he is hated very much in this land."

"So the people here still have not put the war behind them?"

"How could they!" the rabbi exclaimed, holding his hand out in a helpless gesture. "Every family you meet will have lost fathers, sons, brothers. There is still much bitterness against the federal government."

They talked so long that the rabbi said, "It would not be wise to start on your peddling journeys today. Stay the night, and I will take you myself to the outskirts of Norfolk and put you on the main road."

Reisa was glad to hear this and so was Jacob. She was concerned about her grandfather's health, and she tried to make things as easy as possible. In addition to this, she knew that he was anxious to spend time with educated men.

Indeed, it proved to be a pleasant evening. After dinner Rabbi Tichler and Jacob shared passages from the Torah with one another while Reisa repacked their bags.

At one point Jacob asked, "What is your feeling about the Messiah, Reb?"

Tichler gave him a quick glance. "Why do you ask?" he said.

"We are all interested, are we not? When he comes, he will do great things in Israel."

"Yes, that is true, but there is little agreement among our people. What is your own feeling?"

"I have thought much on this and searched the Scriptures. It seems," he said, "there are two Messiahs."

"Two Messiahs!" Tichler was startled. "How do you mean, Jacob?"

"One set of Scriptures seems to identify a victorious Messiah who will come with power and might. The other set of Scriptures speak of one who suffers greatly."

"Yes. That is true, and it has been a trouble to me. I cannot put these two together."

"Nor can I," Jacob sighed.

As the two men talked, Reisa worked through their bags. She was constantly rearranging them so that the goods could be more easily packed and unpacked with speed. She knew there would be times when people could buy nothing—but one could never know.

Dov sat cross-legged watching her. Finally he said, "We leave soon?"

"Tomorrow morning we will be on our way," Reisa smiled.

ॐ

After breakfast the following morning, Rabbi Tichler drove them out of the city of Norfolk and put them on the main road heading west. He blessed them as they left and promised again that their trunks would be safe.

Reisa, Jacob, and Dov traveled hard all morning, stopping many times at houses along the main road. The day was difficult. Reisa was shocked by the poverty of most of the people. They passed the skeletons of many houses. Only the chimneys were left, pointing like a finger toward the sky. Many of the fields were grown up in weeds, and those homesteads where they stopped reflected great poverty.

"We'll ask for a place to stay at this house. It's a nice one and very big," Reisa said late that afternoon. Jacob, she saw, was almost too tired to talk. His bag was very light, for she had arranged it that way. Dov, of course, carried the huge pack as if it were stuffed with feathers. He never showed signs of fatigue.

As they approached the house, a man and a woman came out. Following them were two half-grown children. The man's eyes studied them carefully. "Howdy," he said. "How goes it with you?"

"Very well, sir," Reisa said. "We were wondering if you would like to look at our goods. Perhaps we'd have something you might like."

"My name is Carson. This is my wife, Nellie. You look beat. Why don't you come in and rest yourselves?"

"That's very kind of you, sir," Jacob said faintly.

Carson's eyes narrowed. "You aren't from around here."

"No. We do not speak English well," Reisa said.

"What language do you speak?"

"Well—Yiddish, Hebrew, and Russian, and very poor English."

"Glory be!" Carson's eyes flew open. "You speak all them?"

"I wish we spoke English a little better," Jacob said.

"Then you folks be Hebrews."

"Yes, indeed," Jacob said.

"Well, welcome to you. Look, Nellie, these are God's chosen people! Come inside. You'll stay with us tonight and take dinner. We've got plenty of room."

This freely offered hospitality cheered Reisa, and she said warmly, "Thank you so very much, Mr. Carson."

The rest of the day was a delight for all three of the travelers. They were escorted into the house, their packs were placed in one corner of a spacious parlor, and Boris was given the run of the house.

"We always like cats," Mrs. Carson said. "And I lost mine of twelve years last week."

"Maybe he can catch a few of them rats while you're visitin'," Carson grinned.

Reisa, Jacob, and Dov were able to wash the dust off their faces and hands, and then they were invited to sit down to a dinner.

The table was round and made of heavy oak. Mrs. Carson covered it with dishes, and Mr. Carson said, "It says in the old Bible that you Jewish people can't eat just anything. Do you see anything here you can eat?"

"Oh, yes!" Jacob said quickly. "There's plenty here." There was stewed chicken, beets, squash, corn on the cob, and fresh baked bread.

The meal was punctuated by questions, mostly by Mr. Carson. Reisa answered most of them, explaining why they had left Russia and telling about their stay in New York.

After the meal was over, Carson said, "Let them dishes be, wife. We don't have God's chosen people every day! As a matter of fact, I don't know as I ever seen a Jew before. You don't happen to have a Bible in real Hebrew?"

"Yes, indeed, I do."

"I'd admire to hear you read out of it."

"That will be simple enough." Jacob smiled.

They adjourned to the living room, where for the rest of the evening Jacob and Reisa entertained the family. Jacob read from the Jewish Scripture, and Reisa spoke a great deal of Hebrew. This fascinated the Carsons. Soon Carson had his own Bible out, and he would open it to a passage and say, "Read that for me in Hebrew, Rabbi."

Jacob had given up trying to explain that he was not a rabbi and simply accepted the title. He would read the passage in Hebrew and then give what he thought was the English translation. Then Carson would read from his own Bible and many times would exclaim, "Why, it's the same, ain't it now!"

Reisa unpacked her own pack and found gifts for all of the family. When Carson offered to pay, she said, "No. This is a gift."

She gave the master of the house a new razor and he said, "I'll keep it as long as I live and pass it along to Henry here." For Mrs. Carson there was a brooch that she admired greatly. For the boy who was no more than twelve a fine jackknife, and for the girl a small lightweight doll that fit into her hand.

Finally Mrs. Carson said, "We've kept you up, and I know you're tired. You go to bed now. When you get up in the morning we'll have a good breakfast."

All three of the travelers went to their beds, and Reisa lay down with Boris next to her as usual. He purred and nudged her until finally she embraced him and kissed his nose. "Good night, Boris. It's been a good day."

❧

That day at the Carsons was the best day that they had. From that point on the country seemed to grow poorer. The closer they got to Richmond, the worse the situation.

"These people have almost nothing," Reisa murmured. "The war ruined them. I don't know how we shall do."

Jacob agreed. "But we are here. The great God above will take care of us."

The next night they could find only an abandoned house with most of the roof caved in, but at least they were inside. The following night they had little success, and at dusk slept out under the stars. This was no hardship for Reisa, but she regretted that they could find nothing better for her grandfather.

On the third day they stopped, for the first time, at the home of ex-slaves. The woman that came to greet them had a baby on her hip, one clinging to her skirt, and one about six years old. Reisa introduced herself and asked if the woman would like to look at some things.

The woman stared at her silently, her dark eyes fathomless. "I'm Martha. Martha Grimes. These is my chilluns, and my husband, he's workin'."

"Well, Mrs. Grimes," Reisa said, "I have some very nice things here."

"We ain't got no money. Not much anyways."

"Then you just might like to look," Reisa said. She wanted to know more about how black people felt and opened her pack. Martha Grimes kept looking at Dov and Jacob, who waited just outside the gate.

"Is that your daddy?"

"No. My grandfather."

"He look tired. I wonder would he drink a glass of sassafras tea, maybe?"

"That would be so kind of you," Reisa said warmly.

Indeed, the Grimes had little money, Reisa saw. They did buy a few things for a few coins, and Reisa gave the two older children small gifts.

"You ain't got no caps, is you?"

"I have some in my friend's pack. Dov, come here."

Dov came at once, and the children stared up with wonder in their eyes.

"He big, ain't he?" Mrs. Grimes said.

"Yes, he is, but he's very nice."

Dov opened the pack, and Reisa dug out three caps. "These are only fifty cents apiece." She saw disappointment in the woman's eyes and added hastily, "But you can have one for twenty-five cents."

"That be fine! My husband been wantin' a cap." She took the cap and ran her hands over it, then said, "Don't reckon you got a weddin' ring?"

Reisa nodded. "Yes. I have just two." She went to her own pack and took out the rings that she had wrapped carefully. The black woman took one of them and ran her hands over the smooth metal silently. When she looked up grief was in her eyes. "I ain't got no money for one of these, but some day I get me one." She handed the ring back.

Reisa had an impulse to give her the ring, but it was too expensive. "Maybe I will come back, and we can work out something," she said.

Mrs. Grimes gave them all glasses of buttermilk. "We got plenty," she said. "Got two good cows comin' in fresh." She was silent for a time and then said, "You don't come from around here."

"No. We're from Russia."

"You know about the slaves?"

"Oh, yes. But you're not slaves anymore."

"No, not now, but all them years we wasn't let to marry. Now since we been set free by Mr. Linkum, the first thing Zeke and I do is get married. I be married, but I ain't got no ring."

An idea began to form in Reisa's mind. She said nothing of it, but after they had left the household and made their way down the road, she filed the thought away.

It grew very late, and Jacob, Reisa saw, could go no further. There was no house on the main road, but she looked down a side road and there under a covering of tall pine trees was a house. "There must be some place that we could stay. A barn maybe," she said.

Jacob's face was pale. It was nearly a quarter of a mile to the house. "I'll wait here, Granddaughter. I—can't go any further."

Dov stepped forward and without a word picked Jacob up in his arms. "I carry you," he said.

Jacob smiled faintly. "Makes me feel like a baby."

"Come, Dov. We must find some place before dark."

Dov carried the huge pack and the form of Jacob easily. Reisa was concerned, for she was worried about spending the night under the open skies. As she approached the house, she saw a man with only one leg who was chopping wood. He turned at once and fastened his eyes upon them. As she approached, Reisa greeted him, "Good evening, sir."

The one-legged man did not answer, but at that moment another man came out of the door of the cabin. He was lacking his right arm. He had a cheerful look on his face. Approaching, he said, "Well, you travelers are out mighty late, and you look a little bit peaked."

"My grandfather isn't well."

"Well, bring him in the house. Phineas, why don't you go cook up some grub while I make these folks comfortable."

Phineas did not seem to take kindly to this. "You don't know nothin' about them," he said in a surly fashion. "They may be robbers."

"Now don't act up like that!" Turning to them, he said, "My name's Sam Hall. This here's my partner, Phineas Long. Y'all come in now."

It was a two-story house with windows in the gables. As Reisa stepped in, she found herself inside a rather spacious kitchen with a fireplace that took up almost the whole end of the room. Beside the fireplace sat a blackened kitchen woodstove and on the other side a large cabinet stocked with food.

"You folks come on and set," Hall said pleasantly.

Reisa gave her name, then introduced her grandfather and Dov.

"Well, you are a nice-sized fellow! Put Mr. Dimitri right here while we get some grub cooking."

Dov put Jacob down and then stood up and nodded, saying gutturally, "Dank you ver' much."

"Maybe you folks would like to wash up," Sam said. "And you can't go no further tonight." He laughed saying, "There ain't no place *to* go. Plenty of room here though, ain't there, Phineas?"

Phineas was a larger man than Sam. He was well over six feet, and his left trouser leg was pinned up at the knee. He used crutches and moved easily enough, so it seemed to Reisa. They were a strange pair, and she watched them curiously.

Phineas finally grunted. "Reckon there's room enough for one night."

Indeed there was room, a great deal of it. The two men apparently lived downstairs, but there were two bedrooms upstairs, both with slanting ceilings. Sam led Reisa upstairs and said, "Your granddad and your big friend can sleep here, and you can have this one."

"That's very kind of you, Mr. Hall."

"Oh, everybody just calls me Sam. Come on now. We'll get you all freshened up and get your grandpa rested up. You've come a long ways, I take it?"

"All the way from Russia."

"You tell me that!" Sam was shocked. "All the way from Russia! Think of that!" He studied her carefully. "What's your religion?"

"We're Jewish," Reisa smiled. She was accustomed to the question.

"Well, I'll be dipped! Ain't that somethin!" Sam seem pleased. "I hope you kin stay for a spell."

"That's very kind of you. My grandfather isn't well."

"Well, Jesus can heal him."

Reisa stared at the man. Sam Hall was small, no more than five seven, about Reisa's own height. He had a cheerful expression, and did not seem conscious that he had said anything strange to a Jew.

Going back downstairs, Reisa went to Jacob. "Sam said we could stay the night."

"That is wonderful. Thank you so much," Jacob said to Sam.

Sam shrugged. "Why, no trouble at all. Now, let me give Phineas a hand on this grub."

"You keep your cotton-pickin' hands off of this! I ain't gonna have my cookin' spoiled by you!" Phineas declared.

"In that case I'll just set and talk," Sam said.

Indeed, talk he did! Sam, Reisa soon discovered, did most of the talking for the pair. She found out amidst the tangled thread of his rather loosely joined conversation that Sam and Phineas had both served in the Confederate Army and had both lost a limb. Sam laughed saying, "Between us we make about one good feller. But the Lord Jesus is good to us to let us live through it. So many of my good friends didn't."

The meal was quickly prepared and, as usual, the three ate mostly vegetables. Sam was well aware of the dietary restrictions of the Jews. "We eat pork a lot, but maybe I can kill you a deer. You reckon you could dress it so you's could eat it?"

"Yes indeed!" Jacob said. "But we may not be here long enough for that."

"Well, who knows. The good Lord's got all our ways planned out," Sam said cheerfully.

"Yes." Jacob returned his smile. "The great Creator knows our every move."

"Exactly what I said!" Sam exclaimed.

After supper Reisa put Jacob to bed at once. "Sleep well. We'll rest until you can go on, *Zaideh.*"

Going back downstairs, Reisa offered to help clean up. Sam said cheerfully, "No. That's my job. Phineas cooks, and I clean up. He chops wood, and I bring it in. We got this thing all figured out."

Dov began a conversation with Phineas, which was unusual. "You good men," he said.

Phineas stared at the big man suspiciously. "No better than most, I reckon."

"My English bad. Sorry."

Phineas studied the big man. "How much do you weigh?"

"Weigh?"

"How many pounds?"

"Don't know."

"Well, how tall are you?"

"Don't know."

Phineas found this amusing. "Well, you ain't as big as a steer, but then you ain't a whole lot smaller either."

"Ver' big." Dov smiled. "God made me strong. Tomorrow I help you with work. Pay for supper."

"Ain't no need of that," Phineas said. "How come you're here?"

"I come with the reb and with Miss Reisa."

"But why are they here?"

Dov attempted to explain this, and Phineas seemed interested enough. Dov's poor English did not bother him, and the two sat in the kitchen talking. Phineas puffed on a pipe, and the two seemed to hit it off.

At the other end of the large room, Reisa and Sam observed this. "It's unusual for Dov to take to somebody as quickly as he has to your friend," Reisa said.

"Unusual for Phineas, too. He's as touchy as a bear with a sore toe. But he's got a good heart. He don't know the Lord Jesus, but he's going to one of these days." He turned to Reisa and said, "So, your grandfather. He's a rabbi?"

"No. He taught Hebrew at home."

"Isn't that somethin'! I always wanted to hear some of that. What's it sounds like?"

Reisa smiled. "Well, I can speak Hebrew."

"Say some of it for me, will you?"

"What shall I say?"

"Well, start out in the book of Genesis. I know you folks got that book."

Reisa said, "I'll get the Bible." She went at once to Jacob's pack, pulled the Hebrew Bible out, and came back. She began to read and stopped after a few sentences.

"So that's what it sounds like. Say me some more, will you, Miss Reisa?"

Reisa was amazed by this interest. She remembered Carson being so fascinated by the sound of Hebrew, and she read for some time until finally she said, "You're very interested in the Bible."

"Shore am. Believe it all, too. You ever read any of the new Bible?"

Reisa hesitated, then said, "I read a little bit of a book called John." She explained how the man on board the ship had given it to her.

"That's a good one," Sam said. "Maybe we can read to each other or somethin' while you're here."

Reisa closed the Bible and leaned forward. "It's very kind of you to take us in, Sam."

"Well, the Old Bible says to be kind to widows, orphans, and foreigners. I don't reckon you're a widow, and you ain't no orphan. You're strangers in this land, so I reckon I have to do what the Lord God says."

Reisa felt warmed by his words. "Tell me some more about yourself and about Phineas."

"Us? Well, there ain't much to tell. We ain't got no people left in the world—except Phineas has got a brother somewhere in Georgia, but they don't gehaw together."

"Gehaw?"

"Get along, don't you see? As for me, I never married so I ain't got no younguns. But I got Phineas, and I got Jesus."

Reisa smiled. "You seem very content. You had great misfortune, and it hasn't made you bitter."

"Me bitter! Why should I be bitter? I'm on my way to glory! One of these days I'll walk the golden streets and see my mammy and pappy and won't never be hungry or thirsty no more. I'm lookin' forward to it."

Reisa found the simple faith of Sam Hall intriguing, and she encouraged him to speak of himself. His conversation was studded with Scriptures that she knew must be from the New

Testament, but he knew many from the Old Testament as well. It seemed to her that he had memorized most of the Bible. Finally he said, "Well, you get to bed now, Miss Reisa. We'll get up, and we'll start a new day. May the Lord Jesus give you a good sleep."

"Good night, Sam."

She went upstairs followed by Boris, took off her clothes, and donned a nightgown. She brushed her hair for a while, then put it up again, and then left it out long. She envied the Gentile women who could let their hair down. It seemed it would give her so much freedom. Finally she lay down and went to sleep with Boris purring and heating up her bed like a miniature furnace. Far away she heard the sound of an owl. It had a ghostly sound but not unfriendly, and that sound was the last she remembered.

Twelve

Reisa left her room followed by Boris, who had a bad habit of getting in front of her and stopping. She opened the door to see how Jacob was. He was lying still, his eyes closed, his face turned upward, and the rigors of their journey were written plainly on his thin features. His cheeks seemed to be sunk in, and he looked somehow older. For some reason this frightened Reisa. She knew that some day she must lose him, but that had been a distant event far off in the future. Now the thought of his death brought a cold chill to her heart.

Quietly she closed the door, then went downstairs. She found Phineas and Sam already up, Phineas cooking something on the stove and Sam sitting in a chair tilted back against the wall talking to Dov. He smiled as Reisa came in.

"Morning," Sam said. "I've just been talking to Dov here. He was telling me a little bit about your trip across the big water."

Reisa nodded. "That was a hard trip. If it hadn't been for Dov, I don't know if I would have made it or not. God has sent him to Grandfather and me for a friend."

Phineas looked up from his cooking and said, "What can you eat?"

"We can always eat eggs of any kind."

"Can you eat grits?"

"Grits?" Reisa looked puzzled. "What are grits?"

“They’re corn ground up real fine. You put butter, salt, and pepper on them. They’re real good,” Sam responded. “Phineas makes the best grits in the whole country. I’ll vouch for that.”

The breakfast was simple, composed merely of one egg for Reisa with a mound of grits, and half a dozen eggs for Dov with an even larger mound of grits. For a big man, Dov ate rather fastidiously but rapidly.

“Grandfather is very tired,” Reisa said. “Would it put you out too much if we stayed another day?”

“Why, land sakes!” Sam cried. “It won’t be no put out at all!”

“Perhaps I can help you with the cooking, Phineas.”

Dov said, “I work. Show me what.”

Sam clawed his bristly face and thought for a moment. “Well,” he said firmly. “There’s a stump out there that me and Phineas been hackin’ away at. I ain’t much with an ax with one hand, and Phineas can’t get at it too good hoppin’ around like he does.”

“You show me.”

The two left, and Reisa insisted on helping wash the dishes. She found Phineas not loquacious and knew that they were not as welcome to him as they were with Sam. Still she made the best of it and asked him many questions about their lives. Phineas answered shortly, but he seemed to appreciate the help she gave. Reisa was used to cleaning, and it gave her pleasure to do something to repay the hospitality of the two men.

Soon the sound of an ax came to them, and Phineas shrugged. “Might as well go watch that big friend of yours work.”

Reisa followed him outside and found Sam squatted down watching Dov. It was a massive stump, and a hole had been dug around it. Dov chopped regularly, and Phineas remarked, “The thing’s got a tap root. If we can get that cut through, we can haul the thing out of there. I don’t know as he can do it, though.”

“Yes, he can,” Reisa said loyally. “Dov’s very strong.”

The three watched as the chips flew regularly. The ax looked very small in Dov’s big hands, almost like a stick, and Sam remarked once, "Don't see how that handle's taking it. I hope he don't break it. We don't got no other one."

The chopping went on without a break for over an hour, and Sam shook his head. "Don't that fellow ever get tired?"

Even as he spoke, Dov stopped and laid the ax down. "Almost done," he said. He had gone all the way around the trench, and now he leaned his shoulder against the stump. Bracing his feet, he began to apply pressure. Reisa saw that veins began to grow in his neck, for he wore a loose-fitting shirt exposing the mighty muscles of his neck and shoulders.

"Well, I'll be dipped!" Sam cried. "It moved! I think he's got it!"

"It ain't broke yet," Phineas said roughly.

The three watched as Dov continued to apply pressure. They could see the huge stump move in short increments, and each time it groaned as if reluctant to give up its grip on the earth.

"We'll have to borrow a good team and pull that stump," Phineas said. "He can't break it."

Even as he spoke, Dov seemed to gain fresh strength. He applied pressure, and suddenly there was a cracking sound. The stump sagged, then fell over to its side, and Dov sprawled out on top of it.

"He done her!" Sam yelled. "By heaven, he done her!"

"I didn't think no man on earth could do that," Phineas said. Grudgingly he added, "You're a good man to have around, Dov. Come on in, and I'll feed you another breakfast after all that."

But Dov was not finished. He borrowed a rope, tied it around the stump, and heaved until it had come clear of its hole.

He stood looking down into it, panting for breath. "Now, fill up hole."

"It'll take a while to do that. Look at the size of that hole! That stump's been here many a year. Look at all these rings, Miss Reisa."

They tried counting the rings of the flat section of the stump.

"I reckon that was here when George Washington was crossing the Delaware," Sam said. "Maybe even longer."

"I'm glad to have that pesky thing out of the way," Phineas said. "Now you set and rest awhile."

"Not tired," Dov remarked.

Phineas seemed in a good mood. "You set right over there in that chair."

Dov shrugged and went to take his seat.

Phineas stepped inside the cabin a moment and came back out with a fiddle and a bow in his hands. He gave one of his rare smiles. "I reckon I'll entertain you a little bit now, since you put on a show for us."

He began to play, and Reisa was amazed. The rough-looking Phineas had a touch with a fiddle such as she had never heard. The song he played was poignant and sad, but still it was beautifully done. The notes came sure and pure, and he wove a melody that seemed to cry out for words.

"Oh, that was wonderful, Phineas!" Reisa cried. "You play so well."

"Play another," Dov said.

"Yeah," Sam agreed. "Play a fast one."

Phineas played another song, this time one so rapid you could barely see his fingers move. The bow moved back and forth across the strings, and Sam whispered, "He don't hardly ever play no happy tunes. Mostly them sad 'uns. He makes up a lot of them his own self."

He played for twenty minutes, and Reisa looked up to see Jacob, who had come to stand in the doorway.

"Zaideh!" she cried and went to him at once. "Listen to Phineas play! Isn't he a wonderful fiddler?"

"I have never heard better." Jacob smiled.

He looked tired, and Reisa said at once, "You come and sit down. I will feed you some grits."

"Grits!"

"Yes. You will see. Sit down."

All of them went back inside, and Reisa took over the stove. She soft-boiled two eggs for Jacob, then put grits on his plate, adding butter, salt, pepper, and a piece of bread. "Now, you eat every bite of that."

Jacob ate and looked somewhat better after his meal. Dov was ready to work again, and Phineas left to show him a barn that needed to be propped up, stating it was going to fall over flat if something wasn't done.

Sam made no move to go to work, but after Jacob was finished eating, he began at once asking him questions about the Old Testament.

Reisa moved about finding things to do. She decided she could wash, for she had seen a large black washing pot outside. Going out, she built a fire under it and filled it with water. There was another for rinsing, and soon she was busy rubbing clothes out on a washboard, happily at work. She could see Dov working on the barn, directed by Phineas, and the weather was clear. Although the temperature was warm now, it being August, she wondered how they would fare in the dead of winter in this country. It would not be so bad, she knew, as in New York, and certainly not as frightfully cold as in Russia. But still she was concerned.

Inside at the table Sam was listening as Jacob read the Old Testament. Sam had his Bible out and was trying to follow along as Jacob read in the book of Isaiah. Sam asked, "What do you think about that part in Isaiah that talks about the Messiah?" He opened his Bible and said, "Here in Chapter 42 it says, 'Behold my servant, whom I uphold; mine elect, in whom my soul delighteth; I have put my spirit upon him: he shall bring forth judgment to the Gentiles.'"

Jacob nodded and read the same passage in Hebrew, then translated it freely into English. "All good Jews think of the Messiah. We pray daily for his coming. This passage has always spoken to my heart."

"I guess I'm one of the Gentiles it talks about here." He went ahead and continued to read. "'He shall not cry, nor lift up, nor cause his voice to be heard in the street. A bruised reed shall he not break, and the smoking flax shall he not quench: he shall bring forth judgment unto truth.'"

Looking up, Sam shook his head. "This world has been in a mess for a long time, ain't it, Jacob?"

"A very long time, Sam. But when the Messiah comes, he will bring justice to all people." Jacob looked up, a sadness in his eyes. "We have not seen that, for all people do not have justice. Indeed, the just seemed to be ground into the earth, and the proud rule over them harshly."

Sam studied the old man and said, "What about this one in chapter 61 of Isaiah? It starts out, 'The spirit of the Lord God is upon me.'" He waited until Jacob had found the place in his Bible and then continued. "'Because the Lord has anointed me to preach good tidings unto the meek; he hath sent me to bind up the brokenhearted, to proclaim liberty to the captives, and the opening of the prison to them that are bound.' Now that there is what I call a bodacious good promise!"

"Yes. That will be a good day when it comes. May the Master of the Universe bring it to pass."

Sam said, "Let me read you something from the New Bible. It comes from the book of Luke, the fourth chapter. It was the first time Jesus ever preached. It begins here in verse sixteen: 'And he came to Nazareth, where he had been brought up: and, as his custom was, he went into the synagogue on the sabbath day, and stood up for to read. And there was delivered unto him the book of the prophet Esaias. And when he had opened the book, he found the place where it was written, The Spirit of the

Lord is upon me, because he hath anointed me to preach the gospel to the poor; he hath sent me to heal the brokenhearted, to preach deliverance to the captives, and recovering of sight to the blind, to set at liberty them that are bruised.'"

Sam looked up and saw that Jacob was astonished. "That is what it says?"

"There it is." Sam turned his Bible around, and Jacob began to read. He had never read one word of the New Testament, and his face was a study. "He went into the synagogue on the Sabbath day. He was a good Jew, this Jesus?"

"Oh, yes," Sam said. "He always took up for the law of Moses. When he healed somebody, he would say, 'Go to the priest as Moses commanded you.' All kinds of stuff like that."

Jacob was reading the New Testament passage again and was very quiet. He looked up and said, "Then this Jesus claimed to be the Messiah that Isaiah spoke of."

"Yep, he did, and I found over a hundred prophecies in the Old Bible that fit Jesus down to a T."

Jacob found it difficult to answer. All his life he had heard nothing good of Christians, but somehow this passage had a hold on him. He said, "I cannot believe it, Sam. I am too set in my ways."

"When Jesus came, they were looking for the Messiah then. People kept asking him, 'Are you the Messiah? Are you the one Malachi talked about?'" Sam said quietly. "Some of 'em was lookin' for a great military general to lead the Jews to victory over their enemies, but he never done that."

"There are many Scriptures that talk about this in the Old Testament."

"What do you make of this one?" Sam turned back to Isaiah and read the first line, and Jacob found the place.

"'Who hath believed our report? and to whom is the arm of the LORD revealed? For he shall grow up before him as a tender plant, and as a root out of dry ground: he hath no form nor comeliness; and when we shall see him, there is no beauty that we should desire him. He is despised and rejected of men; a man of sorrows, and acquainted with grief: and we hid as it were our faces from him; he was despised, and we esteemed him not.'"

"That man don't sound like no great conqueror, does he, Jacob?"

"No indeed." Jacob was an honest man, and he said, "I have troubled myself over this passage. How can this be the Messiah? He was a man of sorrows and acquainted with grief. My people are looking for a victorious conqueror."

The two went on talking for over an hour, going back and forth through the Scripture.

Reisa finished her washing, hung it out on the line, and came in smiling as she saw the pair. *This is good for Zaideh,* she thought. *Sam is one of the kindest Christians I have ever seen.* She sat down and listened, picking up on the conversation.

Sam said, "Go back to that part that we read before about he was despised and rejected of men." He waited until Jacob had found it, then said, "Look at what it says after that. 'Surely he hath borne our griefs, and carried our sorrows: yet we did esteem him stricken, smitten of God, and afflicted. But he was wounded for our transgressions, he was bruised for our iniquities: the chastisement of our peace was upon him; and with his stripes we are healed.'"

As Sam read these last words, his voice suddenly trembled, and both Jacob and Reisa looked at him with surprise to see tears standing in his eyes. Pulling out a dirty red bandanna, he wiped his eyes and muttered, "Can't never read that without cryin'. Don't know why. Just to think about Jesus dying for me. That next verse says, 'All we like sheep have gone astray. We have turned every one to his own way, and the LORD hath laid on him the iniquity of us all." He blew his nose, put his handkerchief away, and smiled, but his lips were trembling. "That's what Jesus done for me. I was one of them lost sheep. I'd hate for you to know what a wicked feller I was, but then I called on the Lord, and he saved me. Redeemed me, set my feet on firm ground. He snatched me out of the pit..."

Both Jacob and Reisa were shocked at the intensity of Sam's feeling. There was no question at all about the little man's sincerity.

Later that evening when Jacob and Reisa were alone, Reisa said, "I've never seen a man that loves God more than Sam."

"He is indeed an unusual man," Jacob agreed. "He knows the Bible so well! One would think he almost has it memorized."

Reisa hesitated. "What do you think about his interpretation of Isaiah?"

Jacob did not answer. He merely shook his head and said, "It is something to think on."

~

Reisa, for the next few days, cleaned the house until it shone. Dov had done more work than the two men could have accomplished in many days. He was a tireless machine never stopping. Sam said to Phineas, speaking privately, "That fellow is a hoss! I've never seen the like of him!"

"They've earned their keep." Phineas nodded reluctantly. "The old man ain't too well, though."

"No, he isn't. I'm worried about him," Sam said.

Reisa was worried also. She said nothing, but on Tuesday night she insisted on cooking. "I'm going to cook a good Jewish meal for you. You got plenty of vegetables, and you've got chickens. I'll see what I can do."

That night they all gathered and sat down at the table. "This is stuffed potato cakes. We call them *varnishkes*. This is *borscht*, beet soup, as you would call it. And this is *kreplach*. Just dough filled with chicken. And for dessert we have sweet cake *streudel*."

Sam and Phineas both ate heartily, and Phineas was complimentary. "This is mighty fine cooking, Miss Reisa. I'd like to learn how to make those things."

"I will teach you how, Phineas."

Later that night Reisa said to Sam, "I'm going to make a trip tomorrow. Would you care for my grandfather?"

"A trip!" Sam was surprised. "Where in the world would you be going?"

"I must go sell some things. We came to sell goods to the people, and we must do it. It is not fair for us to be here without paying you."

"Ah, Miss Reisa, don't fuss about that."

"I must go."

"No. I can't let you do that. There's some purty rough people around here. A young woman like you, you wouldn't be safe."

"Dov will be with me. I think I will be safe enough."

"Well, he could whup anybody that came at you with his fist, but there's fellows out there with guns." He thought a minute and said, "Wait right here." He left but was back in a moment. "Here. Look at this." Reisa saw that he had a very small revolver. "It's what's called a pepper box. Fits right in your hand."

It was indeed a small weapon with a circular barrel.

"Shoots four times. Of course, you got to be up close. You take this and stick it in your pocket somewhere. If you get into real trouble, this here little number will discourage whoever's bothering you."

Reisa knew she would never use it, but Sam insisted she take it. Reluctantly, she agreed.

Thirteen

The rank, fetid odors of the cell block had long ago ceased to trouble Ben Driver. Now as he stood staring out of the bars, he studied the blue sky as he had every day for four years, three months, and twelve days. The sounds of other men caged with him came to him, but he had long ago learned to filter them out. The hoarse coughing, the raw cursing, the shoutings—none of them penetrated Driver's thoughts now. His right eye was covered by a black patch, but with his good eye, he saw a red-tailed hawk suddenly fold his wings and descend like a plummet. It disappeared, his dive masked by the leprous gray prison wall, but Driver knew that he had probably made his kill.

"I'm gonna miss you, Ben. But I'm glad you're getting out of here."

Driver turned to the man who sat on a thin mattress covering the steel springs of his bunk. He said, "Charlie, I wish you were—" A spasm of hoarse, deep coughs racked his body, bending him double. He could not get control of himself and leaned against the wall, holding his chest. The coughing spell was so violent that he felt that he was tearing something fragile inside his chest.

Charlie Oats rose instantly and stood there helplessly. Driver was a tall man, an inch over six feet, and when he had entered the penitentiary had weighed a hundred and eighty pounds. Now he was down to one hundred and forty.

"You oughta go to the infirmary with that cough, Ben. I've been tryin' to get you in for two days."

Finally Driver got control. Slowly he straightened up, his face pale and his cheeks sunk in. His coppery red hair with a slight curl he had hacked off himself when it reached his collar. His face was wedge-shaped, and the black patch over his right eye gave him a pirate's appearance. His long lips were now tightened so that they were almost white, and the bristles of a three-day beard glinted in the early morning sunlight that filtered through the small window. He had high cheekbones, a sharp English nose with a break from an old battle, and a scar on the right side of his mouth which drew his lip up slightly. His body also bore other mementos of youthful battles.

"I'm okay now, Charlie."

"You oughta go to the infirmary," Oats insisted. He was a small man of medium build, with a pale face and light blonde hair. He had occupied the same cell when Ben had first come, and the two men had become close. Oats had been glad to get a man like Ben, for he knew there were worse companions. Driver was quiet almost to a fault, but the two got along very well.

"I'll write you, Charlie."

"Yeah. Let's keep up with each other."

Hard heels sounded on the concrete walkway outside the cell and Driver turned quickly. A figure came to a halt before the barred door, and there was a metallic click as he opened the cell door and swung it back. "All right, Driver, come out of there."

Moving to pick up the small bundle on his bunk, Driver turned to shake hands with Charlie, his single eye warm for a moment. "I'll write to you."

"Take care of yourself, Ben."

"Come on out of there, Driver." The guard was a big man with a belly that overflowed his belt. His name was Grooms, and Driver had long been the victim of his sadistic methods. Grooms eyed the tall man who exited from the cell, and his lips twisted. "You'll be back. I can't *wait* for you to get back."

Driver ignored him, and Grooms rapped him sharply across the shoulders. "All right. Get out of here!"

As the two walked down the corridor, men from the cells on both sides called their farewell: "So long, Ben."

"Find yourself a woman—"

"Don't come back, Driver!"

Driver spoke to a few of them briefly. These men had been his companions for what seemed like a lifetime. He followed Grooms, and when they left the cell block, Grooms led him down another passageway.

"Well, Ben. Congratulations."

The speaker was a man almost round in shape. He was so fat that his chins were tripled or even more. They quivered like jelly, but his eyes were warm enough. "Got your goin'-away suit all ready."

Ben took the suit, stripped down, and the trustee whose name was Horton picked his prison clothes up. "Don't guess you want these." He threw them into a basket and watched as Ben put on the suit, which was ill-fitting and cheap. A pair of shiny, flimsy shoes followed, and then Grooms snapped, "All right, get moving—and you get back to work, Horton."

When Ben Driver stepped out of the door, the sun was creeping over the wall. It was a yellow disk that shed brilliant rays over the prison exercise yard. At the gate, Driver found Warden Otis Taylor.

The warden handed him an envelope, then put his hand out. "Ben, you've lost four years of life, but you're a young man. Start all over again. Going home, are you?"

"I guess so, Warden."

"Where is your home?"

"The other side of Richmond."

"Well, don't let me see you again," the warden said. "Open up, Matthews."

A guard opened one of the huge gates and stepped aside. As Driver went through, he nodded and said, "Good luck, Driver."

"Thanks."

Ben turned down the road and walked away. The penitentiary was located just outside of Richmond, and to get home he had a long walk ahead of him. He began coughing again and had to stop once until the spasm passed. His face felt red and flushed, but he ignored that.

Overhead the morning clouds already were a dirty gray underneath, and Driver knew that rain was in the air. He carried nothing but a small sack with his razor and soap and personal belongings. He had collected almost nothing during the four years, and now at the age of twenty-seven he had nothing in the world except a ten-dollar bill and the cheap suit on his back.

Ten dollars in twenty-seven years, plus a cheap suit and a rotten pair of shoes. Not much to show for a life.

He had walked for ten minutes when he heard the sound of a wagon approaching. He did not turn until it was behind him, and when he did wheel around he saw the driver study him carefully. For a moment it seemed that he would pull the team up and offer him a ride, but the woman said something to the driver and shook her head. The man shrugged his shoulders, gave Ben an odd look, and slapped the lines on the team.

Driver had expected nothing else. He knew that people in the vicinity of the penitentiary were wary of the inmates, even though they had served their time. His life had been hard, and now as he trudged along the road under the darkening sky, he tried to put four years of prison life and five years of terrible war behind him. He had learned to do this in prison by reading. He had read every book in the prison library, some of them five times. The choice had been limited, but the printed words seemed to drive away the bitterness that would rise in him if he simply lay on his bunk and thought about what his life had been.

He had walked steadily for an hour when a drop of rain struck his hand. He glanced up and saw that the sky had turned gun-metal gray. The wind was beginning to blow harder, and the drops began to fall more quickly. In ten minutes the drizzle had increased to a slow, steady shower, and he was soaking wet. He did not slacken his pace but pulled the black slouch hat that they had given him down over his face, trudging doggedly along the road. Anything to get away from what had been his "home" for the past four years!

Justin Farnsworth studied the tall figure trudging along the road. He was a cautious man and was going to drive past the man, but an impulse overtook him. He pulled the team down to a slow walk until the traveler turned to face him. "How about a ride?"

"Thanks." The tall man climbed up on the seat beside Farnsworth. He was wearing a cheap suit that had been soaked in the recent shower, and yellow mud clung to his shoes. "Mighty nice of you—" He broke off and a siege of violent coughing doubled him over.

"I hope that ain't catchin'," Farnsworth said nervously.

"I'll sit on my own side so you won't get anything."

"Lot of sickness going around," Justin commented. "Where you headed?"

"My family lives up ahead."

Farnsworth turned to look at him. "I know most folks around here. Who are your people?"

"The John Driver place."

Justin's eyes narrowed, and he chewed his lip thoughtfully. "I know you," he said. "I didn't recognize you. You're Ben Driver."

"That's right."

"I remember when you first came back out of the army. I was just fifteen then, but I saw you win the shootin' match over at Oak Grove at the fair."

"I remember that."

Justin was curious, but it went against his better judgment to ask questions. "Your people will be glad to see you," he finally remarked.

After an extended pause, Driver murmured, "I hope so."

Farnsworth knew a little of Ben Driver's history. He knew that Driver had served honorably and with distinction during the Civil War—but he had also heard that after Appomattox he had turned wild and had drunk far too much. Farnsworth did not remember the details, but he knew there had been a robbery, and that Driver had been involved and been sentenced to prison.

Stealing a glance at the man beside him, Farnsworth kept his silence. He did say finally, "I saw your mother last week. She looked mighty well."

"That's good to hear."

The conversation was one-sided, and Farnsworth shrugged, then kept his silence as the wagon lurched along through the mud. Finally he said, "Well, there's your place." He pulled up, and the team champed and snorted while Driver got to the ground. He looked up and held up his hand. "Thanks for the ride, Mr. Farnsworth." He started coughing then and had to turn away.

"Better get somethin' for that cough. It sounds like it got pretty deep." Farnsworth watched as Driver walked away, then slapped the team with the lines. As they moved forward he thought, *Ben Driver—well, he was a good man once, but I doubt he'll be welcome back here.*

~

Ben walked slowly down the road that led to the house which was set back almost a quarter of a mile. His eyes went over the place, and he saw that the fields were all planted. He knew every foot of this place, which at one time had comprised over a thousand acres. He did not know how much his father had been able to save during Reconstruction. Letters from his mother had mentioned from time to time some of the affairs of the plantation, but he had not had a letter from his father. Not since the judge had sentenced him to prison.

A huge magnolia tree rose up, towering and drooping its limbs in the very front of the yard. Driver stopped in the shade of the tree and stared at the house, its shape pulling old memories out of his mind. It was a large house two stories high with barns and outbuildings kept in the back. Two black men were working in a small garden over east of the house, and on the left was a large pasture where a herd of some twenty beef cattle were grazing placidly.

Ben stood there thinking of how he had spent the happiest days of his life in this place. He had joined the army at the age of sixteen, and that had ended most happiness for him. Now as he stood there, the impulse came to turn and go away. But he straightened up and pulled his hat firmly over his face. He walked quickly up toward the front of the house where two large pecan trees shaded the front windows. He had eaten pecans off these trees most of his life, but they seemed smaller. They had grown, perhaps, in his memory.

When he reached the trees, he paused again. The bitterness that lay deeply buried within him suddenly seemed to rise. He could not move for a moment, and finally he made a half turn, determining to leave. But at that instant he heard a voice crying out, "Ben—Ben!"

Driver turned to see his mother flying down the steep steps of the high porch. She ran toward him, her arms outstretched. Driver caught her as she came, and held her close. He smelled the sweet fragrance of her hair, and he heard her voice crying brokenly, "Ben—oh, Ben—!"

Marianne Driver was sixty, but as she drew back Ben saw that she looked twenty years younger. She looked, he realized with a shock, exactly as she had the day he went off to war. She was one of those human beings over whom time seemed to have no power. She had auburn hair and green eyes, and now she held his hands, unable to speak, her eyes swimming with tears.

"You look wonderful, Mama."

"Ben—" Marianne pulled back, dashed the tears from her eyes, and then attempted a laugh. She took his arm and said, "You come into the house right now! Why, you're skinny as a snake! I'm going to fatten you up."

Ben held back for a moment. "I wasn't sure whether I should come or not."

Marianne's joy seemed to fade for a moment. "Your father will have to change. Come on, you look tired."

Ben began coughing halfway up the steps, and Marianne looked at him with a worried expression. "That sounds terrible. It's deep in your chest. You're going to have pneumonia if we don't take care of it."

"I'll be all right, Mama."

Marianne led him into the kitchen where a black woman, tall and round, turned from the sink. She had a paring knife in her hand, but it dropped to the floor, and she clasped her hands together and said, "Ben! Ben Driver, you is home!"

Ben moved across the room slowly. "Hello, Dorrie," he said.

The black woman came and threw her arms around him. She was a tall woman and powerful, and she hugged him hard, which brought on another spasm of coughing.

"What's wrong with you? You're sick!"

"Just a cold."

"Cold nothin'! You set down there. I gonna make you some of my special toddy."

Ben Driver had never felt so bad in his life. He was lightheaded, and his throat was so sore that he could barely swallow. The women swarmed him, and soon a hot meal was set before him. He ate a few bites, then began to cough. The coughing went into a spasm, and both women were horrified. Dorrie quickly began fixing the toddy.

Marianne put her arm around her son. "Ben, how long have you been sick?"

Ben could not answer for a moment. When he could, he just shook his head. "I'll be all right."

"Here. You drink this."

Ben took the tumbler of amber-colored liquid, drank it down, and then began coughing again.

"You needs to be put to bed," Dorrie said. "You gonna die if you go on like this."

Before Driver could answer, he heard the sound of footsteps. He turned, and at the moment his father entered the room, Driver got to his feet, saying nothing.

John Driver was a tall, erect man, well preserved. His hair was salt and pepper, and his light blue eyes now were fixed on his son. He had served as a colonel under Longstreet throughout the whole war, and had come home to try to redeem his plantation. This had been as bitter a struggle in many ways as the battles he had fought.

Ben nodded and whispered, "Hello, Father."

John Driver said in a short clipped tone, "Eat your meal. But I don't want you in the house when I come back."

"John!" Marianne cried and moved quickly to stand beside him. But her husband shook his head and whirled and left the room.

"Mr. John is wrong! He dead wrong!" Dorrie protested angrily. "You got to be took care of."

Driver had expected nothing less than this from his father. He said, "I've got to go. It's his house." He turned his cheek to his mother, took her kiss, then another from Dorrie, and while the two women both begged him, he turned and walked out of the room.

The women turned and followed after him down the steps, but his long legs carried him away.

Dorrie said, "Mr. John is wrong. We got to do somethin', Miss Marianne!"

"I've tried to get John to see how wrong he is. We've been married a long time, and this is the only thing we've ever disagreed on, Dorrie. He refuses to even talk about Ben."

"I don't understand Mistuh John!"

"He's proud of his family name—too proud, I think. I remember when he drove Ben out of the house. It broke my heart." Marianne's eyes filled with tears. She turned away, her heart so full she could not speak.

Driver walked blindly away from his father's house, almost unconscious of where he was going. He only knew he had to get away. There was no fixed plan, but when he reached the main road, he turned and walked for a mile. To his surprise, a wagon headed in his direction stopped and a tall, rawboned farmer hailed him. "Headed for Richmond?"

Ben nodded, and at the farmer's invitation, he climbed on the seat. "I'm going to Bentonville if that'll help you."

"Be fine—thanks a lot." Driver was desperately tired, and did his best to keep up the conversation. The farmer's name was Silas Tuberville, and he was a garrulous sort. Ben alternated between coughing spells and dropping off into a coma-like dazed sleep. He was vaguely aware of passing through Richmond, but at some point his chin dropped on his chest and he fell asleep.

"Say, young feller, I'm turning off here for Bentonville. You want to go all the way with me?"

Ben's head snapped as he woke out of a dazed sleep. Looking around, he saw the road fork, and scarcely knowing what he was doing, he mumbled, "No, I'll get out here." He climbed painfully out of the wagon, then stepped back as Tuberville waved a hand. "Looks like more rain comin'. Better find a place to get out of it."

Ben was too tired to do more than nod. He took the left fork, having a vague idea that an old companion of his lived in the area.

For a time he followed the main road, then turned off onto a smaller road, a shortcut if he remembered correctly. He had gone a quarter of a mile when he reached a creek, the same creek he had caught sunfish and perch out of as a boy. His throat was swollen and painful, and his lips were dry. He knelt down and tried to drink, but a few swallows were all he could bear. He rose and started across the creek, but the rocks were slippery. He fell headlong and rolled over, getting completely drenched. He struggled to his feet, shook his head, and staggered to the far side of the creek. His path was erratic, and he could not think clearly. He had not eaten anything substantial for twenty-four hours, and his one good eye seemed blurred.

He tripped, falling full length beside the road. Red lights seemed to flash inside his head, and though he struggled to get up, the power seemed to have been drained out of his body. He tried to lift his head, but he was unable to. He let it fall back, his cheek pressed into the yellow mud, then knew nothing. He lay there like a dead man in the road as the drizzle of rain began again.

Fourteen

"We do good," Dov said. He was carrying the huge pack on his back, but it seemed to be no weight at all.

Reisa looked up at him and smiled. "Yes, we did. We must have sold at least twenty dollars worth, and we made some friends."

The two were trudging along the road headed for Sam and Phineas's house. It was late afternoon, and Reisa was tired, for they had walked far and had talked much. Dov, walking along beside her, suddenly said, "Look," and waved forward.

Reisa lifted her eyes and saw there on the road before them a man lying facedown in the mud. Her heart gave a lurch, for she thought at first he was dead. "Come, Dov," she whispered, and the two moved forward. When she reached the man, Reisa leaned over and touched his face. With relief she felt that the flesh was warm, and then he coughed and his body gave a convulsive shudder.

"He's been hurt, Dov. We must get him to the house."

"I take him." Dov leaned over, rolled the man on his back, then pulled him to a sitting position. With ease he lifted him up and draped him over his shoulder. The unconscious man coughed, and his head moved back and forth, then he slumped and lay still.

"It's over half a mile to the house. Can you carry him all that way, Dov?"

"Yes," Dov said. "Is easy."

Dov walked quickly, and Reisa followed by his side. The man's face bumped against Dov's back, but he did not move nor speak.

When they reached the house, Sam was sitting on the front porch. He got up as soon as he saw them and came running to meet them. "Who is this feller?"

"I don't know. We found him unconscious on the road by the creek."

"Well, better bring him inside, Dov."

Dov carried the sick man inside and placed him on the spare bed in Jacob's room. Jacob followed them in, and he reached over and put his hand on the man's face. "He's burning up with fever," he said.

Indeed, the face of the unconscious man was flushed.

"Listen to his breathing," Reisa said. "It sounds rough."

"He's got pneumonia. That's what he's got," Phineas grunted. "You done brought him here to die."

Sam gave his partner an indignant look. "Why don't you look on the bright side of things for once? He won't die."

Phineas snorted, but Sam said, "Let's get them clothes off of him, Phineas. We'll wet some towels with cold water. That'll bring that fever down. And I'll go get my ile."

"Ile? What is *ile?*" Reisa said.

"Ile for anointing," Sam said. "Don't you Jews do that?"

"Oh, *oil!* We do use oil in some of our ceremonies."

Reisa stood by as Phineas stripped the coat and then the shirt from the unconscious man. *He's so thin!* she thought. When Phineas rolled him over, she saw a scar on his back over his right flank. There were other marks, too. This man had been hard used.

Sam returned with a bottle of cooking oil. "Well, I ain't never actually done this, but I know the Good Book says that if a feller gets sick, you're supposed to call the elders of the church and anoint 'em with oil." He looked at Jacob and said, "I reckon you're the closest thing to an elder we got. Would you care to do the job?"

Jacob looked confused and said hesitantly, "Perhaps it would be better if you did it, my friend."

"All right. Here I go." Sam turned the bottle over and poured oil all over the forehead and hair of the sick man. It soaked into his rather curly hair and onto the pillow.

"That's enough, Sam!" Phineas said, snatching the bottle away. "You want to drown him?"

"You can't get too much of a good thing," Sam said. Then without warning, he lifted up his eyes and said, "Lord, you know this man, and we don't. And you know how sick he is, and you done brung him to this place. So I just ask that you do what you done when you was on earth. Reach your hand down and heal him. In Jesus' name. Amen."

"Well, if you'll get out of the way," Phineas said, "we can get down to business."

Without warning, he loosened the man's belt and pulled his pants off with one swift motion. Reisa flushed and turned her head away. "I'll go get a bucket of cool water and some towels," she said.

She went to the well, her face still burning. She could not help but think of the man's body. He was very tall and lean and would have been strong, except he had lost weight until he was almost emaciated. Quickly she forced the sight of his almost naked body from her mind and went to the well, bringing back two buckets of water. She stepped inside the room and set them down, keeping her eyes turned away for a moment. Phineas reached and got a towel, dunked it, wrung it out, and then laid it over the man's legs. He grabbed another and continued until the sick man's whole body was swathed with cool wet cloths.

Now that the man was safely covered, Reisa went to stand just beside Phineas. She studied the face, which was a strong one. The black patch over his right eye drew her attention, and she wondered how he had lost the sight of that eye. *He would be handsome,* she thought, *if he weren't so thin.* She took in the wide mouth and the firm jaw that terminated the wedge-shaped face. The bristles of his beard glistened with the water as Sam laid a cloth on his forehead. "I wonder what kind of a man he is?" she said.

"Probably a no-good one," Phineas grunted.

Sam cast his eyes on Phineas with wonder. "Now why in the blue-eyed world would you say that, Phineas? You don't know nothin' about him."

"Because most people are no good."

"I'd purely hate to have your outlook, Phineas," Sam said. He was standing on the other side of the bed and looked down at the face. "He looks like a right good feller to me. A might hard used, but when Jesus gets him healed up, we'll put some meat on him. Then he'll be a nice appearin' feller. Don't you reckon, Miss Reisa?"

Reisa listened, startled. "If you say so, Sam," she said quietly.

Everything was either burning hot or freezing cold. He moved from one extreme to the other for what seemed like endless time. There was actually, however, no sense of time. The pyramids could have been built while he struggled between the extremes of heat and cold.

At times he would be vaguely aware of voices—different voices—but they seemed to come from far away, and they were not voices that he knew. Most of them were harsh male voices, but one was softer. And he came to associate this softer voice with a touch on his forehead along with a cooling touch of water.

A dream came to him, of the Battle in the Wilderness when he along with Lee's veterans had fought a furious titanic struggle against the enemies dressed in blue. He lived again the time of the roaring of cannons and the whistling of musket balls as they cut the leaves from the trees so that they came pattering down on the ground. He had been knocked to the ground by the concussion of a shell going off. And then the woods had caught on fire. The heat rose, the fire crackling about him with the acrid smell of smoke. He could almost hear the screaming of those men too wounded to crawl away as they burned to death.

Then the heat faded away, and he was cool again.

Finally the world seemed to settle down, and he heard the sound of a bird somewhere singing a song. He opened his eye into a slit. He could not see clearly, and he reached out his hand and touched something soft and yielding. Instantly a blow struck him on the cheek. His hand dropped back, and he fell back into sleep wondering what it all meant...

He slept then, and finally when he awoke his mouth was dry and parched, but the burning fever was gone and there were no chills. Slowly he opened his eye, and as he focused he jerked his head back with alarm. He was looking directly into the green eyes of a jet-black cat who was lying on the bed staring at him intently. Driver watched as the cat stood up, came over, and reached out a paw. The paw touched him gently on the face, and the cat suddenly bared his fangs in what appeared to be a grotesque smile. The teeth were white and sharp, and the eyes larger and more green than seemed possible.

"So, you awake."

Startled by the sound of a voice, Driver rolled over on his back. A young woman was standing there wearing a blue dress with a white apron over it. Her hair was tied up, and she wore a pale green bandanna so that he could not see her hair. He stared at her in confusion, and then he tore his gaze away, staring wildly around the room. There was nothing familiar, and he tried to speak but found that his throat was too dry and his lips too parched.

"You are thirsty." The young woman moved over to a table where a pitcher of water and a glass sat. She filled the glass halfway with water and then looked down. "You must sit up," she said. With one smooth motion she reached down, put her arms around him, and pulled him to a sitting position. Still holding him, she pulled a pillow up behind him and then released him. Taking the glass, she picked up a large spoon and filled it with water and held it to his lips. He opened his mouth and received it—and the parched tissues of his mouth and his throat welcomed the cool liquid. He watched the woman, still confused, as she spooned the water into his mouth.

"Give me the glass," he croaked.

"No. To drink too much is not good. You can have all you want—but a little at a time."

She had a strange accent, one that he did not recognize. Consciousness was sweeping back to Driver now, and after he had taken several more spoonfuls of the water, he said, "Where is this place?"

"It is a place where you will get well."

"How did I get here?"

"My friend and I found you on the road. We brought you here. Now, be quiet." She filled the glass and handed it to him. "Now, you take just a tiny sip. You must eat."

Driver took the glass and watched the woman as she left. She closed the door behind her, and he took a sip of the water and stared around the room. It was plain enough, with pine walls, a high ceiling, and one window over to his left. There was only one decoration, a picture on the wall, a lithograph of General James Longstreet—cut out of a magazine, apparently. A roughly made chest, the bed he lay on, another small bed, and a chair beside it made up the furnishings. There was nothing else, not even a rug on the floor.

Driver took the water in small sips, and memory came back to him slowly. He remembered most of all his father's statement, *Finish your meal and then leave my house.* He remembered bidding good-bye to his mother and to Dorrie, then stumbling down the road. He even remembered falling in the creek and getting up, but he did not remember falling on the road.

By the time he had finished the water the young woman was back. "My name is Reisa Dimitri. What is your name?"

"Ben Driver."

"So, Ben, you will eat." She gave it to him. "Can you feed yourself?"

"Yes." Driver reached out, took the bowl, and realized that he was very hungry. She stood and watched him, however, her eyes vigilant, while he ate slowly. When he was finished, he handed it back. "Tell me again where I am."

"This house belongs to two gentlemen—Sam Hall and Phineas Long. I am a guest here like yourself. My friend, Dov, and I were coming back from Richmond. We found you lying on the road." She held the bowl and studied him thoughtfully. "Do you have a family? Someone we could send word to?" She waited, expecting an answer, but he gave none.

Finally he said without emotion, "I don't have anyone."

Reisa took the bowl. "Do you want to sit up a while?"

Driver realized that he was sleepy again. He shook his head and moved down. She reached forward as she arranged the pillow beneath his head. She said, "You are very thin. You must eat and sleep a great deal to get better."

As she bent over he caught the faint scent of violets, but he was falling into a deep sleep. The last thing he remembered was the cat, for as he turned over on his side the large black feline was still there, his green eyes observing Driver. He thought he saw the cat smile, but he was not sure, for he dropped off into sleep again.

***

When Reisa stepped into the kitchen, she said, "His name is Ben Driver. He just told me."

Sam and Phineas exchanged quick looks. "So the bad penny has turned up," Phineas said.

"Bad penny? What does that mean?"

"Means your sick man is a criminal," Phineas snorted. "He was sent to prison."

"What for?" Reisa asked.

"Aw, it wasn't murder," Sam put in quickly. "I think he held up a store or something." He scratched his chin thoughtfully, then added, "He was a good soldier, but after the war he got into trouble. I hear as how his family kicked him out."

"How awful!"

"His dad, John Driver, has got money. Lives just the other side of Richmond. Ben could have gone home after getting out of the pen. But if the gossip I heard was right, he lit a shuck under his son."

"What that means—'lit a shuck'?"

"Means he ran him off," Phineas grunted. "Don't sound like much of a father to me."

Sam shook his head stubbornly. "The Driver family's always been good folks, Phineas. The old man, he's a little hard-tailed, but a good man deep down."

"What is 'hard-tailed'?" Reisa asked.

"Oh, it means he's a little bit on the hard side—you know, doesn't allow for a body's weakness. Took his boy's going wrong bad, so the talk went. They had another son, Matthew, that died in the war. Heard that the old man was never the same after that."

Reisa listened as the two men talked of the Driver family, and found herself feeling pity for the sick man. She understood better why he was so withdrawn. *Poor man! What if my grandfather would turn me away? How would I feel?*

~

Reisa came back later to see if Driver was still asleep. He was, and she stood there looking down at him. She had a sense of guilt, for once he had flung his arm out and touched her breast, and she had struck out at him instinctively before she realized that his action had been involuntary, that he had not meant to molest her. Now as she looked down on him, she tried to make something out of his face. The sheet that covered his body outlined his tall thin form. His eyes, at least the left eye, were sunken and dark circles were under them, and his cheeks were sunk in slightly on each side. She wondered again how it could be that a man was so alone in the world that he had no family nor friends to send for when he was hurt.

She moved out of the room and found Jacob sitting at the kitchen table with Sam. Phineas was washing dishes at the sink.

"How is he, Granddaughter?" Jacob asked.

"He's asleep. His fever's broken. I think he will be all right." She moved over to where Phineas stood and started to wash the bowl and the spoon, but Phineas took them from her. "I will cook you supper tonight if you don't mind, Phineas."

"Don't mind a bit," Phineas said testily. He turned and studied the two. "I've got to get out of here. They've been arguing religion for the last hour—and they're likely to go on for the rest of the day."

Indeed, Sam looked up and grinned at Phineas. "It wouldn't hurt you to stay and get a little of this. It'd do you good."

Phineas left, however, so Sam turned back to Jacob and said, "Remember, you were reading to me about how the children of Israel disobeyed God, and God sent a pack of snakes to bite 'em."

"Yes. That is in the Law."

"Well, what did Moses do when them people started dying of snake bites?"

"He made a brass serpent, and he put it on a pole."

"And what happened then?"

"Why, the Scripture says that everyone who was bitten and dying of snake bites would look up at that pole, and then God would heal them."

"And do you believe that, Jacob?"

"Certainly I believe it!" Jacob said quietly but firmly. "I believe all that's written in the book of the Law."

"All right. Keep that in your mind now, and let me read you something. This is from the book of John."

Reisa had been washing dishes, but at this word from Sam she half-turned to listen more carefully. She had read her copy of the book of John all the way through, and part of it several times. Now she waited to hear what Sam would say.

"This here part is in chapter three: 'There was a man of the Pharisees, named Nicodemus, a ruler of the Jews: The same came to Jesus by night, and said unto him—'" Sam interrupted himself, "I reckon he came to Jesus by night because a respectable Jewish rabbi wouldn't want to be seen with a man like Jesus."

"The religious leaders did not like Jesus?"

"Well, they thought he'd come to do away with their religion, but Jesus never done that. Anyway, this fellow Nicodemus said, 'Rabbi, we know that thou art a teacher come from God: for no man can do these miracles that thou doest, except God be with him.'"

"That is true certainly. No man can do a miracle of himself. God must be with him."

"This next verse is the part that made me turn to religion. I was a soldier then, and we had a meetin' and a preacher, and he preached on this verse. Here's what Jesus said to Nicodemus." He read again, "'Jesus answered and said unto him, Verily, verily,

I say unto thee, Except a man be born again, he cannot see the kingdom of God.'"

Sam paused, and Jacob blinked with surprise. Reisa had read this passage many times, for it was the part of the Gospel that fascinated—and troubled—her the most.

"That is impossible, Sam! A man can't be born but once."

Sam laughed and slapped his hand on the table. "Now, you said that. Hear what your friend Nicodemus said. 'Nicodemus saith unto him, How can a man be born when he is old? can he enter the second time into his mother's womb, and be born?'"

"The rabbi had good judgment." Jacob smiled.

"But here's what Jesus said, 'Verily, verily, I say unto thee, Except a man be born of water and of the Spirit, he cannot enter into the kingdom of God. That which is born of the flesh is flesh; and that which is born of the Spirit is spirit. Marvel not that I said unto thee, Ye must be born again. The wind bloweth where it listeth, and thou hearest the sound thereof, but canst not tell whence it cometh, and whither it goeth: so is every one that is born of the Spirit.'"

"Those are strange words," Jacob said quietly. "I have no idea what they mean."

"Well, neither did Nicodemus. The next verse says, 'Nicodemus answered and said unto him, How can these things be? Jesus answered and said unto him, Art thou a master of Israel, and knowest not these things?'"

Sam looked up then and said, "That's the Scripture that got me. I didn't see how no man could be born but once. But Jesus said you hear the wind, but you don't know where it's comin' from, you don't know where it's goin'. You don't understand that. And he told Nicodemus that there has to be somethin' happen on the inside of man. Not on the outside. Don't you see? A man's born once into this world physically, but he's got to have a change of heart to get into the kingdom of God."

Jacob's eyes narrowed, and he could not answer for a moment. Finally he said, "I agree with that. A man's heart must be made right. If that is what you call the new birth, then I can see the reason of it."

"So could I, and I gave my heart to Jesus that night."

Reisa listened as Sam talked about his conversion experience—how he had gone to a meeting a confirmed sinner and had heard a preacher speak of Jesus. She listened with wonder as he related how his heart began to melt, and how he felt himself to be a blackened sinner. And then he fell on his face and cried out for God to save him.

"Since that time," Sam said, "I've been a new creature."

"But what does all this have to do with Moses and the serpent?"

"I been gettin' to that. Here it is right here in verse fourteen. After Jesus told Nicodemus how he needed to be changed on the inside, he says right here, 'And as Moses lifted up the serpent in the wilderness, even so must the Son of Man be lifted up: That whosoever believeth in him should not perish, but have eternal life.'"

"So that's what I get out of that Old Testament story about Moses and the snake. Them people were physically bit, and they looked to a physical snake that Moses made of brass, and they were healed in their body. But Jesus said anybody that looks unto me will be healed in his heart. This verse sixteen, I guess, sums up all I know about the Bible." Sam's eyes grew misty, and his voice grew soft: "'For God so loved the world, that he gave his only begotten Son, that whosoever believeth in him should not perish, but have everlasting life. For God sent not his Son into the world to condemn the world; but that the world through him might be saved.'"

Reisa turned and saw once again that there were tears in Sam's eyes. He was, she had learned, a very emotional man, and she honored him for it.

Jacob was deeply moved by Sam's emotion—and by the words that he read. He was quiet for a moment, and he said, "I will think on these things, Sam." He got up and walked outside, his head bent deeply in thought.

Sam watched him go, then shook his head. "He's a mighty fine man, your grandpa. Don't know as I ever met a finer, Miss Reisa."

Reisa came over and sat down and looked Sam in the face. "Are there many Christians like you, Sam?"

Surprised at such a question, Sam shook his head. "I ain't nothin' special, Miss Reisa. I'm just an average, garden-variety Christian, I reckon."

"I've always been afraid of Christians."

"Afraid!" Sam was genuinely surprised. His eyes flew open, and his jaw dropped. "Why in the blue-eyed world would you be askeered of Christians?"

"Because in my country many of my people have been killed by those who call themselves Christians." She went on to tell him of the pogroms that had taken the lives of so many, all carried out by members of the state church, the Russian Orthodox.

Sam shook his head and said loudly, "I don't reckon them folks know much about Jesus. A Christian would never do anything like that to anybody. Jesus never would, and Christians are supposed to be like him."

Reisa reached over and squeezed Sam's hand. He looked at her with surprise as she said, "You've been so good to us, so kind, you and Phineas. God will reward you."

She left the room then and went out to walk beside Jacob, who gave her a strange look but said nothing.

"What do you think about all of this? About what they say about Jesus and—what do they call it?"

"Being born again, they call it. Sometimes he calls it 'being saved,'" Jacob replied quietly. "Other times he calls it 'being converted.' It is very odd. But it is good to meet a Christian who is all that a man should be." They walked for a few more steps, and he turned to face her. "Which of us has the true faith? We shall see."

~

When Driver awoke the next morning, he knew that the worst of the sickness was over. He still coughed from time to time, but it was a minor thing, perhaps nothing but a reflex action. He lay there dozing, enjoying the feeling of good health after such a terrible time.

Hearing the door open, he opened his eye and sat up. The big black cat jumped up and came to him at once, pushing his head against the hand that Driver held out. "What's this critter's name, Miss Reisa?"

"His name is Boris."

"I dreamed he smiled at me yesterday."

"It was no dream." Reisa set a tray down on the table with a plate of scrambled eggs and a biscuit. "He does smile."

"Never heard of a cat smilin'," Driver mused. He sat up, and Reisa handed him the plate and fork, then sat down beside him. He ate hungrily and said, "That was good. I could use more."

"I think you should eat small meals instead of big ones. I'll bring you something else in a couple of hours."

Jacob came in and came near to sit down on his bed. His face was pale and drawn. "How are you, my friend?"

"Better." Driver's eyes reflected a question. "I still don't have it clear in my mind where I am. This isn't your place. Did I hear that right?"

"Oh, no, indeed. I am Jacob Dimitri, Reisa's grandfather. I fell ill on our travels, and we were taken in by Mr. Sam Hall and Mr. Phineas Long."

"It's all comin' back a little, but everything's a little fuzzy."

"They are very kind to strangers. I see your fever is gone, and you are eating. That is a good sign."

"I guess so."

Driver wiped the plate with the last morsel of biscuit, and as he did Sam came in. He was wearing a checkered shirt and a pair of faded jeans with a bright red neckerchief stuck in his shirt pocket. "Well, you ain't gone to be with the angels yet." He came over and smiled down at Driver. "How are you feelin'?"

"All right. Much better."

"Sam here and his partner Phineas were very good," Reisa said. "They bathed you with cold water several times until your fever broke."

Sam shrugged. "Wasn't that. It was that anointing with oil and the prayer. It was Doctor Jesus done the work."

Driver cut his eye around to stare at Sam as if he were some strange creature, but he said nothing.

"How'd you lose that there eye?"

"Got too close to some Yankees at Spotsylvania. Shell blew up."

"I lost this here wing when I was ridin' around with General Nathan Bedford Forrest."

Driver examined the small man with fresh interest. "You rode with Forrest?"

"Yep. Through most of the hull war."

"I've always thought Forrest was the best fighting general on either side."

"You can say that twice." Sam grinned. "I reckon as how he kilt more people personal than any officer in the whole army. Hey, let me show you somethin'!" He left the room and was back at once. "What do you think of this?"

Driver took the pistol that Sam extended to him and examined it carefully. "It's a La Mat, isn't it?"

"Sure is. Fires nine shots as quick as you can get 'em off. The general would go into a battle with two of these things, and I swan if he didn't get eighteen Yankees, he was plumb out of sorts. I reckon you did some fightin' your own self."

"I was with Lee all the way," Driver said.

"You stacked your musket at Appomattox, did ya?"

Driver nodded.

"What does that mean?" Reisa asked.

"Well, a lot of fellers got scared and threw their muskets away. Some surrendered, but some folks like Driver here carried their musket all the way to the very end. General Lee finally had to surrender. Just plumb wore out with a plumb wore-out army. He stacked his musket. About the finest thing you can say of a fella, I reckon."

"It was a hard war," Driver murmured.

Phineas entered, and Sam turned, gesturing toward the recovering man. "Hey, this is Ben Driver. This is my sidekick, Phineas Long."

"Glad to know you," Ben said.

"You keepin' that grub down, are ya?" Phineas asked.

"Yes."

"Well, that's good. I don't want to have to go to the trouble of buryin' you."

Driver's long lips curled up into a small smile. "I'll do my best to accommodate you."

"All of you leave," Reisa said suddenly. "He needs to rest, and he can't get any rest with you clucking like a bunch of chickens." She hurried them out and finally turned and took Ben's plate. "What else can I do for you?"

Ben clawed his whiskers. "Maybe tomorrow I'll shave. Not today though. Weak as a kitten." He turned and reached out his hand and stroked Boris's fur, and Boris obliged him with a mighty purr and a grin.

Driver shook his head in wonder. "Never saw a thing like that in my life."

"Anything else I can get you?"

"Do you have any books?" Driver had read so much in prison he felt unmanned without one.

"Yes. I will bring you something." She left the room and came back quickly. "This is all I have. Phineas and Sam probably have more." She handed him the copy of *Uncle Tom's Cabin.*

Driver looked at it and shook his head. "I don't want to read that. Some people say this is the book that started the whole war."

"It is a terrible book." She hesitated, then said, "I feel sorry for the slaves that were mistreated."

Driver gave her a quick glance, shook his head, and handed the book back. Picking up the other one, he said, *"Great English Poetry."*

"It is a very strange book. I don't know what to make of it."

"Well, I'll try anything once. What's the other one?"

"It is—a book that a man gave me on the ship coming over. You have probably read it."

Taking the small book, Driver glanced at it. "Gospel of John," he murmured. His head came up, and he put his eyes on Reisa. He could not figure the woman out. "You're Jewish, I take it."

"Yes."

"What are you doing reading part of the Bible?"

"I don't know, but I thought you might like it." She was unwilling to talk about the book. "I will see if Sam or Phineas have more." She waited for him to speak his gratitude, but he simply opened *Great English Poetry* and started reading.

Ben was awakened later by the sound of Reisa's voice.

"Are you awake?"

When his eyes flew open, she said, "I brought you a piece of chicken and a boiled potato."

"Sounds good." He sat up, laying his book aside, and took the bowl hungrily. She had brought him a glass of milk, and he drank that as well. When he handed them back, he said, "Much obliged."

"You're very welcome."

"I reckon, if you give me my clothes, I can get out of this bed."

"No indeed!" Reisa said quickly. "You need to rest."

"I'm not much of a one for stayin' in bed."

"You will stay in bed until I say so."

Driver studied the face of the young woman. He wondered what her hair was like, guessing it would be thick and glossy. The quick curves of her healthy, supple body were plain to him under the dress. He studied the depths of her eyes and wondered what lay behind them. There was a serenity to her. She had a long, composed mouth and lips that could charm a man if she so chose. Still, there was an innocence about her.

Finally he said, "I guess you're the boss."

Reisa smiled briefly. "Did you like the book?"

"Can't make head nor tail out of most of it."

"Neither could I, but I learned English from those two books," she said. "A friend of ours had been in America. He taught me to speak. I know I do not speak English well."

"Better than most."

Light pink touched her cheeks at the compliment, and without another word she turned and left the room.

Driver shook his head. "Funny sort of girl," he murmured aloud. He turned and ran his hand over Boris's head. "And you're a funny sort of cat."

As Reisa was helping Phineas fix supper, the two of them talked. She had gotten closer to Phineas. There was an innate sadness in the man, and she had found out that he had been married and had a child, but both had died of cholera while he was serving under Longstreet in the army. That explained a great deal about him—that and the loss of his leg, and the poverty that the war had brought to him. Reisa felt such compassion that she quickly forgave his abruptness and sometimes almost harsh language.

"That fellow, Dov, he's somethin' else," Phineas said. "He's done more work around here than I dreamed a man could do."

"Dov is a good worker and a good friend to me." She related how Dov had saved her from being molested on the ship. "He just picked that sailor up by the neck with one hand and held him kicking there." Her eyes danced, and her lips curved upward. "You should have heard him cry out then!"

"He'd be a bad feller to cross in a ruckus, I'd guess."

"A ruckus? What's a ruckus?"

"A fight."

"Oh. Ruckus—a fight." At that moment a crash occurred from somewhere in the house. "What was that?" she cried.

"Don't know."

The two of them ran quickly down the hall and opened the door to the room that Driver shared with her grandfather. They found Driver getting up painfully.

He was wearing only a pair of long underwear, but still Reisa turned away. "Put him back in bed, Phineas."

Driver insisted, "Give me my clothes!"

Reisa kept her back turned as she said, "I'm washing them, and you're not going to get them until you're stronger. You're getting up too soon."

"Here. Get back in that bed!" Phineas demanded. He grabbed Driver by the arm and even with crutches was able to maneuver him back into the bed. "Now you stay put until Miss Reisa says so."

"Yes. You do that." Reisa left the room and waited outside.

She heard Phineas's voice. "You ain't much for sayin' thanks, are you, Driver? Them folks saved your life."

"What for, I wonder?" Driver said flatly.

Phineas snorted in reply. Reisa stepped aside as he came out of the room.

"That feller's no good," Phineas said.

"He's had great trouble, Phineas," Reisa said quickly.

"Don't matter. He could be decent..."

The next day Driver was sitting in bed fretting when Reisa brought his clothes. They had been washed and pressed.

"Now, I think you may get dressed and sit up," she said.

He did not answer, for he was still put out with her. She left the room, and he dressed. Holding onto the wall, he made his way outside. Down the short hallway he saw the kitchen area and Sam sitting at a table with Jacob. He made his way in, and Sam jumped up.

"Here. Have a cheer."

Dizzy and unsure of his balance, Driver slumped down into it.

He sat there, and Reisa brought him a cup of sassafras tea. "We're out of coffee," she said.

"This will do fine."

"I'm glad you're feeling better, friend," Jacob said.

"Thanks," Driver said but spoke no more. He sat there drinking and studying the people in the room. He was especially interested in Jacob Dimitri. He had known two Jews in the army, but had never been close to one of their educated people. He was amazed to hear Sam, whom he knew to be a devout Christian, and Jacob getting along famously. They would argue at times over the meaning of a passage of Scripture, but still there was an obvious affection between the two of them. He could not quite figure Sam out. He had met religious fanatics before, but Sam did not seem to be one of these. There was a cheerful spirit about him, and once he hopped up to go bring wood in to the stove for Reisa.

Driver sat up for two hours, then grew tired and made his way back to bed.

That afternoon Reisa sat down and listened to Jacob and Sam talk about Jewish customs and traditions. Reisa listened with only half an ear, for she was thinking of how they would manage until Jacob regained his health. She knew they could not impose on the hospitality of Sam and Phineas forever, and more than once she thought, *What are we going to do?* Then she would pray, *Great most high God, you must guide us. I don't know what to do.*

The air turned cool, and darkness began to fall over the homestead. They ate supper together, Driver joining them at the table for the first time. After supper Driver went out and sat on the front porch with the other men. He sat for a long time listening to the other men talk, but finally they came in, leaving him there alone.

Determined to know more about Driver, Reisa went out and sat beside him. He did not speak nor did she for a time, but finally he said, "I thank you for helping me. I reckon I would have played out my string if you and Dov hadn't come along."

It was the most gracious remark Reisa had heard from him yet, and she was surprised. "You would have done the same for us."

"I'm not sure about that."

"I think you would."

"You think too well of people. They'll fail you."

Reisa turned to face him. "Would you have me crawl into a cave, Mr. Driver, and have no friends?"

Driver shook his head. "Ben is good enough." He said nothing for a long time, nor did she. The sound of a dog barking far off with sharp staccato rapidity broke the silence. "He's treed something, I'd guess," Driver observed.

She felt out of place somehow sitting there with him. She was uncomfortable and did not know why.

Finally he said, "I guess I sound pretty hard to you."

"A little bit perhaps."

"I guess I've had a hard life. The army makes a man hard sometimes." He seemed to be about to say something, then changed his mind, saying instead, "I don't have too many answers. Sometimes there's a little sunlight, and sometimes a memory will come. I remember a young girl no more than ten who gave me a glass of buttermilk just outside of Chancellorsville. She smiled at me and flirted a little bit. I still remember that. I guess that's all my life is. Some pictures fading out behind me, and there's not much before me."

"There's much good in the world."

"Maybe there is for some. There are some good men and some good women. But there are so many that are not, and it seems like that's the kind I've bumped up against."

Reisa listened as he spoke, and for the first time she was able to see that beneath his hardness and the caustic manner he sometimes had, there was more. She could not put her finger on it, but she knew that he was a man that longed for goodness, and longed for friends, and perhaps even a wife and family. He would have denied it, she was sure.

Finally she said, "I hope you find your way, Ben. God is real, and love is real."

She turned and moved back into the house, leaving Driver alone with his thoughts.

Fifteen

Large piles of white fluffy clouds raced along the azure skies overhead as Dov and Reisa walked along the dusty roads. The coolness of fall was in the air, for this was September. The hot days of August had faded, and the breath of air that came to them was cool and refreshing. They had seen the cotton fields white with harvest, and Reisa had been reminded of her dream of walking down white fields and seeing black faces. As she moved along, she was suddenly glad that she and her grandfather had followed that dream all the way south.

This trip had been moderately successful. Although cash money was scarce, they had done very well going through a small town nearby and then down lanes deeper into the rural areas. There had been a threat of rain, but it had passed away.

Within a mile of the house, Dov pointed over to his right. "Look—somebody live there."

Reisa turned and saw a winding dirt road that led around a clump of towering pine trees, and caught a glimpse of a house with fields behind it.

"Let's make one more stop, Dov," she said. "We've got plenty of time."

The two made their way down the dusty road, Dov whistling a tuneless melody, as he often did. Reisa was fascinated, wondering exactly what went on in the big man's mind. He seemed simple, but he certainly was not stupid. She sensed that beneath the crude exterior dwelt a sensitive spirit.

When they emerged from the pine trees, Reisa saw a house set back behind a picket fence. It was a small house, one story, with a steep pitched roof covered with cedar shakes.

Over to one side was a pasture filled with several cows and two large horses. On the other side of the house was a cotton field now white and ready to be picked. Behind it she saw the gleam of water of what was apparently a small pond.

As they approached the house, Reisa saw no one. When she knocked on the door there was no answer. Dov called out.

Then they heard someone call. "In back."

Reisa came down the steps and moved around the corner of the house. Dov followed her. She saw the back of a man wearing overalls. He knelt in a pen holding down a squealing pig. Moving to the fence, Reisa said, "Good evening, sir."

Instantly the figure stood and wheeled—and Reisa saw the face. It was not a man at all but a very large woman!

Embarrassed, Reisa did not know how to make apologies. "I'm sorry," she said. "I didn't know—"

The woman was well over six feet tall and broad shouldered. The overalls were worn and thin and revealed the female figure. She was very large, and Reisa saw that her hands seemed to be callused like a man's.

The pig ran away squealing. Reisa said, "I didn't mean to disturb you, ma'am."

For a moment the woman did not speak. Her blonde hair was held in place by a broad-brimmed straw hat. Her eyes were blue, as blue as any Reisa had ever seen. She kept her face turned to one side for some reason and said, "What do you want?"

"We are your neighbors. We are staying with Mr. Hall and Mr. Long."

The woman nodded, and as she did she turned her face so that Reisa saw that she had a bad scar running from the edge of her eyebrow down to her right cheek. She pulled off her hat, and blonde hair cascaded down her back. She had an accent that did not sound like any that Reisa had heard.

Reisa said, "We are peddlers. This is my friend Dov, and my name is Reisa Dimitri."

"I'm Hilda Swenson."

The woman's eyes flickered away from Reisa and rested on Dov. She studied the huge man thoughtfully, then said, "You're peddlers? You're not from around here."

"No. We are from Russia."

"My people come from Sweden."

"Well, we're both newcomers," Reisa said. "If you have time, Mrs. Swenson—"

"It's not Mrs. I'm not married."

"Oh, Miss Swenson then."

The woman appeared to be about thirty and had fair, clear skin. Reisa had to look up to her and had never seen such a large woman—not fat, just large.

"We have quite a few things you might need for your house: spices, sewing goods, needles, thread. I have some fine ribbons that you might use in making a dress."

"I don't need anything for making a dress."

The door, more or less, slammed shut on that conversation, but Reisa set her pack down and began to pull out several items. It became obvious quickly that Hilda Swenson was not interested in any feminine items. She did, however, agree to some needles, several spices that were hard to come by in the stores, and a box of matches.

"That is all I need right now."

Reisa waited until the woman went into the house and came back with some change. "Thank you very much," she said as she pocketed the change and finished packing the items back in her pack. She did not wish to be inquisitive, but the situation was rather strange. She did not see any men working nor any women either, and she asked cautiously, "Your family is here?"

"Only my mother. She is very old. I take care of her and run the farm."

"That must be very hard for a woman."

"I'm a good farmer," Hilda said quickly, as if her pride had been touched.

"I'm sure you are. It must be difficult though all by yourself to take care of a house and farm as well."

"The Lord helps me."

Dov suddenly said, "Maybe sometimes you need man for some things."

Hilda looked over at Dov and considered him. She seemed fascinated by his size. "Sometimes," she admitted. "Right now I've got a wagon loaded out in the field. The wheel came off, and I can't jack it up and put the wheel on at the same time."

"Oh, maybe we can help with that—or at least Dov can."

"Yes." Dov nodded. "Show me wagon."

For a moment the woman looked at them, then nodded shortly. "All right."

As Reisa followed her around the house and out into the field, she noticed that Hilda Swenson walked like a man with long strides. She hurried to catch up with her, trying to make conversation, but got little response.

Finally they reached a wagon heavily loaded with fertilizer. It sagged down on the left side, and beside it Hilda had made a makeshift sort of affair to lever the wagon up into position. "I can't lift it up and put the wheel on it."

Dov took in the situation at a glance. Ignoring the sapling that she was attempting to use for a wedge, he said, "Come. You put wheel on."

"What are you going to do?" Hilda asked. She followed Dov to the rear of the wagon, and the wheel was on the ground beside it.

"I pick up wagon. You put wheel on."

Hilda stared at him, but he did not wait for an answer. Moving around to the front position of the wheel, he got on his hands and knees, crawled under, then turned around. He gathered his legs up under him and said, "You ready?"

Hilda nodded shortly, but shook her head with disbelief. "You can't pick that wagon up."

Dov began to rise up. He braced his hands against his upper thighs, and both women could see the huge muscles bulging in his thick legs. A vein stood out in his forehead, but otherwise there was no sign of strain. He lifted the wagon clear off the ground and said in a conversational tone, "Is this good?"

Hilda gasped, but she wasted no time. Quickly she snatched up the wheel, moved it into position, and slipped it on over the axle. "Now," she said. "You can let it down."

Dov released the weight of the wagon, and Hilda fastened the wheel in place so that it would not slip off. Turning, she looked up at the big man and said, "Thank you." She shook her head saying, "I do not believe there is another man in the world who could pick up that wagon."

Dov smiled at her. "Sometimes when you have things to make—" He hesitated. "No. Things that takes a strong back, you come and get me."

Hilda seemed fascinated by Dov. She looked into his dark eyes for a long time, then said, "I will."

"We'd better be going, Dov. It's going to be dark soon."

"Yah. We go."

They went back to the house, where Dov picked up his large pack and Reisa her small one. Reisa turned and said, "Thank you very much."

"No. Thank you." Her eyes went to Dov. "Thank you again."

"Nothing—nothing at all," Dov responded.

The two left the yard, and Dov turned back once to see that the woman was watching them. "Nice lady," he said. "Very strong."

That night Phineas had cooked potatoes with what he called sawmill gravy for some reason that neither Reisa nor Jacob understood. He had also cooked squirrel and dumplings, which neither guest had eaten before.

"These are plumb sanctified for Jews," Sam said with assurance. "I know you can't eat rabbits and pigs, but this critter doesn't chew his cud, and he doesn't have a cloven hoof. And these dumplins' wouldn't offend Abraham hisself."

Reisa tasted the squirrel and said, "This is fine! I've never had anything better."

"Nobody fixes squirrel and dumplins' like Phineas," Sam said fondly. "The trouble is, we ain't very good at gettin' the squirrels. Phineas there's a good shot, but because of his bum leg he can't go to the squirrel woods. I can get to the squirrel woods, but I can't hit much. Had that trouble all during the war. I had to get up close enough to pepper them Yankees with that La Mat of mine."

"We met a young woman today. The house right back off the road on the west side."

"Oh, yes. That's Hilda Swenson," Sam said. "Fine woman."

"She lives all alone with her mother?"

"That's right. Her pa died about four years ago. He was ailin' for a long time."

Phineas shook his head. "Beats all how that woman works. She does the work of two men, I do believe."

"How old would you guess she is?"

Sam winked at Dov. "How old did she look to you, Dov?"

"Don't know. Good strong woman."

"You're right about that. I think she's thirty nearabouts."

"She's never married?"

Sam and Phineas exchanged glances, and it was Phineas who said sourly, "She was supposed to have been married up with Fred Simmons."

The others waited for him to continue. When he did not, Reisa said, "What happened?"

"He let it get right up to the wedding day and then left her at the church. Run off with that no-count trash Emmy Bradshaw. Three years after she married him, she took everything he had and ran off with a sign painter to St. Louis. Served him right. No-good bum."

"I made a mistake. When I walked up she had her back to us, and I thought it was a man."

"Yep. She wears them overalls except on Sundays. She's got one dress, I think. That's all I've ever seen anyhow," Sam remarked. "She wears that to meetin'."

"How'd she get that scar on her face?" Reisa inquired.

"I don't rightly know. It's been there a long time, I think. She's right sensitive about it. Kind of keeps her hair over it when her hair's down and always turns her face away."

Driver had taken all this in but said nothing.

He ate and then for the first time, he said, "Maybe I can help with the dishes."

Phineas stared at him. It was the first human gesture that Driver had made with the men in earshot, but Reisa turned down his offer. "Oh, no. You men go out on the porch and talk. I don't mind doing the dishes."

They all filed out on the porch, but there were only two chairs. Jacob sat on one and Driver in the other. The other two sat on a box and a keg that served just as well. Sam smoked a corncob pipe, and the talk floated back to Reisa. When she had finished the dishes she went out and sat beside them.

The stars were out overhead. Sam remarked, "Look at all them stars. The Good Book says God knows every one of their names."

"Well, I know that one," Phineas said. "You see that one with three close together and the two at the top and two at the bottom? That's what they call Orion. It's supposed to be a figure of a man—those three stars are Orion's belt."

"Orion. Ain't that somethin'!" Sam remarked. "I wonder how far away they are."

"Further than you can walk." Phineas grinned.

The talk flowed to and fro, and finally Driver stood and walked off into the darkness without a word. They all watched him go.

Phineas said, "He ain't got enough talk in him to make a full-grown man."

"He'll get out of it. He got well, didn't he? He just needs a little encouragement," Sam remarked.

Reisa did not speak, but later on she thought of this, wondering what would bring the tall man out of his silence.

Three days later Ben Driver insisted on helping around the house. He only had the clothes that he had worn from the prison, but when Dov went out to build a fence he came out and said, "I can help a little."

Dov stared at him. "Maybe not. You been sick."

"I can do something," Driver insisted.

Dov shrugged his massive shoulders. He picked up a wedge and a fifteen-pound sledge. He handled the sledge as if it were a tack hammer and with one hand drove the wedge in. He added another one, then a third, and with a few hard blows the tree split in two. He quickly split these until he had a small stack of fence posts.

"Those locust posts will last forever and a day after that. Fine for fence posts," Driver said. He managed to dig a hole for one, and then Dov took the post-hole digger, and the dirt simply flew.

The two worked together, Dov doing ninety percent of the work.

Finally they stopped to rest—at least Driver did. He went and sat down under the shade of a sycamore tree. When Dov sat down some time later, Driver said, "What do you want, Dov?"

Dov stared at him. "You mean—now?"

"No. I mean for the rest of your life."

"Food to eat, place to sleep—friends."

"That's all?"

"What else is there?"

At that moment Reisa came out of the house bearing a bucket of water. "I thought you might be thirsty," she said.

"I am. Sometimes I forget to take a drink and dry myself out." He drank deeply from the pitcher, then handed it to Dov. The big man simply turned the bucket up and drank deeply.

"What's all this about Jews can't eat certain things?" Driver asked curiously. "The fellows in our outfit nearly starved to death, the two men who were Jews. I knew they couldn't eat hog meat. What *can* you eat?"

"We can't eat anything that chews their cud or has a cloven hoof."

"You mean like a deer?"

"Oh, yes. We can eat a deer."

"Well, I think it's about time I paid my way." He left the two and went up to the porch. Sam was sitting there with Jacob, and, as usual, they were discussing Scripture. Driver interrupted, "I'm going to get a deer."

Sam nodded. "That'd be mighty fine. Like I said, I can't shoot much, and Phineas can't get to 'em. Just a minute."

Sam entered the house and came back quickly with a rifle.

"This is a Spencer I took off a dead Yankee. You think you can hit anything with it?"

"Well, I got seven chances." Ben grinned. "I saw lots of deer tracks down by the creek. I won't come back until I get something. Dov, you come along to carry the critter back."

The two turned and left.

~

Reisa sat down on the porch beside Jacob, and Sam went inside, leaving them alone.

Reisa shot a cautious glance at her grandfather. He was pale and drawn. She knew he was not eating well and was growing weaker, but she did not mention this.

"*Zaideh,* I know we can make money, but we need to be able to carry more goods." She sighed deeply. "What we need is a wagon and a good team of horses."

Jacob smiled at her. "Well, God owns the wagons in a thousand wagon yards. He can surely spare one if you ask." He paused, then spoke. "I've been thinking about what you said about the ex-slave women wanting wedding rings, and the men wanting hats. The hats are easy, but the wedding rings would be easy to carry, and you should sell them on credit."

Reisa nodded. "That would be good, but where is the money to come from to get started? A wagon and a team costs more than we would ever have. And as for the rings, how much would they cost?"

"I do not know, but I will write a letter to our friend Rabbi Isaac Tichler in Norfolk. He, no doubt, will be able to find out something for us."

Reisa did not comment on that. It just seemed too big to take in.

~

It was four o'clock when the two men returned. Dov was carrying a fat deer over his shoulders, and he smiled broadly. "We have food!"

Sam came down the porch quickly. "Fine fat deer," Phineas said.

"Well, Jacob," Sam said. "How do we dress this deer? You will have to tell us how to do it right."

Jacob said, "That I will do."

They all went around to the back of the house, where Dov strung the deer up by his hind legs.

"You must drain all the blood out," Jacob said. When this was done, he said, "Now it is safe. We feel that the life of the flesh is in the blood, and no Jew will eat blood if he is a good Jew."

Reisa watched as the deer was dressed. "Give me some fat steaks, and I'll start them cooking." She waited until she had plenty of fresh meat, then she went into the house and started the meal.

It turned out to be a fine supper. All of them ate a great deal except for Jacob.

While they were lingering over the table, Sam said to Ben, "Did you ever get shot in the war?"

Driver nodded. "Three times. The first time was at Shiloh. We were chargin' the Yankees, and I came on a Yankee lieutenant who was down. He seemed to be bad off. He was beggin' for water, and I stopped to give him a drink. When I left him, I turned my back and started away. He pulled out a pistol and shot me in the back."

Reisa was horrified. "How awful!"

"What happened to that fella?" Phineas demanded.

Driver was silent for a moment, then shook his head. "He didn't make it."

Reisa cleaned the kitchen, as usual, while the men talked. Reisa started to wash the dishes, but Sam interrupted. "Nope. Me and Phineas will do them. You've done 'em every night. You go sit on the porch."

As soon as she had left and Jacob had gone to his room, Sam began to wash the dishes. Phineas said, "How long do you reckon they'll stay here, Sam?"

"Until Jacob gets able to move on, I guess." He gave Phineas an odd look. "You don't mind it, do you, Phineas? I mean, after all, they just take up a little food, and it don't cost much."

Phineas scratched his chin and stared down at the dishwater. "I don't know as I mind it all that much. Driver—well, I dunno."

"He's kind of a lost fella wanderin' around and don't know what to do with himself. You know how it was right after the war—so many of our friends just had nothin' left to go home to. Almost like ghosts, they were."

The two stood there talking quietly, and finally Phineas looked over at Dov, who was sitting on the floor with his head pressed back against the wall. His eyes were closed, and Phineas said, "You finish these dishes. I'll go play that feller a tune."

He moved over to a case where his violin lay, picked it up, and went over and sat down in front of Dov. "Like to have a little music, Dov?"

"Yes," Dov said brightening up at once. He sat there and listened while Phineas played song after song. Sometimes he would sing the words, and Dov would beat time with his fists against his meaty legs.

Outside on the porch, Ben and Reisa stood looking off into the gathering dusk in the trees. Reisa's voice came to Ben through the darkness. "Phineas plays so well."

"Yes, he does," Driver agreed. "We had a fellow in our outfit that played a banjo like that. He could almost make that thing talk."

"What are you going to do, Ben?"

Driver turned to face her, although he couldn't see her clearly in the darkness. They were isolated for the moment, and she was sitting close enough that he could smell the violet scent that she used. Once again he wondered about her hair. He could see that it was black and wondered what it would look like if it were loose. "I don't know," he said finally. "I've been thinking I'd go out to the coast to California."

"California. Where is that?"

"Three thousand miles away."

"What would you do when you got there?"

"I don't know. The same as here probably."

Reisa turned to face him. "Don't do that, Ben."

"Why not?"

"There's nothing for you in California that isn't here. This is your homeland, isn't it?"

"I used to think it was."

She did not answer, and the two of them stood there very close together. It had not been planned by either of them, but they were standing almost shoulder to shoulder. Ben knew that if he moved slightly, her arm would be pressed against his. He held himself back. Finally he said, "What are you going to do, Reisa? You and your grandfather."

"Oh, I have a dream." She laughed softly, a good sound on the night air. "I have lots of dreams. You'd think I was a silly woman if I told you."

"Try me. What is it?"

"Oh, I'd like to have a wagon. Not just an ordinary wagon, Ben, but one with compartments in it. You may have seen them. I saw one last week. It was all divided up. In one compartment was clothing. In another was groceries and household things. In another there was tools for the men, and still in another there was jewelry for the women. It was beautiful." She turned to him and was facing him. Her eyes seemed to glow in the faint light of the moon.

Driver said, "That's not a bad dream."

She laughed and said, "You haven't heard all of it."

"What's the rest?"

"All of the ex-slave women want wedding rings. They couldn't buy them before they were set free, you know."

"I never thought of that."

"No, they weren't even allowed to marry in many cases. Now they're married, but very few of them have wedding rings."

"So you'd like to sell wedding rings to them?"

"Yes, but most of them don't have enough money. But if I had enough money, I could buy up a group of wedding rings and go sell them on credit. They could pay a dollar a month or whatever they could afford."

"That'd take a big investment and a lot of work."

"I wouldn't mind it," Reisa said simply.

From far off came a mournful sound. Reisa said, "What's that?"

"Coyote."

"Are they dangerous?"

"No. Very shy. You hardly ever see one."

"What do they look like?"

"Like a small, skinny dog. A fox maybe. The only time they're dangerous is when they go mad."

They stood there on the porch, both of them soaking in the sounds of the night air and the coolness of the fall wind. Finally Driver said, "I owe you, Reisa."

"No. Not really."

"Yes, I do. I've done wrong a lot of times, but I always like to pay my debts."

"Please don't worry about that, Ben."

And then as they suddenly faced each other, Ben was caught again by the strangeness of this woman who stood before him. He had noted before that she was a woman of depth and also of pride and capable of great emotions. Her lips and eyes usually were carefully controlled as though she feared to reveal herself. Now suddenly he saw a break in her reserve, and she looked at him with her eyes full open—the eyes of a woman in all her fullness and mystery and beauty.

Without thought Ben reached forward, took her shoulders, and pulled her toward him. Her soft form rested against his chest, and his lips fell on hers. Driver had kissed other women, but somehow this young woman seemed so innocent and so virginal. Her caress sent something almost like an electric shock through him. He felt her return his pressure for a moment, and then she put her hands on his chest and pulled away. He saw that there were tears glistening in her eyes.

"Please," she whispered. "Please—don't ever do that again!" She turned and left, going back into the house.

Driver stood in the darkness, wondering why this woman had the power to stir him so much. He did not know what was happening, and he was not a man who liked mysteries.

Reisa went to her room without another word. When she got inside her room, she shut the door and leaned her head back against it. She was thinking, *That's twice I let a man kiss me. First Benjamin and now Ben.* She shut her eyes tightly, compressed her lips, and then she whispered, "Am I a bad woman? Oh, God, don't let me be bad!"

Sixteen

The following morning when Sam Hall came out of the house, he found Driver leaning up against the large elm tree that shaded the yard. Something about Driver's expression and his posture brought a question to the mind of the small man. He moved over toward him. "How's it goin', Ben?"

The sun was bright overhead, but the wind was turning cold. Mid-September had brought cooler breezes, and the sky overhead was a light blue and looked hard enough to scratch a match on. Driver lifted his head, and his voice was tense. "Getting restless. Reckon I'll be moving on."

"You ain't ready to be movin' nowhere. You need to put some meat on your bones."

As he spoke, Sam studied the figure of Driver. The tall man was wearing a pair of worn jeans that had belonged to Phineas and a gray cotton shirt from the same source. Phineas was a heavier man, and his legs were not as long as Driver's, so the clothes were ill-fitting. Boots had been another problem, for the cheap shoes that Driver had arrived in were not suitable for working. Phineas had found a pair of worn boots and had patched them together as best he could. All in all, Driver did not make a prepossessing figure. Still, he was stronger now. His neck had filled out, and the hollows in his cheeks were gone. The one eye which was a startling bright green, and sometimes seemed to have light blue around the pupil, was alert. Sam had watched Driver shave, stripped to the waist, and noted with approval that the muscles were building up. He was a lean man and never would be fat, but he was still not over his bout with sickness.

"I'm going into town. Why don't you go with me? I get tired of my own company."

"All right. I've got two whole dollars. I may go on a wild spree."

Sam laughed. "Well, I've got two, so both of us may do the town. Come on, you can help me hitch up the team. With one wing it ain't too easy."

The team was composed of two ancient blue-nosed mules named Betty and Heck. Sam swore they were owned by George Washington. Quickly Driver hitched the team to a ramshackle wagon. As he got in, it sagged and creaked ominously under his weight. "I hope this thing holds together."

"More likely them mules will die first," Sam said cheerfully. He said, "Get up, Heck! Come on, Betty!"

The mules stepped out obediently and did not offer to run away. Driver grinned suddenly. "I reckon they're pretty safe now, these two."

"They're old friends of mine. If one of 'em died, I expect the other would just up and decide to die, too. They do the best they can, though, and that's all you can say about any mule—or any man."

The wagon clattered along, and neither man spoke until they got to the small creek. A brisk wind was running its breath over it, and the clear water made a sibilant murmuring as Sam stopped at the water to let Betty and Heck drink. As they sat there waiting for the mules to finish refreshing themselves, a bird suddenly appeared, perching on the branch of a large hickory tree beside the road.

"Listen to that bird," Sam said, turning his eyes toward the tree. "Sounds like he's saying, 'Get out! Get out!' I always call him the 'Get Out' bird. Don't know what his real name is."

A small smile pulled at the corners of Driver's broad mouth. "Seems like I've been told to get out a few times."

"Well, who ain't?" Sam shrugged his scrawny shoulders. "I remember once we was gettin' surrounded by a bunch of Yankees, and General Forrest, he said, 'Men, let's skedaddle! We ain't welcome here!'"

"What'd you do, Sam?"

"Oh, we skedaddled all right. I got to where I wasn't ashamed of runnin' away. There was so many of them blasted blue bellies and so few of us. Guess you felt the same way."

"I guess I stopped feeling somewhere after Antietam."

"I wasn't in on most of that. We was guardin' the flanks, but we didn't get into the hard fightin'. I hear it was bad. You wasn't at that bloody angle, was you?"

"Yes."

The tone of that single word was as cold as an iceberg. Sam shot a quick glance at Driver's face, which was set. The planes of his face even seemed to grow harsher. He removed his hat, and the breeze blew his crisp, slightly curly, auburn hair across his brow. He brushed it back and shook his head. "I don't like thinking of those times."

"Me neither, most of it. But that's all over now."

"No, it's not over. Not for some of us."

"Best to try to put all that behind us, Ben."

As the mules picked up their pace slightly, Sam studied the fields that spread out on each side—some grown up with weeds and untended, but here and there cotton fields white as the whitest clouds in the sky.

Ben turned to put his eye on Sam. "Sometimes I feel like a man who's in the middle of a bridge, and I've forgotten both ends of it. I'm just standing there looking down at a river and not knowing which way to go."

Well, that's the most revealin' thing he's ever said, Sam thought quickly. Aloud he said, "Well, you'll git off that bridge, Ben. Time goes on, and we put things behind us."

"I was in prison before I came here, Sam. For four years. A man doesn't just blot that out of his life."

Sam allowed nothing to show on his thin face. Shrugging he said, "You ain't the first to do time, I reckon. But you didn't kill nobody, did you?"

"No, I was in for armed robbery." Driver put his hat back on and pulled it down over his brow, his one eye searching the landscape ahead as if something dangerous might appear. He had a way of letting his body go lax, but that one green eye would search around never settling on anything, but always looking, expecting some sort of trouble.

"I kept myself from going crazy by reading books. We didn't have many, and I read some over and over again. There was one in there by a Russian called Dostoevsky. He told about a man that was given a choice. Either to die at once or to stand on a ledge throughout eternity."

Sam shivered. "That gives me the willies. You don't need to be readin' no books like that."

Driver did not respond, but when they had passed several minutes in silence, he said, "I think I'd rather die than stand on a ledge waiting for something that never happens."

"You ain't standin' on no ledge. What about your folks? They godly people?"

"Yes, my mother especially. Every time I have doubts about heaven and God and the Bible, the picture of my mother comes to my mind." He shook his head and murmured, "I can doubt the Bible at times, but I can't question her life." Then he turned and said with a half smile, "Yours either, Sam. I don't agree with you, but I'll say one thing. You're always the same. Good or bad, storm or calm. You're always praising God even when you don't have much reason to."

"Me!" Sam said with astonishment. "Why, Ben, I'm plumb fine. I've got my health, I've got friends, I've got a place to stay, an' I got Jesus."

"That's about what Dov said. I wish I was as simple as he is."

"Don't put Dov down. He don't say much, but he thinks some stuff that you wouldn't dream."

"I'm not putting him down, Sam. I like him a lot."

The two talked intermittently until finally they pulled into the outskirts of Richmond.

"Reckon you know this town, Ben?"

"Pretty well." Ben did not tell the whole truth—which was that he knew every corner of Richmond, having spent his life there until he had left to join the army. Now he sat loosely in the seat until Sam pulled up in front of a hardware store. "Come on in, Ben. Won't take long."

"Nope. I'll just wander around a little. Well, I'll probably go over there, find a saloon, and drink up this two dollars that's burnin' a hole in my pocket."

"I wouldn't do that. Tell you what, let me get my buyin' done, then we'll walk around and maybe go into a cafe and have a real fancy meal. Maybe with a good-lookin' waitress to make up to us."

"All right, Sam. I'll be around."

Driver walked the streets of Richmond for a time, shocked at the devastation that had not yet been repaired since the war. Some businesses that he had known were simply cavernous holes in a line of those still standing. He remembered one that had been a clothing store where his father had brought him to buy his first grown-up suit. It was gone now, nothing but an empty hole filled in with bricks and rubble.

The years of Reconstruction he had spent in prison. He knew only sketchily that there had been a fierce struggle between President Johnson and Congress about how best to bring the southern states back into the Union. Finally military governors had been appointed by the federal government. Ben had heard some of the excesses and injustices that went on in the South. Civil rights were often flagrantly ignored, and the legislators of

Georgia, Alabama, and Louisiana were purged—simply set aside—as were many of the state laws. An army of occupation twenty thousand strong aided by Negro militia enforced this harsh military rule.

Virginia had been reconstructed in the previous year, but still the so-called carpetbaggers could be seen, as were federal soldiers, many of them black, who remained in the South. Grant had been elected in 1868, and already rumors of his inept and even devious plan of leadership were being whispered of in the South.

A faded sign hung over the sidewalk, one that Driver remembered. It said *The Wild Horse Saloon,* and it brought back a sudden rush of memories. He had taken his first drink of liquor in this place, played his first game of poker—and lost every dime he had, sitting at a table with older men. He suddenly remembered the distaste, the cheap painted women that were available, and quickly shoved that out of his mind.

A whimsy took him, however, and he went inside. The place seemed unchanged. The long bar with the mirror behind it still occupied the east side of the building. Round tables for poker and blackjack were scattered around, with mismatched chairs and a few men sitting at them. There were no women, for which he was glad. He stood for a moment and then walked over to the bar. A burly man with a bright yellow shirt and blue arm garters said, "Help you?"

"Whiskey."

The bartender turned, pulled a bottle from the shelf, grabbed a tumbler, and poured it full. "That'll be two bits."

Ben pulled out a dollar. When the bartender started to make change, he shook his head. "Give me another."

"Right." The bartender filled up another tumbler and left it in front of Ben.

He stood there at the bar, his mind filled with memories of these past days. He remembered a fight that he had and touched the scar beside his cheek where Juke Powers had left his mark on him. He had staggered away from the fight bloodied and bruised, but he had beaten Powers, which was quite a feat in those days. He had only been sixteen when that had happened. He was too young to be in a saloon, but he had been a wild boy.

And then abruptly, he thought suddenly of his brother Matthew.

Four years older, Matt had been steady and the pride of his father's heart. Matthew had wanted to be a lawyer, but left school to join the army. He had served with his father, becoming a captain, but had been killed at Cold Harbor. Not only had Matthew died, but some of his father died with him. Ben had always realized that. Now he thought of Matthew and wondered why it was that he, Ben, was left, the profligate, the jailbird, while Matthew, the upstanding citizen and pride of his family, had been shot down in a senseless battle.

Driver stood there staring down into the amber liquid, taking it in sips. The liquor hit his stomach quickly, burning its way down. And by the time he had finished the second glass, when he had tapped the glass on the surface of the bar, there was a numbing sound, and he knew that he did not need anything more to drink. He reached into his pocket, pulled out the one dollar that was left, and then looked across the room. He had been watching, intermittently, a blackjack game dealt by a short fat man with a red face and a pair of cold blue eyes.

Might as well try it. He moved over to the table and sat down.

"Howdy. My name's Chandler."

"Ben Driver."

"Glad to know you. New in town?"

"Yes. Pretty new."

"You want to take your try?"

Driver was good at poker, but blackjack was not his game. A dollar was not enough to get into a poker game, however, so he nodded.

He looked at the nine on top and when he turned it over he found another nine. "I'll stand on these."

"I'll take another." Chandler turned the card over and shrugged. "You win."

"Let it ride."

Once again the dealer busted himself, so now Driver's wealth had grown to four dollars. He played one, lost, and then played two and won.

He began to pay more attention. He needed a stake, and aside from robbery the only way he knew how to get it was gambling. He settled down in his chair, his green eye fixed on the cards and on Chandler's expressionless face. Finally he said, "This is pretty slow. How about a hand of poker?"

"Suits me."

They gathered a group of four other men. Driver won the first two hands, lost a small pot, then won three in a row. *Maybe my luck is changing,* he mused. He bought another drink, leaned forward, and put his mind on the game.

Glancing at his next hand, Driver said, "I'll stand fast."

The man to his left studied Driver, then threw his hand in. "I'm not chancing it."

The other, a tall dignified man, said, "I'll take one card." He took the card, and a flicker of disgust washed across his face. He was not a good poker player, which Driver soon discovered. There were, in fact, only two good poker players—Driver himself and a man called Ridley. Ridley was a young man no more than twenty, Driver guessed, but he had sharp gray eyes and played his cards well. His stack was about the same as Ben's. The two were winners, the others were losers.

Ben had drunk more than he should. Because he was still thin, the liquor hit him hard.

The game went on, with Ben winning. Finally he turned to find Sam standing beside him, disapproval on his face.

"Hello, Sam. Sit down. I'll relieve you of some of your money."

"Time to go, Ben."

Driver snapped, "Don't tell me what to do, Sam!"

Sam frowned, but he shrugged and backed off. "All right. It ain't none of my business."

"That's right." Driver turned back to his cards.

Sam interrupted again. "Reisa and Dov saved your life. Don't that give you no ideas?"

Driver held fast. "If you don't like it, get out!"

Sam left the room in disgust. But for Driver the fun had gone out of the game. The others were watching him, and he said, "I'll raise ten dollars."

"Too rich for me," Ridley said. "I think you're bluffing, but I'm not going to lose money on it."

The others dropped out, all except a roughly dressed man named Nance who was down to his last chip. "I ain't got the money, but I got a pair of mules that I'll put up."

"What kind of mules?"

"Steady mules," Nance said. "Young. About five years old, both of 'em in their prime. I got you beat this time, Driver. You'll never see them mules."

"I call your bet."

He laid down his hand, which was three of a kind, but Driver laid down four of a kind. "Game's over. I've had enough."

Ridley protested. "You've got to give us a chance to win some of that money back."

"You had your chance," Driver said. "Come on, Nance, introduce me to those mules."

Nance grinned at him broadly. "Happiest day of my life to get rid of them mules."

"They sick or broke down?"

"No, they ain't. They're strong, but they're the meanest pair I ever had in my life!"

Nance led Driver to the stable where he had left the mules and turned over their reins. When one mule tried to bite him and one tried to kick him, he found out that Nance had spoken the truth—both mules were as mean and treacherous as it was possible for animals to be. But they were healthy, strong, and in fine condition. He'd find some way to control them.

Reisa's face came to him, and he thought of how she had murmured wistfully of her dream to have a team and a wagon. Acting on impulse, Ben took some of his cash and purchased a wagon from the stable owner. It took all his money, but he had a team and a wagon.

Finally, with the help of the stable owner, Ben wrestled the two mules into harness. The liquor slowed down his reflexes, and he was breathing hard by the time he succeeded.

Climbing up on the seat, he nodded. "Much obliged."

"Watch out for them critters," the stable owner said, handing him the reins. "I've knowed mules to be good for five years just to get a chance to kick a fella once."

"Sure."

Driver held the lines firmly, and as expected the mules tried to bolt. He leaned back and pulled their heads cruelly, but it took all his strength to get them to stop.

That struggle was continued all the way back to the house. By the time he pulled up, he was exhausted. He drew up in front of the house and sat there staring at the mules.

Reisa came out of the house at once, her eyes shining, and she started for the mules.

"Stay away from those animals!" Driver called out sharply. "They'll bite a plug out of you!"

Reisa stopped reluctantly. As Ben held the mules, she called, "Ben, where did you get them?"

"Won 'em in a poker game and bought the wagon with the rest of the money. Now you got what you wanted."

Reisa came near the wagon. Driver held the mules carefully, as they were still full of life and meanness. "Oh, it's wonderful! Now we can start fixing it up."

"Fixing it up!" Driver said in confusion. The liquor had worn off, but he was at the end of his strength. "What do you mean, fixing it up?"

"Oh, we'll have to fix the compartments in it. I told you about that," she cried excitedly. "But we can do it!"

"Do it with *what?* If you got it fixed up, you won't have any money to stock it with. I don't have a dime left."

Ben looked down, and Reisa's face filled his vision. She had a marvelous expression of gaiety in her eyes, and somehow a provocative challenge. As her quick breathing disturbed her breast and color ran freshly across her cheeks, he knew that this woman had something for him that no other woman had ever had.

"All right," Driver said with resignation. He looked up and, seeing Dov, said, "Dov, go up and see if you can hang onto the heads of these two critters. If they fool with you, bust 'em in the nose." He waited until Dov had the mules in hand before he climbed from the wagon.

Close now to Reisa, he looked into her sparkling eyes, noted her excitement, and suddenly, for the first time in many years, felt good that something had gone right.

"I don't know how we'll do it, Reisa," Ben said. "But somehow I know you'll find a way."

"God will give us what we need," she stated confidently.

Seventeen

A week had passed since Ben had brought the mules and wagon from town. He had spent a great deal of time trying to gentle the pair, but with little success. Still a little peeved at Ben for his gambling, Sam had enjoyed watching Ben's struggles hugely.

One day Jacob and Sam sat out on the front porch enjoying the breeze. Inside they could hear the sounds of Phineas playing his violin for Dov, and from far off came the cry of a pack of hounds pursuing something. "The New Year's coming up," Jacob said.

"New Year? Whatcha talking about, Jacob? It's only September!"

"I'm talking about the Jewish New Year, Sam. It doesn't always fall exactly on the same calendar date, but the first days of our New Year are called the Days of Awe. And days one and two are called Rosh Hashanah."

"Well, I'll be dipped!" Sam said. "I just figured we had the same calendar."

"No. Ours is somewhat different. On the tenth day we celebrate Yom Kippur."

"And what's that for?"

"That's the Day of Atonement. Probably, to many of us, the most important day of all."

Sam listened as Jacob explained the meaning of the holy days, and finally he said, "Well, you can't have much of a celebration out here in the back side of nowhere."

"No. I would like very much to go to a synagogue. I miss meeting with my people."

Sam scratched his head so hard that his eyes were pulled together. "Well, drat it, I don't know why you can't! There's a synagogue in Richmond, ain't they?"

"So I've heard, but I've never been there."

"Well, I've heard it, too, so we're gonna up and go. How about today?"

Jacob was shocked. In all truth he had no thought whatsoever of going to Richmond, but now that Sam had brought it up, he began thinking about it. "But it's a long trip."

"Why, it ain't no piece." Sam shook his head. "We got that wagon and that team of mules." A sly grin touched his lips, and he said, "Of course, that wagon and team is probably the way to sin, seein' as how Ben won 'em at a poker game. You don't reckon it would unsanctify you to ride in such a sinful thing, do you?"

"I do not think that would be a problem, but can it be done?"

Sam leaped up and ran inside. He stopped to tell Reisa what her grandfather wanted, and she was very pleased. "Oh, it would be wonderful, Sam, but can we do it?"

"You go get yourself all prettied up and get your grandpa ready. I'll have Ben hook up them mules, and I'll go along with you. I always wanted to go to that synagogue, but I never had the nerve to do it by myself."

When Sam broached the idea of driving Jacob and Reisa to Richmond to worship at the synagogue, Ben seemed surprised. He thought for a moment, then shrugged. "Well, they may get ready in ten minutes, but it'll take longer than that to get those ornery mules hooked up."

"I kind of like the names Miss Reisa gave 'em. Samson and Delilah. Don't you?"

"I've called 'em a lot worse." Ben grinned. Then he said, "I'd better go get a two-by-four in case I have to persuade them a little bit."

Nevertheless, in less than an hour the party left. Nobody but Ben could handle Samson and Delilah. He had rigged a buggy whip and could reach out and snap it so that it touched their sensitive ears when they tried to get rambunctious.

"Them mules is just like a woman, Ben," Sam said. He was sitting in the backseat with Reisa, and he winked at her. "A little correction every now and then does 'em good."

Reisa made a face at him, but clearly she was happy. Jacob, too, looked better than he had in days. Evidently he had missed the ceremonies of the synagogue.

Reisa leaned over, put her arm around Sam, and gave him a hug. "You're an angel, Sam."

"Well, I've been called lots of things, but never an angel. But I'm right glad you think so, Miss Reisa."

They reached town, and as they entered the synagogue Rabbi Eli Altschul welcomed the party with a broad smile. He did not fit the typical image of a rabbi, for he was a powerfully built man with a head of thick black hair and large brown eyes. He had a determined chin and a slight hook to his nose, and as the spiritual leader of the small community of Jews in Richmond, he greeted the visitors royally.

As they prepared for the service, he asked Jacob, "You were a teacher of Hebrew in the Old Country?"

"Yes, I was," Jacob replied.

"We could use a man like you in this synagogue. I'm ashamed to say that some of our young people have begun to follow the Reform Movement, turning away from the old ways."

"I'm afraid I won't be able to help a great deal, but whatever I can I will do." Jacob hesitated, then held out a box that he had brought with him. "I thought this might be interesting to you, Rabbi."

Altschul took the box, opened it, and exclaimed, "A shofar, and it looks very old."

"I was told it came from the Holy Land itself from the very shadow of the Temple. It has been my most prized possession for many years."

"Indeed! I must prevail upon you to do the honor."

Blowing the shofar, which was a ram's horn, was one of the traditions associated with Rosh Hashanah. There was no explanation in the Torah for what blowing the horn meant, but most rabbis arrived at the conclusion that it was to wake the slumbering conscience. Others said it called the people to war against evil.

In any case, when the service began, Driver and Sam sat with the men, while Reisa sat with the women, as the custom was. There were no more than thirty people in the synagogue. At least ten men were required, and there were fourteen including the rabbi.

Lifting the shofar to his lips, Jacob began to blow. First he blew a loud clear blast which was called the *tekaiah.* Then when that faded away, he blew a series of three short notes called the *shevarim.* Finally he blew a quick staccato series of nine short notes in a row, which was called a *teruah.*

Jacob bowed to the congregation, and there were murmurs of appreciation. He took his seat, and the sermon went on, which included many Bible readings and songs which neither Driver nor Sam could understand because they were in Hebrew. Many of the songs were sung by a cantor, a young man with jet black hair and liquid brown eyes, whose voice was as clear as a striking bell.

Finally the service was over. As they left the building, Ben murmured to Sam, "I didn't understand much about that service, but it did Jacob and Reisa a lot of good."

They passed out into the sunlight and walked down to the street where Driver had hitched the team. They were only ten feet away when three men suddenly came out of a saloon. At once Driver drew himself up.

The leader of the three was not a tall man, but he was massively built. His head was joined onto his body with a neck so thick it was impossible to tell where it began or where it left off. His lips were thick, and his eyes an odd color, more hazel than anything else. His face changed, and he suddenly moved to stand in front of Driver. "Well, look who's back in town. I heard you got out."

"Hello, Fears."

"Don't reckon you know this fella, Alf." He turned to a tall, lanky man with cold blue eyes and a mouth like a catfish. "This here's Ben Driver, the great soldier. He won the war all by himself. Ain't that right, Ben?"

Driver did not answer. His glance flickered over the three, and he nodded to the smallest of the trio. "Hello, Vic."

"Hello, Driver." Vic Giles, undersized with light brown hair and blue eyes, wore a forty-four prominently displayed on his hip. It had a pearl handle, and the holster was of exquisitely tooled leather. "When did you get out of jail?"

Driver was not looking at Reisa, but he could sense her stirring at the threatening tone in the man's voice. He didn't want to bring her or the rest of them into this, so he kept his voice carefully neutral. "How have you been, Vic?"

Honey Fears said, "You're lookin' peaked. They didn't treat you good up at the pen, I reckon."

"It was all right." Driver kept his eye fixed on Fears. The man was a bruiser and was the bully of the county. He had whipped every man that had ever come up against him, often breaking them up so badly that they never recovered. He had kicked one man to death in a fight years before. He had also been the leader of a group of wild young men, and it was this same group—of which Driver was a part—that had robbed the store. Fears and the others had escaped, and Driver alone had taken the fall. He had never identified the others, but he saw now that this made no difference to Fears.

Driver waited for Fears to speak, but the big man merely shoved his way through the small group. "Come on. It looks like the fighting Ben Driver's been tamed. They say the state pen does that for some fellows."

The three left, and Driver did not speak. Sam helped Jacob in and then Reisa, then climbed in himself. Driver unhitched the mules and with a quick bound got into the seat. They reared up as they often did, but he jerked them back. "Delilah—Samson, behave!"

The ride out of town was rather quiet. Finally Sam spoke up. "I don't know how that Fears fellow stayed out of jail. Maybe because he's a friend of Vic."

"Why would that keep him out of jail?" Reisa asked.

"Because that's Vic Giles. The little one with the gun. His daddy is Sheriff Charlie Giles." Sam shook his head in utter disgust. "Them three have been into everything for the last three to four years, but they never get hauled up. Everybody's scared of Honey Fears."

"What about his friend, the one they call Alf?"

"That's Alf Despain. He killed two black men and one white man. Never got convicted neither. Should have been, though."

Driver bit his tongue and said nothing.

The following day, Driver was in a dark mood. He remained quiet, staying out in the woods with Dov hunting. Late in the afternoon he brought back a sack full of squirrels which he carried, and Dov carried over his broad shoulders the carcass of a large ten-point buck.

As Phineas helped with the dressing of the meat, he said to Ben, "You must be the world's greatest shot. Look at these squirrels. Every one of 'em shot in the head. And I keep up with the shells. You never miss!" He shook his head in wonder. "Beats me how a one-eyed man can do that!"

Ben Driver smiled slightly for the first time all day, but all he said was, "I noticed yesterday that the mules need to be shod. Don't know where I'll get the money for it, though."

Phineas nodded. "Something'll turn up," he said.

Hilda Swenson was sitting beside her mother. Hilda was sewing, and Mrs. Emma Swenson was listening as Hilda spoke from time to time. Mrs. Swenson was a frail woman of sixty-four with white hair and faded blue eyes. Her health had deteriorated a great deal in the past year so that now she had to walk painfully with a cane. She also had memory lapses which troubled her a great deal.

Hilda broke off suddenly, for a knock had sounded at the door. "Who could that be, Mama?" she said.

"I don't know. You'd better go see."

Laying the sewing aside, Hilda moved toward the door. She was wearing overalls, as usual, but her long blonde hair was tied at the nape of her neck and came halfway down to her waist. When she opened the door, she blinked with surprise. "Well, hello, Dov," she said.

"Miss Hilda." Dov nodded. "Ben kill a deer, and I think you like some fresh meat."

Hilda kept her head turned to one side to conceal the scar, but she smiled. The simple smile made her look much younger and changed her whole appearance. "Come in. I'll put the meat where the flies can't get at it."

Dov had to stoop to get through the rather low doorway, and he stood there until Hilda returned.

"My mother would like to meet you."

Dov followed Hilda into a well-furnished, large, airy room with high windows.

"This is my mother. And this is Dov Puskin."

Mrs. Swenson smiled. "I'm happy to know you." She still had a Swedish accent after so many years, for both she and her husband had come to this country speaking no English at all. "My daughter has told me how much you helped her with the wagon. It was very good of you."

Dov smiled and nodded at the frail woman. "Your daughter works hard. I glad to help. My English bad."

"No worse than mine when we first came here. Tell me about yourself, Mr. Puskin."

Dov waved his massive hand. "Please. Just Dov." He smiled, and his teeth were very white against his swarthy skin and black beard. "That mean *bear* in Russian. People say I like bear."

Hilda said, "Please take a chair, Dov. I've fixed some tea, and we have sweet cakes."

Dov did not protest, and the women watched—Hilda with some amusement—as he drank cup after cup of tea and fairly demolished the sweet cake.

"Good!" he exclaimed. "You make?"

"Yes. I made them."

"You good cook."

Hilda Swenson sat back in her chair, not knowing exactly how to treat this man. She and her mother had few friends although, of course, she knew all the people in the neighborhood. She attended church, but this huge man was different from any man she knew. For one thing, he made her feel small! She was accustomed to towering over most men and being broader than all except the huskiest. As a result she had given up feminine ways long ago.

Now she mostly sat and listened as Dov entertained them with stories of Russia.

Finally Dov stood up and bowed slightly. "I go now."

"I'll show you out," Hilda said quickly.

Dov bowed again and said good-bye to Mrs. Swenson. He followed Hilda outside and then stopped as they stepped off the porch. "You have some work I can do?"

Hilda chewed her lower lip. She thought for a minute and then said, "Well, I can do most of the things, but I'm not a blacksmith. My father was, though. There are some metal things that need to be done. I have to take them into town to the blacksmith."

"Show me."

Hilda led the smiling giant to the barn, which turned out to be a fully equipped blacksmith shop. It had not been used for a long time, but Dov suddenly laughed. His laughter startled Hilda, for it was booming but quite merry.

"Guess what I do in Russia?"

Hilda's eyes flew open. "You weren't a blacksmith, were you, Dov?"

"Best blacksmith in my village." He laughed again. "I the *only* one in my village, too." He looked around and said, "You have good place. I fix what is broken."

It turned out to be a fine day for Hilda. Dov fired up the forge, and she helped with the bellows. She had the material on hand, and he fixed those small items which she had been unable to do. Finally he shoed both of her horses. He was quick, expert, and so strong that the horses had no chance at all.

Finally it was growing dark, and Dov said, "I go now."

Hilda did not know how to thank him. Finally she put out her hand as a man would. It was swallowed up by Dov's massive paw, and she felt the power in the grip, although he was holding her hand gently. He did not turn her loose, and when she looked up into his eyes, she saw that they were studying her carefully.

"I thank you, Dov. Anytime your friends need any blacksmithing done, feel free to come and use my father's equipment."

Dov still held onto her hand. It was firm and hard and muscular. He seemed about to say something, but stopped himself. He squeezed her hand once, then nodded. "Good-bye, Miss Hilda."

Hilda Swenson watched the big man as he made his way, taking long, firm strides down the road. She watched until he disappeared around the group of pines that marked the road. Even then she stood. "He's so big and so kind," she whispered. "I've never known a man like him."

Eighteen

Would you have some more tea, *Zaideh?* Or maybe some coffee?"

"Tea would be nice."

Reisa rose from the kitchen table where the two were sitting, moving quickly to the stove. She heated the water, and when it was boiling she poured it into a pan, added the tea, then came to sit down across from Jacob. "It's so quiet around here. Usually it's noisy, but with everyone gone it seems almost strange."

Driver and Dov had left early to take the new mules over and get them shod at the Swenson place. Dov had told them about the blacksmithing tools, and Driver had said, "We've got to get those mules shod and right away." They had left right after breakfast. Phineas had gone to borrow some lime from a neighbor, and Sam had gone fishing down at the river.

As Jacob picked up his tea, Reisa noticed how thin his hands seemed. He had always been a spare man, but now he seemed almost emaciated. A coldness came to her as the thought pressed itself on her mind, *He's going to die soon.* It was a fear that had come to her often of late, and now she shook her head slightly and sipped her tea.

Jacob looked around the room and turned to face Reisa. "We've come a long way from Russia." He spoke in Russian, for the two often used that language when they were alone.

"Yes, we have. I think often of how strange it is to be in this place."

"We had little choice, but I still miss our friends back in our village. I fear that many of them have suffered from the government."

Reisa did not answer. She looked down into the teacup and was silent for so long that Jacob lifted his eyes and studied her. After a moment, he said, "What's wrong, Granddaughter?"

"Nothing."

"Come now, something is troubling you. Do you think I don't know when my granddaughter is having a problem? What is it?"

"I have been troubled about something," Reisa said reluctantly. "But I didn't want to trouble you about it. "

"Gai shoyn, gai." Jacob lapsed into Yiddish, then shook his head and returned to speaking Russian. "Don't be silly," he interpreted his own words. "What are we for if not to lean upon one another? You and I, we ought never to hold back anything from each other. Sometimes we take our troubles and put them in a large box and lock them up, hoping they will go away. But we know all the time that they're still there. Now, my Reisa—" And here Jacob reached over and put his hand on her arm. "Unlock the box where your troubles are and give them to me. Does not the Scripture say that two are better than one?"

Jacob's words brought a tremulous smile to Reisa's lips. "You are right, but it is hard sometimes to know when we're being a burden with our troubles."

"Tell me. What is it?"

"Do you remember I told you of the Christians on the *Jennings* when we came over the ocean?"

"Yes. You've mentioned them many times."

"I have thought of them often—of their fearlessness. How much faith they must have had to be so joyous even when the storm was at its worst."

"Yes." Jacob nodded quickly. "That is something I admire as well."

"There's one thing I didn't tell you. For some reason, I thought you might be displeased if you knew it."

"That is not likely, my Reisa."

"As I was leaving the ship, the leader of the Christians gave me a gift. It was wrapped in an oilcloth for protection, and I barely had time to thank him. He said it had been a great treasure to him, and that God told him that it would now be a great treasure to me."

"That must have been encouraging to you, and it was a fine gesture."

"Yes, I was grateful, but after I saw what the present was I wasn't so sure."

"And what was it?"

"Just a minute. I'll go get it for you." Rising, Reisa went into her room, picked up the gospel of John, and brought it back. When she sat down again, she put it before Jacob and waited as he picked it up. She saw him look at the first page where the title was and then leaf through it.

"This is part of the Christian New Testament," Jacob said.

"Yes. It's called the gospel of John. I do not know exactly what *gospel* means, but it was written by a man called John, and it's about Jesus."

"And why did you think I would be troubled?"

Reisa shifted uneasily. "Because I know that our people have been treated terribly by some who call themselves Christians."

"And there are some who call themselves Jews that are not what they should be. It is not only Christians who have their evil men and women."

Seeing that Jacob was not angry, Reisa grew more talkative. "It is a strange book. I do not know what to make of parts of it, but there is one thing that surprised me greatly about the book."

"I think I can guess what it is."

"You can?"

"Yes." Jacob nodded. "You are drawn to the man called Jesus."

Reisa's eyes flew open with astonishment. "Yes. How did you know?"

"Because Sam has been reading to me from his Bible. Some of the passages concern Jesus, and like you, I have felt a strange admiration for him."

"But, *Zaideh,* it cannot be, can it? All that this book says?"

"I have been thinking much about this. I think our friend Sam has been a great influence on me, and on you, too, perhaps. He is such a good man! He lives for God. His ways are rough, and his speech is crude at times, but there is a love for God that burns within him like a flame."

"Yes, *Zaideh,* that is true. I have seen it myself."

Jacob bowed his head and thought for a moment. A silence fell over the room so all that could be heard was the friendly ticking of the clock up on the mantel. Finally Jacob lifted his head, and there was trouble in his eyes. "The Christians believe that Jesus is the Messiah, and they believe that the Old Testament points to this."

"Yes. I have read many times in this book of John where the writer would point out that Jesus fulfilled a prophecy concerning the Messiah."

"Sam knows a great many things about these prophecies, and I have been surprised at how many there are."

"What have you found?"

"Well, a prophecy said that the Messiah was to be born in Bethlehem, and Jesus was born in Bethlehem. Another prophecy says that he would go down to Egypt, and according to their Scripture the parents of Jesus took him to Egypt. The Messiah, as you well know, was to be born of the tribe of Judah, and both of his parents were born of that tribe." He continued for some time naming off various prophecies. Evidently Sam had impressed him much, and finally he paused and was silent.

"I did not know all of that, and I am not qualified to judge the Scripture, for I do not have your learning, *Zaideh*. But I know one thing—when I read of how Jesus loved people, and how good he was to them, I cannot help but—" She broke off and could not finish.

"You were going to say you cannot help but love him?"

"Maybe that is wrong, *Zaideh.* I know many wrongs have been committed by his followers. But I do not believe that Jesus would have done such awful things. Listen to this: 'And the scribes and Pharisees brought unto him a woman taken in adultery; and when they had set her in the midst, They say unto him, Master, this woman was taken in adultery, in the very act. Now Moses in the law commanded us, that such should be stoned: but what sayest thou? This they said, tempting him, that they might have to accuse him. But Jesus stooped down, and with his finger wrote on the ground, as though he heard them not. So when they continued asking him, he lifted up himself, and said unto them, He that is without sin among you, let him first cast a stone at her. And again he stooped down and wrote on the ground. And they which heard it, being convicted by their own conscience, went out one by one, beginning at the eldest, even unto the last: and Jesus was left alone, and the woman standing in the midst. When Jesus had lifted up himself, and saw none but the woman, he said unto her, Woman where are those thine accusers? hath no man condemned thee? She said, no man Lord. And Jesus said unto her, Neither do I condemn thee: go, and sin no more.'"

Reisa looked up, and tears glistened in her eyes. "Is that not wonderful, *Zaideh?*"

"Yes, indeed. I have not heard that particular story."

"It is so dramatic, this gospel of John! I can almost *see* it happening. Those awful men with their hard eyes who want to kill Jesus. And they bring this poor woman in, a sinner no doubt. But, *Zaideh*. . ." At this point Reisa clasped her fists together, and her eyes flashed. "If she was taken in adultery, there must have been a man, no? Where is the man? Why didn't they bring *him* to Jesus?"

"I see your point. Obviously they want to force Jesus to pronounce judgment on the woman. And, indeed, Moses' Law did say that one taken like that should be killed."

"But that would be so cruel, wouldn't it?"

"The Law is cruel in a way, Reisa. The judgment of God against sin is cruel. We cannot forget that."

Reisa struggled for a moment, seemingly unable to find the words, then she said, "But Jesus did. He forgave her."

"Yes, and he was entirely correct when he said, 'He that is without sin cast the first stone,' for all of us are sinners, Reisa. The Scripture says all have sinned, and that is very plain in the Law." Then he said, "It is strange how the men who brought that poor woman all left. I wonder what it was he wrote in the dust of the ground?"

"I have thought that perhaps he wrote the names of some of the men that had brought the woman. Perhaps he wrote their sins in the dust."

Jacob smiled faintly. "It may be. In any case, their consciences condemned them, and they left. It is a dramatic scene, and exactly the sort of thing that would draw any decent man or woman to Jesus."

Reisa put her finger on a verse. "The next verse says, 'Then spake Jesus again unto to them, saying, I am the light of the world: he that followeth me shall not walk in darkness, but shall have the light of life.'"

"What a strange saying! Sam read me a verse yesterday from the Christian Bible in which Jesus said, 'No man cometh under the Father, but by me.'" He shook his head saying, "How can that be true?"

"It cannot be—unless Jesus was who he said he was."

For some time the two sat there speaking about the words of Jesus. Finally she said, "I have read the last part of this book many times. It describes how Jesus died. *Zaideh,* I can never read it without weeping! They beat him with a whip. They shoved a crown of thorns on his head. They spit in his face. They mocked him, and yet he never said one word to them."

"I know. Sam has read it to me."

"And one verse stays with me. I cannot forget it. As Jesus was on the cross dying, he said, 'Father, forgive them; for they know not what they do.' That verse rings like a bell in my mind, *Zaideh*. It is not the cry of a man consumed with hatred for his enemies, as most of us would be. It is ultimate love, and that is why I have thought so hard on all of these things. Listen to this: the Bible says that after Jesus was dead, 'Then came the soldiers, and brake the legs of the first, and of the other which was crucified with him. But when they came to Jesus, and saw that he was dead already, they brake not his legs; But one of the soldiers with a spear pierced his side, and forthwith came there out blood and water. And he that saw it bare record, and his record is true: and he knoweth that he saith true, that ye might believe. For these things were done, that the scripture should be fulfilled, A bone of him shall not be broken. And again another scripture saith, They shall look on him whom they pierced.'"

"Is that true, *Zaideh?*" Reisa asked. "Does the Law say that the Messiah will be pierced and that not a bone of him would be broken?"

"It says so indeed."

Reisa whispered, "It is strange, is it not?"

"Yes. And even more strange is that which follows."

"You mean the story that says that Jesus rose from the dead?"

"Yes. That is what I mean. If Jesus rose from the dead, then indeed he must be the Messiah, the Son of God."

Reisa gasped. "But—that goes against all of our religion."

"Not against all of it. From what Sam has told me, Jesus honored the Law of Moses always."

"But how can all this be?"

"I cannot say, but my heart has been troubled for days now. And I see that you are troubled as well, but we must trust God. Whatever the truth is, that is what we want."

Reisa reached over and grasped Jacob's arm. Squeezing it hard, she said, "But how are we to know?"

"How does any man know the truth? He seeks God, and God will give it to him. That is what I'm doing now, my granddaughter. Seeking God for the truth."

"Then I will seek the truth also, *Zaideh.*"

Nineteen

A cold wind whistled around the house that evening, but the group sitting around the table paid no heed to it. The stove had warmed the kitchen, and the food on the table sent a delicious odor that filled the room. Reisa had cooked a Jewish dinner using the fish that Sam had caught. She had stuffed them with chopped onions and seasoning and cooked them in salt water. There was a cold spinach soup that she called *tshav* that had astonished Phineas, who had sworn nothing good could be made out of spinach. It was delicious, however, and it disappeared quickly. She made *grieven*, fried chicken skin, which surprised Sam. "I usually throw the skin away and eat what's under it," he remarked. "But this is mighty good." She also made a bread suet pudding with raisins, which was called *kugel*.

Phineas had made pumpkin pie, which neither Reisa nor Jacob had ever eaten before.

"Why, this is delicious, Phineas," Reisa said. "You're a fine cook."

Phineas shrugged. "Do the best I can with what I got."

Sam bragged on all the food and then remarked, "Sure was better than what we got in the army, wasn't it, Ben?"

"Better than anything I ever got," Ben said.

Sam turned to Phineas, and the two talked for a while about their experiences in the army. Neither of them seemed to be particularly bitter, having apparently been able to put the war behind them. Sam mentioned the Battle of Antietam. "You wasn't there, Phineas, but it was the worst." He turned and asked, "Were you at Antietam, Ben?"

"Yes."

"Was it as bad as they say it was?"

Driver did not answer for a moment, and Reisa saw that he did not like to talk about it. But to the surprise of everyone, he began speaking of that time. "I never quite understood what General Lee had on his mind at that time," he said quietly. "I guess men have been arguing ever since the battle about why he stayed on there to fight when he was so badly outnumbered. We was worn down to nothin'. I think altogether we wouldn't have had forty thousand men, and we knew McClellan had nearly ninety thousand and more comin' up. And yet General Lee decided to stay and fight. I remember talking with a lieutenant, one of the smartest officers I ever saw, who loved Lee. He said it was a mistake, but he told me not to tell anybody else."

Leaning forward on the table, Driver locked his hands together, seeming to gather his thoughts. The planes of his face were highlighted by the oil lamp. He had filled out since his sickness, and Reisa, as she watched him, saw that his shoulders and arms were stronger, for he had picked up some muscle.

"We was sure a ragtag bunch. I don't think any of us had on any underclothes. All I had was a ragged pair of pants and a stained jacket and an old slouch hat with the brim pinned up with a thorn. I was carryin' a grimy blanket over my shoulder, a grease-smeared haversack full of apples and corn, my cartridge box, and a musket. I was barefoot, too, as many of our men were, and I had stone bruises on both feet. I think we'd been run in by the police if we had appeared on the streets of any city. We sure weren't much to look at!

"I remember we got there, and it was a beautiful day. Antietam Creek was all that separated our armies. We could look across sometimes and see the blue, and we knew they would be comin' at us."

"I heard Stonewall took care of a lot of those Yankees," Sam said.

"Yes, he did. Once I was close enough to reach out and touch him. He was suckin' on a lemon, and from time to time he would hold his right hand up in the air." Driver smiled. "He said it equalized his blood or somethin' like that. Strange man, Jackson. Calm and quiet when there was peace. But when the battle came his eyes blazed, and he was a cold killer. They called him 'Old Blue Light' because of those eyes.

"Well, there we sat on the side of a big cornfield with stalks higher than a man's head."

"Yep, I was with Jeb Stuart over on the flank." Sam nodded. "I remember that real well. There was open pasture rolling off to the hills. I never will forget that whitewashed Dunker church out in the open grove of trees."

"That's what it was like." Driver nodded. "I remember our lieutenant got us all in a line in that cornfield because we knew that an attack would come through there. We heard that Hooker was going to lead it. They called him Fighting Joe Hooker. He was a fighter that day, all right! He put three dozen field pieces on a low ridge, and he had the gunners blast that cornfield out. It laid it level, and most of us that were in it either got killed or had to back off."

"I heard them guns," Sam said. "It sounded like the world was comin' to an end."

"Well, finally the attack came, and it was rough. They pushed us back—all the way back to that Dunker church where Jackson had some of his infantry." He smiled. "The Yankees were about to overrun us when John B. Hood from Texas sent his men into action. They were mad as hornets because just when they were cookin' their first really good breakfast in a week, they had to leave. Well, they came runnin' in there and formed a line.

I never saw such volleys! It tore that Federal column all apart. All of us were screamin' and yellin', and then D. H. Hall came in and run 'em off."

Everyone waited for Driver to finish. He said slowly, "I never saw anything like that cornfield. You could have walked across it on the bodies of men, theirs and ours, without touchin' the ground. I went over that battlefield later, and the bodies were so swollen and black, covered with dust and crushed, that they looked more like clods of earth. Had to look twice to be sure they were human bein's."

Apparently that was all of the story, and Dov, who had been listening, said, "Did you win the battle?"

"Well, they didn't run us off, but we lost a fourth of our army, Dov. The worst day of the whole war. I learned one thing, though. We had always said one Confederate could whip four Yankees. I found out different that day, all right. Those boys in blue fought like men possessed. Charged right into us. I never believed after that that we had a chance. There were too many of 'em, and they were just as determined to win as we were."

Suddenly Driver looked up and laughed shortly. "Always swore I'd never be one of those veterans sittin' around lyin' about how they won battles. I'm gettin' talkative in my old age."

He lapsed into a long silence. Then, his voice quieter, he asked, "How does God let things like that happen?"

Sam said, "You can't blame God for what men do."

"That is right, my son." Jacob nodded. "Man is evil, but it was not God who made him so."

Reisa saw that Driver was disturbed by his memories and changed the subject. "We're all going into town tomorrow for the celebration."

"What celebration?" Dov asked.

"Didn't I tell ya?" Sam said. "Why, it's Founder's Day. I can't even remember the feller's name, but every year everybody in the whole county comes. They have all kinds of contests, runnin' and wrestlin' and horse races. All kinds of food. They get some acts sometimes to come—tumblers and circus folks and like that."

"Good excuse for people to get drunk." Phineas sniffed.

"You got to go this year, Phineas," Sam said. "You ain't been out of this house in two months."

Phineas shrugged, but finally said, "I reckon I will. Somebody's got to be responsible for this bunch."

Later that night, Driver was reading, as usual. He'd borrowed a book called *Oliver Twist* from Phineas. Reisa came to sit across from him. She spoke up over the voices of Sam and her grandfather, who were once again discussing the Bible. "Do you like the book, Ben?"

"It's pretty grim. It's about an orphan that gets shoved around."

"I don't know why people write sad books."

"I guess because that's the way things are."

"But things are nice, too, sometimes. Like tonight. It's been such a good day. We got out and worked, and we had a good supper, and now everything is all right. Nobody's sick."

Closing the book, Driver looked across at her. After studying her for a moment, he said, "You always think things will turn out well, don't you?"

"I try to."

"I'm glad you think that way, Reisa," Ben said quietly. "And I hope you always will."

"I dreamed about a wagon and team, and I got them, didn't I?"

"Well, you got the wagon, but you don't have nothin' to go in it. You can't go out and sell anything with an empty wagon. I've heard you say that yourself."

"We'll get it. I believe that it will come."

Ben noted her shining eyes and smooth skin. "What does your hair look like?" he asked suddenly.

"What?" Reisa asked, surprised.

"I'd like to see your hair down sometime. It's always tied up under a scarf. It looks pretty, what I can see of it."

"It's black," Reisa said shortly.

"I can see that. How long is it?"

"Why do you care, Ben?"

"I don't know. Just that I'd like to see it. A pretty woman doesn't have any business hiding her beauty."

"Favor is deceitful and beauty is vain. That's in the Scripture."

"Nice to look at though." Ben grinned.

"Are you going into town tomorrow?"

"Yes. I've got to get some clothes to wear. I've worn out these old rags. Maybe I can get some credit at the store."

"I have money," she said. "After all, we're partners."

Ben studied her. "All right. Lend me ten dollars. I'll pay you back. Maybe I'll get in another poker game."

"No. Please don't do that."

"I won't, but I do need some work clothes."

"Will ten dollars be enough?"

"For what I need it will be."

As usual, Samson and Delilah gave Driver a hard battle. He fought them until finally all three of them wore themselves out. Dov finally came over, and with his mighty hands jerked Samson's head down and held him so tightly he could not lift it. "Now you be good," he said. Quickly Driver hitched the mule up, then Dov simply grabbed Delilah by the ear and led her out. She squealed and tried to kick, but when he twisted her ear, she uttered a pitiful cry. "You hush. I won't hurt you."

Driver hitched Delilah up and then grinned. "From now on this is a two-man job. I'm tired of these critters."

Driver got in the seat and drove the team out in front of the house. The others came out, and Reisa got in front with him. Jacob, Sam, and Phineas sat in the backseat, while Dov sat with his legs straight out in the wagon box, occupying nearly the whole width of the wagon.

The trip to town passed pleasantly enough. Phineas had brought his fiddle, for there would be musicians there, and he liked to play with them. He played many songs for them on the way. Once Dov called out, "Play the bean song, Phineas."

The bean song was sung by the Confederates. As Phineas had told them, they had often pooled their beans and baked them in a bean hole in the ground:

There's a spot that all soldiers love,
The mess tent's the place that we mean,
And the dish we best like to see there
Is the old-fashioned army bean.

As he swung into the chorus, Sam and Dov joined with him:

Tis the bean that we mean,
And we'll eat as we ne'er ate before.
The army bean nice and clean
We'll stick to our beans evermore.

There were many verses to this song, and finally they reached the last:

The German is fond of sauerkraut,
The potato is loved by the Mick,
But the soldiers have long since found out
That through life to our beans we should stick.

Then everybody joined in, even Driver, who had heard the song many times during his service.

Tis the bean that we mean,
And we'll eat as we ne'er ate before.

The army bean nice and clean
We'll stick to our beans evermore.

"I recollect that was the last song I sung in the army," Sam said. "We was trapped there at Appomattox, and we all seen our time was up. Every boy was feelin' pretty low, so I started up this song, and we sung it." He looked off into the distance and said, "Them was hard days, but somehow I miss 'em."

ↄ

As they pulled into town, Ben saw that it was crowded indeed. He drove down the main street and finally found a place to hitch the mules. He was helped by Dov, who got out and did some more ear twisting. Delilah squealed, but she stood still until they were firmly tied.

The whole party walked along together, and Sam and Phineas spoke to a great many people. Phineas was dragged away by a man with a banjo, and they all followed as he found his place with a small group already filling the air with song.

Driver listened, and from time to time he glanced down at Reisa. She was wearing her only good dress, which was light green. The color brought out the gray-green of her eyes, and he noted again the jet-black hair that crept out from beneath the scarf that she wore over it. He wished again that he could see it down her back, imagining how beautiful it must be.

They had been there only half an hour when suddenly Ben tensed. Reisa, who was standing beside Driver holding his arm, looked up at him.

"What's wrong, Ben?"

Ben couldn't tear his gaze away. Reisa, he knew, saw only a tall man and an attractive woman walking toward them. They were well-dressed, and as they approached he saw recognition come to both of them.

It was his parents.

His father said nothing—in fact, turned his head away. But his mother whispered as they passed, "Hello, Ben."

Ben returned her greeting but said no more.

"What a fine-looking couple," Reisa said. "Who are they? Do you know them?"

Ben turned, and his face was drawn. "My parents," he said in a tight voice.

"Oh, I didn't mean to pry."

The fun had gone out of the festival for Ben, but he shook it off. "I was bound to meet them sometime," he said. "Now that's over."

Rarely did Hilda Swenson attend anything such as a festival, but the neighbor from down the road had offered to stay with her mother, and she felt lonely. Loneliness was something that she knew how to handle, for she often felt that way. Nevertheless, the feeling seemed to be heavier than usual. So she donned her one dress, the one that she wore to church, and she exchanged her men's boots for shoes and made the trip to town driving her team.

For almost an hour she wandered around, pleased just to hear the music and to be with people. She was a woman who craved companionship and talk and music, but that had been taken out of life by her appearance—or so she thought. Now she simply enjoyed herself.

There had already been several races, and then she heard someone say, "The wrestling match is almost over. Let's go take them in."

She followed the crowd who had gathered at the edge of town where there was a slight hillock. The hill was full of people, and out in front was a large man with his shirt off. He was blonde haired, smiling, and his white teeth showed against his sunburned face. He was a powerful man with a deep chest and heavily muscled arms, yet he gave the appearance of swiftness.

"Hello, Hilda."

Taken off guard, Hilda turned quickly and found Reisa Dimitri, Ben Driver, and Dov Puskin approaching. Glad to see someone she knew, she said rather shyly, "Hello."

"Come to see the wrestling?" Ben smiled.

"Oh, I suppose so. He's a very strong-looking man."

"That's James Kincaid," Ben observed. "I grew up with him. He put us all on our back even though he was younger than we were. I thought I was something. He just picked me up, slammed me down like I was a baby. I think he's beat every man in the county now. Powerful man, and a good fellow, too."

At that moment a man stepped out wearing a light gray suit with a string tie and a white broad-brimmed hat. He called in a bull-like voice, "Well, I reckon it's about over, folks. James here has put every man that challenged him down. Looks like he's gonna win this nice heifer." He turned, and a young man wearing a straw hat came out leading a beautifully proportioned calf.

"Oh, she's beautiful!" Hilda said. "Isn't she beautiful, Reisa?"

"I think she is."

"You want calf?" Dov said suddenly.

Hilda's eyes blinked with surprise. "What did you say, Dov?"

"You like the calf?"

"Oh, yes."

"I get her for you." Without another word he strolled toward the contest, calling, "Wait! I will wrestle."

The crowd murmured, for indeed Dov Puskin was a sight to behold. He still wore the pants that he had worn from Russia now tucked in the top of his boots. He wore no hat, his black hair shone in the sunlight, and his beard covered his face.

"Look at the size of that fella," Hilda heard a man standing close beside her say. "Who is he anyway?"

"I don't know, but he looks big enough to give Kincaid a throw."

"He can't whip James Kincaid," the first man said firmly. "Nobody can."

Hilda watched as Dov approached the man apparently in charge. "I wrestle," he said.

"What's your name? I don't remember you."

"Dov Puskin. Come from Russia."

"This is for local folks."

A voice called out. It was Sam. "He's local. He stays with us, Franklin."

Franklin turned to the wrestler, who stood there eyeing Dov cautiously. "What do you say, James?"

"He'll have to take off that shirt. It'd get in my way," Kincaid said. There was confidence in his tone. He had never been beaten, and although the man was big, he had wrestled big men before. He knew all the holds, was lightning fast, and now he smiled and said to Dov, "Good luck to you."

Dov nodded. "God bless you, sir."

His mild words surprised Kincaid, and then Dov drew off his shirt. A murmur went around the crowd for, indeed, the massive trunk that seemed to swell upward ended in a pair of oak-like arms and a strong, firm neck that swelled out from his shoulders.

Mr. Franklin said, "You know the wrestlin' rules?"

"No," Dov said. "Tell me."

"No gouging."

"What is gouging?"

"You can't use your thumb to pull a man's eye out."

"No, God forbid!" Dov said, shocked by the idea.

"No biting."

Dov bared his white fangs. "Not even a little one?"

"None at all," Mr. Franklin said. "The man that gets pinned loses."

"What is pinned?"

"That means if this man can put your shoulders on the ground, he wins. If you can put his shoulders on the ground, you win."

"Da, I understand."

"All right." Franklin stepped back to the edge and said, "Start!"

Dov stood bolt upright, his dark eyes watching James Kincaid. He was perhaps the calmest man in the crowd, for there were bets being made now. It had been difficult to find anybody to take a bet against Kincaid, but now some offered two to one, and a few hardy souls chipped in.

"Give me that ten dollars you were going to give me for clothes, Reisa."

Reisa fished out the ten dollars, and Driver turned to the man. "Two to one on the Russian."

"Done." The tall man with a heavy cavalry mustache grinned. "You'll lose your money, son. Kincaid ain't as big, but he's strong and fast as a bolt of lightnin'."

"He put me on my back enough, but I feel he's about due for a lesson."

As for Hilda, her face flushed as she watched Dov. Kincaid slowly circled him, bent over in a crouch with his arms out. He made a feint at Dov, but Dov never moved. This, for some reason, disturbed the smaller man.

"He's never seen anybody like Dov before, Hilda," Driver said. "What he tries to do is to get a man to make a move at him—stick out an arm or something. When he does, he's a goner. Kincaid's so fast he can grab that arm and flip a man over his shoulder before you can blink."

Again and again Kincaid tried to feint the huge man before him out of his position. It all failed, however, and finally the crowd began to grow impatient. "Come on, Russian, do somethin'!"

Dov, despite the calls, did nothing. He simply turned slowly, his feet planted firmly on the ground.

Finally Kincaid saw that his tactics would not work. He moved so close that Dov stuck out both arms to catch him, and instantly Kincaid grabbed Dov's forearm. He turned himself and heaved—and that was when he got the biggest surprise of his life. Many a man he had thrown over his shoulder and pinned, but this was like trying to pull a tree. He gave a tremendous lunge, but Dov simply stood there.

And then suddenly Dov reached out and got his hands on James Kincaid. Kincaid struggled and fought, but Dov had him by the upper arms. He slowly began forcing Kincaid down, and Kincaid kicked and tried to throw Dov off balance. But it was no use. Inexorably Dov forced him down.

When Kincaid was on the ground, he held one shoulder up. Dov simply leaned his full weight on him until Kincaid could not hold him.

"Pinned! He pinned him!" Sam Hall yelled. "He wins!"

A cheer and applause went around, for while James Kincaid was a well-liked man, it was always good to see that a champion isn't absolutely unconquerable.

Franklin came out and slapped Dov on the back. "All right. Let him up. You win."

Dov rose and picked Kincaid up and set him on his feet. "You good man," he said. "Ver' strong."

Kincaid was a study in astonishment. He shook his head silently, then said loudly, "Me? I'm nothin' but a baby. I thought I was half a man at least. What's your name again?"

"Dov. Dov Puskin."

"Well, Dov, give me your hand. You're a better man than I am."

A cheer went up at Kincaid's good humor, and then Dov turned to the boy with the calf. He took the rope and led the calf to Hilda. Every eye was upon him as he handed her the rope. "Here, Miss Hilda. Your calf."

Hilda looked up at the big man, who now smiled down at her. Tears came to her eyes, and her lips quivered. She could not speak, for no one had ever done anything like this for her before.

She knelt and put her arm around the calf, burying her face against the silky hide. The calf twisted her head and turned to lick her in the face. Aware of the murmuring around her, she did not know what to do. She hated being looked at, and now half the people in the county were there.

When she rose, her eyes swept the crowd, and she saw many people smiling and heard them whispering. Taking a deep breath, she held out her hand, which was taken immediately. Dov's big paw enclosed hers and held it with a reassuring warmth. "It was—it was noble, Dov," she whispered. "No one ever did—such a thing for me."

He did not release her hand for a moment but squeezed it, exerting a fraction of his powerful strength. "Come. We will tie her to the back of your wagon."

The afternoon sped on, and finally it was Phineas who said, "I got me an idee. I'm tired of you goin' around lookin' like a ragged bum, Ben."

"Well, that's all right. I won some money on that wrestlin' contest."

"You need more than that. You can use some ready cash. You done enough work around the place that I felt bad we wasn't able to pay ya."

"That doesn't matter, Phineas."

"Come on."

"Where to?"

"The last event's always the shootin' contest." His eyes gleamed, and he said, "The way you bring them squirrels home, I figure you got a pretty good chance."

"I got no gun."

"Well, I have. Come on."

Driver followed the one-legged man to the wagon. Phineas had mastered the crutches so that he could swing along at a more rapid rate even than ordinary so Ben had to stretch his legs to keep up. When they reached the wagon, Phineas reached over and pulled out a long object in canvas. "See what you think of this," he said, unwrapping the object.

"Why, this is a Whitworth!" Ben exclaimed.

"You bet it is. I left a leg in that war, but I brung this gun home. Ain't used it much, but I always keep it in first-class condition. Come on now."

"I don't know. There'll be some good shooters there."

"Give her a try, Ben."

Suddenly Driver felt good. "All right," he said. "I will."

The two made their way to the site of the shooting match, where a huge crowd had already gathered. "This is always the big show," Phineas said.

Indeed it was a big show, for at least twenty men were already lined up in position to shoot at the target. "It costs a dollar entry fee."

"Well, I got that. If I lose it, I'm not out much."

"You ain't gonna lose," Phineas said. "Come on now, get to it."

Phineas moved across the field, for he had seen Sam, Jacob, and Reisa. He moved to stand beside them and said, "Ben's going to shoot."

"Well, by gum, that's a good idea!" Sam exclaimed. He nudged Reisa with his elbow. "That feller was a sharpshooter during the war. He don't boast none about it, but he was. They made only the best shots sharpshooters in our army."

"Oh, I hope he wins!" Reisa said.

"Got a good chance," Phineas nodded. "But there's some mighty good shots here, too."

Driver, at that moment, was paying his fee. The man that took it looked up at him. He was the sheriff, Charlie Giles. He blinked with surprise when he saw the tall man standing in front of him. "I heard you was back, Driver. It didn't pleasure me none."

Ben did not answer. He simply put the twenty dollars down.

"I got to take your money, but I'm warnin' you, Driver. You give me any trouble, and I'll see you go back to the pen."

Driver did not even nod. He took the receipt that the sheriff offered, watched his name being written down, then turned to go to the line of men. He had not gone far when a voice caught him up.

"Driver!"

He turned to see Alf DeSpain and Vic Giles standing there. He half expected to see Honey Fears, but the muscular man was not present. DeSpain was a tall man, even an inch or so taller than Driver. He was lean as a snake, and he had a wide mouth like a catfish. "There ought to be a law against lettin' convicts in this match," DeSpain sneered.

Vic Giles snickered.

DeSpain continued, "But I think I can beat a one-eyed man."

The two continued to make loud remarks so that soon everyone was aware of the situation. Driver clamped his temper down tightly. He did not even answer the two and stood there waiting quietly until the contest started.

The men shot in groups of five at targets set a hundred yards away. Each man had three shots, then the totals were counted up. The first five shot, and one man was the winner. Then another five took their place. This went on for some time with cheering and moans of grief and shouting. Driver quietly stood there watching until his turn came. He was in the last group of five. Giles had been eliminated, but Alf DeSpain had won from his group.

There was a familiarity to the feel of the Whitworth. He had used one in the war, but then he had been shooting at men instead of a target. For a moment it disconcerted him, but that passed. Coolly he put his three shots so close together in the center that it could have been covered by a dollar.

"Ben Driver's the winner," the sheriff announced. "Now the semifinalists will shoot."

There were five semifinalists, and out of these, two would be chosen to shoot for the finals. The target was moved back twenty yards, and once again Driver coolly planted his shots in a neat triangle in the center. The sheriff announced the winners, and discontent was in his voice. "The two finalists are Alf DeSpain—and Ben Driver."

"Show 'em how it's done, Ben!"

Driver recognized Sam's voice and smiled, looking over toward the sound of it. He saw Reisa holding onto her grandfather's arm, and when he caught her eye, she waved at him. He nodded and turned back and stood beside DeSpain. The target was moved back another twenty yards.

"I don't aim for you to win this match, Driver." DeSpain's voice was cold, and there was a look of hatred in his blue eyes.

Ben said absolutely nothing. He had made up his mind not to be drawn into any trouble with anyone. He well knew that he could be sent back to the penitentiary, and he also understood that Sheriff Charles Giles would be glad to be the man to do it.

DeSpain shot first, and one of the men at the target examined it. He called out, "Dead center!"

"You're beat, Driver." DeSpain grinned.

Ben lifted the rifle and held it. He looked down the long barrel, and when he saw the line of light not moving he knew his hand was steady. He squeezed the trigger gently, heard the explosion, and felt the rifle kick up. He stood back then, waiting while the judges at the far end congregated. There were three of them: the mayor, the banker, and a big plantation owner.

One of them advanced forward, and when he got close enough he said, "A dead heat."

Cheers went up, but DeSpain said, "Move the target back another ten yards."

Driver said, "That's fine with me."

They moved the target back, and DeSpain took more time. His shooting was good, as always, but one of his shots was at least three inches off center.

Driver did not hesitate. He sent the three shots one after the other.

The judge, a tall man named Aaron Coats, came with the targets. He held them up and the men gathered around, reading the names written on the target. Coats said, "DeSpain—two dead center, one three inches off—" He turned. "Ben Driver—three dead-center shots."

A cry went up, and he recognized Reisa's voice. The crowd followed him, men pounding him on the shoulders, until he got to the table where the sheriff sat. Sheriff Charlie Giles looked as if he had bitten into a sour plum. His lips were puckered. With great reluctance he took the money out of a box, threw it down on the table, and said, "Take your money, Driver."

"Much obliged, Sheriff."

Picking up the money, Driver stuffed it into his pocket. The crowd was still there, men offering to buy him a drink. Many of them he knew from old times. Most had been his friends, and a good feeling washed over him.

Fifty feet away from the sheriff's table his arm was grasped, and he was whirled around. He saw Alf DeSpain, whose eyes were blazing with anger. He cursed Ben vilely, his voice rising with anger.

"Cool off there, DeSpain," one of Ben's old friends said. "He won fair and square."

"He's a stinkin' convict and a dirty yella' coward!" He waited then, cocked and ready for the blow that he was sure Driver would send at him.

Ben knew he could not strike the man, for it would surely buy his own ticket back into the pen. "I don't want any trouble, DeSpain."

"I'll give you trouble." DeSpain struck quickly like a snake. The blow caught Ben flush in the mouth and was a disaster. He fell backwards, but he had consciousness enough to roll himself over and double up, preparing for the kick he knew would come. It caught him on the hip, and he gasped with pain. Rolling over, he got to his feet and was swarmed as DeSpain came after him. He was also aware that from nowhere Honey Fears had come and struck him a blow from the right.

There was no beating the two men. They struck him blow after blow, driving him backward. He was only half conscious as he struck the ground, but he was aware that he had fallen on something hard. Rolling over he saw it was the Whitworth, and in desperation he picked it up and got to his feet. He swung the rifle blindly and heard it connect with something. When he looked down he saw Alf DeSpain, but he had no time to think, for Honey Fears leaped at him and knocked him to the ground with a single blow.

"I'll kick your brains out, you stinkin' con!" a voice cried.

Ben looked up just in time to see that Sam had pulled out his pistol and was pointing it dead on at Fears.

"You just make one move, Honey, and I'll see how big a hole this Le Mat will make in your stupid head," Sam warned.

Fears turned his head slowly. The round bore of a pistol was pointed right at his nose. "You're askin' for trouble, Hall," Fears said. "I'll stomp you."

"You won't stomp nobody. Now get out of here."

At that moment a commotion came as a man thrust himself through the crowd. Sheriff Charlie Giles came hustling forward, and he drew his gun. "You put that gun up, Sam." He took one look, and he said, "Who put this man on the ground?"

"Driver did," Fears gritted between clenched teeth.

"He did?"

"Yes. He hit Alf with that rifle. He ain't moved. I'm afraid he's hurt bad."

A light of pleasure touched Sheriff Giles's eyes. He was a corrupt man, taking bribes, and he was not popular. He had served in the Confederate Army, but only as a guard at Andersonville Prison. He had been put in office by the carpetbaggers with help from powerful Federal friends. Now he pointed the gun at Driver and said, "Drop that gun, Driver."

Driver reversed the weapon and held it by the stock. "Here, Sam," he said with resignation. He knew what was coming.

"You can't arrest him, Giles," Sam said loudly.

"You shut up or I'll arrest you, too! Now come on. You're going to jail."

"He didn't do nothin'," Hall protested. "DeSpain picked the fight."

"That don't sound likely."

"No use arguing, Sam. I'll go along with the sheriff."

There was yelling, some for Ben but a few against him—mostly those who had lost money and who hadn't seen the action.

Ben made his way through the crowd, and as he passed by he saw Reisa, her eyes filled with fear.

Twenty

The following morning Reisa washed her hair, using rain water captured in a large barrel. As she worked the soap into her long black tresses, she looked up to see Boris watching her carefully. His eyes were fully opened, and he seemed to find interest in what she did.

"What goes on in your mind, Boris?" She spoke in Yiddish, her voice soft and gentle. "Do cats think—like people?"

Boris suddenly opened his mouth in a tremendous yawn, exposing an amazingly red throat and two rows of gleaming white teeth.

Reisa laughed at this display. "I'm boring you, aren't I? Why don't you go catch a mouse or something."

The faint sound of a fiddle came to her, and she turned to listen. Phineas played some very sad songs, and this one she didn't know. The melody floated to her, and she soaped her hair, listening to the plaintive sound. Finally she rinsed her hair in a separate bucket of water, and moved to the window to look outside while she dried it with a worn gray towel.

Her hair was difficult to dry, and she longed to go outside and let the sun pour its warm rays on it. But Jewish girls didn't do things like that. She suddenly remembered how Ben had asked about her hair, how long it was, and then had said, "It's a shame to hide anything beautiful." The memory of the scene was etched in her mind, and she wondered, *Would it be wrong to let my hair down?* The desire was suddenly there, but she knew she never would. She was a good Jewish girl and would keep to the old ways.

Finally her hair was merely damp, and she put on a kerchief and moved outside carrying the two buckets of wash water. She dumped them in the back yard, then set them down by the well. Phineas was sitting in a chair beside the house, pulling the bow across his fiddle. His eyes were closed, and he seemed half asleep. Sam sat beside him, lazily scuffling at the dirt with his boots.

Reisa moved to stand in front of him. "Phineas, play me a song."

Phineas opened his eyes to twin slits. "What kind of a song?"

"A happy song."

"Maybe you don't need a happy song."

"Everyone needs happy songs."

"Sam read me a verse in the Bible a while back. Said something like—let's see—what was it, Sam?"

Sam shrugged.

"Oh, yeah, I remember," Phineas said, and quoted, "'It is better to go to the house of mourning, than to go to the house of feasting.' Sure sounds mournful, don't it?"

"I suppose we need to think about sad things—but right now I need a happy song. Please, Phineas!"

Phineas began playing a fast tune, and when he finished, asked, "That happy enough for you, girl?"

"Yes! What's the name of it?"

"Ain't got one. I just made it up."

"Why, Phineas—that's wonderful! How nice to be able to do such a thing!"

"Don't pay too well." Phineas grinned. He continued to play softly, and finally he gave her an odd look. "What you think about the mess Ben's got himself into?"

"I'm worried," Reisa said instantly. "It wasn't his fault."

Phineas nodded in agreement.

"He won't go to prison, will he?" Reisa asked.

"I hope not," Phineas said gloomily. "Trouble is, the sheriff's crooked. Judge Bell ain't the best one to go up against, neither. He's liable to listen to the sheriff."

Reisa turned to Sam. "Is that true?"

Sam dropped his head and wouldn't look at her. "Let's just say his chances ain't good."

Reisa stiffened. "Well, we can't just let Ben get thrown back into jail. We've got to do *something!*" She paced the yard in front of them for several minutes, then turned suddenly. "I know!"

"Well," Sam said, "spit it out, Miss Reisa. What you gonna do?"

"I'm going to see his parents. I know Mr. Driver is an influential man. He's got to help Ben—he's just got to!"

"That might help," Sam agreed. "I think it's worth a try."

"Do you know where they live?"

"The Driver place? Why, sure."

"Do you think that Heck and Betty can make it that far?"

"It might be a strain on old folks like them. You get ready, and I'll go hitch 'em up. We'll go as far as we can with 'em. Then we'll walk the rest of the way."

It had not been necessary for Sam and Reisa to walk. Heck and Betty had made the trip through Richmond and the eight miles past it on the north where the Driver place was located. They walked along now at an even pace, until finally Sam gestured at a large white two-story house set far back off the road. "That's the Driver place. Pretty, ain't it?"

Indeed, it was a beautiful house. To Reisa it seemed like a mansion. "They must have a lot of money."

"Did have before the war. Of course the Yankees ruined everything. A wonder they didn't burn the house down. Only reason they didn't was they used it for a field headquarters. Just about tore the inside of it out, so I hear tell. When John Driver came back from the war he was like everybody else. He found it a wreck. He's worked like a dog ever since. I remember him as a younger man. He sure has aged since he come back from the war."

"Why is he so hard against Ben?"

"Well, I don't rightly know. That's family business. Of course, rich folks like that, they don't look favorably when their son gets sent to prison. I guess that was mostly it. But Marianne Driver, she might be different. Mothers always have a soft heart for their sons."

Sam drove the mules around into the circular driveway that arched in front of the house. Reisa got out, looking up at the tall pillars and the long windows evenly spaced across the front. Her courage failed her for a moment, but she turned and said, "Sam, you wait here. I may not be long. Mr. Driver may not see me."

Sam leaned back against the wagon seat and scratched his chin thoughtfully. "I reckon you've sold to some mighty reluctant buyers. You stick your head in there, girl, and don't leave until they throws you out bodily." A grin flashed across his face, and he nodded. "I don't reckon he's liable to do that."

"Thanks, Sam." Reisa returned his smile. She straightened her back, turned, and walked up the steps. There was a brass knocker in the center of the huge door, and she gave it four firm raps, then stood back to wait. The wait was not long before the door opened, and Reisa recognized Marianne Driver. She had only seen her once, and that fleetingly, but the memory of the woman had stayed with her. She was a fine-looking woman with auburn hair, and the same odd-colored green eyes that she had seen in Ben's remaining eye.

"Yes? May I help you?"

Trying to think of some way to approach the subject, Reisa decided that there was no easy way. "You're Mrs. Driver, aren't you?"

"Yes, I am. Do I know you?"

"No, ma'am, you don't. My name is Reisa Dimitri. My grandfather and I are staying with Sam Hall and Phineas Long on the other side of Richmond."

"I don't believe I know them either."

"No, ma'am, I guess you wouldn't." Reisa straightened her back, and said, "I've come to talk to you and your husband about your son."

The words seemed to strike against Marianne. Her lips tightened, and she said, "You know my son?"

"Yes, I do, Mrs. Driver. And I think he's in trouble and something's got to be done."

"You'd better come in," Marianne said quietly. She stepped back, and Reisa walked inside. She took one quick glance around at the shining hardwood floors, the paintings on the wall, and the glass chandelier overhead, then the woman said, "Come along. We'll go to the parlor."

As Reisa moved slightly behind Mrs. Driver, she formulated in her mind what she would say. It seemed this woman and her husband were rich and powerful—and she was a nobody, a foreigner not even able to speak the language very well. Still, she set her jaw, and when Mrs. Driver said, "Sit down there, my dear," she sat down but kept her back straight.

She waited until Marianne took a seat and then said at once, "I suppose you're wondering how I know your son, Mrs. Driver."

"Yes, of course, I am. We don't—" Marianne broke off for a moment and then finished her sentence. "We've—we've not been close to Ben in recent years."

"Yes, ma'am, I know. But let me tell you how I met Ben." She launched into the story of how she and Dov had found the sick man, taken him home, and nursed him.

When Reisa finished telling of her meeting with Ben, Marianne said, "I'm very grateful to you, Miss Dimitri. From what I understand, Ben would have died if you hadn't found him and taken him in."

Reisa's face flushed. "Well, it was really Sam and Phineas who provided a place. My grandfather and I don't have anything. They took us in, too, as a matter of fact."

"Where are you from? I don't recognize your accent."

"From Russia. I don't speak too well, but I'm learning."

"How did you happen to come to this country?" Marianne Driver listened again as Reisa gave her a brief sketch of her history, and Reisa was encouraged by her sympathetic gaze.

When Reisa finished, Mrs. Driver said, "You said that something must be done, and I agree with you. I don't know much about politics, but from what I hear, Ben doesn't have much chance unless something is done."

"Could I talk to your husband?"

Mrs. Driver seemed to hesitate, and at that moment Reisa understood—the problem lay with Mr. Driver, not with this kind, yet cautious woman.

Marianne Driver herself confirmed her thoughts. "You must understand. My husband has been very hard on Ben since he was sentenced to prison. He thinks Ben's failed the family. He's very proud of his family name, and he thinks Ben has ruined it. But we will try."

She rose and beckoned for Reisa to rise as well.

Reisa followed Mrs. Driver down the hall until they stood before a closed door. Marianne knocked, and Reisa heard a voice say, "Come in." She followed the woman inside and found herself in a large room obviously used as an office. Books lined the wall, papers were everywhere, maps were rolled up, and one large map of the county was fastened to the wall with tacks. She paid little heed to the surroundings, however, but fastened her eyes on a tall man, who rose as they entered.

"John, this is Miss Reisa Dimitri. My husband, Mr. John Driver."

"Well, I'm glad to know you, Miss Dimitri," John said. There was a formal manner about him, but his eyes were merely curious. He obviously did not remember Reisa.

Before she could get too nervous, Reisa spoke. "I know this is, perhaps, wrong, but I'm very worried about your son, Mr. Driver. I think unless something is done he is going to go back to prison."

Instantly a change swept over John Driver. The warmth seemed to vanish, and he said, "I hardly see how that's your affair."

Marianne intervened. "John, she's a good friend of Ben's. She and her friend found him when he was sick and dying. If they hadn't taken him in, I don't think he would have lived."

Mr. Driver shot a sharp glance at Reisa. "Well, I'm grateful for that, but as for doing anything else, I must decline."

Reisa took a deep breath. She was intimidated by this big man, but she knew she must not be. Quietly she faced him, and her eyes locked with his. "Sir, he's your son, and he's in trouble. Can't you find it in your heart to help him?"

John Driver dropped his eyes for a moment, and hope came to Reisa. But it was only a brief moment, and when he looked up his mouth was set firmly. He studied her for a few seconds, then shook his head. "I think this is none of my affair."

Reisa knew she had been dismissed. She was not by nature a bold girl, but now she was desperate. "Mr. Driver, I myself am not a Christian. My grandfather and I are Jewish, but you are a Christian, are you not?"

Surprise washed across Driver's face. "Yes," he said reluctantly. "Why do you ask?"

"I have been reading some in your Bible. Not long ago I read that Jesus told a story about a man who had a son who went wrong. I can't remember all the details. The son went away and fell in with bad companions, but he also was sorry, and he went home. And the story said, I believe, that the father ran and greeted him, put his arms around him, and welcomed him home."

A silence fell over the room, and Marianne Driver's eyes were fixed upon her husband. Reisa saw how Ben's mother longed for her husband to show her son mercy. But then, like a curtain, bitterness fell across John Driver's face. "Sorry, Miss Dimitri. It's none of your affair, and it's none of mine. I must ask you to leave."

Reisa, crushed, turned to leave. She walked down the hall almost blindly, her thoughts and emotions in turmoil.

When she reached the front door, she heard a voice saying, "Miss Dimitri, wait, please." She turned and saw Marianne Driver approach her, her face working as if she were about to weep.

"I'm sorry for the way my husband answered you. If it were up to me, I would do anything—but he's my husband. You must believe he's an honorable man, but he has a blindness about Ben. I've been praying for years that he would open his arms and take our son back. And I believe that he will yet."

Reisa warmed to Mrs. Driver. "I hope so. Ben's a fine man."

"Now let me tell you what you must do," Marianne said, her voice low. "It's possible that we can help Ben, but I must not be involved. There's a man in town called Colonel Randolph Fisher. He's a lawyer, and he was Ben's commanding officer in the war. He's always had a great heart for men that served under him. He's helped many of them. I want you to go to Colonel Fisher and tell him that he must defend Ben. Tell him I will pay his fees, but he must get Ben free. Can you do that?"

Hope came to Reisa then, and she smiled. "Ben has a good mother," she said simply. "I lost my own mother when I was very young, but I'm glad that Ben has you."

Tears came to Mrs. Driver's face. To Reisa's amazement, the older woman suddenly reached out and embraced her. "Help my son all you can, Reisa," she whispered. "Help him."

"There's a young woman to see you, Colonel Fisher."

Colonel Randolph Fisher looked up from the papers he was examining. His clerk, William Dokes, stood just inside his library entryway.

"A young woman?" Fisher barked. "What's her name? What does she want?"

"She's a foreigner, Colonel. She speaks with an accent. Her name is Dimitri. Rita Dimitri, I think. She wouldn't say what she wanted."

Colonel Fisher straightened his already military-straight back. At the age of sixty-three, he was vigorous and put in longer hours than most men half his age. He shook his head. "Well, I don't have time for her."

The clerk hesitated. "I think you might want to see her," he said cautiously.

"Why do you think that, Dokes?" Fisher stroked his neatly clipped beard.

"Well, she's very demanding for one thing, and she's dressed like a foreigner with a handkerchief over her head, but she's a good-looking woman. I can't imagine what she wants, but whatever it is, I think it would be interesting."

Fisher leaned back at his desk and smiled. "Good-looking, you say?"

"Very attractive, Colonel."

"Well, send her in. I'm tired of looking at your ugly face."

Dokes smiled. "Yes, sir. I'll send her right in."

Getting up from his chair, Fisher moved around the desk. And when the young woman was ushered in by Dokes, he thought, *Well, Dokes was right for once.* He advanced, saying, "My name is Randolph Fisher. I believe your name is Dimitri."

"Yes. Reisa Dimitri, Colonel."

"Not a colonel any longer. Sit down, Miss Dimitri, and tell me what this is all about."

Ten minutes later Fisher had the entire story. He was an expert at extracting information, and he found out very quickly that it was Marianne Driver who had sent the girl and offered to pay his fees. He did not ask about John Driver, for the two were friends. He knew that Driver had a blind spot about his son. It was a matter that Fisher had once spoken to Driver about and had been rebuffed rather harshly.

"And so," Reisa said, "Mrs. Driver said you could help. I wish you would, sir."

"Your name is Rita Dimitri?"

"No, sir. Reisa. R-E-I-S-A."

"Is that Russian?"

"Oh, no. That's Yiddish. It means 'rose.'"

"Well, that's a well-chosen name. Now, Miss Dimitri, I want you to go to Ben and tell him that I'll be handling his case in court. Try to encourage him all you can. Tell him I'll be by to see him late this afternoon."

"Oh, thank you, Mr. Fisher!" Reisa stood at once and came over, offering her hand as a man would. Her eyes danced, and her lips were caught up in a smile. She was, indeed, a beautiful young woman, and unusual to say the least. "I'll go now and tell Ben."

Fisher watched her run out of the room leaving the door wide open, then turned to the window. He waited until she came rushing out of the building holding her skirts and running directly toward the location of the jail.

"Well, was she interesting, Colonel?" Dokes spoke from behind him.

Fisher turned and nodded at his clerk. "Very interesting. I'm taking Ben Driver's case."

"Not much money in that," Dokes remarked.

"No. But a great deal of enjoyment. They're trying to do one of my boys in, Dokes. I won't stand for it!"

"No. I don't think you will, Colonel. Do you want me to get all the facts?"

"Yes. Turn over all the rocks you can and see what falls out."

"Yes, Colonel. I'll see to it."

Fisher suddenly laughed aloud. "I was going to take Ben's case anyway. I've been waiting for his father to come to me, but apparently he won't do that. It's good to know, though, that his mother still believes in him."

Ben had been lying on his back staring up at the ceiling, and when he heard the outer door unlock he did not move. It was not time for a meal, and he was not hungry anyway. But when he heard a voice say "Ben," at once he swung his feet over the bunk and came to his feet.

"Reisa!" he said, going over to the cell door. He grasped the bars. Staring at her, he said, "What are you doing here?"

"I've been to see your old commander, Colonel Fisher. He's going to defend you, Ben."

Driver blinked with surprise. "Why, I don't have the money to pay him! He's a high-priced lawyer."

"That's all taken care of."

"You can't use your money for this. I'm going to be convicted anyway."

"No, you're not. Colonel Fisher says he's going to get you off, and I believe he's a man who does what he says he will do."

"You're right about that," Ben murmured. "But you can't spend your money. You've got to make a living."

"It's not my money. Your mother agreed to pay for it."

Driver's jaw dropped. "How did she happen to do that?"

"Don't be angry with me, Ben, but—I went to see them."

"You went to my parents' house?"

"Yes. I've been so worried about you. So I talked to your mother—"

"And did you talk to my father? You didn't get a welcome there, I don't guess."

Reisa tried to think of some gentle way of putting it, but nothing came to her. "No, he wasn't willing. But your mother was," she said quickly. "She sent me to see Colonel Fisher and to tell him she would take care of his fee, and I did."

Ben had been severely depressed, knowing he would likely end up back at the penitentiary. Now he could not speak for a moment. Finally he reached out and put his hand on Reisa's cheek. It was smooth and warm, and at his touch he saw her eyes suddenly grow large. "Thanks, Reisa," he whispered huskily.

Reisa did not move. Instead, she reached up and put her hand over his, holding it tightly against her face. "It'll be all right, Ben. You'll see. Everything will be all right!"

A week later, Ben's trial was held in the Richmond Township courthouse. The courtroom itself was large, its high ceiling painted white. Every one of the oak benches was packed, for Ben Driver had been well known in the county.

"Third Federal District Court, Richmond Township, Judge Marion Bell presiding. All rise!"

Reisa quickly got to her feet and glanced at the judge who had come in from a door behind the platform at the front of the courtroom. She searched his face anxiously and saw nothing there to reassure her. He was a cold-eyed man of some fifty years, and the black robe that he wore made him look even more sinister.

"That there's a hangin' judge," Sam whispered as he stood beside her. "But we ain't gonna worry."

"Be seated!"

As they settled themselves into their seats, Reisa felt the pressure of Marianne Driver's arm touching hers. She turned and gave the woman a smile and thought again how very much she liked Ben's mother.

Glancing to her right, Reisa saw Ben sitting at a table with Colonel Fisher. He turned his head suddenly, and their eyes met. She smiled reassuringly and nodded. He returned the nod.

The judge said, “The case of the State against Benjamin Driver. Assault with a deadly weapon. Is the prosecution ready?”

A small man wearing a buff suit, a white shirt, and a string tie leaped to his feet. “Yes, Your Honor.”

“Then you may proceed. I want this case over with as quickly as possible, Mr. Danvers.”

The district attorney, Tyler Danvers, reminded Reisa of a small feisty dog. He was no more than five feet six inches tall and small-boned. He moved, however, very quickly, and seemingly every nerve in his body was connected with his vocal organs. Whenever he spoke he had to be moving and twitching in some area—his legs, his feet, his torso, or his head. Now he went quickly to stand before the jury and said, “Ladies and gentlemen of the jury, this is a simple case. It will not occupy a great deal of your time. The facts are very simple. Benjamin Driver, a former convict—”

“Objection!”

“Objection overruled, Mr. Fisher.”

Danvers smiled at Fisher. “My worthy opponent would like for you to ignore the fact that the defendant, Ben Driver, is a convict. He would also like you to ignore the fact that he was sent to prison for armed robbery. So we have here a man who is capable of violence. The State will prove, therefore, that Ben Driver maliciously and without cause struck Mr. Alfred DeSpain, causing serious injury. Such a man as this is unfit to have his freedom. We will ask that you convict the defendant of this charge and have him returned to the state penitentiary.”

Reisa knew absolutely nothing about courts of law. There was something frightening about the courtroom scene—as if a giant machine were in operation and nothing could stop it. From time to time she would look for reassurance to Marianne Driver or towards Sam, but she knew that Ben’s fate lay in the hands of Colonel Fisher—and Judge Bell.

The prosecution called its first witness, Mr. Honey Fears.

“Mr. Honey Fears, will you please take the stand.”

Fears, dressed neatly for once in a blue shirt and a pair of wool trousers, rose and took the stand. He put his hand gingerly on the Bible that the officer of the court held, took his oath to tell the truth, and then sat down.

"Mr. Fears, will you tell the court where you were on the afternoon of September the twenty-nine. That's last Thursday."

"I was at the doin's at the festival," Fears said. He had slicked his hair back with some kind of grease and shaved his beard, but still he was a brutal-looking man.

"And, Mr. Fears, after the shooting contest—will you describe what you saw for the jury?"

"I seen him, Ben Driver, hit Alf DeSpain with a rifle. Like to have killed him, he did."

"And what provocation did he have?"

"What's that mean?"

"Why did Ben Driver hit Alfred DeSpain?"

"Why, he didn't have no cause at all. He just up and hit him."

"And what did you do?"

"Why, I think he would have beat poor old Alf to death if I hadn't jumped in and stopped him."

"So you attempted to restrain Ben Driver?"

"Yes, I did."

"And then what happened?"

"The sheriff, he come and arrested Driver."

"Very good." Danvers turned and said, "Your witness, Colonel."

Fisher arose and walked leisurely toward the box. He looked Fears squarely in the eye for such a long time that Fears began to fidget. "Mr. Fears, have you ever been in jail?"

"Objection!" Danvers called out at once.

"Objection overruled," the judge declared. "The witness will answer the question."

Fears twisted around. "Yes, I have. Once or twice."

"It's more like seven times, isn't it, Mr. Fears?" The colonel said easily, "I have the records here if you'd care for me to read them to the court."

"Maybe it was seven."

"Was it seven, or was it not?" the colonel snapped, his eyes suddenly flashing.

"Well, it was seven."

"And on four of those charges you were convicted of beating men almost to death."

"I get into a fight now and then."

"And in two of those fights the men were permanently injured because you used, in one instance, the butt of a gun on one victim's head. And then another time you kicked the man nearly to death. Is that correct?"

"You know how it is in a fight."

"No, I don't. Not if it means kicking a man who's flat on his back."

"Objection!" Danvers shouted. "This trial's about Ben Driver, not Mr. Fears."

"Are you going somewhere with this, Colonel Fisher?" the judge asked.

"I will change my line of questioning, Your Honor." Fisher turned and said, "How long have you known the defendant, Ben Driver?"

Fears shot a baleful glance across the room at Driver. "A long time," he said.

"You've had trouble with him before, haven't you?"

"I never liked him. He never liked me neither."

"In fact, you got into a fight with him several years ago in which you were badly beaten. Is that correct?"

"I'd been drinkin' that day."

"But you were badly beaten."

"I reckon I was."

"And you threatened to get even with him. Is that true?"

Fears looked quickly across the room at the sheriff, whereupon Fisher said, "Look at me, please, and answer the question. And I must remind you that the penalty for perjury is severe. I have witnesses who have heard you threaten to get revenge on my client. Did you threaten him or not?"

Fears had nothing to say except to grunt, "Yes. I did."

"No further questions."

As soon as Fears left the witness box, the district attorney called for two other witnesses, both friends of Honey Fears. They both swore dutifully that Ben Driver had started the fight.

In both cases Colonel Fisher said, "No questions, Your Honor."

The next witness for the prosecution was Alf DeSpain himself. He wore a white bandage on his head and used a cane as he made his way to the box. As soon as he was sworn in, the district attorney immediately began to question him. DeSpain sat in the box answering briefly. Yes, Driver had struck him with a rifle. No, there had not been any provocation. He didn't know what came over the man.

"Your witness," Danvers said.

Colonel Fisher moved to the front and began firing questions. "Have you ever been arrested? What were the charges? Have you ever spent time in jail?" The questioning was brief, and DeSpain got angry. When he was dismissed he quickly left the witness box. The colonel watched and said loudly, "You do very well without that cane, don't you, DeSpain?"

Laughter went up all over the courtroom, and DeSpain's face flushed as he was forced to return and get the cane. He had hobbled up to the stand as a man badly injured, but on leaving he had forgotten to limp.

"That concludes the case for the prosecution, Your Honor. I think the evidence is clear," Danvers declared.

"Colonel Fisher, are you ready?"

"Oh, yes, we are, Your Honor."

"The first witness I call will be Mr. Jack Connerly."

Jack Connerly, a tall well-dressed man of some fifty years, approached the bench. He was the mayor of Richmond and had served in the Confederate Army with great distinction under General Hood. He was a popular and well-known man noted for his integrity.

"Mr. Connerly, you were at the celebration under discussion."

"Yes, I was."

"Did you observe the conflict between my client and Mr. DeSpain?"

"Yes. I had attended the shooting contest, and I saw the whole thing clearly."

"Would you describe what you saw to the jury."

Connerly turned to face the jury. He had clear blue eyes and a ringing voice. "Ben Driver received the prize and was walking away. Alf DeSpain came out of the crowd and started cursing him and abusing him."

"Did Mr. Driver respond?"

"No. He turned and tried to walk away, but DeSpain hit him in the face."

"And what did Ben Driver do?"

"He didn't strike back. He said, 'I don't want trouble.' But he was knocked to the ground. And then Honey Fears joined in, and the two started beating him. He was pulled to his feet, and he struck out with the rifle in his hand and hit DeSpain."

"Then my client did not start the argument?"

"He did not."

"Your witness, Mr. Danvers."

Danvers was a politician above all things. He knew that most of the men on the jury were Confederate veterans who admired Jack Connerly. He also knew that Jack Connerly was incapable of lying, so he had no choice but to get rid of this witness as quickly as possible. "I have no questions."

"My next witness is Mr. Sidney Taylor."

In rapid order Fisher called five men, all men of prominence in the community noted for their honesty. Each had seen the fight clearly, and they reiterated what Jack Connerly had said. When the final man sat down, Fisher said, "I call Charles Giles to the stand."

A murmur went over the courtroom as Sheriff Giles, his face flushed, made his way to the front. He took his place in the witness box and was sworn in. When he sat down he twisted nervously as Fisher approached him.

"Sheriff, did you witness the fight in which Alf DeSpain alleges he was struck without cause by my client?"

"Well, I didn't exactly see it—"

"You didn't *exactly* see it! How can you not *exactly* see something? You either saw it or you didn't. Which was it?"

Giles's flush became even more pronounced. "I got there right after it happened."

"And what did you see?"

"I seen Alf DeSpain on the ground, and Ben Driver with a gun in his hand, so I assumed—"

"You assumed!" Fisher said in disdain. "Did you ask anybody what had happened?"

"No, I didn't."

"Why not?"

"Well, I've known Driver a long time, and he's a bad one."

"How long have you known him?"

"I knew him before the war."

"You served in the army, I take it?" Fisher knew very well that the sheriff had escaped active duty by serving as a guard at Andersonville Prison.

"Objection!" Danvers screamed. "That has no bearing."

"I withdraw the question," Fisher said. He gave the jury a wry smile. "If a man doesn't want to testify as to whether he served the Confederacy or not, that's his business." Since he knew that every man in the jury box was well aware of Giles's record, he knew that he had made his point.

"So, you did not see anything, and you did not ask anyone what had happened. You simply arrested a man because he had been in the penitentiary."

"I guess so."

"Did you know that Alf DeSpain had been in the penitentiary?"

Giles was trapped. "Well, not exactly."

"You didn't *exactly* know. Well, *inexactly* what did you know?"

"I heard he had been, but I didn't know it."

"I see. So two men with records get in a fight, and you just choose one. Is that about the size of it, Sheriff?" He waited as Giles stumbled to come up with an answer. Finally he said, "I think the jury will know how to assess your evidence. Your witness."

Danvers jumped up and tried to make something more out of Giles's part in the affair, but the more he talked, the worse it got. Finally he sat down sullenly.

"Do you have any more witnesses or any more evidence?" the judge asked.

Colonel Fisher said, "No, Your Honor, the defense rests."

"Then the jury will retire," the judge said. He gave them a few instructions. As they trooped out, he got up and left the room.

"What happens now?" Reisa said.

"The jury will talk about the case, and they'll decide whether Ben is innocent or guilty," Mrs. Driver said.

"How long will it take?"

"There's no way of telling. It could be more than a day, but I don't think so."

To Reisa's relief, Mrs. Driver was right. In less than ten minutes the jury came trooping in. Many of the spectators, thinking the jury would be out for some time, had gone outside to smoke and to get refreshments, so the courtroom was only two-thirds full when the jury returned.

The judge took his position, and he said, "Gentlemen of the jury, have you reached a verdict?"

A lanky man with a sunburned face and a pair of steady blue eyes said, "We have, Your Honor."

"How find you?"

"We find Ben Driver innocent."

Sam Hall let out a loud screech, and the judge at once said, "Order in this court!" He turned to Ben, who had stood to hear his sentence. "You are found innocent and are released from this court. Court adjourned!"

Reisa found that Marianne's arm had gone around her as the verdict was being rendered, and suddenly she turned and threw her arms around the older woman. They stood there for a moment, and then Reisa whispered, "This is your doing. Thank you! Thank you!"

"I can't go to Ben," Marianne said. "But you must."

Reisa hesitated, but as she moved out, Ben saw her. He looked past her and saw his mother, and for one moment their eyes met. He went to her at once and whispered, "Thank you, Mother."

He embraced her, and she whispered, "God bless you, Ben. But it was Reisa who did it all."

Reisa was watching this. She saw Ben turn, his eye filled with something she could not quite understand. He came to her and took her hands, and for a moment the two stood there isolated in the busy courtroom. Then he smiled and said, "Well, you've made a habit of saving my life, Reisa. Thanks again."

Reisa wanted to reach out and touch his face, but she knew she must not. "I'm so glad, Ben—I'm so glad, Ben!"

Twenty-One

For the week following the trial, Reisa was aware of a sense of well-being and happiness that seemed to go deep down into her spirit. Perhaps it had been Ben's decision to give her most of the prize money that he had won in the shooting contest. He had come to her the morning after the trial and said briefly, "I don't like to be in anybody's debt, so I'm going to use the money I won to convert that wagon to whatever it is you want for your peddling."

Reisa had tried to refuse, but he had smiled at her crookedly. "Don't worry about it. I'll get it back. We're going to be partners."

"Partners!" Reisa had exclaimed. "What do you mean, Ben?"

"I mean that I'm the only one that can fix that wagon up, and I'm the only one who can drive those ornery mules. So we're partners. Right?"

Reisa remembered that time warmly, and all week long remodeling the wagon had been the chief activity around the homestead. Sam and Phineas had thrown themselves into it. Phineas actually helped to do the work, and Sam mostly got in the way and offered a multitude of suggestions.

They worked all day on it, and at night sat around the table drawing up plans for new modifications. It had been a happy time, and Reisa had seen that Ben had somehow been changed by the trial. She suspected that it was the sight of his mother and the love she had shown to him. Whatever it was, he had thrown off the dark spirit that had possessed him and had spoken no more of going to California.

As soon as Reisa awoke on Thursday morning, she shoved Boris aside. Ignoring his protests, she dressed quickly and went at once into the kitchen. The air was fragrant with the odor of bacon, and Reisa wondered what it would be like to eat such good-smelling food.

Phineas looked up and said, "Breakfast is ready. Sit and eat."

Reisa went to the table where the others were all waiting and patted Dov's shoulder as she sat down beside him. "How are you this morning, Dov?"

"Good. How are you?" Dov said the words carefully, pronouncing each syllable. He was not quick with English, but all four of his companions were coaching him constantly so that he was getting better each day.

As usual, Sam asked Jacob to say the blessing, which he did, and then they all began to eat hungrily. Reisa looked over at Ben and asked, "How much longer will it take to finish the wagon, Ben?"

"Well, the way suggestions have been coming in from all sources"—Ben paused to grin at Phineas and Sam—"I expect in about six months we ought to be almost finished."

"Oh, Ben, don't be foolish!" Reisa exclaimed. "Really. How long will it be?"

"We're ready for sunup tomorrow, I guess," Driver remarked, smiling at her enthusiasm.

Reisa clapped her hands in anticipation. "Let's go out and see it one more time."

"All right," Driver agreed. He got to his feet and headed to the door, Reisa following him.

As they walked to the wagon, Driver asked, "Do you think your grandfather will be able to make the trip?"

Reisa shook her head sadly. "He wanted to go, but he's not strong enough yet. I'm praying that he'll be able to go with us soon."

When they reached the wagon she began to go over it. "This little compartment will be just right for jewelry," she said, opening a hinged door. Ben had found some seasoned walnut and had it planed. She saw again what a good carpenter he was, and exclaimed as she went over all of the compartments. Some were large enough to hold clothes; others were designed just the right height for spices. Along both sides of the wagon there were small modules, and compartments had been fitted together all the way to the top of the sides. The top of the wagon itself had a sort of fence built around it where other boxes or chests could be fitted. At the very back he had fitted in a false rear that would drop and was held into place at waist level by two sturdy cords. There Reisa could lay out her goods on the improvised table for prospective buyers. Also on the back was a single board across the high top of the wagon into which could be inserted brooms or other long articles which would be awkward to carry.

"I'm glad you made it so nice for traveling, Ben," Reisa said. She was on her knees looking at a small cabinet which would hold their food and cooking supplies. "We can carry all the food we need and the cooking equipment on top, and I can sleep in here. It'll be so nice to have a place to sleep."

Ben had insisted that Reisa make a mattress for herself, and Phineas had shown himself able in this way. They had fashioned a cotton mattress small enough to pack away in one of the compartments but just right for Reisa. She also had a small pillow and blankets, for the weather was growing cooler.

"It's just wonderful, Ben!" Reisa exclaimed. She got to her feet and came to stand by him. "God is good to give us such a thing." She turned to look at him, and she said sincerely, "Thank you, Ben."

He returned her gaze. Something serious in his eye, something hungry and lonely and mysterious, caught at her.

"Why are you looking at me so strangely, Ben?" Reisa asked.

Ben blinked and looked away. "I guess I just always wonder what you'd look like with your hair down."

Reisa flushed, for he had mentioned this before. "Jewish women don't do that. We always wear kerchiefs in public."

"Then I guess your husband will be the only man that'll ever see it."

"I suppose so." The words disturbed Reisa, as had Driver's intent gaze. Now she nervously moved away, leaving Driver standing there looking after her. She had been aware for some time of his attention to her, and it had troubled her. She tried to put the gaze of that one attentive eye of his out of her mind. She did so by thinking, *We still don't have enough money. I've got to find enough to stock our wagon—especially with gold wedding rings for the women who want them so much.*

Aaron Coats had been a banker most of his life. He had started out by sweeping the floors of the bank, and had gradually moved into the position of teller. He had moved rapidly ahead, being interrupted by the war when the banking business had crashed. But since the war he had prospered, not becoming rich but at least becoming comfortable. Now as he sat there looking across at the young woman who had come in, he wished somehow that he could help everyone that came into his office.

The young woman had introduced herself as Reisa Dimitri, and there was something about her accent and her appearance that appealed to Coats. He had seen her at the festival, and remembered how distraught she had been when Ben Driver had been arrested by the sheriff. She wore a scarf and looked very young, but there was something most appealing in the way she had simply asked for a loan. She said, "I do not know how to do this, but my grandfather and I want to expand our business, and I need money."

Coats listened as she explained their venture with excitement. She told how Ben Driver had fixed the wagon up, and now they were ready to go, except they had no money left for stock. Finally she said, "I do not know about banks and borrowing money. I have never borrowed any, but if you could help us, Mr. Coats, it would be God's blessing."

Coats was touched by her appeal, but he had no choice. "Miss Dimitri," he said gently. "You must understand one thing. The money in this bank is not my money. It belongs to the people who deposit their money here. One day"—he smiled encouragingly—"you will be successful, and I trust you will let us handle your funds. If you do, you would want me to lend money only to enterprises that are certain. And your business has not proven itself."

Coats went on for some time trying to break the news as gently as he could. But after he had finally made it plain that he could not grant the loan, he saw disappointment touch her fine eyes. "I'm so sorry, Miss Dimitri," he said. "I wish it were different."

Reisa tried to smile and rose at once. "I understand," she said quietly. "Thank you for your time, Mr. Coats."

Coats watched the young woman leave. Suddenly he struck his rosewood desk with a gesture of anger. "Blast it all," he muttered. "Sometimes I hate being a banker!"

Crushed, Reisa left the bank. She realized that it had been a wild idea, but she had known nothing else to do. Now she would have to go on the first trip without much more stock than she and Dov could have carried in their packs. She had sold her inventory down until there was little left, and she and Jacob had insisted on paying Sam and Phineas something for their room and board, despite their objections. Now as she left the bank and turned down the walk, she was absolutely devoid of ideas. *We'll just have to go with what we have,* she thought. *We'll sell a little, come back and buy a little bit more—but it will take a long time.*

"Reisa, how good it is to see you!"

Reisa, who was deep in thought, suddenly looked up and saw Marianne Driver standing in front of her smiling. She was wearing a light brown dress with gold piping along the round neckline, and once again Reisa was struck with what an attractive woman she was. "Hello, Mrs. Driver," she said. "It's good to see you, too."

"What are you doing in town? Buying supplies? Did Ben come with you?"

"No. He didn't come this time. He's home putting the finishing touches on our wagon."

"Walk along with me, and tell me about what you are doing."

Reisa, willingly enough, fell into step with the woman, and began to outline what she and Jacob hoped to do. She found Marianne Driver an interested listener, and before they had walked a block along the wooden sidewalk, she had told her a great deal of how Ben had thrown his lot in with her. "We're partners, you see. We couldn't have done it at all without Ben. He'll be going with Dov and me on the trip. He's the only one that can handle Samson and Delilah."

"Samson and Delilah?"

"Oh, they're the mules that Ben bought. Nobody can handle them but him. They're the meanest things you ever saw!"

"Come inside and have a cup of tea. I often stop at the restaurant here. They make excellent tea and usually have good tea cakes."

The two women turned inside the Elite Cafe. They were greeted by a tall smiling man who nodded. "Good morning, Mrs. Driver. Good to see you."

"Do you have any of those good tea cakes and some fresh tea, David?"

"Yes, I do."

"Bring us a platter full and an ocean of tea."

"Yes, ma'am. Right away."

The restaurant was pleasant with the hum of quiet talk, for several customers had scattered themselves among the tables that filled the floor. Marianne led Reisa to a table beside the window where they could look out and watch the traffic. "It's such a pleasant place," Marianne said as they sat down. "Now, go ahead and tell me about your venture."

Reisa had discovered that talking to this woman was a pleasure, and as she leaned forward, she lost herself telling all the plans that she had. The tea came and the cakes, and Reisa found that they were very good indeed. She ate four of them and drank three cups of tea.

Marianne seemed to get caught up in Reisa's excitement. "So you and Ben and Dov, is it, will be going out selling gold rings to the ex-slaves. I think that's a marvelous idea."

"Well, that's not quite the way it is, Mrs. Driver."

"Couldn't you call me Marianne?"

Reisa gave the woman a rather startled look. "Why, yes, ma'am, if you'd like. Anyway, we won't be selling any gold rings—not for a while."

"Why not?"

"They're very expensive, and we don't even have enough money to stock the usual things: ribbons, thread, spices. We'll just have to go with what little we have and save up."

Marianne looked down at her teacup, quiet for a moment. Then she lifted her head and looked directly at Reisa. "Would you consider a silent partner, Reisa?"

"A silent partner? What is that?"

"Someone who puts money into a business but doesn't actually take part in it. In other words, I would advance you the money to buy the rings and the supplies. But, of course, I would never see any of them or go on any of the trips. Mercy, wouldn't I be a sight in a peddler's wagon!"

"Why, I couldn't let you do that, Marianne." She laughed suddenly. "It's hard for me to call you that. I always call older women *Mrs.*"

"I like it. I have only one daughter that I don't see often, so it's very nice to have a young woman treat me like a mother."

Reisa was startled at the words. She stared at Marianne Driver and finally shook her head. "I couldn't let you put your money into it. We may lose it."

"Don't be foolish. You're not going to lose money. You're going to be very successful." She grew sober then and reached over to place her hand over Reisa's. "I'm doing this for you and your grandfather—but, of course, I'm doing it for Ben as well. He needs so much to have something go right. He was such a fine, happy, young man before the war. And even during the war he didn't lose the joy of living—until somewhere along the end. I think he became a silent man, and there was a sadness in him. Maybe it was losing the war. Maybe it was all of the death and suffering that he saw. Whatever it was, I want to see him become what he once was, and I think he can. So you *have* to take the money."

Reisa was touched by Marianne Driver's words, and it gave her a new insight into Ben. "All right. If you like, we can pay you back in weekly payments."

"Don't worry about that. Pay it back as you can. Come. You'll have to go to my home."

They left the restaurant, and as they got into Marianne's carriage, she said, "The only thing I've ever done that I haven't told John about is that I've kept money out for a long time from housekeeping expenses, and when he gave me little gifts of money. I've got nearly a thousand dollars now."

"That's a lot of money, Marianne!"

"I always had one thing in mind—to use it to help Ben. And now," she said, turning her full smile on Reisa, "I'm going to get to do it."

Aaron Coats looked surprised and then harried. Reisa Dimitri had come into his office, and he assumed she had come to beg him to lend her the money. He rose. "Miss Dimitri."

"I have some money to put in your bank to start an account." Reisa held up a leather purse that looked very heavy. She poured it out on Coats's desk and said, "Tell me how I can spend it on merchandise."

Coats quickly counted the money and said, "Why, you have nine hundred dollars here!"

"Yes, and now I need to buy rings and other things."

"Well, I'm so happy! You came by this money very quickly," Coats said. He raised one eyebrow, hoping she would tell the source of her good fortune.

Reisa merely smiled. "Yes. God provided it. Now, can you show me how to handle this?"

Coats liked the young woman more than ever. "I can indeed! Several of the wholesalers are customers of mine and good friends. We'll put this money away and I'll get you a checkbook. Then we'll go visit my friends, and I'll ask them to make you the very best prices possible."

"That's so good of you, Mr. Coats."

"Indeed, no. It's my pleasure."

~

The rest of the day went very quickly for Reisa. Mr. Coats took her to several wholesalers, including those who sold gold rings. He stayed with her as she made her orders, all of the time urging the merchants to do better with their prices. One of them finally said, "Coats, will you please get out of here. I'm going to lose money on this sale if you don't leave me alone!"

Coats merely laughed.

In the carriage on the way to the wholesalers, Coats taught Reisa how to write checks and keep a balance. She spent nearly six hundred dollars of the money, and he advised her to keep a balance. But she had ten gold rings and plenty of other supplies to stuff the wagon nearly full.

When she arrived home, her eyes blazing with excitement, the men gathered around her, and she told them what she had done.

Ben said, "I never knew a banker to lend money without security. How'd you do it?"

Reisa longed to tell him that it was his mother's money, but Marianne had sworn her to secrecy. So she merely said, "Women have secrets, Ben." Even as she said this, she determined that very soon she would find some way to persuade Marianne to let her tell the secret.

"We'll pick up all of the supplies tomorrow, and we'll leave early in the morning the following day," she said.

Reisa slept little that night, but finally she drifted off, her last thought being a vision of the sweet face of Marianne Driver.

The first four days of travel had been easy, and the small company had sold considerable stock. They had fallen into a pattern, traveling throughout the day, stopping at houses, or occasionally at a small village, setting up shop on the main street. Neither Ben nor Dov ever tried to sell anything, but they helped Reisa unpack and show her wares and then repack the wagon. In the evening they camped, whenever possible, by a stream. Ben picked their stops, for he knew all of this country like the back of his hand.

On the evening of the fourth day, they set up camp in a pleasant meadow beside a small stream. Darkness had already come, and Dov was sitting on a box in front of the campfire roasting quail. Ben had gone hunting while Reisa set up shop in a small village. He had killed a dozen quail, and he and Dov had cleaned them. They were spitted, and Dov was watching carefully as the meat turned a golden brown.

Reisa came out of the wagon where she had been brushing her hair, drawn by the smell of cooked meat. She had, as usual, put on her kerchief, and now she came to stand beside Dov, patting his shoulder. "That smells good, Dov."

"All done," he said. He reached over and stirred the beans that were bubbling in a pot. Reisa took out three plates and forks and spoons. There was a coffee pot balanced on the grill that they had brought along. Dov took two quail off the spit, put them on Reisa's plate, then added beans. "I hope it good," he said. "I never cooked birds except ducks."

Reisa sat down cross-legged beside Ben. The fire was a dot of red and yellow brilliance, throwing its welcome heat outward. Reisa touched the quail. "Ow, it's hot!"

"Nothin' better than fresh quail," Driver said. He began to eat, hot as it was, and he showed Reisa how to break the legs off. Tiny though they were, they were delicious. "About all there is to these birds is the breast," Ben said. "But it's mighty good."

Reisa found it delicious. Being out in the open air all day and then sitting around the campfire eating gave her an appetite. "I'm going to be fat if I keep on eating like this," she said between bites.

"You will never be fat."

"How do you know that?"

"It's a gift I have." Driver smiled at her, his teeth bright. His single eye gleamed by the light of the fire, and he said, "I can always look at a woman and tell what she'll be like at sixty."

"You can't either!"

"Yes, I can."

Reisa laughed. "All right. What will I be like?"

"Just like you are now, with silver hair instead of black."

Reisa considered this, then said, "No. I'll have wrinkles. Everybody gets wrinkles when they get older."

"Guess you're right."

They ate their meal leisurely, but it was still too early to go to bed. Dov, however, always loved to go to bed after eating at night. He crawled under the wagon with his blankets and settled in.

Ben remained behind, sitting cross-legged staring into the fire. Once he reached out and took a twig and set the end of it ablaze. He watched it until it burned down, then tossed it back into the fire.

Reisa was sitting next to him. She had a cup of coffee and sipped it from time to time. Finally she asked, "What was it like during the war? You rarely talk about it."

"No. I guess I don't. It was all right at first," he said quietly. "Everywhere we went we were heroes. Young women met us and kissed us and gave us donuts, and there were bands playing battle songs. We thought it was a good world for young men then."

Reisa listened as he spoke, wondering what he was like during those times. His mother had said he was full of joy, but she could not see this in him now.

For a while Ben talked about the war, and then finally he said quietly, "I guess I lost my taste for the war when my best friend got killed. The battle was over, and we had come through it again. We were just standing there trying to catch our breath after it all. A shot rang out, and Paul fell down dead—victim of a sniper. That took everything out of me. I went on through Appomattox, but I didn't care much about anything. My lieutenant said I was tryin' to get myself killed exposing myself. Maybe I was."

"I'm so sorry about your friend."

"I lost a lot of good friends."

"What about your family?" Reisa asked.

"I had one brother Matthew, but he was killed in the war. He was the one who should have lived. He was the good one, and I was the black sheep, always into some kind of mischief, but nothing really bad until after the war."

"You have no other brothers or sisters?"

"Yes, I have one sister named Prudence. She married a real fine man named Martin Rogers. They have three children now."

"Where do they live?"

"In Washington. He's a doctor—and a fine one, too. Prudence and I were really close, and I liked her husband a great deal."

"You haven't seen her in a long time?"

"No, not in a long time."

"I like your mother very much. I had tea with her the last time I was in town."

"Did you?"

"Yes. She's such a good woman and a fine-looking woman, too."

Ben suddenly smiled. "All Drivers are good-looking people." Then the smile left. "I don't guess you saw my father?"

"No, I didn't." Reisa hesitated. "It's a shame you two don't get along."

"I don't blame him. He's always been proud of the Driver name, and I dragged it down in the dirt."

Quickly Reisa knew she had to change the subject. She watched as Ben stood up and stretched. She stood up with him, and for a moment the two stood there. He turned to face her and said, "I'm glad you like my mother. You'd like Prudence, too."

Reisa felt a surge of pity go through her for this tall man. He had endured a great deal of hardship, and yet she knew that deep down in his spirit there was goodness. She put out her hand almost involuntarily and laid it on his arm. She felt the strength and thought for a moment how thin he had been when she had found him in the road.

He turned suddenly to face her, and as he did she saw something in his expression that startled her. She expected him to kiss her, but he did not. They stood there silently, and then Reisa did something that she had never done, and she did not know why she did it. She untied the knot of her scarf, and then pulled the pins out of her hair. It fell over her back, and she said, "I wish I could wear my hair like this all the time. You always wanted to see it. Well, there it is."

The woods were silent around them except for the sound of some hunting owl that made a sudden soft cry that broke the silence. Overhead the stars looked down, but she saw that he was not looking at the stars but at her. He reached out, ran his hand over the glossy blackness of her hair. It fell almost to her waist, and somehow she felt that she had opened herself to him more, perhaps, than was proper. It gave her an odd feeling to stand there with her hair down and to look up at him.

She saw him reach out and then felt his hand on her hair. She felt helpless before him and knew that if he pulled her close, she could not resist.

But he did not. He pulled his hand back and held her gaze for a moment. Then he turned away saying, "Better get to bed, Reisa. We've got to get up early tomorrow."

As he moved away from her, Reisa stood there feeling somehow that she had been rejected. She quickly moved to the wagon, pulled the canvas over the front, undressed, and put on a gown. She went to pull the blankets over her and lie down, but she could not forget the scene. She could almost feel his hand on her head, but she could not help but think, *I must not be attractive to him.* Somehow the thought troubled her deeply, and she lay awake for a long time thinking of what it would be like to be attractive to a man.

Twenty-Two

Jacob often grew lonely while Reisa was off on her trips with Dov and Ben. They never stayed longer than a week, yet he missed them all. Phineas and Sam were not bad company—especially Sam, who was willing to spend twenty hours a day talking about the Bible. He never seemed to tire of listening to Jacob speak of the Old Testament, and was always quick to locate New Testament Scripture to fit that which Jacob read.

At the moment both of his hosts were outside tending to the morning chores, and Jacob sat alone at the kitchen table. Sam had spent a great deal of time on the Hebrew version of Isaiah 53. It was his favorite book in the Old Testament, and many times he had asked Jacob to read it to him in the original, then to translate it. Something that Sam had said just before going out had troubled Jacob greatly. They had read the whole chapter together, and Sam had insisted that Jacob read verses ten through twelve twice. Jacob had read it, and Sam had said eagerly, "Well, what do you make of that, Jacob?"

Jacob had replied, "I'll admit it seems to fit the death of Jesus."

Sam had smiled with delight but then had left. Now Jacob sat down reading the English translation in Sam's Bible.

> *Yet it pleased the LORD to bruise him; he hath put him to grief: when thou shalt make his soul an offering for sin, he shall see his seed, he shall prolong his days, and the pleasure of the LORD shall prosper in his hand.*

He shall see of the travail of his soul, and shall be satisfied: by his knowledge shall my righteous servant justify many; for he shall bear their iniquities.

Therefore will I divide him a portion with the great, and he shall divide the spoil with the strong; because he hath poured out his soul unto death: and he was numbered with the transgressors; and he bare the sin of many, and made intercession for the transgressors.

Jacob kept his eyes fastened on the passage, and his lips moved as he whispered softly, "When thou shalt make his soul an offering for sin..." He closed his eyes and leaned back. *What a tremendous thing! That God would make a man an offering for sin. All of the thousands and even hundreds of thousands of lambs slain on Jewish altars, but they did not atone. And here God says that the Messiah will bear iniquities, that he will make his soul an offering for sin.* His eyes dropped to the last verse. *And he bare the sin of many, and made intercession for the transgressors.*

For a long time Jacob sat there, his face fixed as he resisted what seemed to be the obvious meaning of the passage. He had tried to push the thought away many times. *Jesus may be the one spoken of in Isaiah. He surely was despised and rejected. He was brought as a lamb to the slaughter. He was cut off from the land of the living. Every verse seems to point to him, and yet can it be? Can I have been this wrong all of my life? Can all of my people be wrong?*

His thoughts were interrupted as a faint knocking on the door brought him back to the present. He lay the Bible down, got up, and walked to the door. Opening it he found Hilda Swenson standing there holding a paper sack in her hand.

"I baked this morning, Mr. Dimitri. You know we Swedes love pastries, so I thought you men might be getting hungry for something sweet."

"Come in, Miss Swenson. Yes, indeed. I do have a sweet tooth, and so do the others. Here, sit down and let me fix you some coffee or maybe tea?"

"I like coffee a great deal, but I can't stay long."

Jacob busied himself with making the coffee, then when he sat down, he opened the paper sack. Taking one of the round, fat pastries, he bit into it. His eyes opened with surprise. "This is delicious! You are wonderful cook, Miss Swenson."

"Oh, not really. My mother was, but of course, she's not able to cook anymore. She did teach me how to make these sweet rolls."

Jacob ate two of the pastries and attempted to engage Hilda in a conversation. He found her to be very shy at first. It was the first time he had ever been alone with her, but soon she began to speak more freely.

"And how is that yearling that Dov won for you at the fair?"

"Oh, she is the sweetest thing!" Hilda exclaimed, and her eyes brightened. She was, as usual, wearing overalls and a straw hat to keep her blonde hair up. But now she took it off and her hair fell down her back. She had beautiful hair, blonde and clean with a healthy glow. She was not a pretty woman, but there was a goodness in her face that pleased Jacob a great deal. Of course she was large, much larger than Jacob himself, but he could tell that she was well formed—not fat in the least—no indeed! Her forearms were as strong as a man's, it seemed. Her shoulders were broad, and she gave the impression of great strength.

Jacob Dimitri was a wise old man. Some would even call him crafty. He had learned long ago how to draw people out of their shells, and soon without her realizing it, Hilda was telling him a great deal about herself.

When Jacob asked almost casually if she ever thought of having a husband and a family, she flushed and shook her head. "No. I don't think of that."

"I don't see why not. It's natural enough for a healthy young woman to want such things."

"It's—it's not for me, sir. No man would ever have me."

"Why not?"

"Why not! Why, look at me. I have this bad scar—and I'm big as a house."

"No, no, child, you are not. Large perhaps, but healthy and strong."

Hilda suddenly laughed. She had a good laugh, and her eyes grew merry. "Yes. I'm large enough, all right. I think if I had wrestled that man instead of Dov, I might even have won. But no man wants a cow like me for a wife." She suddenly grew more serious. "I would never say so to anyone else, but your granddaughter is such a beautiful young woman. She will find a husband, and she will have fine-looking children and be happy. And I'm glad for her."

"With God anything is possible. Don't you agree?"

For a moment Hilda dropped her head, hiding her eyes. She put her hands together and clasped them, and Jacob saw that her hands were clean although obviously callused. The nails were pink, and the white moon shone. She had really beautiful hands—not feminine, but not masculine either. "I am a Christian," she said finally. "And I know the Bible says that we can pray for what we want."

"And do you believe that?"

"I—I don't know, sir. It seems too much."

"Too much for God! Oh, surely not! He was able to feed the children of Israel for forty years with bread from heaven. Surely he can find a man who would love you and care for you."

Hilda shook her head and smiled. "That day is gone for me. That's for young girls. I'm thirty-one years old now. What man would want me?"

Jacob saw that she was uncomfortable, and he regretted it. He knew she would make some man a wonderful wife, and he determined privately to talk to Reisa about it. She was a woman and understood such things better than he.

"I've been studying the Bible, the New Testament, with Sam. Of course, I only knew the Old Testament, but he's been showing me some wonderful things." He hesitated and then said, "How is it that you became a Christian? Were you baptized when you were a baby?"

"Oh, no. I didn't know the Lord until I was fourteen years old."

"Can you tell me how you came to be a Christian?"

"Well, I've heard several people tell what an awful time they had becoming a Christian. An evangelist came through and told about how he drank, and he killed a man, and he went to jail. Oh, it was awful! And it took all that to bring him to God. But I wasn't that way at all." She smiled shyly, and her voice was mild. "I began listening to the preacher and to my father, who was a fine Christian man. I heard that Jesus died for our sins, and one time when I was just past fourteen the preacher preached a sermon on the suffering servant. His text was 'He shall see the travail of his soul and shall be satisfied.'"

Jacob's eyes blinked, and Hilda asked, "What's the matter, Mr. Dimitri?"

"Oh, nothing, Miss Swenson. It's just that I'd been reading that Scripture just before you came."

"Well, the preacher said," Hilda went on, "nothing man ever did really satisfied God. No matter how good he was, or how many offerings he made, or how much money he gave. Even if he went to church and did many religious things, he was evil. He said that all had sinned and come short of the glory of God."

"That is in the Old Testament as well as the New."

"Is it? Well, it made a great impression on me. I knew I was a sinner. Then when the preacher said, 'Jesus died for us' and also 'God saw the travail of his soul and he was satisfied,' oh, that pleased me! How I wanted to satisfy God! I was out in a cotton field the next afternoon chopping cotton, and as I went down the row the verse kept coming to my mind. 'God will see the travail of his soul and will be satisfied.' And finally I just stopped in the middle of that field. I was all alone that day. I remember it was cool, the wind was blowing, and I just knelt down right between those rows of cotton. The fields were white and the sky was blue, and I just prayed a simple prayer."

"Can you remember it, my dear?"

"Oh, it was something like 'Jesus, I'm a sinner. I know that, and I can't help myself. So I ask you to forgive me. You must love me because you died for me.'"

"And that was all."

"That was all."

"Well, what happened? Did you feel any different?"

"Not right away. I was a little disappointed. I got up and began hoeing cotton again. It was about ten o'clock in the morning. At noon it was time to get lunch, and after I ate and went back I thought all afternoon about what I had done. And I said, 'God, I don't feel anything. Shouldn't I shout as some people do?' But nothing happened—except I began to feel—oh, I don't know, Mr. Dimitri. I'm not one to show my emotion much, but I began to think about Jesus again, and as I did I began to feel very relaxed and very happy. I even began singing a song in the cotton field." And she began to sing.

"What can wash away my sins?
Nothing but the blood of Jesus.
What can make me whole again?
Nothing but the blood of Jesus."

"I sang it over and over all afternoon." Hilda's eyes were shining now, and she leaned forward, clasping her hands together. "And ever since that day I felt, somehow, that my soul is safe in his hands. I don't show it much, I suppose, but sometimes I think about what Jesus did for me. And when I read about it my eyes begin to fill up, and I know what I did when I was fourteen years old is still good."

Jacob was intrigued with this young woman's testimony. He had listened carefully, and now he said, "It's somewhat like Sam's testimony. He was in the army, and he went to a meeting. A preacher preached, and Sam said he just fell on his face and began to cry and beg God to come into his life. And he says that God did it! When he knelt down, he said, he was a sinner, and when he got up, so Sam says, he was a saint." Jacob rubbed his hands together and shook his head. "I wish my own longings for God could be that simple."

"I know you're a scholar," she said, "and can speak other languages and can read the Hebrew in the Bible. My father used to tell me that sometimes smart people have a harder time finding God. He said they get caught up in their search, and they forget to look for the person."

"Your father sounds like a very wise man."

"Oh, he wasn't educated, but he was wise. I've noticed that simple people find God quicker than those that have a lot of education."

Jacob was feeling rather uncomfortable. Everything seemed to be closing in upon him. "I've always been taught to keep the Law. I've believed that if I kept the Law, kept the Sabbath, and tried to obey God, when I stand before him I'll be all right."

Hilda shook her head slightly. "If we could be saved from our sins simply by keeping the Law, why did Jesus die?"

The simplicity of her question caught at Jacob sharply.

"Everything hinges on Jesus," Jacob finally said slowly. "He is either the Son of God—or he is not. If he is not, many people are confused and misled. But if he is, then many more are misled in not believing him. With God as my witness, I want to know the truth!" He lifted his sad eyes, and asked directly, "Is Jesus real to you, Miss Swenson?"

Instantly Hilda nodded. "When I pray, I know he is there. When I am lonely and grow afraid, I pray—and suddenly he's there, though I can't see him. But, Mr. Dimitri, Jesus is more real to me than—than *you* are. He's more real to me than my own flesh."

Jacob Dimitri had never heard of anything like this, but it had the absolute ring of truth. He said heavily, "Thank you for sharing this with me, Miss Swenson."

"I must go now," Hilda said. She stood, headed for the door, but then turned and said, "I'll be praying for you. You are a good man, and your granddaughter is a wonderful woman. I want you both to know the Lord in your hearts."

After she left, Jacob could not be still. He paced the floor for a long time, then finally left the house. He had put on his coat, for the October wind was getting colder, and he did not bear cold weather well. He walked down to the small creek that wound around the cabin and followed it upstream, not paying attention to the world about him, for his mind was concerned with the world within. He prayed, or tried to, but it seemed there was no answer. Never had he been so confused, and finally, wearily, he turned back home.

He said little the rest of the day, and both Sam and Phineas noticed at lunch that he was quiet. Sam asked if he wanted them to study together, but Jacob said, "No, not right now, I think, Sam."

All afternoon he kept to himself, sometimes sitting on the porch staring out into the distance. Twice he got up and took a walk, came back, and resumed his vigil.

At supper time he ate but little, and shortly after that he said, "I think I will go to bed."

"Good night, Jacob," Sam said quickly. "I hope you feel better tomorrow."

"Thank you, Sam."

He undressed quickly and went to bed. As always, he tried to pray as he lay awake on his pillow, but thoughts of Isaiah 53 kept coming back to him. He had memorized it by this time, for he had an excellent memory, and the words kept coming back to him: *He hath no form nor comeliness—he is despised and rejected of men—surely he hath borne our griefs and carried our sorrow—he was wounded for our transgression*—over and over again the words seemed to come until Jacob grew almost distraught. He simply could not get the matter of Jesus Christ out of his mind.

For a long time he lay there tossing and turning, but never did he fall into a sound sleep. Finally after two hours of restlessness, he threw the cover back and knelt beside his bed and began to pray. "Oh, God," he whispered, "please, speak to me. You know I want to do your will. I just don't know what it is." He hesitated for a moment and then prayed the prayer that he had tried not to pray for the past weeks. "If Jesus Christ is the Messiah, let me know it."

For a long moment he knelt there as if expecting God to speak audibly—but nothing happened. He remembered Hilda saying that after she had prayed nothing had seemed to happen. Again and again he lifted his voice, not loudly but in an agonized whisper. Finally he thought of Hilda's simple prayer, and pressing his face into the cover of his bed as he knelt there, he began to weep. Finally in a broken voice, he said, "Oh, God, I open my heart to you. I cry out to you, Jesus. Help me, for I put my trust in you."

Over and over again he prayed this prayer. He remained on his knees until they ached and then went numb. Repeatedly he called upon God, confessed that he was a sinner, and asked that he find peace. And over and over again he called upon Jesus.

Finally, weary in body and exhausted in mind, he simply slumped there half asleep, totally enervated. But as he lay there something happened. He could never explain it afterwards, but he remembered what Hilda had told him—that she had known God was in her by the peace that came into her spirit.

Jacob Dimitri heard no voice, but he somehow, for the first time in his life, knew with an absolute certainty that God was pleased with him! He knelt there simply letting this assurance grow, and he knew without any doubt whatsoever that something had taken place that would change his entire life.

Getting to his feet slowly, for his limbs were aching, he fell into bed and covered himself with a quilt. He lay there expecting the peace to go away, but it did not. He began to praise the Lord and to thank him for his goodness. And as the peace soaked into his spirit, he smiled and went to sleep as if he were a little child.

Part Three

Twenty-Three

Reisa returned from their fourth trip bubbling over with enthusiasm. They had sold all the gold rings on credit and much of the rest of their merchandise. They celebrated a victory dinner that night with Phineas trying his hand at some Jewish cooking. Reisa had taught him very well, and he served them *k'nishes*, Jacob's favorite dish, consisting of baked dumplings filled with meat and liver. He had also tried his hand at what Reisa called *kugel* but was simply a bread pudding with raisins.

Jacob, more excited than Reisa had seen him, could not say enough to Reisa and the two men. He seemed almost as happy, if not happier, than Reisa herself.

The following day Reisa simply relaxed. She did take some time to make lists of merchandise and supplies for their next venture out with the wagon, but mostly she spent time with her grandfather, talking or simply sitting together. It pleased her that Jacob looked much better than usual.

Late that afternoon she mentioned this to Sam. "Don't you think Grandfather looks better?"

"He sure does. He's eatin' better, and he sure could use a few pounds."

"I haven't seen him so relaxed and happy in a long time. He was worried about money, and now he's relieved that our peddling has turned out so well."

"I don't reckon that's it."

"You don't?"

"No, I don't."

"Well, what do you think it is?"

"I don't think it's money," Sam replied slowly. The two were sitting in the kitchen as Reisa peeled potatoes. Sam, having only one arm, was not much good at this, but he was good at talking. Handing her a potato, he said thoughtfully, "If money would make people happy, there wouldn't never be no miserable rich people. And you know that ain't so, Reisa."

"No, it's not."

"And if it took money to be happy, you'd never see anybody that was poor with any spirit about them. But that ain't so either, is it?"

"No, Sam. You're right about that."

"So I don't think it's the good luck you've had with your trips and your sellin'. As a matter of fact, I think that was all God's doin'."

"You think *everything* is God's doing."

"Why, certain I do! Ain't nobody ever gonna convince me no different, neither." Sam paused to take a bite out of one of the peeled potatoes. Reisa clucked her tongue, took the potato, and carved out the bite. He grinned for a moment, then became more serious. "No. I figure your granddad's got somethin' a lot more than a little cash to make him happy. I think he's got his ducks all in a row with God."

As usual, Reisa was confused by the many idioms of Sam Hall. "Got his ducks in a row?" she said. "What does that mean?"

"Oh, it's just an old sayin'. It means everything's all been arranged right, and somehow I think your granddad's gettin' right with God."

Reisa continued slowly peeling a long strip that reached the floor. Finally she looked up to fix her eyes on Sam. "What makes you think that?"

"Well, I've allus noticed what a heavy burden he's had on him ever since you two come here. Now it's like that burden's been done lifted off. And the only one I know that can really do that is Jesus."

"Oh, come, Sam! There are people who are happy without Jesus."

"I'll not argue that with you, but you know somethin'? I found out there's a big difference between joy and happiness."

"What sort of difference? I thought it was the same."

"Nope. The Bible says the fruit of the Spirit is joy. It's somethin' God gives. Now you take happiness. As long as everything's goin' all right, we got plenty to eat, no big problems on the horizon, why, we're happy. But what happens if you lose some of that and bad times strike? Tell me that."

"Well, we're not happy anymore."

"Exactly right! But the joy of the Lord ain't like that, Reisa. It comes from the Lord, and it's downright permanent. So when we got the joy that God gives us, even if somethin' terrible happens, that don't have nothin' to do with the joy we feel. As a matter of fact, I think somebody can be unhappy and have lots of joy. That is, he can be plumb disheartened about losin' his arm or somethin' like that, but deep down he knows it's all right."

Reisa continued peeling potatoes, and finally Sam got up to get firewood for the stove. He paused at the door to make one final remark. "I think your grandpa looks an awful lot like a fella that's done met up with Jesus. He's the only one that can give a feller bone-deep joy!"

The following day, Reisa went into Richmond to buy supplies from the wholesalers. The first thing she did, however, was to make a deposit at the bank. Mr. Coats was so happy to see her he came over and took her deposit personally, saying, "I want to congratulate you on your venture, Miss Dimitri, and I'm sure you'll have many more good times ahead."

After she left the bank, Reisa went to see several wholesalers and found them to be most helpful. All of them were encouraging and interested in her venture. One of them remarked, "You know, Miss Dimitri, Ed Stevens who runs the general store isn't too happy about what you're doing—but Ed's so tight he'd steal flies from a dead spider!"

Reisa laughed out loud, for this was such an odd way of putting it. "I'll try not to put Mr. Stevens out of business."

She finished her business and found Sam waiting. "Sam, will you go by and pick up the merchandise I've bought? Then come to the Elite Cafe. I'm going to get some tea and something sweet. Come in when you're done, and I'll buy you something."

Sam agreed, and Reisa went to the Elite Cafe. As she walked in, the manager greeted her. At once she saw Marianne Driver sitting at the same table where they had lunched. Marianne spotted her and motioned her over. "How nice to see you, Reisa. Please join me."

"I was going to write you a letter," Reisa said as she took a chair, "but now I won't have to." She reached into her purse and pulled out a checkbook. "I can make a payment on the loan that you gave me."

"Oh, not now," Marianne said quickly. "Business will fluctuate. It's getting to be winter time, and you may have some lean months ahead. Don't even talk about paying me back for at least six months."

Reisa protested, but Marianne would have it no other way. Finally Marianne ordered, and as she drank the tea and ate the sweet roll, Marianne asked her about Ben.

"He's so wonderful, going with Dov and me! No one else can handle Samson and Delilah as well."

"I think those are lovely names. Which one is the mean one?"

"They're both just awful! They'd run away in a minute, but Ben can jerk them up short. Dov is learning to handle them, too. He just goes and gets one of their ears and twists, and they cry like babies. It's enough to make you laugh. They'd bite me anytime if they got a chance."

"Then you let Dov and Ben take care of them." Marianne took a sip of tea, then asked quietly, "How is Ben doing?"

Reisa knew instantly what Marianne meant. "Not very well, I'm afraid. Oh, he seems to be content enough at times. He enjoys it when Phineas gets his fiddle out, and they sing songs they sang at the war. But he's not happy. I wish," she said wistfully, "I could do something to help him."

"You *have* done something. You saved his life, and he thinks a great deal of you, I'm sure."

Reisa lowered her head.

"You think a lot of him, don't you, Reisa?" Marianne asked softly.

The question took Reisa aback. She could not think for a few moments of how to answer, and finally simply nodded. "Yes, Marianne. I like him very much."

"Well, there have been a lot of prayers sent up for that son of ours. And I've got good news."

"Good news? What's that?"

"My daughter Pru and her family are coming to see us."

"Pru? That's a funny name."

"Well, it's short for Prudence, but everyone calls her Pru. She's married to Martin Rogers, a fine man, a doctor. They have three beautiful boys."

"I remember—Ben told me about them."

"They get down to Richmond at least twice a year. John and I have been urging them to move back. Martin could have a wonderful practice here. He wouldn't make as much money, but we'd be near the grandchildren, and I think children need their grandparents."

"I'll agree with that. My grandfather's all I have. When will they come?"

"They're not sure, but when they do come, you can just know Pru will come hunting Ben up. The two of them were always closer to each other than to anybody else. Matt was always so serious."

"That was your older son who died in the war?"

"Yes. There's not a day gone by, Reisa, that I don't think about him. But he was very different from Ben." Marianne's eyes grew thoughtful as she continued. "We always knew that if there was any mischief, it would be either Ben or Pru. Usually both of them. Pru was one year older, but they were much more like brothers than brother and sister."

"I hope she'll visit Ben," Reisa said. "I know he gets lonely for his family." She wanted to say more about John Driver, but she knew that it would be out of place. "We'll be leaving soon. I'd hate for Ben to miss her."

"As soon as she comes, I'll get word to you."

That evening when Reisa got home, she went to Ben at once. "I have good news for you. Your sister is coming to see you."

"Pru? How do you know that?"

Reisa admitted, "I ran into your mother when I was in town today. She told me."

"I'll be glad to see her. We were always close."

Reisa studied Ben's face, glad to see the good effect the news had on him. She thought again what a shame it was that he had to wear an eye patch. Now that he was filling out, there was a lean handsomeness to him. The patch gave him a rakish look, and she grieved over it. He had told her once that it was a good thing it was his right eye. When she had asked why, he had answered, "Because I'm left-handed. I use my left eye to sight a rifle with. So even after I lost my eye, I stayed with my outfit. I couldn't have done that if it had been my left eye."

The two were interrupted by Sam, who stuck his head out the door and said, "Come and get it before we throw it out."

The meal was excellent, and afterwards Phineas got his fiddle down and played for a long time. Sam whispered to Reisa, "He hasn't played like that in a coon's age. You folks are good for him."

"I feel like we're imposing, Sam."

"Not a'tall! Why, we're all just one big family here now."

"What a nice thing to say!"

Later on, just as Reisa was getting ready for bed, a knock sounded at her door. She went at once to open it and found Jacob there. "What is it, *Zaideh?*"

"I must talk with you, Reisa."

This had a serious sound to it, and Reisa said at once, "Come in. Sit down on the chair, and I'll sit on the bed."

The two could still hear the voices of Phineas and Sam downstairs. They were arguing about one of the battles in the war—one of those interminable arguments that never got settled. "What is it, *Zaideh?* You've been feeling well lately, haven't you?"

"Better than you might believe."

A smile touched his lips, and Reisa felt relieved, but she still asked, "Is anything wrong?"

"I don't know whether you'll think so."

"Why, anything that pleases you pleases me. What is it?" she asked.

Jacob's eyes were bright, Reisa saw, and she could not imagine what he was going to say.

"I have come to believe, my dear Reisa, that Jesus Christ is the Messiah."

Reisa stared at her grandfather. For one wild moment she thought he was joking—but he would never joke about a thing like this! "Why, *Zaideh,* that can't be!"

"I'm afraid it is. Let me tell you about it." Jacob began speaking of how it had all begun with his talks with Sam. "The more I studied the New Testament," he said quietly, "the more I recognized that this Jesus seemed to fit so many prophesies that

I had pondered over in the Law and in the prophets. Sam read me one verse out of the New Testament. I can't remember the location, but I remember the words. It said, 'To him give all the prophets witness, that through his name whosoever believeth in him shall receive remission of sins.' That's not exactly right, but the first part is. 'To him gave all the prophets witness.' It's true, Reisa! Jesus was born in Bethlehem exactly where everyone expected, and he was born of a virgin, exactly as Isaiah foretold: 'A virgin shall be with child.'"

"But do you really believe that Jesus was born of a virgin?"

"I would not have believed it some time ago, but after looking at his whole life—how he poured himself out for all people—I firmly believe it now."

Reisa had never been so confused. "And do you believe that he rose from the dead?"

Jacob did not answer for a moment. "I have struggled with this, and it is this one thing that has made me a believer in Jesus. There have been other prophets, other men claiming to be the Messiah. There will be many more. There have been other religious leaders such as Buddha and Mohammed, but all those men *died*. You can go to their tombs and say they're there, but if you went to the tomb where Jesus was placed, it would be empty. I believe that with all of my heart."

Reisa felt a great fear, somehow. This thing that had happened to her grandfather went against all she had ever learned. She remembered all of the stories she had heard of Christians persecuting the Jews, but when she brought that up, Jacob said, "Jesus is not responsible for what his followers do. I believe he is the Prince of Peace that the prophet foretold. His followers may betray him. Indeed, one called Judas sold him into the hands of his enemies."

"Yes, I read that in the little book of John."

"Judas was wrong, and others have been wrong. But that does not change what Jesus is."

Reisa had never seen her grandfather more excited. Still she was afraid. "Are you sure, *Zaideh?* Somehow I feel this will separate us."

"No, that must never happen! I cannot force you to take this new way, Reisa. No one can force another to do this, but I tell you with all honesty—I have peace in my heart for the first time in my life. Every day, for a time after I called on God in the name of Jesus, I expected to wake up and find this peace gone. But it never is! It's there every morning. It will be there until I die. This way—it is the right way."

Reisa began to tremble. Jacob reached out and took her hand in his. His hands were frail and weak while hers were strong. But the strength was in his spirit, not in his hands. "This will not make me love you any less—indeed, I love you more than I ever did. I seem to love all people more. I don't know why that is. Sam says that when one becomes a Christian, the Holy Spirit of God comes within him and puts within him those things that I've always longed for—love and joy and peace. But never be afraid that I will love you any less."

He rose, and Reisa rose with him. He kissed her tenderly, then she asked, "Have you told anyone else about this?"

"No, I have not."

"Why not, *Zaideh?*"

"I can't say. At first I was cautious—and I'm still cautious. But every day I read the New Testament, and more and more I am drawn to Jesus. There was never anyone like him, Reisa. Never—never!"

Reisa watched as her grandfather left, and then she sat down on the bed, her legs weak. She did not know what all this meant, but she knew her grandfather would not deceive her. He would not deceive himself either. This thing that had happened to him was real, and she knew that the peace he had was not feigned.

She sat there for a long time, and Boris crawled into her lap. She stroked his black fur and finally shook her head. Getting up and putting Boris down, she began to undress. She put on her gown, got into bed, and Boris came to nuzzle at her side. She put her arm around him and held him, and he began to purr. For some reason tears came to her eyes. She did not know why, but the news that her grandfather was forsaking the old way and turning to a new way frightened her badly.

She prayed, "Oh, God, take care of me! Take care of my grandfather! I can't do anything but beg you for this, oh great Creator of the Universe!"

Twenty-Four

"What's wrong with you, Miss Reisa?" Sam asked. "You look plumb down in the mouth."

Reisa and Sam were washing the dishes up after breakfast. The others had gone outside to do their chores, and Jacob was up in his room reading the Bible.

"Down in the mouth? What does that mean?"

"Why, it means you look like you feel bad."

Reisa looked at Sam and said, "My grandfather is changing, Sam. I'm worried about him."

Sam Hall nodded and studied her, a fond and almost fatherly expression in his eyes. "Why, he's all right. Matter of fact, he looks a lot healthier than he did when you two first come here."

"Oh, he's better physically, but he's not the man I grew up with. He took care of me, Sam, when I had nobody at all. You don't know what it means to be a Jew. We don't have much, and my people have suffered terribly—but at least we knew who we were. Now I'm afraid. My grandfather"—her voice trembled—"he talks about Jesus all the time."

Hall put his hand on her shoulder. His voice was soft as a woman's as he spoke, and his eyes were gentle. "I wish you could see this like I do. It's hard to see change, but this is a *good* change, Miss Reisa. Jesus makes people feel better, not worse."

Reisa did not answer but dropped her head. She wanted to weep, but knew that she must not. The fear that had come to her was like nothing she'd ever experienced, and as she stared down at the soapy dish water, she wished desperately they'd never left their homeland.

The rising sun climbed steadily, glowing bright, and from far away came a thin cry of a dog. "Thet dog's on a trail," Sam remarked. "And yore grandpa's on a trail, too. He's after God, and anytime a feller gets after God, he'll find him. I reckon you'll find Jesus one day."

Reisa shook her head and dried off her hands. She was fond of Sam, but she wanted to hear no more of Jesus. Going to her room, she shut the door and flopped onto her bed. She clung to Boris, who purred and touched her face with a soft pad.

"You're the same, Boris—I wish *Zaideh* was!"

Sam went outside, where Ben was repairing a fence. He stood over him, saying abruptly, "Ben, Miss Reisa's havin' a hard time."

Ben looked at him with surprise. "Why, things are going well for us, Sam."

"Maybe in some ways—but thet girl is worried."

"About what?"

"She's afraid of whut's happenin' to her grandpa."

Ben frowned and gave the barbed wire a tug, then drove a staple in before he answered. "He seems fine to me. Matter of fact, I've been glad to see how well he looks."

"It ain't his health she's worried about."

"What then?"

"Ben, I ain't ever pestered you with religion, but I'm curious. You ever been saved?"

A long silence greeted this question, and finally Ben said, "When I was young, I thought I was. But then everything changed. The war just about tore me up inside, Sam. Guess it did that to lots of men. I tried to follow the Lord, but I guess I saw too much killing. I couldn't see God in any of it."

"Lots of fellers had that problem."

Ben did not respond for several seconds, but finally he shook his head. "After the war, I was just crazy, Sam. Took to drinking and running with a wild bunch. It nearly killed my folks—but somehow I just couldn't get on the right track."

"It's not too late, Ben," Sam said quietly.

Ben turned to face the smaller man squarely. "What do my wicked ways have to do with Reisa?"

"Just this—if you was right with God, Ben, I think you'd see she's hurtin'."

Sam's flat statement took Ben hard. His lips tightened and a troubled light came to his good eye. "In that, I guess you're right, Sam. Drunks don't care about anything but themselves and getting the next drink. I'm not a drunk—don't care for liquor that much. But something's wrong with me, Sam. I don't know where God is—and I don't know what I am."

Sam nodded slightly, and suddenly he put his one hand on Ben's shoulder. "I lost an arm and you lost an eye in the war. But we both make out right well without 'em. But when a man loses God, Ben, he can't make it."

The pressure of Sam's hand on his shoulder warmed Ben, and he said slowly, "I guess God's not lost, Sam—so it must be me. And for a long time I've been trying to find what I had once." He looked up at the sun wreathed in skeins of ragged clouds. Finally he whispered, "I'm sorry for Reisa, Sam. But I can't even help myself!"

Sam started to reply, but Ben turned abruptly and walked rapidly away.

For a long moment the small man watched him, then shook his head sorrowfully. "Lord, Ben's in a mess. But like he said, *you* ain't lost. I'd shore appreciate it, Lord, if you'd bring 'im back to the fold!"

From somewhere outside in the distance, John Driver heard a voice lifted in some sort of admonition. He knew it was his servant Trask correcting his young son and smiled for a moment. Trask and Dorrie had been with his family for many years. He had given them their freedom before the Civil War as he had the rest of his slaves. Now he leaned back in his chair and thought about what a tragedy the war had been. He had said once to Jefferson Davis, "It would have been much better if the North had just paid slave owners for their investment."

Now the house was quiet, and Driver had set apart this time every day to read and to work on his books. The books were done, and now he was reading a sermon by a British pastor—Charles Haddon Spurgeon. Spurgeon's sermon was taken from Psalms 30:5, "Weeping may endure for a night, but joy cometh in the morning." Driver read the sermon as he always read this minister's words, with great attention, for he had found that Spurgeon knew how to touch the heart as well as the head. For days his heart had been heavy, and now he read hungrily as Spurgeon spoke to the problem of depression:

> *... let us go on boldly; if the night be never so dark. The morning cometh, which is more than they can say who do not know the Lord Christ. It may be all dark now, but soon it will be light; it may be dark now, but it will soon be happiness. What matters it*

though "weeping may endure for a night" when "joy cometh in the morning"?

Reading these final words, John Driver shut the book and sat with his eyes closed. As always, he never wanted to be ungrateful to God. He remembered the terrible dark days of the war when all was lost, and so many of his friends had gone down to unmarked graves. He thought of the women today who had no husbands, and children who knew no fathers. He had never gotten over the loss of his son Matthew, and he felt that he never would. But as he remained still in the quietness of the room, he prayed, "Lord, I don't want to be ungrateful. You've given me so much. Help me to continually give thanks unto you..."

Even as he prayed suddenly he heard an unusual sound, small light feet running down the hall. He opened his eyes and rose as the door burst open, and the room suddenly seemed to be full of little boys.

"Grandpa! Grandpa!"

Driver's three grandsons—Johnny, David, and Robert—swarmed him. He knelt down to get on their level. Johnny was twelve, David ten, and Robert eight. He encircled them all with his arms, and his heart was lightened as he heard them all trying to talk at the same time.

"Boys, you're going to smother your grandfather!" Prudence entered the room with her husband, Martin. She was a tall, well-formed woman with auburn hair. Martin was a man in his early forties with blonde hair and blue eyes. He had served with Pickett in the war as a surgeon.

Quickly Driver peeled off the boys and went over to embrace Pru and take her kiss. He turned and shook hands with Martin. "I'm heartily glad to see you. We've missed you all so much."

"Granddad, you promised to take us fishing," Johnny said. Like the other boys, he had dark hair and blue eyes—almost electric eyes they were so bright.

"Yes, Grandpa. We want to go now!" Robert was by far the loudest of the trio, and now he said, "I'm going to catch the biggest fish of all."

"Boys, your grandfather can't take you fishing right now."

"No, but we will go this afternoon."

"Can we see the horses?" David said. He was the scholar of the family, with a keen mind and a rather quiet personality.

Prudence said at once, "Martin, why don't you take the boys to see the horses while I help Mother with dinner?"

"All right, I'll do that. Come along, boys." He herded them outside, and Driver stood listening until the door closed and shut off their voices.

"I'm glad to see you, Dad," Prudence said. She patted his arm affectionately and asked, "How have you been?"

"Oh, I'm always well. And the boys look well. Good to have a doctor for a son-in-law."

"Sit down and tell me everything you've done. It seems like it's been a year since I've been here."

The two sat down on the small divan and talked until they caught up on the news. Finally Driver asked eagerly, "Have you and Martin talked any more about moving back to Richmond?"

"Yes, we have. A great deal, as a matter of fact."

"Do you think there's any chance of it?"

"I think so. Neither of us like Washington. I don't think it's good for the boys to grow up in the middle of a big city."

"We've got plenty of country left around here." Driver smiled.

"Martin would make less money, of course."

"Well, money's not everything."

"No, it's not. We know that."

"I need you here, Pru. And so does your mother." Driver put his hand on her shoulder and squeezed it. He was a man who did not like to ask favors, but the words had come out almost without volition. "And I—I need my grandsons here. I miss those rascals every day."

"I think it will work out. It will be Martin's decision, of course. He's the one that has to make the living, but I know he'd like a quieter life." Pru looked at John Driver, studying his face. Then she said without preamble, "Ben's back, isn't he? How's he been? Have you seen him?"

Instantly Driver stiffened. He shook his head. "Yes, he's back. He's living on the other side of Richmond. I've just seen him a couple of times in passing."

"But hasn't he been here?"

"Pru, I don't think he needs to come here."

Prudence started to speak, then shook her head. Instead, she simply leaned over and kissed him and said, "I'll go help Mother with dinner. It's just like cooking for a regiment. Those boys eat like starved wolves."

"All right, I'll go out and find Martin and the boys. Maybe I'll take them riding."

Driver watched as his only daughter left the room. It felt good to have one of his children back in the house. Now, if only Matthew were still alive, and if only Ben hadn't. . .

No. He shut his thoughts off. If onlys would get him nowhere. He left the room, in search of his energetic grandsons.

Prudence went at once to the kitchen, where her mother and Dorrie were busy stirring up a meal. Dorrie came over, took Pru's embrace, and said, "Them boys is gonna put a little life in this old house, Miss Pru."

"Dorrie, we've all missed your cooking. We're going to work you to death."

"No, you ain't. Now, you and your mama go talk. I can fix this myself."

Pru said, "But I need to help."

"You mind what I say! I was cookin' when you wasn't no bigger than a nubbin'. Now you 'uns get out of here."

Marianne laughed and said, "Well, when Dorrie speaks it's done. Come along."

The two went into the parlor, and almost at once Pru said, "Dad won't talk about Ben. What's wrong with him?"

"I don't know. You know how bitter he was over the loss of Matthew. And somehow I think he feels that it should have been Ben. I know that's a hard thing to say, but Matthew was his favorite."

"He's bitter. I can see that."

"Yes, he is—and it grieves me."

"Bitterness has killed more people than bullets," Prudence said slowly. "Dad knows that. Why can't he see what he's doing?"

"Well, the devil knows our weak points, Pru. Your father was able to put aside his bitterness toward the Yankees—but he's blind as far as Ben is concerned." Marianne reached out and took Pru's hand. "Go see him, Pru. You two were always such good friends. He's very sad, and I don't know anyone that could cheer him up better than you."

"All right," Prudence agreed, nodding her head thoughtfully. "I'll go first thing in the morning."

❧

The trees were turning red and gold and scarlet, and Pru looked up with keen enjoyment as she drove the roan mare along the road. Winter would come soon, but now was the finest time, in her opinion, of the whole year. The air was clean and fresh, scented with the smell of burning leaves. Pru slapped the mare's flanks with the line. "Get up, Ruby! You can do better than that!"

Ruby, indeed, could do better and broke into a fast trot. She was a lively mare, but Pru was an excellent driver. This drive pleased her, for she was tired of the confines of Washington.

She had left the house immediately after breakfast and driven through Richmond, emerging on the east side. She had always liked Richmond, and now it grieved her to see the damage that had been done by the Union troops. The war had left ugly scars that would take decades to heal, but here in the country the wounds were less evident. The fields spread out on either side of the road, and from time to time she passed houses or small cabins, many of them occupied by ex-slaves. She stopped only once at a small store to ask the owner if he knew Sam Hall and Phineas Long.

"Yes, ma'am, I do. You go on down this road another two miles, take a left by the Jeffrey place. That's a big white house on the left. Take the left there, and it's another three miles on that road."

Pru had made the turn, and now as she followed the winding road that led between cotton fields and many acres of second-growth timber, she saw a house that looked much like the clerk's description. "Come on, Ruby," she said. "We'll find out."

Pulling up in front of the house, she tied the lines, then got out and walked around to pat Ruby on the side of the face. "Good girl," she said. Turning, she started toward the house, and as she did a young woman came out. She wore a scarf over her head, although her very black hair escaped in wisps.

"Yes, ma'am. Can I help you?"

"I'm looking for Ben Driver."

The woman looked surprised and curious. "Why, this is where he lives, but he's not here. He's gone over to the neighbor's to get some mules shod. He should be back very soon. As a matter of fact, I've expected him for some time."

Pru studied the young woman and remembered her mother's description of her. "Do you think I might wait?"

"Oh, yes. I'm Reisa Dimitri." She hesitated a moment, then said, "I'd guess you're Ben's sister, Mrs. Rogers."

Pru smiled. The girl was very sharp indeed. "Yes, I am, Miss Dimitri."

"Please just call me Reisa. Everyone does."

"Good. And I'm Pru."

"Come inside. We could drive over to where they're doing the shoeing, but we'd probably meet them on the way. If you come inside, I can fix some refreshment."

"Some tea or coffee or even water would be nice."

Reisa started to turn when Sam exited from the house. He stopped and gave the visitor a keen look. When he was introduced, he said, "That hoss looks like she needs a little waterin' and maybe a little feed."

"Would you be so kind?" Pru smiled. "She's a wonderful animal."

"Be proud to. Come along, missy." Sam took Ruby's lines and led her over to the trough, where he allowed her to drink.

When they stepped inside, they found Jacob and Phineas sitting at the table. "This is my grandfather, Mr. Jacob Dimitri, and Mr. Phineas Long. And this is Mrs. Rogers, Ben's sister, *Zaideh.*"

Jacob rose and bowed slightly. "It's an honor, Mrs. Rogers."

"Pleased to meet you, ma'am." Phineas nodded. "Excuse me, but I got some chores."

He left the room, and Pru said to Jacob, "Please, keep your seat."

"Yes. Sit down, *Zaideh.* And you, too, Prudence. I'll fix something."

Prudence sat down and found herself intrigued by the pair. She had heard their basic history from her mother, but she was impressed at the gentle manners of the grandfather. She found that although his English was less than perfect, he had a sharp inquiring mind.

Soon Reisa had hot tea. As she poured it, she said, "I wish we had our samovar."

"What's a samovar?" Pru asked curiously.

"Oh, it's just something to make tea in. It's one of the few things we brought from our home when we had to leave, but it is stored."

"My mother told me how much you two did for Ben. I'm very grateful to you."

"We only did what anyone would have done," Jacob said mildly.

"Perhaps so, but you were there, and you did it. And we're very grateful to you." She took the tea, sipped it, and then nodded. "This is very good."

"We'll be having lunch in about an hour," Reisa said eagerly. "I hope you'll be able to stay."

"Well, I do want to see Ben."

"He'll be anxious to see you, too. He's told me about you," Reisa said.

The three sat there talking, and soon Reisa was giving her version of their business. She spoke of how it had been Ben's willingness to help that had provided a wagon. As she spoke, Prudence admired the beauty of the young woman, and she also noted that she was not completely indifferent to Ben Driver.

They were on their second cup of tea when suddenly boots sounded, and Reisa said, "That's Ben."

Pru rose at once, and when Ben came in he smiled broadly, came over, and put his arms around her. He picked her completely up off the floor and kissed her on the cheek. "Pru!" he exclaimed. "It's been so long!"

"It's been too long, Ben, but it won't be anymore." Pru stepped back from his embrace and said, "You've lost weight."

"You should have seen me before Phineas started fattening me up. I looked like a snake." Ben sat down and pulled Pru to his side. "Now, tell me all about my nephews and that husband of yours and about yourself."

"Zaideh," Reisa said, "would you come upstairs with me? I want you to help me write some letters back home."

Jacob rose and said, "Of course, Reisa. Excuse us, please."

As soon as the two were gone, Prudence turned and took Ben's hand across the table. "How are you, Ben?"

"Oh, I'm all right."

"Now, Ben, we've always been able to talk straight to each other. Don't you remember when I was sixteen and madly in love with Farley Stapleton? You sat me down and told me what a fool I was making of myself."

Ben could not help smiling. "I was too rough on you."

"No, you weren't. I *was* being a fool."

"We could always talk, Pru." Ben held her hand in his and studied it. "We used to have some mighty long talks, didn't we? Well, I'm treading water, Pru," he said slowly. "Nothing has gone right—and I don't see any happy ending."

"Have you given up on God?"

"No, but I expect he must have given up on me."

"That's foolish talk, Ben!"

"I expect you're right."

"From what I hear he saved your life."

"Reisa and Dov did that."

"Your theology has gotten pretty bad. God used them, but he cares about *you.*"

Ben shook his head. "I expect my theology went down the drain some time back during the war when I lost friend after friend for a lost cause. I just seemed to lose all hope, Pru. Then when I lost Paul Jennings there at the very last, life caved in on me. It was only two weeks before the war was over. We'd gone through the whole thing together. I thought it was all over. We'd lose the war, but Paul and I would make it through. Then when a sniper got him, it was like his bullet hit me, too. I haven't cared much about anything since then."

Pru did not answer for a time, and then she said directly, "What about Reisa?"

Startled, Ben blinked and stared at Pru with a strange expression. "What about her?"

"What do you feel for her?"

"Why, I'm grateful, of course. She saved my life—she and Dov."

Pru said, "I thought we were going to talk straight."

"What do you expect me to say, Pru?" Driver said almost roughly. "I like the girl a lot, but she's Jewish, and I'm a backslider. What can be made of that?"

"I can't make anything of it, but God can. In any case, I'm glad to see you."

"How long will you stay with Mother and Father?"

"A week at least."

"Good. I want to see those nephews of mine."

Suddenly Pru knew she had to say something about their father. "Dad will change, Ben."

"I don't think so."

"Yes, he will. He's a strong man, but God will break him down. That's what I've been praying for—that whatever it takes, no matter how hard, Dad will learn to act like a father and not like a judge."

"That's hard talk, Pru."

"I love Dad, but he's wrong. And when we're wrong with God, whatever he has to do to bring us back will be for our good."

At this point footsteps interrupted them, and Sam and Dov entered.

Dov pulled off his cap and smiled. He seemed to fill the whole room, but there was a soft look in his eyes, and he smiled but said nothing. Ben introduced them, and Pru was impressed with this gentle giant who shook her small hand so carefully.

"You'll stay and take lunch with us," Sam said, and his tone permitted no denial.

Pru did stay, and the meal was very good indeed. She allowed Ben to take her on a tour of the place, and then Reisa proudly showed her their wagon.

Finally Pru had to leave, for it was a long drive back. Sam brought the mare and wagon around, helped her in, and stood beside her for a moment. "What's this about some boys you got, Miss Pru?"

Ben answered for her. "They're my nephews, Sam. I sure would like to see them."

Sam Hall didn't hesitate. "I want you and your husband and your boys to come out here and spend a day. We'll take those boys of yours fishing."

"Well, that would be very kind of you, but we wouldn't want to put you out," Pru said.

"There ain't no put out to it. You bring them boys out here, and we'll go coon huntin' and trot linin' in the river."

Pru looked over at Ben and saw the eagerness in his face. "You don't know what you're asking for, but we'll be glad to do it," she said.

"When could you come, ma'am?"

"I suppose the day after tomorrow, if you're sure. Just after lunch."

"I'm plumb sure! Why, I'm just lookin' for an excuse to get out of work. Just think of all the loafin' we can do with them young fellers. Right, Ben?"

"I expect you're right about that, Sam."

They all laughed merrily. And Pru left them that way, her heart a little lighter.

ঌ

John Driver watched from his study window as Pru drove up the long drive. Several minutes later, when he heard her steps in the hall, he went downstairs to greet her.

"Why, Pru, you've been gone. You been to Richmond?"

"No. I went to see Ben."

John Driver hesitated but could not think of an answer. He turned and would have left, but Pru took his arm. "Walk with me a bit."

Driver wanted to refuse, for he knew what was on Pru's mind. Nevertheless, they stepped off the porch and walked slowly toward the big grove of trees that shadowed the house. They reached there without either saying a word, but finally Pru stopped, and he turned to face her.

"Dad, I'm taking Martin and the boys to see Ben the day after tomorrow."

"You're a grown woman, and you do as you think best." He was unhappy, but he knew he could say no more.

Pru said quietly, "You're wrong, Dad. Very wrong."

Driver could not answer this. He simply stood there, unable to speak. Pru suddenly stepped forward and put her arms around him. She put her head on his chest and held him tightly, and when she spoke her voice was very quiet. "I've always respected you, Dad, and loved you. You gave me a father to use for a model when I chose a husband, and I'll always be grateful to you for that. And I'll always love you."

Without another word Pru turned and walked away.

John Driver suddenly found himself crushed by her gentleness. He would have taken it better if she had lashed out at him, but she was her mother's daughter. They both had a gentleness in them that he had always loved. There was a directness, too, and Pru's words struck him with great force. He turned blindly and walked away, not knowing where he went. He had been so happy when Pru and Martin and the boys had come, but now everything seemed to have turned bitter in his mouth.

Twenty-Six

Marianne stopped at the door of her husband's study and knocked gently. When his voice answered, "Come in," she stepped inside and found him standing in front of the large bay window. At once she noted that he was distressed, but she crossed the room to stand before him.

"I wish you would reconsider, John. It would mean so much to Ben if you'd come with us."

Driver had slept poorly the previous night. When Marianne had told him just before going to bed of her plan to go along on the visit to their son, he had been visibly upset, saying at once, "You'll have to go without me."

Marianne's heart was grieved as she studied her husband's face. She loved him, but now she said quietly, "John, anything else that you ask of me, I'll do it—but I must see Ben. He's our only son now, and I love him dearly."

"You must do as you think best, Marianne."

For one moment Marianne considered changing her mind, but her desire to encourage Ben was very strong. "I think we'll probably stay for dinner; I don't know exactly what time we'll be back."

"All right."

Driver's tone was clipped, but Marianne ignored his obvious displeasure. Leaning forward she kissed him, then turned and left the study.

When she reached the kitchen, she found Dorrie with what seemed to be a pile of food on the table.

"What in the world is all this, Dorrie?"

"You cain't go bustin' in on folks with a whole army without takin' some vittles. These is jist a few things I throwed together."

The "few things" involved three pies, a cake, a quarter of beef, and several large bowls of cooked vegetables.

Trask grinned and winked slyly at Marianne. "She don't cook this good fo' me."

"You don't need it! You gettin' fat as a possum! Now you load dis on the wagon for Miss Marianne."

Picking up a bowl of black-eyed peas, Marianne went outside with Trask and Dorrie to the large carriage where Martin was waiting. The boys were already running around like wild Indians, shouting and shoving each other.

Martin asked, "What's that?"

"Dorrie thought we should take some food."

"Not a bad idea. Those poor fellows don't know how these boys can eat. Let me help you load that, Trask."

Soon the food was loaded, and the boys were placed inside the large buggy. It was a covered buggy in case of rain, with curtains that could be drawn. Martin helped Marianne to climb in the front, then placed Pru and the boys on the back seat. Picking up the lines, he spoke to the team, "Get up there!"

The buggy jerked as the horses leaped forward, and Marianne caught a glance of John peering out the window of his study. "I'm sorry John wouldn't go with us," she said quietly.

Glancing at Marianne, Martin didn't answer at once, but when they pulled off on the main road, he said, "He'll come around."

As they moved along the dirt road at a brisk pace, Johnny insisted on singing songs. He started the song "Dixie," and the other boys joined in.

His voice masked by their singing, Martin added, "I've been praying that John would see how much Ben needs him—especially now."

Marianne was very fond of Martin. He was a fine husband and a devoted father, and she knew that he loved John. "He's making a terrible mistake, Martin."

"Well, God can do wonders. We'll just have to keep on praying that he'll work on John's heart."

Ben was splitting white oak for the cooking stove, a job he enjoyed. He and Dov had sawed the logs into eighteen-inch lengths, and he lifted the splitting maul, bringing it down firmly. The white oak split as cleanly as if it were rock. He'd always liked splitting wood, though sawing the logs into the proper lengths was tedious. He raised the maul again, quartered the log, then split it into smaller sections. When Reisa came to watch, he smiled at her. "You want to try it?"

"All right." She came over and took the splitting maul from Ben, but it was so heavy she could barely lift it over her head. He laughed and came to reach around her. Gripping the handle he lifted it, saying, "Just let it drop on the wood."

"Like this?" Reisa let the maul drop, conscious of his arms around her. The wood split, and she turned with a smile saying, "I did it!"

Driver was standing so close he could see the iris of her eyes and thought how clear they were. He felt the turbulence of her spirit as a man might feel strange currents of wind blowing across him. He felt suddenly that she was a light in darkness to him, a personality, a fragrance, and a will. He had noted that this woman constantly searched the world for color and warmth, treasuring these things as other women valued clothing and fine furniture. He felt also that Reisa longed for the comfort of a man's closeness that would end the solitary quality of her life.

Reisa asked uncertainly, "What is it, Ben?"

"Nothing. I was just thinking how strange it is that you and I met. Doesn't seem very likely—you in Russia, and me in jail in America. But somehow we came together."

"Our people have a story about men and women in love."

"What is it?"

"It tells about the time God made a creature, a beautiful creation. But somehow the creature displeased God, so he tore it in two. One half of it was man and one half was woman." Her eyes were thoughtful as she spoke, and a slight smiled turned up the corners of her lips. "Each of these was incomplete, so they wandered all over the world looking for their other half. Only one would fit; none of the rest would match what they were. And if they found each other, they were joined again and were very happy."

"Nice story," Ben remarked. "Most people don't find the right parts, seems to me."

"But sometimes they do. My grandfather and his wife were like that—and my parents also."

Ben suddenly reached out and touched the single lock of raven hair that had escaped her blue headscarf. She looked at him, saying nothing—but a woman's silence meant many things. He was not sure what she was thinking, but something in this woman pulled at him like a mystery. Whatever it was disturbed his own solitary way, and as they stood there under the pale early November sun, Ben Driver knew that he had never met a woman exactly like this one.

A sound caught Driver's attention, and he turned away to look across at the buggy that approached. "There they are," he said, "One o'clock, right on schedule." He leaned the maul against the wood pile. With Reisa at his side, he walked over to the drive, waiting until the buggy came to a stop, then called out, "Hello!"

The boys came pouring out of the buggy, then Martin leaped out and stepped forward to shake Ben's hand with a hard grip. "Good to see you, Ben," he smiled.

"You're looking fine, Mart," Ben said, then went to help his sister and his mother out of the buggy.

"This is your Uncle Ben, boys," Pru said quickly, then placing her hand on their heads, introduced them. "Ben, this is Johnny, this is David, and this is Robert."

Robert, the youngest, stared up at Ben, saying in a loud voice, "Hello. What happened to your eye?"

"I had an accident."

"Are you really my uncle?"

"I really am," Ben grinned. "Are you really my nephews?"

"Yes, sir," Johnny said quickly. "It's good to meet you." At the age of twelve, he felt it necessary to be somewhat of a role model, and put his hand out. Ben shook it and then did the same for the other boys.

Marianne came over and embraced Ben, who kissed her on the cheek. "Hello, Mother. It's good to see you." Then he turned to Pru, noting the warm light in her eyes. "Sis, I can't tell you how much I appreciate your coming out."

"Oh, we came out to have a good time," Prudence smiled. "Martin, this is Reisa Dimitri. Come along, and I'll introduce you to her grandfather."

❧

The room had always seemed very large to Reisa, but it seemed to grow smaller somehow as the visitors entered. The boys darted everywhere looking at everything and talking loudly. Dov was standing with his back against the wall, smiling slightly. Robert came to stare up at him, his eyes large. "I'd like to be big like you when I grow up," he announced.

Dov smiled down at the small boy, then suddenly knelt to one knee. "It is not always good to be big. It's hard to find a bed big enough. Better you should be like your father."

Sam and Phineas were dressed in their Sunday clothes for the occasion. They had both shaved, and for once their hair was combed. When Phineas discovered that Martin was a doctor, he said instantly, "I've got this here ache in my shoulder, Doc. You think it could be rheumatism?"

Sam spoke up with irritation, "Will you hush! He always thinks he's ailin' with somethin'. Jist don't pay him no never mind."

Pru said to Reisa, "We brought some food. Nobody could feed an army like this. Would you help me bring it in?"

"I will bring," Dov said. He went out quickly, followed by Robert, who was fascinated by the huge man. The youngster fired questions incessantly, Dov doing his best to answer as many as he could.

The room was a beehive of activity, but when it sorted itself out Martin said, "Mr. Dimitri, I wonder if you would give me a little help."

Surprised, Jacob said, "Why, anything, sir."

"I've been asked to teach a class of men in my church concerning the Jewish sacrifices in the Old Testament."

"Ah, that is most interesting."

"Well, I've got a great many books, but Pru tells me you're a scholar in the Jewish way."

"I have studied somewhat."

"Would you be willing to help me? I'm bogged down in all the old sacrifices. I can't really get it all together in my mind."

"Oh, certainly!"

Soon the two men were sitting at the table, Sam close beside them, anxious to miss nothing.

Reisa said to Marianne, "You have not seen our wagon that Ben bought and fixed up."

"I'd like to see it very much," Marianne said.

Reisa led Marianne outside, and proudly pointed out the fine points of the wagon. Marianne opened and shut the compartments, oohing and ahhing at the workmanship. "It's wonderful, Reisa," she smiled. "Did you design it?"

"Oh, we all worked on it—but Ben did the compartments. He's such a good carpenter."

For a while Reisa talked with animation of the experiences she'd had on the trips she'd made with Ben and Dov, but finally Marianne asked gently, "Are you happy here, Reisa? It must have been very hard to leave your homeland."

"I am content."

"I'm not sure I would be, but I'm glad you are."

"I worry about my grandfather. He's getting on, and he's all I have."

"That comes to all of us—but you will marry."

Reisa smiled then, spreading her hands in a quick gesture. "Marry who? There are few Jewish young men here."

Marianne asked, "Would you consider marrying a Gentile?"

A tremor of fear swept through Reisa's heart. "Oh, I could never do that," she said firmly. "Such a thing would never make me happy."

The day passed agreeably for everyone. Ben took the boys out to where the flat-bottomed boat was tied up on the river, and they ran the trot line. He had deliberately chosen not to run the line for twenty-four hours so that there would be a catch for the boys. Sure enough, the lines were half full, and the boys were thrilled as they moved across the river removing catfish. Ben had to warn them to be careful because they seemed to be fearless.

When they returned with a burlap bag full of fish, Ben taught them how to clean them. Cleaning catfish was a difficult matter, but Ben had learned to skin them with little trouble. He had caught a large bass the day before, and had kept it for Jacob and Reisa, knowing they would not eat catfish.

When the fish were cleaned, Sam came ambling over to say, "Ben, why don't you teach the boys how to shoot?"

Pru, who was taking the fish inside to prepare for cooking, said at once, "Oh, they're too young for that."

"Let them learn, ma'am. At least they can watch."

Of course all three boys were excited about this. Sam went inside to get his Le Mat, and he also brought the Whitworth that Ben had won the shooting contest with. Dov accompanied Ben, Sam, and the boys out to a clearing far from the house.

For over an hour Ben amazed the boys with his marksmanship. He knocked down cans that he had saved for target practice with the pistol, and then he handed Robert a can. "Toss this up in the air and see if I can hit it."

Robert threw the can high in the air, and Ben, apparently without aiming, lifted the Le Mat and fired. The bullet struck the can, sending it flying. When it was almost to the ground, Ben fired again, the slug driving the can farther along. He shot three more times, each time hitting the can. Turning, he saw the boys' eyes all big.

Johnny demanded, "Teach me to shoot like that, Uncle Ben!"

"Yes, me too!" David said. Of course Robert could not be left out, so all three were pleading with him.

"I'll tell you what, fellows, this gun's too big for you, but the next time you come, I'll have a small pistol, and then I'll start teaching you how to shoot."

When they returned to the house, the smell of frying fish was in the air. The boys all tried to outshout each other, telling their parents what a wonderful shot Ben was.

Pru moved closer to Ben, smiling and squeezing his arm. "I think you are going to be a *wonderful* uncle, Ben!"

"Well, I don't have much practice at it, but they're fine boys, Pru. You and Martin are to be envied."

"You'll have your own boys one day, Ben," Pru whispered.

Dinner was wonderful: fried catfish and bass, hushpuppies, green onions, and Dorrie's vegetables. All this was followed by the cake and pie that Marianne had brought.

With a little persuasion from Ben, Phineas got his fiddle down and played for the boys. All the men except Dov and Jacob knew the war songs, many of them comic, and they joined together to sing for the visitors. Phineas finally said, "This here song's allus been my favorite." He started singing, joined by Sam and Ben:

O, I'm a good old rebel,
Now that's just what I am,
For this "Fair Land of Freedom"
I do not care at all;
I'm glad I fit against it,
I only wish we'd won;
I don't want no pardon
For anything I've done.
I hates the Constitution,
This Great Republic, too,
I hates the Freeman's Buro,
In uniforms of blue;
I hates the nasty eagle,
With all his brags and fuss,
The lyin', thieving Yankees,
I hates 'em wuss and wuss.
I followed old Marse Robert
For four year near about,
Got wounded in three places,
And starved at Point Lookout;
I cotch the roomatism
A campin' in the snow,
But I killed a lots o' Yankees,
I'd like to kill some mo'.

Finally Robert said, "Uncle Ben, Mother said you were a good soldier. Did you kill lots of Yankees?"

Ben had been smiling, but now he sobered up. "Robert, they were fellows just like us. I always hated it when I had to shoot at them. I hope you never have to go through a thing like that."

"I hope so, too," Martin said quickly.

Phineas put his fiddle away, and they all filed outside on the porch as the evening closed down. There they said their good-byes, shaking hands, hugging, the boys still talking a mile a minute.

When they were in the carriage and rolling down the road toward home, Pru turned and faced Martin. "What did you think about Ben?"

"There's a great sadness in him, isn't there?"

"Yes, there is, but he'll get over it."

"He won the boys over so easily. I can't believe it."

"They need an uncle. If we move here, I know they'll get to see him often." She sat silently for a while, then she asked, "What did you think about Reisa?"

"About Reisa? Why, she's a nice girl."

Pru struck him playfully in the chest with her fist. "You are a fine doctor—and a rotten observer! Don't you have any romance in your soul? Can't you see the way they look at each other?"

Martin was not as obtuse as she implied. "I caught some of that, but nothing can ever come of it."

She put her arms around him and drew him close to whisper, "Yes, it can. If a man and woman love each other, there'll be a way. And I think they love each other."

Twenty-Seven

The following morning Dov set out for the Swenson house. The sun had just risen, tinting the eastern landscape a delicate crimson. He carried in his hand some pieces of iron for repair at the forge. Two days ago, when he and Ben had gone to shoe the mules, Mrs. Swenson had been too ill to see him, and Hilda had told him with fear in her eyes that the doctor was very concerned. Dov had tried to be as encouraging as he could, but he saw that Hilda was frightened by this sickness. So he was using the iron repairs as an excuse, really wanting to check up on Hilda and her mother.

Going at once to the forge, he lit the fire, and as it caught, he moved outside to glance toward the house. With some surprise he saw that Hilda was standing on the front porch. At once he moved forward, and when he was twenty yards away, lifted his hand to greet her—but then he saw that something was odd about the way she stood. Moving closer, he saw that she was leaning against one of the pillars and her face was very pale and worn. Mounting the steps quickly, Dov said, "Miss Hilda—is something wrong?"

Hilda did not move, in fact she did not seem to hear him. Her body was stiff, but Dov saw that her hands were trembling almost violently.

"What is wrong?" he repeated gently.

Hilda started, then turned her face toward Dov. Her eyes were staring blindly, and her lips were pressed tightly together.

She swallowed hard, then whispered hoarsely, "Mother—she is dead."

A cold shock ran through Dov. He had not known the woman well, but had admired her gentleness and the stoic way in which she bore her painful illness. "I ver' sorry," he said quietly. He was not a man to whom words came easily, especially words in a language not his own. He longed to comfort her, to say something, but for the life of him could not think of a word.

Hilda stood motionless for a moment, then her shoulders began to shake. She closed her eyes tightly, but tears coursed down her cheeks. Her body trembled violently, and she swayed uncertainly, seemingly about to fall.

Dov Puskin was not an eloquent man, but he did have enormous sympathy for anyone who suffered. He was fond of this woman in a way that he could not explain, and now he simply reached forward and put his arms around her. "Maybe," he said quietly, "I can help."

Hilda came against him helplessly. It seemed that all strength was gone, for she nearly fell. Dov held her, and as she put her face on his broad chest, she clutched his shirt desperately. And then great tearing sobs from deep down inside began to shake her body.

Dov held Hilda tightly, a great pity welling up in him. *Her mother was all she had. Now she's all alone.* His mighty arms held her as easily as if she were a child, but he said nothing.

Finally the deep sobs began to modify, then finally ceased. Hilda put her hands on Dov's chest and stepped back. He released her but held to her upper arms. "Come. Sit down," he said gently. He guided her to one of the three rockers that sat on the front porch and helped her sit down. He himself was too large for any normal chair, so he simply knelt down on one knee and took her hands in his. "When did it happen, Miss Hilda?"

"Sometime just before dawn. She—she was feeling so well last night." Here the tears began to flow again, and Hilda bowed her head and groped in her pocket for a handkerchief. She found one and for a moment did not speak. Finally she whispered, "Last night she ate a little, and I thought she was better. She went to bed, and I sat and read to her out of the Bible for almost an hour."

It seemed to Dov that it was good for Hilda to talk as much as possible. He stayed on one knee beside her, his hand on the chair arm, listening as Hilda related how strange it had been that her mother was free from pain.

"She had been hurting so bad for so long, but last night it was as if God took it all away. After I read the Bible, she wanted to pray, so I knelt down and we prayed."

"What you pray, Miss Hilda?"

"I just prayed that God would be merciful and take away her pain for good."

"And the good God has done that. She has now no pain."

Quickly Hilda looked up into the broad face of the big man. Reading the compassion in his dark eyes, she whispered, "Thank you, Dov."

"It is nothing—but now we must do things. I will hitch wagon and take you to Reisa."

"No! I must stay with Mama!"

"No. You will with Reisa stay," Dov said firmly. He took her hand and said, "You have done all you could for your mother. The good God—he has seen all that; he has her to himself taken. Now, you must stay with Reisa. I will do what is to be done here. Do you have other people?"

"No."

"Then I will tell the neighbors. I will get the doctor—and minister?"

"Reverend Luke Berry. He lives across from the white church on the road by the river."

"I know church. You wait—I get wagon."

Dov left, and Hilda sat quietly in the chair. Finally he came back with the team, pulled it up, then jumped out. She followed him to the wagon, and all strength seemed to have left her. "I don't know what's wrong with me," she said holding onto the side. "I feel—"

"You ver' weak." Dov suddenly reached down and picked her up as if she were a child. He seated her in the wagon, then smiled. "All right?"

"Yes. I'm all right."

Dov nodded, then went around and climbed in. He spoke to the horses, and as they moved out, Hilda said, "She always wanted to be buried by the river in the cemetery down by the church."

"I will tell minister. All be done."

Hilda said nothing for ten minutes. Dov stole glances at her, and finally she spoke haltingly, "I'm—I'm all alone now, Dov."

Dov Puskin extended his right hand, placing it gently on her shoulder. "No, my Hilda, you not alone—never while Dov is here!"

Reisa spotted the wagon coming down the drive, carrying Dov and Hilda. Sensing something was wrong, she went outside to meet them. Quickly, Dov explained the situation.

Reisa turned to Hilda, who by this time had more control of herself. "I'm so sorry, Hilda. What can I do for you?"

"I would like to go back to my house—if you would go and stay with me."

"Of course I will. Dov, let me tell Grandfather what has happened. I'll have Sam go for a doctor. I'm sure there has to be a certificate." She turned and went quickly into the house. Jacob looked up from the kitchen table as she came in. "It's Hilda's mother—Mrs. Swenson. She died last night."

"How terrible for Hilda," Jacob said quickly. "What can we do?"

"She wants to be in her own house with her own things. I'm going with her, *Zaideh,* if it's all right with you."

"Of course. What else can we do?"

"I'm sure arrangements will have to be made, but I'll send Dov to do whatever needs to be done."

"Let us know if we can do anything."

Going back to the wagon, Reisa climbed into the seat beside Hilda. Dov said, "I will take you back. Then I will go find the minister."

Dov turned the horses around, and they began the journey back. Reisa put her arm around Hilda and squeezed her. The woman was very large, but now she was like a child. Hilda's face was stiff, and Reisa well understood that she was grieving deeply inside.

When they reached the house, Dov jumped down. He handed Reisa down, then carefully lifted Hilda. He held her arms until they had ascended the porch, and then he took her hand. "Your mother is with God," he said simply. "I go find the minister."

As Dov left, Reisa saw Hilda looking after him in a peculiar fashion.

"What is it, Hilda?"

"It is so strange."

"What is strange?"

"When we left here I was too weak to get into the wagon, and Dov reached down and picked me up as if I were a child. No man has ever done that. There was no man strong enough."

"He is a giant, but with the gentle spirit of a woman," Reisa said warmly. "Come now, you must change clothes. Dov will see some of the neighbors and find the minister."

Hilda continued to talk. "While we were going, I told him I would be all alone. Do you know what he said?"

"What? What did he say?"

"He said, 'You'll never be alone—not while Dov is around.'"

"He's very sweet, and you won't be alone. You'll have me and Grandfather and Phineas and Sam and Ben, so many of the neighbors, and you have many friends in church. You won't be alone, Hilda."

Jacob sat in the pew next to Reisa. On Reisa's right Hilda sat quietly, with Dov on her right. Sam, Phineas, and Ben were seated just beyond Dov. Since there was no family, Reisa had insisted that they all sit with Hilda.

Jacob glanced over his shoulder, noting that the church was almost filled. Dov and Sam, he knew, had gone throughout the country notifying people of the funeral. Jacob, who had never been to any funeral except a Jewish one, sat quietly taking it all in.

Everyone was quiet, and then a door beside the platform opened. A tall man in his forties came to Hilda. Leaning over, he said something to her in a gentle tone. Hilda bowed her head and nodded, then the minister, Reverend Luke Berry, walked to the small platform and sat down. A short man with a handlebar mustache stood up in front of the congregation and began to sing. There were no books, but everyone except the visitors seemed to know the songs well. Jacob listened intently to the words. Most of them were about heaven—a subject that interested him greatly. He could not see the faces of those behind him, and he wondered if they were as sure of their place in this heaven as the song seemed to indicate one might be.

Finally Berry rose and in a clear voice read from a single sheet of paper the facts of Mrs. Swenson's birth, briefly mentioning her departure from this life. He opened a worn black Bible and stood loosely before them for a few moments. Jacob studied his face and found him to be a man of true compassion, if a countenance can reveal such a thing.

Reverend Berry began to read Scripture. He read quite a few of them, remarking once, "These are all Scriptures that our dear sister loved greatly. She left behind a note giving instructions that the songs that we have just sung would be sung at her funeral, and the verses that I have just read were favorites of hers. She also asked me to speak on the resurrection of the dead."

A silence fell over the church as the preacher's voice seemed to fill it. Reverend Berry had a powerful voice, and Jacob had the impression that if he chose to lift it, he could have been heard a mile away. Still there was a warmth and an intimacy in his tone, and his eyes often fell on Hilda as she sat drinking in his words.

"It is always a joy to me to speak on the resurrection—especially at times like this when one of our own has passed onto the other side. Naturally we are sad and grieved, but that's the human side of us. Our dear sister suffered so much while she was alive that not a one of us would wish her back again to endure that pain—least of all this precious daughter of hers."

Jacob glanced quickly at Hilda's face, noting a peace that had not been there the previous day. The shock of her mother's death had devastated her, but now a calmness seemed to surround her as she listened.

"The apostles always spoke of the resurrection of Jesus—and of the resurrection of all who believe in him. When they chose another apostle to replace Judas, he had to be one who had been a witness of the Resurrection. When Peter stood up before the multitude, he declared unto them that they had killed 'the Prince of life, whom God hath raised from the dead.' When Peter and John were taken before the council, the great reason for their arrest was that the rulers were 'grieved that they taught the people, and preached through Jesus the resurrection from the dead.' After they were set free, the Scripture tells us, 'With great power gave the apostles witness of the resurrection of the Lord Jesus: and great grace was upon them all.' When Paul mentioned the resurrection in Athens, some laughed, but others were touched, and when he stood before the council of the Pharisees, and the Sadducees, he said, 'Touching the resurrection of the dead I am called in question.'"

Jacob's retentive mind soaked up the Scriptures as the minister went through the Bible, the Old Testament as well as the New, giving evidence of the resurrection of the body. He was intrigued when Reverend Berry recounted the story of Abraham offering up Isaac. "Abraham believed in the resurrection of the body," Reverend Berry said firmly. "He told those servants that had accompanied him to wait, that he and his son would return again. At that time he firmly believed he would have to slay Isaac, but over in the book of Hebrews it tell us that he 'accounted that God was able to raise up Isaac even from the dead.' His grandson Joseph believed in the resurrection, otherwise he wouldn't have been so careful of his body, insisting that it not remain in Egypt but be buried with the rest of his family. And our friend Mr. Dimitri, no doubt, could render the Hebrew of Job's triumphant word: 'For I know that my redeemer liveth, and that he shall stand at the latter day upon the earth: And though after my skin worms destroy this body, yet in my flesh shall I see God.'

"David believed firmly in the resurrection, for he sang of Christ: 'For thou wilt not leave my soul in hell; neither wilt thou suffer thine holy One to see corruption.' The prophet Daniel believed in the resurrection, for he said that, 'Many of them that sleep in the dust of the earth shall awake, some to everlasting life and some to shame and everlasting contempt.'"

Jacob smiled at Reverend Berry at the mention of his name, and he was amazed at how firmly the resurrection was built into the New Testament. The resurrection, he was well aware, occupied a minor place in the Old Testament. As he had been reading the New Testament, however, he saw that the entire structure of Christianity was firmly built upon this one fact—that Jesus was risen from the dead.

The preacher did not speak long, and his sermon consisted mostly of Scriptures. Finally he said, "Do not weep because this dear sister is before the throne. You weep because her body will go to the grave, but I have comfort for you." Berry's voice rose. "This very body will rise again; this cold hand will be held out in affection once more. This very hand, those cold claylike arms, shall be strong, and these still fingers will sweep the living strings of golden harps in heaven!

"Here is comfort for all of us. Scarcely a day goes by but most of us are tormented with some suffering or another. Our dear sister is past all this. This worn body will grow warm, and it will live again. All who have put their trust in Jesus shall feast at the wedding feast of the Lamb.

"I would close with one passage from the book of John, chapter eleven. You are familiar with the story. Jesus was very close to a family there, a man named Lazarus whose sisters were Mary and Martha. He often went there to find rest from the crowds that pressed in upon him.

"We read that Jesus received word, verse three, 'Therefore his sisters sent word unto him, saying, Lord, behold, he who thou lovest is sick.'"

Reverend Berry raised his head. "What would any of us do if we received the message that one that we loved was very sick? Would we not go at once? Is it not what we expect that Jesus will do? But in verse four we find something quite different. When Jesus heard that he said, 'This sickness is not unto death, but for the glory of God, that the Son of God may be glorified thereby.'"

Looking around the congregation, Reverend Berry shook his head. "Our ways are not God's ways, and his ways are not our ways. Verse six tells us that after Jesus heard that his friend was sick he stayed two days, and it was not a long journey. You could walk the distance from where Jesus was located to where Lazarus lay sick in Bethany in an hour. But Jesus did not go for two days." He paused and said, "Have you ever wondered what Lazarus must have thought at this time? He knew, probably, that he was dying. He knew that his sisters had sent for Jesus, and he believed that Jesus would be able to heal him of his sickness—yet Jesus did not come."

Jacob exchanged a quick glance with Reisa. They had talked about this very Scripture more than once, and now Reverend Berry brought up a thought they had never considered.

"It must have been very painful for Lazarus, knowing that Jesus was so close and yet chose not to come. But I think there's a lesson for us here. Have we not all had times of sorrow, of grief, of pain, when we called upon God begging him to come—and he did not come? I think we can all sympathize with Lazarus. But Jesus said that the sickness of Lazarus was for the glory of God. It's hard for me to understand that, but it must have been much harder for Lazarus.

"But I think you know how the glory of God was made manifest. The Scripture says that Jesus did go to the home of Lazarus. He met Martha, and he met Mary, who both wept and said, 'If you had only been here our brother would not have died!'

"So we find Jesus saying in verse twenty-three, 'Thy brother shall rise again.' And Martha said unto him, 'I know that he shall rise again in the resurrection at the last day.'"

At this point Reverend Berry suddenly lifted his hands and lifted his voice: "Praise be to God for the next verse. It says, 'Jesus said unto her, I am the resurrection and the life. He that believeth in me, though he were dead, yet shall he live.'

"This is the hope of every believer—that even though we must die, yet we shall live again. This sorrow is for the glory of God, for our dear sister was a faithful follower of the Lord Jesus.

We will miss her, but we would not have her back. This daughter knew her suffering more than any of us, but she knows now that her mother is free of all pain. Let us pray."

They all stood, and Reverend Berry asked one of the deacons to say a prayer.

When the service ended, they went out to the edge of the small cemetery located not far from the church. Dov kept very close to Hilda as the pallbearers brought the coffin. As it was lowered into the grave, suddenly Hilda reached out, and Dov took her hand, holding it firmly. Reverend Berry said, "Ashes to ashes and dust to dust, but we trust in the Lord, the living God. This mortal must put on immortality, and surely our dear sister has done that. So now, Lord, we commit her into your hands until the time when we shall meet her once again."

The song leader lifted his voice in one of the old hymns, and afterward everyone came by and spoke to Hilda. She could not answer them, but Dov, who stood slightly behind her, was happy to see that she was in control of her emotions.

After everyone had passed, Reverend Berry stopped long enough to say quietly, "I'll be calling to see how you are very often, sister Hilda."

Reisa came to her. "Come and stay with us, Hilda."

"No. I must go home."

Dov said quickly, "I will take you home." He took Hilda's arm, and as they moved away, Dov said over his shoulder, "I will be late tonight."

Jacob, who stood beside Reisa, said, "He has a heart as big as his body."

"She will be very lonely," Reisa said sadly.

Jacob shook his head. "She will see her mother again—just as you will see your father and mother—and I will see my Leah."

Twenty-Eight

Over the next week everyone made special attempts to see that Hilda had plenty of company. Sam and Phineas invited her over for a meal several times, and once she fixed a big meal for all of them. Hilda was flustered with so much company, but Phineas had taken his fiddle, and they'd had a wonderful time.

One day Ben entered the house, back from a trip to Richmond. He found Reisa washing dishes. When she turned to greet him with a smile, he said, waving a paper in his hand, "I've just gotten a letter from Pru, Reisa."

"Oh, that's good. How is she?"

"Well, she's taken with you."

"That makes us even. I think she's wonderful."

"I'd let you read it, but you'd be swollen up with pride," Ben teased. "Where's Dov?" he asked.

Sam, who was sitting at the table reading the Bible as usual, looked up. "Gone over to fix a fence for Hilda."

Ben's eyebrow raised. "I don't think he's missed a day going over there since her mother died."

"That feller's got a big heart," Sam nodded. "I think he's good for her. She's bound to get lonesome."

Ben moved over to the window and stared outside. The dark days of November had come, bringing a chill to the air. The clouds were a dirty gray as they scudded against the backdrop of the bleak horizon. Finally he turned to Reisa. "I don't know as there's much point in going out to sell things in this weather."

"Oh, we must go," Reisa said. "With one thing happening and another, we haven't been on the road for almost two weeks now. I'm trying to save as much money as possible. Winter could be long, and if it gets very bad, I won't be able to go out at all. I'm sorry you have to go with me."

"I don't mind," Ben said quickly. "I get restless around here. Shall we leave tomorrow, then?"

She nodded. "Tomorrow."

The trip was hard, and their sales were not great that week. It was, as a matter of fact, the least lucrative of any of the trips they had made. Many of the women who had bought wedding rings did not have the money to make their payment. Reisa was not demanding on any of them, for she understood how hard times were.

On Wednesday afternoon they stopped at a small town called Pine Grove. As usual, they set up near the center of town. Ben and Dov let the back table down, then helped Reisa to set out the merchandise. Ben said, "I'll just walk around a little bit and stretch my legs. You don't need me here."

"You go right ahead, Ben," Reisa said quickly. "Dov and I will take care of things here."

Dov never got too far from Reisa when they were traveling, and this day he came to stand beside her. When there were no customers he talked freely of Hilda. "I worry about her," he said. "She is ver' good woman."

"Yes, she is, Dov. I know she gets lonesome."

Dov did not answer this, but though he said no more Reisa knew that Hilda Swenson was much on his mind.

The doors of a saloon located half a block down the street burst open, and Honey Fears stepped outside with a companion. They came down the street, both of them talking loudly. They met one man whom Fears simply shouldered aside, nearly upsetting him and knocking him off of the boardwalk. Fears looked at him eagerly hoping for trouble, but the man simply ducked his head and moved away.

As they came close, Fears's eyes lit on the wagon and then fastened on Reisa. He grinned broadly and said, "Looky there, Ike. There's that little Jew girl."

Ike Green was one of Fears's long-time companions. The two had been involved in several shady activities, and now Green stared over at the wagon. He grinned loosely, revealing yellow teeth. "Come on, Fears. Let's have some fun." He was a dark-skinned man with close-set brown eyes and had not shaved in several days. He was drunker than Fears and came toward the wagon weaving.

Green pulled himself up in front of Reisa, then deliberately looked her up and down. "Hey, Fears, is these Jew girls good sleepin'?"

Suddenly Dov moved very quickly for such a big man. He put himself between Reisa and Green and looked down at the smaller man without saying a word.

Green was a high-tempered individual, but if he had been sober, he would never have done what he did next. He began to curse Dov, and when Dov did not respond but simply stood there, Green struck him directly in the jaw. Green was a powerful man, the victor of many barroom brawls. Suddenly Dov doubled his fist up and struck Green in the chest. It seemed a light blow, but it drove the man backwards full length, and he could not catch his breath.

Honey Fears fancied himself the best brawler in the country. Dov was turned sideways, and Fears took his swing, striking

Dov in the neck. He was such a powerful brute that even Dov was driven off balance. Honey began to rain punches on Dov, and Reisa cried out, but Fears paid no heed. Dov's face was bleeding, for Honey was a fast man with his fists.

Dov did not strike back, but suddenly his hand shot out and one of Honey's fists was completely enclosed. Dov said nothing, but his eyes glittered. He began to squeeze, holding the hand high in the air.

Honey Fears was a strong man. He could put a wrapping around his fist and break a two-by-six simply by striking it. Always he had won his battles by sheer brute strength and a thick skull that deadened all of his opponents' blows. He tried to wrench his hand away, but it might as well have been encased in cement. He struck Dov in the face with a blow that would have felled a lesser man, but then suddenly the pressure on his hand increased.

Honey's jaw sagged, and he gasped, "Let go of me!"

But Dov, for once, had lost his even temper. The insult to Reisa had inflamed him, and now he simply tightened his grip.

Fears cried out, "You're breakin' my hand!" He clawed frantically at Dov's massive paw with his free hand, but it did no good. The pressure kept increasing. Honey Fears then did what he had never thought to do. He began screaming, for his bones were literally being crushed.

Reisa ran to Dov crying, "Let him go, Dov! Let him go!"

Dov looked down at her, and reason came back to his eyes. A crowd had gathered around—including Ben, who stood there like a cocked gun watching the scene. When Dov released Fears's hand, the big man held it to his chest, and the look that he gave Dov was pure venom. His face a dirty white, he whispered, "No man does that to me! I'll kill you!"

He turned then and walked away, and Green staggered to his feet to follow him.

The crowd was murmuring, and Reisa felt very faint. Ben came over to stand beside her. "Are you all right, Reisa?"

"Yes." Reisa turned to Dov and put her hand on his arm. "Dov, you must be careful."

"He say bad things about you."

"I know, but you must be careful. You could hurt somebody."

Ben stared at Fears and Green as they staggered away. "You'll have to watch out for those two, Dov."

"They could never whip Dov," Reisa declared stoutly.

"No, but they could shoot him in an ambush. I think they've done it before."

This frightened Reisa, and she said, "Let's pack up and leave."

"Suits me," Ben said, and he and Dov fell at once to repack the merchandise.

❧

The cold wind tossed the tops of the pin oaks that sheltered the wagon. The three had already eaten supper, and Dov, as usual, had crawled under the wagon, wrapped up in his blankets, and fallen asleep instantly.

Reisa was sitting beside Ben, soaking up the warmth of the fire. Both had wrapped blankets around their shoulders and were watching the fire send up pointed yellow and red tongues of flame. Occasionally a gust of wind would catch the fire, sending myriads of golden sparks high into the air, swirling like a miniature whirlwind. Reisa watched them for a time, then murmured, "Look at those sparks. They look like they're going to join the stars overhead."

"They are pretty, aren't they? I've always loved the stars. I've envied sailors knowing the names of them and how to use them to navigate."

The two talked for a time, but finally Reisa fell silent. She had been shaken by the encounter with Fears and Green. "You don't really think Fears would shoot Dov, do you?" she asked finally.

"If they got a chance and could get away with it, they would."

"How can men be so evil?"

"The Bible says it's because Adam and Eve fell."

"I know that story." Reisa was very lonely and did not want to go to sleep. As a matter of fact, for some reason she had been despondent for some time. The fight with Green and Fears had merely brought her more and more into a depressed state.

Her head dropped, and when Ben looked over he saw, by the light of the fire, that her face was sad.

"Don't worry about it," he said. He moved closer to her and suddenly did something he had never done before. She looked so helpless, forlorn, and depressed that he put his arm around her and squeezed her shoulder. "It's all right, Reisa. I'll keep an eye on Dov. We won't let him go anywhere alone."

"That's good of you, Ben. I don't know what I'd do if anything happened to him."

"That's not all that's worrying you, is it?"

For a moment Reisa hesitated. The weight of his arm was comforting to her. She turned, and he was aware of the smooth roundness of her shoulders and the straight lines of her body. The light was kind to her, and he was aware of her womanliness in breast and shoulder.

She seemed to be unaware of his gaze by that single eye. "I'm worried about my grandfather. I have been ever since Hilda's mother died. She's all alone—and I would be, too, if anything happened to him."

"You mustn't dwell on that. He may live for many years yet. He could live to be ninety." He did not remove his arm but kept it across her shoulders. "Don't worry," he said. "I hate to see you troubled."

"You know that book, Ben, about poetry, that I brought from Russia?"

"Sure. It's a good book. I don't know much about poetry, but I've read some of it. What I understand is good."

"There's a poem in there that's always held me somehow or other. It's a sad poem, and I didn't memorize it on purpose, but I read it so many times that it's just burned into my mind, it seems."

"What is it? Say it for me."

She began to say almost in a whisper the words of the poem:

So, we'll go no more a roving,
So late into the night,
Though the heart be still as loving,
And the moon be still as bright.
For the sword outwears its sheath,
And the soul wears out the breast,
And the heart must pause to breathe,
And love itself have rest.
Though the night was made for loving,
And the day returns too soon,
Yet we'll go no more a roving,
By the light of the moon.

"It sounds good," Ben said quietly, "but the fellow that wrote it must have been mighty sad."

"It's those two lines that bother me. 'The sword outwears its sheath, and the soul wears out the breast...' I can't get away from those lines, Ben. They seem to haunt me."

"Hate to see you troubled," Ben murmured.

"You've had more trouble than I've ever had."

"Doubt that. I never got run out of my country afraid of gettin' killed like you and Jacob."

"Death concerns me, Ben. I'm afraid of it."

"I guess maybe everybody backs off from death a little bit."

"You saw so much of it in the war—so many men killed. Were they all afraid?"

"Some didn't show it, but I was. I was pretty good at puttin' on a front. A lot of us joked to cover up what was inside when the cannons began to go off and the musket balls began to whistle around our heads."

"But you're a Christian, aren't you? Christians believe in the resurrection."

Ben Driver was silent for a long time. "When I was thirteen years old I found the Lord—or thought I did. I stayed close to him, although I had some bad ways. I always knew that I was trusting Christ, but then the war came along, and I began to doubt. I still doubt him, I guess. I don't doubt that God's there, and I don't doubt that Jesus is the Savior. What I doubt is—am I one of his sheep or not?"

The fire crackled, throwing its warm breath toward the two. The blanket was comfortable to Reisa, and she was totally aware of the strength and warmth of Ben's body. She felt safe and secure for the moment, but still the sadness when she thought of the possible loss of Jacob was almost overwhelming. They sat quietly for a long time, and finally she began to weep—something she had rarely done. The tears rose in her eyes and ran down her cheeks. Her shoulders trembled slightly, and Ben turned quickly and looked at her. "What is it, Reisa?"

"I—I don't know, Ben. I'm so afraid!"

Ben Driver knew something about loneliness, for he had known little else for many years. Even in the busy bustle and action of the war, he had felt somehow alone. The prison years had caused him to build a wall around himself, but now with the warmth of the fire and the warmth of Reisa's form held in his embrace, he suddenly felt a strange emotion. Partly it was compassion for this girl so lovely and with all the graces of womanhood. Partly it was the old hungers that rise in a man that turn him toward a woman and draw him when he himself is almost unaware of the drawing. He knew she was a good woman, and this also drew him toward her. He had known women who were not good, and had nothing but distaste for them. But now he reached out with his other hand and drew her around so that she faced him. "Don't be sad, Reisa," he whispered. "We're all alone in some ways, but we can believe in each other."

She lifted her head, and her eyes sparkled with the tears, and her cheeks were damp. Compassion came to him and something more than that. Lowering his head, he pressed his lips against hers. She was so brokenhearted and lonely that she came to him, and as he kissed her, she put herself against him. Driver knew they were on the edge of some mystery that every man and woman face, neither knowing what good would come of it or what tragedy would come of it. Her nearness sharpened all his long-felt hungers, and the shape of her lips and the lovely turnings of her body stirred him as nothing ever had before. She had a woman's fire and spirit with a woman's soft lips, and she was almost totally unaware of her beauty and of her power to stir him.

Reisa had not resisted. Her hand rested on the back of his neck, and somehow she knew there was more than a wish to comfort her lying behind Ben's embrace. He was a strong man in the prime of life, and Reisa knew enough to understand he was holding her as a man holds a woman that he desires.

She gave herself to him freely as she never had to any other man. A confusion swept through her, and she was conscious only of his lips on hers and of his strong arms around her.

Then suddenly Ben stiffened. He drew back, drawing his hand across his forehead in a strange gesture. Reisa felt him remove his arm, and the abruptness of his gesture troubled her. "Why did you stop, Ben?" she whispered. "Don't you want me?"

Ben turned and saw the poignant light in her wonderful clear eyes. "Yes, I do."

"Why did you stop then?"

"Because I had to, Reisa." He struggled to find the words. They were difficult for him. He had been locked up away from women for four years, and now that she was beside him in all of her richness and warmth, he knew that he had to draw back.

"I don't know if I can make you understand this, Reisa," he said slowly. "You're a good woman. Maybe the best I've ever known except for my mother and Pru. But you're innocent, and I'm not. You don't know what a life I've led, and I'd hate for you to find out." He turned to face her then, but kept his hands locked together. "A woman should be better than a man," he said finally. "All men are squirming around in the dust fighting lust and every other ungodly thing that comes into our minds! But a woman should be better than that—and you are. That's why I drew back, because I didn't want to spoil you. You're a woman who has to have God, and I'm not a man of God."

Reisa did not understand this. All she understood was that for the moment everything in her cried out for Ben to hold her in his arms. This frightened her also, and she dropped her head, saying quietly, "Good night, Ben."

"Good night, Reisa."

Making her way to the wagon, she lay down fully dressed, pulled the blanket around her, and closed her eyes. She had no hope of going to sleep at once as Dov did. She was shaken to the very core of her spirit by Ben's caress. She knew she could not ever forget what had risen in her, a desire for him such as she had not known in her young life. She was ashamed of it—yet at the same time there was a queer streak of pride, for she realized that she was capable of being stirred physically. She had heard of women who could not be, and she had always feared that she might be one of these.

She stayed awake a long time, until finally from exhaustion she began to drift off. As she did, she prayed, "Oh, God, who are you? Where are you? I'm so confused! I love this man—but I can never have him! And I love you—but I don't know who you are!"

Twenty-Nine

Reverend Berry had preached his usual fine sermon, despite the fact that it was a cold morning in mid-December and the crowd was off. Many of the congregation were down with sickness, but Berry had been warmed by the sight of Jacob Dimitri, who had been brought by Hilda Swenson and Dov Puskin. Reisa also had joined them and, as usual, had a scarf on, a bright green fabric that brought out the green of her eyes. The grandfather and granddaughter added a colorful flavor to the congregation with their foreign air. He noted that Reisa clung tenaciously to the old ways. He could not help but admire her, and from time to time during the sermon his eyes would flicker over to where the group sat.

As usual, Sam sat directly on the end of a pew. He loved to take up the offering. Sometimes he disturbed Berry, for if Sam felt that some wealthy individual was not giving enough, Sam was not above advising him that God blessed a cheerful giver. Berry could never restrain a smile when he thought of the time the church was taking an offering for missionaries in Africa. Sam had shoved the plate under the nose of a wealthy land owner, and the man had stared angrily at him and shaken his head. "I'm not putting anything in," he had said.

Sam had shot right back. "Take some out then. It's for the heathen."

The sermon was simple enough. It was a simple message on Jesus as Savior. At one point Berry said warmly, "When John the Baptist first sought Jesus, he said, 'Behold, the Lamb of God that taketh away the sin of the world.' Every Jew that was in hearing distance of John knew exactly the ceremony to which John referred. The Paschal lamb had been slain ever since the Passover days of Israel in Egypt. The head of the family would bring a lamb, and it would be sacrificed by the priest. Symbolically the sins of the people would rest upon the lamb who died, taking their sins with him. Of course, every thinking Jew knew that the blood of an animal could not possibly take away sin. So now John is saying, 'You've slain a thousand thousand lambs, and not all the blood of all these lambs would take away one sin, but now God has sent the one who is the reality. Those other lambs were mere pictures and shadows and types, but now the reality, the Lamb of God, has come.'"

He had gone on to trace Jesus' death on the cross, and the congregation was stirred, for Berry was a warm-hearted, fervent man of God.

Finally when the sermon ended, he said, "There may be one here this morning who has not found his way. Jesus is the way, the truth, and the life. I invite you to come and make public your decision. Jesus died for you. Will you trust in him?"

The song leader began "Just As I Am." Reverend Berry was stunned when Jacob Dimitri stepped out and came toward him. Berry was so confused for a moment he could not think, but he took Jacob's thin hand, asking, "Why do you come forward, Jacob?"

Jacob had planned this for some time. He had read over and over in the New Testament how Jesus asked his disciples to follow him publicly, not secretly. Now he smiled and said, "I will not be like Nicodemus who came secretly to Jesus by night. I have taken the Lord Jesus Christ as the Lamb of God. I called on him, Reverend, and he has forgiven my sins. Now, if I understand the Bible, he asked those who do this to be baptized."

"That is right, Jacob." The pastor's eyes filled with tears, for he had grown to love this man. "Is that your desire?"

"Yes, I wish to be baptized as soon as possible."

Reisa was staring, her eyes enormous and filled with apprehension. Dov put his hand on her shoulder. "It is all right, my Reisa," he whispered. "Your grandfather is a wise man."

Reisa had somehow expected this and yet dreaded it. She herself had prayed, but her prayers seemed to rebound from a heaven made of brass and iron. But she could not deny the light that had been in her grandfather's face, and the excitement and joy that was his even though he was not healthy. She simply stood there unable to believe it.

When the verse ended, Reverend Berry said, "We are so happy that our brother, Jacob Dimitri, has found Jesus. He has given his testimony to me, but perhaps you would like to hear it. As you know, Jacob has been an orthodox Jew all of his life, but now he feels that he must confess Jesus as Savior."

Jacob spoke briefly and simply. His eyes moved over the congregation, and finally came to rest on Reisa. "It will be hard for me, for I am an old man, and the old ways die hard. But the Bible says that you cannot put new wine in old wine skin, so I come ready to taste the new wine. Sam has told me how he was baptized in a river when he was in the army, and I desire to be baptized as soon as possible."

Reverend Berry's face instantly assumed a worried expression. "But, brother Jacob, it's so cold out there! We couldn't possibly baptize you in the river."

Jacob said, "Nothing is impossible with God. Does not the Bible say that, Reverend?"

Sam Hall suddenly jumped up. "It shore does—but I can fix it. You give me an hour, brother Berry, and we'll have us a baptism right here in this church!"

Shock ran over the congregation, for all the baptizing had been in the local creek or in a pond. But Sam Hall was off and running. "You come with me, Dov. Phineas, you get a fire built up outside. Some of you womenfolk get somethin' to heat water in. We're havin' a baptizin' quicker than Moody's goose."

Sam's work had been done well. A large horse trough had been emptied and brought into the church and placed front and center. It was filled with warm water heated on a quickly built fire outside. The women from close by had brought pans and kettles, and now Jacob Dimitri was standing in the water. It was only two feet deep, but Sam had said, "That's deep enough to get him under, Preacher. Miss Reisa, you hold that blanket ready. We got some fresh clothes when he gets out, right in the back there."

Reisa's hands were unsteady as she held the rough blanket. She was standing over to one side, but she could see Jacob's face clearly. There was a peace and joy in his features such as she had never seen.

Brother Berry stepped forward and smiled. "I've baptized a thousand people, perhaps, in my life, but never have I been as happy to baptize anyone as I am this dear brother." He had Jacob lock his hands on his own left wrist, then put his hand behind Jacob's back. He was a big man, and Jacob was small. Lifting his hand, Reverend Berry cried out with a loud voice, "And now in obedience to the command of our Lord and Savior Jesus Christ, I baptize you, my brother Jacob Dimitri, in the name of the Father, in the name of the Son, and in the name of the Holy Ghost."

Carefully Berry lowered the old man down into the water. Jacob clung to the pastor's wrist, and was completely immersed. Berry pulled him quickly forward, and Jacob wiped his face. Sam shouted, "Hallelujah! Praise the Lord! Glory to God and the Lamb forever!" Others in the church were shouting and praising God fervently.

With the pastor's help Jacob stepped out of the tub, and Reisa was there at once. She wrapped the warm blanket around him. *"Zaideh,* you must get on warm clothes."

"I'll see to that, Miss Reisa." Dov was there and led Jacob into the back room. A fire had been built there so that it was warm, and clean clothes had been provided by one of the members.

Reisa was feeling rather forlorn when an arm came across her shoulders. She turned to find Hilda, her eyes filled with tears. "It is wonderful. Your grandfather has found Jesus." Hilda threw her arms around the younger woman, and Reisa simply felt engulfed as she was held firmly against the big woman. It was something she needed, and she put her head down on Hilda's breast and tried to keep fearful thoughts from racing through her mind.

Soon Jacob came out in dry clothes with his hair combed, and he quickly came to her. "So, we go home now."

"Yes, *Zaideh.*"

Jacob reached out and took his granddaughter's hand. "I know you are sad and you feel left out, but God has told me that you will not be left out for long. Come. We will go home now."

As Ben Driver made his way down the main street of Richmond, he was thinking of Jacob and the joy that the old man had shown at his baptism. The scene had brought back fine memories, and he thought, *I guess I'm not entirely dead. Thought for a while I'd break down and cry. And that wouldn't have been too bad, I guess.*

He had come to town with Sam to get supplies, and had taken time to buy a new shirt. He was on his way back to the stable where Sam waited with Samson and Delilah hitched to the wagon. It was a cold day with a hint of snow in the air, but Ben was unconscious of this. He wore only a flannel shirt, a pair of new jeans, and his half boots were warm and snug, for he was wearing the new boot socks that Hilda had knitted for him, as she had for all of the men at the house.

Driver was also thinking of that moment beside the fire in the wilderness when he had held Reisa in his arms. It was a troubling thought to him, and one he could not shake off. He knew that he loved her, but he could see no good ending for such a love. Years of disappointment and hardship had conditioned him to think of the dangers and the gloomy side of life.

As he approached Bell's Hardware Store, a couple came out, and he was quickly drawn from his thoughts when he faced his father and mother. His mother smiled as soon as she recognized him. "Hello, Ben. How are you?"

"I'm fine, Mom." Then Ben Driver looked at his father and saw the discomfort in John Driver's eyes. He had planned to go see his father someday and talk with him, but now he said quietly and simply, "Dad, I've been a rotten son, a disappointment to you, and a disgrace to the Driver name. I'm sorry. I know you find it hard to forgive me, for you're a proud man, but as best as I can I'll try not to disgrace your name anymore."

Without another word he brushed past them and did not look back.

John Driver turned to stare after his son. He felt his wife's hand on his arm and knew that she was waiting for him to speak. "That was fine of Ben, wasn't it, John?"

"He seemed—very honest."

"He is honest."

John Driver was still struggling with himself. He was unhappy with his own spirit, and he knew that somehow at the heart of his discontent lay his harshness toward Ben. He could not speak for a moment, and then he turned, saying, "He seems different."

"He is different, John. You'll see."

Sam was aware of Ben's silence on the way home. He knew that something had happened and longed to know what it was. Being an inquisitive man, he finally could refrain no longer. "The cat got your tongue, Ben? You look plumb down in the mouth."

"I saw my father and mother in town." He hesitated and then said, "I've been intending to go see him to tell him what a rotten son I've been to him and how sorry I am."

"Did you tell him?"

"Yes, I did."

"Well, then you'll have to let him come to his own conclusions." Sam Hall was a practical man, and now as he sat on the seat beside Ben, he said, "It's a hard row to hoe, raisin' children. I gave my daddy fits, and I'm right sorry for it." His cheerful face assumed a frown. "He died afore I found the Lord, and I never got to tell him what a good dad he was and how sorry I was." But he straightened up then and slapped his single hand on his knee. "When I get to the streets of glory, right after I say hello to Jesus, I'm lookin' Pa up, and I'll bet he'll be right glad to see his wanderin' boy made it after all."

The two were halfway to home on a little traveled road. Both were sitting loosely on the wagon seat, Sam chatting idly, when suddenly two horsemen came out of a grove of hickory trees. Instantly Ben drew up, for he recognized Honey Fears and Alf DeSpain. Instant regret flashed through him that he had no gun, for he saw that both men had pulled their revolvers and were holding them right on him.

"Pull up, Driver," Fears said. He held the revolver in his left hand. His right hand had never recovered from the terrible crushing force of Dov's mighty grip. "Get out of that wagon!"

"There's no point in this, Honey," Ben said calmly, coming out of the wagon.

Fears had dismounted and so had DeSpain. Honey handed the reins of his horse to his companion and said, "Hold the horses. I'm gonna gun-whip this man. If Sam up there gets involved, shoot him."

DeSpain shook his head as if he disagreed, but he took the reins of Fears's horse.

"What's wrong, Honey?" Ben asked.

"You know what's wrong. You always thought you were the big dog, but I guess prison has taken some of the starch out of you, and I'm going to take the rest. And when I find that big Russian I'll put a bullet in him."

"You can't stand it when a man can whip you, can you, Honey?"

"Well, I can whip you. I always could."

This was true. The two had had three fights back in the old days, and each time Ben had been beaten—not badly but definitely.

Fears moved forward and said, "I'm gonna beat your brains out, Ben."

At that moment Sam called out, "Ben!"

DeSpain's eyes had been on Fears and Driver. Sam had reached down under the seat and pulled out the Le Mat nine-shot revolver.

Ben heard his name and saw Sam toss the gun. It seemed to come to him very slowly, making a single turn in the air. He simply reached up and plucked it out of the air. Instantly he wheeled and struck Honey over the head with it. The blow drove Fears to the ground. Quick as lightning, Ben aimed the Le Mat at DeSpain, saying in a hard voice, "Either shoot or drop that gun, DeSpain!"

"I'm out of this," DeSpain cried instantly and dropped his gun.

Stooping over, Ben picked up Fears's gun, then retrieved DeSpain's. He got back in the wagon saying, "I'll drop these off at the sheriff's office. You can pick them up there if you've got the nerve. Let's go, Sam."

As they pulled off, Fears was getting to his feet. Blood matted his hair and ran down past his ear onto his shirt. He began cursing, "I'll kill you for this, Driver! I'll kill you and that Russian, too! There's plenty of places to get you!"

Ben held the Le Mat in his hand and said, "Thanks, Sam. I think he would have killed me."

Sam Hall said, "Well, I don't know if I done you a favor or not."

"Of course you did."

"Look at the chambers of that Le Mat, Ben."

Driver looked at the chambers and then gasped, "It's not loaded!"

"No, I took it to the gunsmith, and he cleaned it. I ain't loaded it up yet." He smiled and said, "Honey would be even madder if he knew you bluffed him with an empty gun." Then he sobered up. "You know Honey, Ben. He means what he says. Sooner or later he'll try to kill you."

"I expect he will, Sam. But at least he didn't do it today."

Thirty

"Do you want anything special from town, *Zaideh?*" Reisa had put on her heavy coat, for the weather outside was getting colder. It was not like the Russian winters, to be sure, but both she and Jacob had had their blood thinned by the hot summer. Now she touched Jacob, who sat at the table with Sam. "What about if I try to find salmon?"

"I doubt if you'll find salmon this far inland," Jacob said mildly. "If you do, it would be nice. Is Ben going with you?"

"No, just Dov and me."

Reisa left the house and found Dov in the wagon. He had learned to handle the unruly team of Samson and Delilah. When they tried to pull their tricks on him, he simply pulled back on the lines so hard their necks were arched backward and they squealed in fear and anger. If he was on the ground, he grabbed an ear and twisted it, jerking the animals down almost to their knees. The pair had learned to fear Dov, but still only he and Ben could drive them.

Leaving the house, they started to town. But as they passed by Hilda's house, Reisa said, "Let's go see if Hilda wants anything."

As it developed Hilda needed nothing, but she had an invitation. "I want all of you to come for a big supper tomorrow night. You must help me cook it, Reisa, so that you and your grandfather have something you can eat." She turned to Dov. "You'll have to be sure and come, Dov. I'm cooking your favorite pumpkin pie."

Dov, who could annihilate a pumpkin pie singlehandedly, grinned. "Yes. I will come, Hilda."

As they pulled out, Reisa passed a sly glance at Dov. "You like Hilda, don't you?"

"Yes. Good big woman."

"Do you know she's worried about herself?"

"No. What she worried about?"

"Oh, women worry about things that men don't think about. She worries about that scar on her face. She thinks it makes her ugly."

"Not ugly."

"And she thinks she's too big."

"She is not as big as I am."

Reisa suddenly laughed aloud. "Of course she's not as big as you are, Dov, but she's larger than most women."

"What does that matter?"

"Well, women like their men to be bigger than they are so they can protect them. Don't you understand that, Dov?"

The wagon rolled along, and Dov said nothing. But as Reisa glanced at him from time to time, she saw that what she had told the big man was working in his mind.

"Come on, Fears. You've had too much to drink."

"Shut up, DeSpain! I'll tell you when I've had enough."

Alf DeSpain shrugged his shoulders and stared at the big man with something like anger. Ike Green and Deuce Farley, two of Fears's regular companions, were with them. At the moment Green had gone to the bar and was talking with another man. The four had been there for several hours, and all of them were more or less drunk. Fears, who did not handle his liquor very well, had reached the point where his speech was slurred, and he fumbled with the cards that he attempted to deal on the table.

"This place is dead," DeSpain complained. "Let's get out of here."

At that moment Green came back, a grin on his loose lips. "Guess what I heard? The Jew girl's in town with that big bruiser, the Russian, that messed your hand up."

Fears at once clamped his hands together. It was still painful, but more than the pain in his hand was the knowledge that the big man had bested him publicly and had made him cry out. "I've been waitin' to get even with him," he breathed. He started to get out of his chair.

Deuce Farley, a small man wearing a tight leather coat, said, "If you get into any trouble in town, you'll get busted for it."

"That's right, Fears. Let it go," DeSpain said quickly.

"I ain't lettin' it go," Fears stated flatly. "Ike, you go find them. When they leave, they'll be in that wagon of theirs. When they leave town, come and get us."

The four men waited on their horses in a clump of alders that bordered the river. It was after two o'clock now, and Fears had sobered up somewhat. He still took a pull from a bottle that he kept in his saddlebag, but the wicked anger that coursed through him had not diminished in the least.

"I think I hear a wagon comin'," Deuce said. His eyes were good, and he drove his horse forward and leaned over the mare's head, peering down the road. "It's them," he said, straightening up, his eyes glinting. He loved trouble, especially where there was no danger involved, and he saw none here.

"All right. Let 'em get even, and we pull out and stop 'em."

"What are you going to do, Fears?" DeSpain asked quickly.

"What do you care? You ain't no kin to the Russian, are you?"

"It's not smart," DeSpain said. "Everybody saw us ride out of town together, and everybody knows you got a grudge against the Russian."

"Shut up, Alf!" Fears grunted. He pulled the forty-five out of his belt and said, "I'll handle this. You just put your guns on them two."

The sound of the wagon rumbling over the frozen road came closer. When it reached the group of alders, Fears said, "Now! Get 'em!" The four men rode out and surrounded the wagon. Dov pulled up at once, for Honey Fears had drawn his horse up directly across the road and was pointing the gun at him. "Get out of that wagon!"

Dov stared at the gun, but said, "Go away and leave us alone."

Honey Fears lifted his gun and let off a shot. The slug struck Dov, driving him back. He fell backward off the seat, and his back struck the wagon bed.

"Dov!" Reisa screamed. She scrambled to the back and found that Dov had been shot high in the chest. Blood was staining his shirt, but he struggled to his feet and stared at Fears. "You let this girl alone," he said, ignoring the wound.

"The next bullet will be right in your head! Take that girl out of that wagon!"

Fears guided his horse around and reached over and pulled Reisa from the wagon. She started to beat her fists against him, but he simply squeezed her with his massive strength so that she gasped.

Dov started to get out of the wagon when Deuce let off another shot. It stung Dov's neck and left a bloody furrow. "Now, you stay right there, Russian!" Fears grinned. "You're gonna be a messenger boy. You tell Driver if he wants to see this woman alive again, to come to the hanging tree. And tell him to come alone. If he brings anyone with him, we'll kill the girl first. Now, let's get out of here."

Dov watched helplessly as the men rode away. His chest wound was bleeding badly. The wound on his neck was minor. He got into the seat, picked up the lines, and slapped the mules. "Go!" he shouted, and when he struck the mules with the line they shot off in a wild run.

DeSpain looked back to see the wagon headed down the road bouncing over the ruts.

"This ain't smart, Fears," he said. "It's bad business to fool with a woman."

"You got no guts. That's your trouble, DeSpain. Now keep your mouth shut or I'll give you what I gave the Russian!"

Ben was reading a book when suddenly he lifted his head.

Sam caught the motion and asked, "You hear somethin', Ben?"

"Wagon coming fast." Ben came to his feet and left the room. He was followed by the three men, and as soon as Ben saw Dov bouncing along on the seat he knew something was wrong.

"Dov's been hurt," Phineas said. "That's blood on his shirt and his neck."

Dov pulled the mules up, and his face was pale, what could be seen of it around the beard. "Bad men. They took Reisa."

"Who was it?" Ben demanded.

"Man whose hand I hurt. Honey Fears and three others."

"Get down out of the wagon. We've got to patch that wound up," Phineas said sharply.

Dov got down and stood on his feet unsteadily. They led him into the house where he lay down, and Phineas began stripping his shirt off. As he worked on the wound, Dov said, "Fears—he say for Ben to come to hanging tree."

"Where's that?" Jacob said. His face was pale.

"It's a place in the bend of the river," Sam said. "Five horse thieves were hanged there once."

Ben looked at the wound and said, "How bad is it, Phineas?"

"It's not too bad. It didn't hit a lung. This on his neck's just a scratch."

"I want your Whitworth."

"It's over in the corner. Ammunition's on the shelf. "

"Let me have your Le Mat, Sam."

"I'm going with you," Sam said.

"No, you take Dov to a doctor. I'll go after Reisa."

"How'll you get there?"

"I'll borrow Hilda's gelding. Dov road him home yesterday."

Jacob looked at the stern face of Ben Driver. His heart knew fear, but he quickly said, "Ben, let us ask the Lord Jesus to give you a victory."

Ben Driver had not prayed for a long time, but now he stopped dead still. "I think that's a good idea, Jacob." He bowed his head while Jacob came over and stood beside him. When Jacob had finished the simple prayer for the rescue of his granddaughter, Ben said, "Amen." Then, grasping the Le Mat and the Whitworth, he hit the door running. Quickly, he saddled the gelding and stuffed the Le Mat into the saddle bag and the Whitworth into the rifle boot. Without a backward look, he kicked the flanks of the horse.

Jacob stood watching as Ben leaned forward in the saddle urging the gelding to a dead run. His whole hope was in the goodness of God now—and in the guns of Ben Driver.

Reisa was thrown across the front of Fears's horse. He held her with an iron arm, and she had stopped struggling. He was too strong for her, and now she simply lay there pressed against him unwillingly. It seemed that the horses had traveled for hours, and she was stiff and terrified. Her mind raced to and fro, but there was no hope in her own strength.

After what seemed like an eternity, Fears said, "There's the cabin."

"Good thing, too. I'm gonna build up a fire," Ike Green rumbled.

Five minutes later the horse Fears rode drew up to a halt, and Honey stepped out of the saddle. Reisa was jerked to the ground and placed on her feet. She almost fell when he released her, and Fears reached out and jerked the scarf from her head. Her hair fell down, and he grasped her by pulling her close and turning her face upward. "What are you worried about?" he said. "You got big, bad Ben Driver to protect you, don't you? Come on."

Reisa was half-dragged into the cabin, and one of the men began building a fire. She looked around, seeing beside the front door there was only one more room, which presumably was a bedroom. The furniture, such as it was, was broken down and patched together, and there was a fetid smell about the place.

"Where is this place?" she asked nervously.

"What do you care, sweetheart? You just don't try to get out that door. You wouldn't get far."

Deuce came by and brushed his hand across Reisa, causing her to recoil. Deuce laughed. "Well, I don't believe it! We got us a shy, young, innocent Jewish girl here."

Reisa backed up against the wall, breathing hard.

Fears went out and came back with a whiskey bottle almost full, sat down, and began to drink. He stared at her steadily, a dull light of hatred in his close-set eyes. "So you're Ben Driver's girl."

"No, I'm not."

"Don't give me that! I hear the talk about you two. I don't reckon you're as innocent as you make out." He turned and said, "Get that fire started! It's cold in here!"

"We can't stay here, Fears," DeSpain said. "Driver will come and bring others with him."

Honey shook his head. "You don't know him like I do. He'd never ask any help of anybody. That's why I told him to come alone—because I knew he would anyhow." He took a pull on the whiskey bottle, then handed it to Deuce and Green, who also took long pulls on it.

"You can't kill him, Fears," DeSpain said. "The big Russian knows where we are. Even if Driver don't spill the beans on us, somebody else will. Let's leave the girl and get out of here."

"You're a lily-livered sort, ain't you?" Deuce said in disgust.

"I got sense. I know what happens to men that get caught foolin' with a woman—good woman, that is. You don't talk your way out of that." He nodded saying, "That hangin' tree's still out there. They'd hang us all in a minute if we hurt this girl."

"Shut up, DeSpain!" Honey growled.

"I'm gettin' out of here."

Honey drew his gun and held it on DeSpain. "You ain't goin' nowhere! Sit down over there."

DeSpain knew that Honey Fears would not hesitate to shoot him. Clamping his jaws together, he said in disgust, "You'll get us all killed, Fears."

Three of the four men got into a poker game, all drinking heavily. From time to time one of them would look at Reisa and make a raw remark, at which the others would laugh coarsely.

Finally DeSpain said, "Go in the other room, girl."

Honey looked up and laughed. "Yeah. Go in the other room. There's a bed in there. You'll have some company pretty soon."

Reisa quickly went into the room and shut the door. There was a window, but it was small and apparently nailed shut. There was a single bed and no other furniture. It was dirty, littered with trash of all sorts. Reisa's mind raced. She searched every wall, looking for a loose board, but there was no way out.

As the night drew on, the men in the next room got drunker, and the shouting became louder. Reisa knew that at any moment the door might open, and that Honey Fears would come in, and she would lose her innocence. The thought of it chilled her, and fear weakened her so badly that she could not stand. She was not afraid of death, but she could not bear the thought of what the evil men would do to her. She sat down on the bed, bowed her head, and tried to pray, but nothing came. For a long time this went on, it seemed, and many times she thought she heard the door opening.

Reisa knew that there was no hope for her. Ben could not get here in time, and if he did, what could he do against four men? She had seen that the house was up on a high rise, and nobody could approach without being seen. At one point she had heard Honey tell Ike Green to get out and keep watch for Driver.

Sitting there in the dusky room illuminated only by one small window, Reisa Dimitri knew that unless God helped her, she was lost. Suddenly she fell on her knees and began to pray aloud in an intense voice. "Oh, Lord, I am helpless! These men will do worse to me than kill me. I could not bear it, my Lord. Will you help me?"

A long silence came, broken by the voices of the men in the next room. Reisa closed her mind to that and continued to pray. But as she did, suddenly she remembered a word that her grandfather had given her. It was the day after his baptism. The two had been walking along the road, and he had suddenly turned to her saying, "Reisa, I have always believed in God, but I have found it to be—not enough. It is Jesus, the Son of God, that the Creator has used to draw me into himself. Jesus is indeed God, and he brings us to the Father. If ever you are in trouble, and I cannot be there, and there is no hope, please, Reisa, call upon the name of Jesus."

Her grandfather's words came to her clearly, and she, in desperation, said, "I have so little faith, but I call upon you, Jesus. My grandfather says you are the Son of God, and I want to believe that. I am so alone and so afraid. Please, Jesus, bring peace to my heart as you have brought it to my grandfather. I give myself to you. Save me from everything that weighs me down."

She stopped praying aloud, but she remained kneeling, for she was aware that something was happening. She could never describe it afterwards, but it was a sudden stillness that came into her spirit. Her mind had been battering wildly seeking an escape, and now it was as though her mind and her heart suddenly became still. In wonderment she knelt there, and finally she realized that God was doing something in her.

"The danger is still here, Jesus. The men are still there, but I believe that you have come to me. I give myself to you so that whatever happens I will believe that you love me, and that you care for me."

Ben galloped the gelding all the way through the streets of Richmond. When he emerged on the north side, he took the highway that led directly past Rosewood. He knew that the chances of his being alive the next day were not good, and he had one more thing to do. It was firmly in his mind, and he knew that God was in it. It was the first time in years that he had felt God doing anything in his life, but now he pulled up in front of his home and tied the panting horse to the porch rail. As he took the steps two at a time, he was met by his mother.

"Ben!" she exclaimed. "What's wrong?"

"Is Dad here?"

"Yes. What's the matter? Are you sick?"

"No. But I need to talk to both of you."

Even as he spoke the door opened, and John Driver stepped out. Ben turned to face him and said without preamble, "Honey Fears and his gang have captured Reisa. They shot Dov, and Fears said for me to come to the hanging tree or we wouldn't see Reisa alive again. I've got to go."

"Get the sheriff, Ben." Marianne said at once. "He'll have to help."

"You don't know Honey like I do. He'd be apt to shoot Reisa. I know him."

"But you can't go alone," Marianne said.

Ben suddenly took his mother in his arms and kissed her. "I've got to go, Mother." He released her, turned, and said, "I came to say good-bye, Dad. I've told you before how sorry I am, but I wanted to say it again. I've been wrong through and through. I'd like to go back and live life over again, but I can't. So I'm asking you to forgive me. It's the last thing I'll ever ask of you."

John Driver stood for a moment as if transfixed, then suddenly he cleared his throat. Words came to him with difficulty, but finally he said, "I've been wrong, Son. I'm sorry I've been so bitter and hateful. I'm the one that needs forgiveness, not you. Will you forgive an old man?"

Ben stepped forward and put his arm around his father. The two men embraced, and Marianne, not given to shouting in the least, suddenly cried out, “Oh, thank you, God! Thank you, God! Thank you, God!”

Ben felt his father’s arms around him, and he knew something had changed in his heart. He clung to him for a time and then stepped back. He swallowed hard, then said, “I guess I’ve been wrong with God all these years. Somehow, Dad, when you put your arms around me, I felt like God himself had forgiven me.”

“That’s good, Son. I know he has.”

Ben straightened, and then he said, “Good-bye.”

“Good-bye, my foot!” John Driver said. “You wait right here.”

Ben stared at his mother, and their glances were puzzled. John Driver disappeared inside the house, and Marianne said, “What’s he doing?”

“I have no idea.”

He soon found out, for John came out carrying the pistol he had carried throughout the war. He was strapping it on, and there was a light of battle in his eyes. “I guess I’m ready, Son.”

“No. You can’t go, Dad.”

“And you can’t stop me.”

The two strong men stared at each other, and suddenly Ben laughed. “No, sir, I don’t reckon I could stop you if I wanted to—and I don’t want to. Let’s go then.”

John Driver turned and kissed his wife, and she threw her arms around his neck. “Be careful—oh, be careful, John.”

Then she turned to Ben and held to him for a moment until he pulled her arms away. “Be careful, both of you.”

John called Trask to saddle two fresh horses. Marianne stood watching as the two men mounted and rode off. She turned then and went inside the house. She went at once to the drawing room, fell on her knees by the sofa, and began to call upon God.

Thirty-Two

"There it is—right in the open. No way to get closer without being seen."

Still in the shadow of a grove of willows, Ben gestured toward the one-story house, and John Driver squinted, leaning forward in the saddle. The moon was full and the house and open ground around it were revealed by its brightness. "Almost as bright as day," John muttered. "They'll be watching for us, Son, and that moonlight makes for good shooting."

Ben nodded. "There's no easy way to go about this. I'll just have to ride on in."

John said, "I wish we had just one company from my old outfit."

"It wouldn't do any good. Honey Fears is crazy," Ben said quietly. "He'll shoot Reisa if we give him any chance."

"There must be a better way to do this."

"I don't think there is. This is one of those times when there aren't any options." His expression broke, and he added, "It's a little bit like being back in the war. I was playing a game, but nobody had really taught me the rules. Maybe there weren't any rules."

John Driver shifted uneasily. "I keep trying to think of something, Son, but I can't. Just when I see you and find out what a fool I've been about the way I've treated you, then this has to happen." He dropped his head for a moment and shook it in a small gesture of negation. "Sometimes a man bends to pick up something that fell out of his hand—and when he gets up the world has changed."

Both men sat there waiting for the inevitable. Sooner or later they both knew that Ben would have to walk up to that cabin—and they both knew what was inside waiting for him.

Ben felt a need to say something to his father, but it was difficult. He checked the loads in the Le Mat. "I'd better get this done," he said quietly.

The older man sat there, grief mixed with anger—the grief for the wasted years he had spent cutting himself off from this tall man who sat beside him—the anger that he might lose him, and there was nothing he could do about it. As Ben turned to walk toward the shack, he caught his arm, turning him around.

"You know," he said, "when people ask me whether they should have children or not, I never tell them what to do. You never know how a son or a daughter will turn out, but there's no other way to find out. There's no substitute for it. You can't do it with a friend or with a lover. You have to have that boy or that girl to find out what it is really like."

Ben listened carefully and then asked, "Would you do it again, Dad?"

Instantly John Driver nodded, and turned his eyes on his son. "Yes, I would. I made so many mistakes with you. I want time to make them right."

"Maybe we'll have it. You never know how things will turn out. I remember that second day at Gettysburg. We all knew that most of us weren't going to come back from that charge up the hill. I didn't expect to."

"I didn't either," John said, "but we did."

"Right." Ben stirred, then said, "Well, let's get this thing over."

"You care for this girl a great deal?" John Driver asked.

Ben touched the Le Mat in his belt. "Yes, I do, and I've never told her. If this—doesn't turn out right, you tell her that I thought she was the finest woman I ever knew."

John Driver could not answer. He nodded his head, and as Ben turned away and walked steadfastly out of the shadow of the trees, he had an urge that had come often to him in the war. At times of battle he had to hold himself back from rushing ahead blindly at the enemy. That was in his mind, and in his heart, and in his spirit as he watched Ben cross the meadow and head up the hill toward the cabin.

As Ben walked steadily up the hill, neither hurrying nor holding back, his attention focused on the windows of the cabin. He had done this many times during the war. Serving as a scout, being sent out to draw enemy fire, he remembered once he had crossed a cotton field in Tennessee. The day before the Yankees had been at the other end in great numbers. He knew they had sharpshooters just as his own side did, and every moment he expected a bullet to tear his body into a lifeless hulk. He had walked to the end of the field and had discovered that the enemy had abandoned their position during the night.

Now as he advanced and the cabin seemed to draw nearer to him, looming larger, he waited for the bullet to strike him—but it did not happen. When he was thirty yards away the door opened, and Honey Fears stepped out. He was holding Reisa by the arm, and three other men fanned out behind him. They were all holding their guns, and Ben stopped twenty yards away. His gaze went at once to Reisa, and he saw that she was exhausted—but he saw hope in her eyes. He had expected her to be terrified as most women would have been, but she simply stood there, not struggling, her gaze fixed steadfastly on him. Even under the pressure of the moment he admired the ivory shading of her skin and the lovely turnings of her strongly rounded body. Her hair, a dense black, fell loose against her own will, he was certain, but there was something in her eyes that he had never seen before. Perhaps he had missed it, but as he watched her, he felt the vitality leap out of her eyes and knew that there was never another woman like this one.

At that moment Ben Driver knew the strange thing a man feels when he looks upon beauty and knows that it will never be for him.

"Just throw that pistol down on the ground, Ben." Fears grinned as he spoke, and absolute certainty tinged his voice. He waited until Ben leaned over and placed the Le Mat on the ground.

"I guess I've been waitin' for this a long time," Fears said, and the hatred that lay deep in him flared in his eyes. "You always had to be the top dog, but you ain't the top dog no more. I'm gonna kill you, Driver."

Suddenly DeSpain stepped forward. "Fears, don't be crazy! We'd never get away with it, not in a hundred years!"

"Aw, shut up, DeSpain!" Fears's laugh made a meaningless sound.

Farley said wickedly, "You take the first shot, Fears, then I'll put my slug in him."

Fears turned his attention back on Driver. "I'll kill you, and I'll keep the girl! The big Russian ain't here now, so we'll take what we want from her."

Ben was thinking quickly, and he spoke up clearly, "DeSpain, you'll hang alongside of Fears if you don't stop him."

"Shut up!" Fears exclaimed.

DeSpain was not drunk, and he well understood that if Fears had his way, they'd all hang sooner or later. He knew also that Farley was past reason, as was Fears. "Ike," he said suddenly, "are you in this?"

Ike Green was not as much of a drinker as the others, and he had been listening to DeSpain, who had warned him that they would hang along with Fears unless they pulled out. Green turned carefully and checked the odds. He knew Fears and Farley were wild and reckless men, but the shadow of a noose had forced him to a sudden decision. He was on the left side of Fears and Farley, and DeSpain was on the right. They had the two flanked if it came to shooting. "DeSpain's right, Fears. You don't talk your way out of ruining a woman—not in this county. You remember Fingers Duvall? They didn't bother with the trial after he raped that woman over at Fenton! I'm not lettin' that happen to me."

Fears cursed and glanced at DeSpain. Whatever went through his mind no one ever knew. He saw that the odds were no more than even, for both DeSpain and Ike were good shots, and at this range they could not miss. He saw that Farley was ready to fight, but something changed in his face. A crazed light appeared in Fears's eyes, and he suddenly turned and shouted, "You've rubbed my face in the dirt, Driver! Now you're a dead man!" He lifted his pistol and fired.

Ben saw the move, twisted, and fell to the ground. The bullet passed so close it seemed to brush by his ear with an audible hissing sound.

Sprawled on the ground he saw the Le Mat five feet away, and knew that there was no time, for Honey was lowering the pistol, cursing as he did so. Desperately Ben lunged forward and even as he did, he knew that he was a dead man.

His eyes were fixed on Honey even as he reached for the Le Mat. Fears's gun exploded again, but it was pointed down at his feet. A black hole suddenly appeared over the big man's left eyebrow, and he seemed to freeze. At that instant Ben heard the retort from the Whitworth and knew that his father had killed Fears.

Deuce Farley turned his pistol toward Ben, but by that time Ben had snatched up the Le Mat. He took a snap shot at Farley and saw the slug hit and drive the man backward to the ground.

He came to his feet and saw that DeSpain and Green had both thrust their hands high in the air. "This wasn't our idea, Driver," DeSpain cried instantly. "You saw me try to talk him out of it!"

"Just drop your guns. You, too, Ike, on the ground." He waited until they did, then turned to see his father hurrying forward, a pistol in his hand.

"Are you all right, Ben?"

"Yes, thanks to you." He suddenly smiled. "That was a good shot."

John Driver's face was pale. "I didn't see any other way."

"There was no other way." He turned to look at the still figure of Honey Fears, who had fallen on his back. His eyes were open, and he stared blindly at the sky above. "Somewhere he must have had parents that loved him and a woman that cared for him, but he never showed any concern for anybody but himself," Ben remarked. He moved over to where Farley was bleeding profusely from a slug he had taken in his left shoulder. It was not fatal, and Ben said, "You won't die from that, Deuce."

"What are you going to do with us?" Ike asked nervously. His glance went involuntarily to the hanging tree.

Ben did not answer. He had turned to Reisa. He stepped to her side, stuck the Le Mat in his belt. He reached out and took her hand. She returned his pressure, and they did not speak for a moment. Then he asked, "Did they hurt you?"

"No, I was terrified at first. I thought they would—" She could not finish the sentence. "But I'm all right." She nodded toward DeSpain. "He's telling the truth. He tried to get Fears to let me go."

"What do you think, Dad?" Ben asked.

John Driver spoke up. "You two take Farley and get him patched up, then get as far away from here as you can. If you're still in the county day after tomorrow, there'll be a warrant out for attempted murder and kidnapping. You'll hang."

An expression of relief swept across the faces of the two men, and DeSpain said, "Come on, Ike. Let's get Deuce to a doctor." He turned then and said, "Don't worry. You'll never see my face again."

They watched as the two patched up the wounded man. They stopped the blood flow, then helped him get into the saddle. Farley's face was pale, and his eyes were shut. His lips were clamped tightly together, and he did not say a word as they left, DeSpain leading his horse as they rode away.

"Reisa?"

Reisa turned then, and she smiled. "I knew you'd come, Ben."

Ben glanced at his father and smiled. "It's my dad you have to thank."

Reisa went to him at once and looked up into his eyes. "Thank you for coming. Thank you for what you did."

John Driver took the hand of the young woman and for the first time looked at her carefully. He had the feeling that he was going to know her much better, and now as he studied her features they were almost serene. He saw a fire in her that made her lovely—a beautiful and robust woman.

"I've asked Ben to give me another chance. I've been the biggest fool God ever made. If Ben will let me, he'll see a difference."

"I'm so glad," Reisa said, and her smile brightened her entire face. She hesitated, then said, "Something happened to me." For one moment she paused, then she squared her shoulders. "I was terrified when they brought me here, but when they put me in the room alone I knew it would be only a matter of time until they came to hurt me. So I began to pray, and for the first time in my life I called for Jesus—and somehow he was there. I did what Sam did and what Grandfather did. I asked him to come be with me, that I needed him—and he did."

John Driver was touched by the young woman's words. "I'm so glad, my dear," he said gently.

"And now your grandfather will be happy, too," Ben smiled. Then he said, "Come along. He must be terribly worried about you."

The three left, and as they walked down across the open plain the moon came out from behind a cloud and cast its silver beams over them.

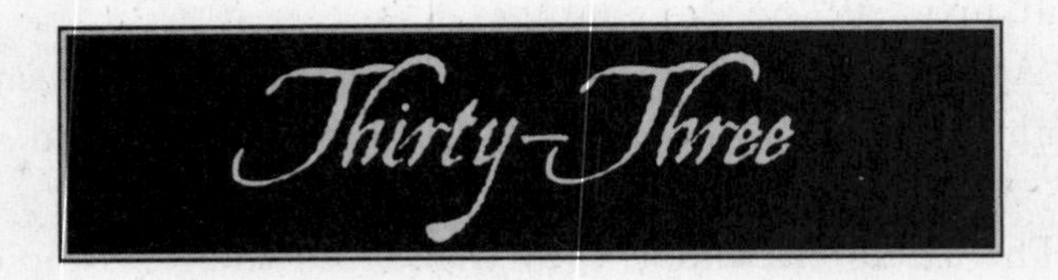

Thirty-Three

"It was generous of Ben's family to invite us all to their home for Christmas," Jacob said. He was sitting at the kitchen table drinking tea while Sam and Phineas busied themselves cleaning up the house.

"Well, I reckon they're so happy to have Ben back," Sam replied, "that they want to let everybody know how grateful they are."

Reisa was washing dishes, and she looked over her shoulder. "Pru and all her family will be there. It will be good to see them again. Ben says that they're going to move here, and her husband will be a doctor in Richmond."

The talk went on for some time, mostly about the Christmas celebration. It was the twenty-fourth, and they were due to go that day and spend the night.

Dov had said little during this time. Seated at the table, his huge fists almost swallowed the large coffee mug that he used for tea, and now he cleared his throat and said suddenly, his deep voice cutting through the others, "I must shave."

Everyone turned to stare at the big man.

"Shave!" Sam exclaimed. "Why, you ain't never shaved!"

"Well, I think that's a wonderful idea," Reisa said quickly, having some idea where the idea had originated.

Sam persisted, however. "What do you want to shave for? It's just a pain in the neck!"

Dov became more embarrassed than ever. He stared down at the cup and mumbled, "Hilda say I would look more better."

Phineas suddenly grinned. "I think she's showed a little sense there. You look like a grizzly bear. Come on over here. I reckon I can do the job."

"You are a barber?" Dov asked with surprise.

"I shaved half the fellows in my company through the whole war," Phineas said. "Now, you come here and set."

Soon the water was heated, and the scissors and Phineas's razor lay on the table. Taking the scissors, he grinned, saying, "Say good-bye to this mess. It looks like you have enough to stuff a mattress."

Reisa watched with interest as Phineas performed the operation. He proved to be quite an apt barber, as he had boasted. With the scissors he trimmed the beard down as close as he could to the skin, then he took his brush and shaving mug and worked up a rich lather. Dov watched him cautiously as he dipped a towel into a basin of boiling water. "What that for?" he demanded.

"Soften up them whiskers of yours. Now just lay your head back there." When Dov docilely obeyed, Phineas carefully lowered the hot towel, leaving just room for his nose. As he waited, Phineas remarked, "He ain't shaved in so long them whiskers are probably about like wire. But I got a razor that will do the job." He plucked up the razor, tested the edge on his own arm, then said, "She'll cut right through." Removing the towel, he lathered up the face again, then put his hand on top of Dov's head. "Don't you move," he said. "I'm liable to cut your throat." Expertly he drew the razor down the side of Dov's left cheek, leaving a clean track.

Reisa exclaimed, "Why look, his skin's so white!"

"It ain't never seen the light of day," Sam grinned.

They all watched as Phineas worked carefully. Finally he was finished. Taking the towel, he cleaned Dov's face. "Well, look at that. You ain't scary enough to frighten the young 'uns now."

"No!" Reisa exclaimed. "You look so—so *different*, Dov! Let me get a mirror." She dashed away and soon returned. Dov, still sitting, stared at his reflection. He had not seen his face in so long without whiskers that he could hardly believe it. He drew his fingers across the tender skin. "Burns like fire," he said.

"You look wonderful," Reisa said. "I can't believe a beard makes such a difference."

"You do look very good, indeed!" Jacob said, staring at Dov. The big man had looked rather fierce ever since he had known him, and now the missing beard revealed a face with a mild, rather gentle expression. "People won't know you," he remarked.

As Dov stood, towering over the others and stroking his face, he said, "It feel funny."

"Dov, when you're ready to go, Hilda and I finished that suit. Go put it on and see if it fits. I may have to take a few more stitches."

Dov followed Reisa into Jacob's room, and there on the bed lay trousers, a new white shirt, and a coat. The coat and pants were made of a light gray woolen material that Reisa had bought at a bargain. She and Hilda had made the garments together. She shook her head. "It's the first suit either one of us ever made, but put it on, and we'll see."

She left the room and found the men laughing about the change in Dov. "Don't you laugh at him when he comes out. If that suit doesn't fit, it won't be his fault," she said.

But when Dov came out, once again, they were all rather shocked. The suit did fit reasonably well. They had never seen him in anything but the huge loose-fitting trousers and the shirt that he simply pulled over his head. Now he looked somehow smaller.

"You look beautiful, Dov!" Reisa exclaimed. "But where's your tie?"

"Tie?"

"Yes, the tie."

"Oh, I forget him."

"I'll get it." Reisa went and got the tie, and since she had trouble reaching up to Dov, she made him sit down. Carefully she tied it, and then said, "Now, stand up and turn around."

Awkwardly Dov stood up and turned around, and Jacob nodded. "You look very much like a gentleman, Dov."

Dov felt the material of the coat and stretched his arms. "Thank you, Reisa."

"It was mostly Hilda. You'd better let her see it."

Dov seemed anxious to get away. "Yes, she is going to the Christmas party. I drive her in wagon." He started for the door.

As soon as he was out of earshot, Sam said, "Well, ain't he a caution now. He don't look like the same feller."

"I hope Hilda will like him," Reisa remarked.

The dress that Hilda had made for herself was of a soft blue, almost the color of her eyes. She and Reisa had picked out the material at the store, and for days now she had worked on it. She stood there for a moment in her petticoat, held it up, then quickly slipped it on and fastened it. She turned to the mirror and anxiously surveyed her image. A smile came to her lips. "It's such a pretty dress," she said. "I hope Dov likes it."

She had bought a pair of new shoes as well, made of soft black leather. She slipped her feet into them and buttoned them up and stood. They were the first high heels she had ever bought. Before, she had always worn flat-heeled shoes to make her height less noticeable. Reisa, however, who had helped her choose the shoes, had said firmly, "These are beautiful, and you must have them."

Going to her room, she pulled out a carved walnut chest, opened it, and pulled out a smaller box. Opening it, she looked down at the blue earrings and the matching necklace on a fine gold chain. She put the earrings on, fastened the necklace, then moved back to the mirror. They were very old stones, having come all the way from Sweden. They had belonged to her grandmother, and her mother had given them to her when she was seventeen. She had worn them only once, and since then they had lain in their case in the same chest. Now she stood looking at herself nervously.

The invitation to the Drivers had been a surprise to her, but Ben, who had delivered the invitation, would take no protest. "We're all going. You make Dov shave that beard and dress up, and you put on that pretty new dress that Reisa's been telling me about."

Even as she stood there, Hilda heard the sound of a voice. Flushing slightly, she replaced the chest and moved quickly to the front door. It was very cold outside, and snow was expected. For one moment she felt so nervous she could hardly stand. Being a woman of firm word, she thought, *Stop acting like a baby, Hilda. It's only Dov.* She opened the door and looked up at the big man waiting for her, who stood looking down at her.

"Dov!" she exclaimed. "You shaved!" Involuntarily she reached up and touched his smooth cheek. With embarrassment she giggled and drew her hand back. "I can't believe it's you! Come in and let me see your suit."

Dov stepped inside the door and stood there as she moved around him admiring the workmanship of his suit. "You look very good. I want you to always shave."

Dov did not speak, for he was taken aback by the woman before him. His usual picture of her was of a woman in overalls and men's shoes. On Sundays to church she wore the same gray, faded, and rather shapeless dress. But this was changed now! The woman who stood before him was feminine beyond any vision he had had of her. The dress revealed the mature curves of a woman in the prime of her life. He was almost shocked to see that her waist was so small. The curves of her upper body thrust against the dress, and as she turned around, Dov shook his head. "You look ver' pretty, Hilda."

"Oh, Dov, do you think so really? I'm so embarrassed to go to the Drivers'."

Dov shook his head, still staring at her. "You look pretty," he said. "I never saw woman look so pretty."

These words fell on Hilda's ears and brought a strangeness to her. It was the sort of thing that she knew men said to women, for she had heard other women talk, but except for the one time in her life, just before she had been jilted, no man had ever called her pretty. Her pale skin suddenly glowed, and her lips made a small change at the corners and became soft with the interest of a mature woman. She held her head still and looked straight up at Dov, not smiling exactly, but the thought of a smile was a hint at the corners of her mouth and the tilt of her head.

As for Dov, he was always a silent man. He struggled to find words. The fragrance of her clothes came powerfully to him. She was, he saw, not what he had thought. He had not cared whether she was attractive or not, but now she stood before him, a well-shaped woman, her features quick to express her thoughts, and the love of life lying impatiently behind her eyes waiting for release.

Finally Dov took a deep breath and said, "Are you ready to go?"

"Yes. Let me get my coat." She turned to go, but suddenly Dov caught her arm. Surprised, Hilda turned around and looked up. "What is it, Dov?"

"You know me well, Hilda."

"Do you think so, Dov?" Hilda was pleased at his remark. Indeed, the two had become very close. "And I suppose you know me, too."

"Do you remember once I tell you, right after your mother died, when you cried—and I say you never be alone as long as Dov was here?"

The memory had never left Hilda, and she nodded. "Yes, Dov," she whispered. "I remember."

Dov had no words, but he put out his hands suddenly and placed them on her shoulders. Startled, Hilda looked up and saw something in his face that caused her to tremble. The face was unfamiliar, but the eyes were always the same—always kind—and now they glowed with something she had always longed to see in a man's eyes. She saw, however, that he could not speak and knew that she would have to take the initiative. "Do you care for me, Dov?" she asked quietly.

"Yes! I always have—and I always will."

Hilda Swenson then reached up and put her arms around Dov. She pulled his head down and kissed him on the lips. She clung to him, pressing against him, and as his strong arms went around her, she felt small and fragile against his mighty strength. His arms closed in on her, and when he finally lifted his head, he said, "I want us to be together always."

Hilda instinctively realized what he was saying. "Shall we be married then, Dov?"

"Yes. We will be married." Suddenly relief seemed to wash through him. He swept her off her feet as easily as if she were a child and danced around the cabin.

For Hilda this was a miracle. She had never had this sort of attention, but this big man had come to fill a place in her heart that had long been hungry.

"Put me down, Dov," she laughed. And when he did, she reached up and put her hand on his cheek. "We will be married in the church. Now, let us go."

As they left, she said, "You must tell everyone tonight while we are at the Drivers' what has happened."

Dov laughed. A sense of freedom had come to him. He nodded. "Yes. I tell them in the church we will be married."

⁂

Marianne Driver's face was radiant. Her eyes danced, and she looked almost like a young girl again as she came up to her husband.

"Well, I guess my Christmas present is a beautiful wife," John said. He reached out, drew her to him, and kissed her.

Marianne held him for a moment and then cried, "Isn't it wonderful, John, to have Ben back, and Pru and Martin moving back with the grandchildren? Oh, I'm so happy!"

"So am I, sweetheart," John said. Indeed, the two of them had been closer together than they had for years. The reconciliation with Ben had worked a miracle in John Driver's spirit. He had not realized how that bitterness had dragged his spirit down, and now his back was straighter and his light blue eyes shone as he held Marianne and said, "Listen to that noise. Isn't it beautiful?"

The noise, indeed, came from three lively grandsons who were playing some kind of a game in one of the rooms. Even as the pair stood there, they came flying out chasing each other and yelling at the top of their lungs.

"Ben has been so good with the boys, hasn't he?" Marianne said. "They fell in love with him in no time."

Indeed, Ben Driver had won the hearts of his three nephews. The last few days he had spent practically all of his free time playing all sorts of games with them, taking them out for rides, fishing with them in the river, although it was too cold to stay for long, and then he had taken them out to find a cedar tree. Martin had gone along, and the five of them had come back dragging a huge tree that now stood in the largest of the two parlors. It almost brushed the ceiling, and the decorating was part of the fun.

⁂

Ben, at the very moment his parents were watching the boys, was standing outside with Pru looking out across the fields. He said suddenly, "Everything seems so dead now, but in the spring everything will be green, and the ground will have a good rich smell to it when it's broken." He turned to Pru. "I'm glad you and Martin are moving back. I need you, Sis."

Pru put her arm around him and hugged him tightly. "And we need you, too, Ben." The two stood looking out over the fields, and soon she asked, "What will you do? Keep on selling out of that wagon with Reisa?"

Ben laughed. "No. The only reason I went was because nobody could drive the mules except me. But Dov can do that as well as I can now." He looked down fondly at her. "I think you could probably guess what I want to do, can't you, Sis? You always could figure me out."

"I'd guess you want to stay here and help Dad with the plantation."

"It was all I thought about during the war. Just get back home and plant cotton and corn and raise horses. Then when I crashed I lost all that. It's come back to me though. Lately all I can think of is this place and working and being with the family."

"Well, nothing you could do would make Mom and Dad happier."

At that moment a faint cry came to them, and Ben looked up, squinting his one eye. "There they are. Some of them, any-how."

They went at once to meet the wagon. Ben reached up to help Reisa to the ground. He was a little shocked at her appear-ance. "You're not wearing a kerchief," he said. Her black glossy hair glowed in the sun, and she reached her hand up almost in embarrassment.

"Since I'm a Christian woman now I don't have to wear a scarf, just dress modestly."

"I like it," Ben said.

"You have such beautiful hair," Pru said, coming to give her a hug. "And that dress. It's new, isn't it?"

"Yes. I bought it from the dressmaker last week. I'm shocked at how much I spent on it."

The dress was made of dark green satin with a high collar trimmed in white lace, long tight-fitting sleeves, and a long skirt. The bodice had tiny pin tucks down the front and ended at the waist in a "V," where a small red satin rose with green and white ribbons hung loosely down the front of the skirt. She had on a pair of high-heeled black leather shoes and carried a matching bag.

Jacob had stood beside Sam and Phineas taking all this in, and he suddenly said, "I'm afraid we're bringing a lot of hungry mouths."

"There's plenty of food. Don't worry about that," Pru said. Then she asked, "Well, where's Dov?"

"Didn't he get here yet?" Reisa asked with surprise. "He went by to pick up Hilda and bring her."

Ben suddenly grinned and winked at Sam. "I guess they got delayed somehow."

Sam and Phineas both laughed, and then they turned, for John and Marianne had come out to greet them. They were followed by Martin and the three boys, who pulled at Reisa, trying to tell her that she would have to help them decorate the tree.

"I've never decorated a tree," Reisa said to Robert.

This stunned Robert. "Never decorated a tree! Where have you been?"

"Well, I've been in Russia, and my grandfather and I were Jewish. And, of course, Jews don't have Christmas trees."

"You missed a lot!" David exclaimed. "Come on. We're ready to get started again."

They went inside the house, and John Driver at once approached Jacob. He shook hands with him warmly and said, "I've got a favor to ask of you, Mr. Dimitri."

"Oh, Jacob, please."

"Fine. And I'm John. Would you consider teaching the Old Testament to a group of men of our church? And other churches would like to join in, too. I've been doing a little asking around."

Jacob beamed. "I would be happy to, but really, I am the one who should learn the New Testament."

Reisa whispered to Ben, "Isn't that wonderful? It will give *Zaideh* something to do."

"I'll sit in on that myself, I think," Ben smiled.

They were standing close together, and Pru's sharp eyes took it in. She nudged Martin and winked, and he said loudly, "What?"

"Oh, hush!" she said. "You're blind as a bat, Martin."

Martin, in confusion, followed his wife up into the house.

The decorating went on for some time and was interrupted when Sam looked out the window. "There comes Dov and Hilda."

Everyone waited until Marianne went to the door and came ushering the pair in. They seemed to dwarf everybody else in the room.

Johnny cried out, "Where's your whiskers, Dov?"

"Phineas shave them off. How I look?"

Robert said, "I liked you better with them. I liked to pull on them."

"Well, you can pull my hair. How's that?" Dov reached out and picked the small boy up, tossed him in the air, and caught him as he came squealing back to his arms.

Everyone had to admire Dov's shave and his new suit and Hilda's new dress. Pru murmured to Reisa, "Isn't Hilda attractive? She doesn't look a day over twenty-five, and she's so well formed. For some reason I didn't think she would be. Every time I saw her she was wearing those awful overalls."

Finally Marianne said, "Ben, you take these boys outside. If we're going to have a dinner here, we can't have all of you underfoot."

Instantly the boys began pulling at Ben, and he allowed himself to be hauled outside. The other men followed, and for the next hour all of them practically exhausted themselves trying to satisfy the boys' games.

Dov amazed them by picking up a yearling calf. He simply stuck his head under her, grasped her forelegs, and picked her up. She kicked and bawled, but he merely laughed at her. "I pick her up every day, and someday I pick up a nice, big cow!" He laughed, his eyes sparkling.

Inside, Hilda was helping with the meal.

Marianne said, "You look so pretty, Hilda. I hope you'll burn those old overalls."

Hilda flushed and said, "I might do that, Mrs. Driver."

Reisa and Pru, who were standing across the table working on the meal, glanced at each other. Both of them felt that there was more to Hilda than a new dress.

~

The dinner itself was a masterpiece. Dorrie had outdone herself. She rustled as she walked around, loading the table with food, for Ben had given her her Christmas present already—a new taffeta petticoat. She pretended that it was nothing, but she was proud as punch about it. When he had given it to her, she had unwrapped the package and stared at the petticoat, then gave a slight scream and covered her mouth. "You ain't changed one bit, Mr. Ben! You ain't, indeed! You jist as bad as when you was sixteen years old!"

As they settled at the table, John Driver said, "Jacob, would you ask the blessing?"

Jacob Dimitri looked startled, but he immediately bowed his head and prayed a brief prayer. "We thank thee, Oh God, for this day, for this food, for this friendship. We thank thee for the birth of your son, Jesus, and it is in his name we ask all blessings. Amen."

An *amen* ran around the table, and they immediately sat down. Looking at the spread on the table, Sam's eyes twinkled with mischief. Turning to Jacob he said, "I reckon this will be a day to be remembered for you, Jacob."

"How is that, Sam?"

"It'll be the day you took your first bite of ham. Now that you ain't bound to the law no more, set your teeth into this."

Sam forked a slice of ham and put it onto Jacob's plate. Jacob looked startled, but then he smiled. "I have always wondered what pig tastes like. Here, Reisa, we'll eat our first bite of pork together."

Reisa took half of the slice of ham, and both took a bite.

"It's salty but good!" Reisa exclaimed.

"Oh, you got lots of treats comin'," Sam said. "Now you get to eat catfish. I'll set you down to some first chance we get."

The meal went on, and it was a noisy one. The room was full of the smell of cooked meat and fresh bread. Everyone spoke loudly, and finally it got so that they could hear only the person next to them.

When Dorrie started bringing in the plates of pumpkin pie and chocolate cake, Dov suddenly stood up. His action took everyone off-guard, for he always made an impressive figure. "I have something to say."

Everyone waited expectantly, but Dov appeared to have lost his power of speech. He turned his head to look at Hilda, who smiled at him, and then he said, "Hilda and me—we are going to be married—in the church."

Instantly the cheers broke out, and the two were swarmed as the visitors got up. Dov was pounded between the shoulder blades, and Hilda was hugged and kissed repeatedly.

Finally, when they took their seats again, Reisa, who was sitting next to Ben, said, "Look at Hilda. She's so happy."

"Dov, too. I reckon if two people were ever meant for each other, there they are."

"Do you think people are meant for each other?" Reisa asked suddenly. She turned her large eyes upon him, and for a moment he could not answer.

Finally he nodded. "I think so."

~

The house was quiet now, for it was late. The boys had protested to the very last, begging to stay up for just one more half hour, but their pleas had not prevailed.

Now as Reisa sat in the small room on the third floor that had been provided for her, she brushed her hair out, sitting on the bed. She was wide awake, thinking of all of the things that had happened. Boris had taken up station on her lap, and purred with contentment.

Suddenly a small tapping caught her attention. Putting the brush down, she went to the door and opened it.

"Ben—what are you doing here?"

"Come with me," Ben said. He was smiling faintly, and when she hesitated he took her hand and simply pulled her out of the room.

"Ben," she whispered. "What are you doing? Everybody's asleep."

"No, they're not. I'm not and you're not."

Reisa had no choice but to follow him. He drew her down two flights of stairs, both of them tip-toeing instinctively. Ben turned down the hall. He finally pulled her into the smallest of the parlors where there was a fire burning in the grate. It sent up small tendrils of yellow and red flame and threw a warmth over the room.

"Ben, what are you doing bringing me down here?"

Ben suddenly reached out and caught both of her hands. "I've been having a talk with your grandfather."

Suddenly Reisa grew very still. She looked up at him, and her heart seemed to beat more rapidly.

"About what?"

"Can't you guess?"

"N–no," Reisa said, and then at once she knew for a certainty. But she waited for him to speak.

"I asked him if he would give you to me, Reisa. I want to marry you and spend the rest of my life with you."

Somewhere deep within Reisa's being a warmth began to grow. She could not speak for the happiness that had come to her, and now she simply stood there looking up at him. When she saw that he was smiling at her in a peculiar way, she asked, "What did he say?"

Ben's smile became more pronounced. "What if he said no?"

She had no chance to answer for suddenly Ben swept her into his arms, and she came to him willingly. She had known for some time that she loved him, but she had not known for certain how he felt about her. Now all of that seemed irrelevant, and as his lips pressed against hers, she knew that she was a woman desired, and this sent a song through her body.

The kiss lasted long enough so that by the time Ben lifted his head, Reisa knew that she had found what her heart longed for.

"Jacob said he thought it was God's will. Will you have me, Reisa?"

A thought crossed Reisa's mind, and with her hand on his shoulder, she said, "Did I ever tell you about my goose?"

Ben's jaw dropped. "I'm asking you to marry me, and you want to talk about a blasted *goose?*"

Reisa could not help but laugh. She felt as though she were made of feathers and fire on the inside. She could not help it and pressed her face for a moment against his chest. When she lifted her head, her eyes were glowing. "I know it doesn't sound very romantic, but there was an injured goose..." She told the story and finally when she finished, she said simply, "I wondered so many times if he found his way, and if he ever found his mate. I've heard they mate for life."

Ben had listened with great joy. This woman was rich in a way a woman should be rich, and now she was showing him the mysterious glow of a softer mood. He knew that the old hunger in him for her would never grow less—and it would never be satisfied. Always she would have the power to stir him, to deepen his hungers and drive his loneliness away.

"I don't know about your goose, but I found my way. And it's for life. I'll never let you get away, Reisa."

And then Reisa came against him. She put her cheek against his chest, and his arms went around her. They stood there for a long time, and he stroked her long raven hair gently. Finally he heard her whisper, "No, we will hold to each other, Ben, as long we live."

Boris, his large eyes taking in the pair, walked over and lay down before the fire. His head nodded as the heat toasted his side, but hearing a slight cry from his mistress, he turned to take in the pair. For a long moment he studied them—then he grinned, exposing his sharp fangs. Finding everything to his liking, he yawned enormously, then closed his eyes and promptly went to sleep.